Count Geiger's Blues

Orb books by Michael Bishop

Ancient of Days (forthcoming)

Philip K. Dick is Dead, Alas

COUNT GEIGER'S BLUES

(A COMEDY)

MICHAEL BISHOP

A TOM DOHERTY ASSOCIATES BOOK ■ NEW YORK

COUNT GEIGER'S BLUES

Copyright © 1992 by Michael Bishop

This book was originally published as a Tor hardcover in July 1992.

This book is printed on acid-free paper.

Cover art by Tom Canty

An Orb Edition
Published by Tom Doherty Associates, Inc.
175 Fifth Avenue
New York, N.Y. 10010

Library of Congress Cataloging-in-Publication Data

Bishop, Michael.
    Count Geiger's blues / Michael Bishop.
        p.   cm.
    ISBN 0-312-89008-7
    1. Heroes—Fiction.   I. Title.
PS3552.I772C68   1994
813'.54—dc20   94-2341
                                                                 CIP

First Orb edition: June 1994

Printed in the United States of America

0 9 8 7 6 5 4 3 2 1

For George Zebrowski,
this tardy experiment in literary synergism

Prologue:

"Regulated Medical Waste"

The vehicle backing into the loading dock at the rear of the cancer clinic looked surprisingly like a U-Haul van painted a flat silver. Its paint job gleamed dully in the floodlights washing the dock, and its only visible marker was an exhaust-stained sticker on a rear door: REGULATED MEDICAL WASTE. The sticker was so small you could read it only if you were within a car's length or so.

Once the truck was parked, with a ramp linking its cargo bay to the loading dock, the driver went to the clinic's door and traded a few words with the matronly-appearing administrative nurse waiting there for him. He and his partner had come for the cancer clinic's radium waste, as stored in lead cylinders about a foot across and eighteen or twenty inches tall, and the administrative nurse seemed glad to see him.

"I was starting to think nobody would come for this stuff," she said. "It took me three years to find a firm like yours."

"Yeah, well, we're sorta new," the driver said.

"No one wants used radioactives anymore. No disposal firm. No disposal site. I was getting frantic."

"Nothing to fret now, ma'am. Jack and I know what we're doin', we do it awl th' time."

"Where will you take it?"

"Hanford 'Tomic Energy Reservation in Woshington State. They know us there. Got us a long-term contrack wi' them."

"They told me no a dozen times. So did sites in South Carolina and Idaho. I was ready to try France."

"Don't mean to rap the Frenchies, but why go to furriners when you can deal wi' Americans?"

The driver, a middle-aged man with short reddish hair, and his partner, who might have been a trainee, put on butyl-rubber suits. The suits were more protection than they needed, but their company, Environomics Unlimited, the driver said, liked to play it safe. The administrative nurse, Teri-Jo Roving, led the EU disposal men in their balloon suits into the clinic, where they took a service elevator to the basement.

Here, the only sound was the sluicing of wastes—human, not radioactive—through an organ-pipe assembly of bracketed overhead tubes. Nurse Roving took the men into a storage area posted with stenciled cloverleaf warnings and unlocked the door to its central vault. Soon, using a furniture mover's hand truck, the men began emptying the room of the cylinders containing the discarded radium needles. In less than an hour, they had transferred every cylinder from the vault to the rear of their silver truck.

"Sign here," the unsuited driver said, handing Nurse Roving a daunting stack of forms. She signed in all the specified places and tore off a batch of copies for the clinic's records. *"'At's awl there is to it. Bye-bye, unwontered hot stuff."* The driver looked at Nurse Roving. *"I need our payment, ma'am—first half of 'er, anyways."*

"Of course. Sorry." She handed the driver a cashier's check for $2,500. The clinic would authorize another payment of a like amount as soon as it had official acknowledgment that the shipment had reached its destination. A paper trail would document the rad waste's movement from Salonika to the Pacific Northwest.

"Thanks," the driver said in his idiosyncratic Oconee accent. *"Bet you're gonna sleep good t'night, ain' jur?"*

"I will," Nurse Roving said. *"I certainly will."*

Down-shifting on an upgrade northeast of the city, the driver noisily sucked his teeth. Jack, who was reading the funny papers from yesterday's Salonika Urbanite, didn't notice. The driver smiled. Mr. F.'s people had thought of everything, including a way to fake the mandated check-offs from Memphis, Wichita,

Denver, Boise, and the other major sites en route to the dump site. It was all a matter of contacts. . . .

"Hey, Will," Jack said an hour or so later, having polished off the last of his comic strips. "Where are we?"

Will didn't answer. They were in the Phosphor Fog Mountains, a dozen or so miles from Placer Creek, and he was looking for a turn that would carry them past a rotted-out mill on a branch of Placer Creek itself. He found the turn and gunned the van along the muddy ruts of the sweetgum-bordered road. It was late autumn and rainy. Moist foliage scraped the van, and, despite the rain, a section of sky ahead of them pulsed yellow, as if urine-tinctured or faintly beer-polluted.

"Will—my God, Will, what's that?"

"'S Plant VanMeter. Con-Tri's a-building it."

"Jesus, Will, what're we doin' up here?"

"This is where we're gonna dump them little lead barrels Nurse Roving jes' signed off on."

"Dump 'em? Up here? What for?"

"Old Mr. F.'s people don't wont us wasting our time truckin' cross-country when we can do what needs doing closer to home. And if any of the hot stuff from them'ere radium needles shows up in the atmosphere, well, Plant VanMeter'll cotch the flak for it. Hot stuff's hot stuff, right?"

Will drove the van into a tight clearing overlooking the upper reaches of the millrace, then backed it around so that they could shove the radium-waste drums out the rear without any lifting or toting. To Will's disgust, Jack refused to touch a single cylinder until he'd bundled himself in his butyl-rubber suit, by which time Will had already wrestled three cylinders to the edge of the cargo bay and launched them like radioactive depth charges into a pewter-colored rock pool far below the wooded cliff. The cylinders were almost gone from sight before they actually hit the creek, but Will could hear them breaking the icy water and sliding irretrievably into it. When Jack lumbered up to help, Will shooed him away.

"You're too late. Besides, this is more fun 'n a scroffy wort like you deserves to have."

He unloaded the rest of the cylinders himself, even carrying a few to different parts of the cliff so that they wouldn't land atop one another and build an upjutting reef in the pool. The effort wore him out, but it was kind of a kick too. There was something *to be said for playing bombadier. It was almost as much fun as an evening at the Grand Ole Opry.*

The rock pool in the creek was deep. The discarded cylinders plummeted down through its waters, in unseen tumbling slow motion, until they could drop no farther. One of them, after bouncing a few times on the creek's nearer shore, didn't reach the water. It lodged among a colony of pigwort and ferns, a bomb with an internal timing mechanism. . . .

1

A Superior Man

Xavier Thaxton viewed himself as a superior man. But because he earned his living as a journalist, he sometimes had doubts about the degree of his superiority, recalling Oscar Wilde's remark, "The difference between journalism and literature is that journalism is unreadable and literature is not read."

Even more damaging to Xavier's confidence was the fact that he wasn't a bona fide reporter or an editorial writer, but a . . . well, a reviewer, a critic. Which left him open to jibes that he wasn't a real newspaperman. One colleague liked to bushwhack him with a James Russell Lowell couplet: "Nature fits all her children with something to do; / He who would write and can't write, can surely review."

Even so, Xavier persevered in the notion that he was a superior specimen of humanity. For one thing, he wasn't only a reviewer. He was the Fine Arts editor at the *Salonika Urbanite.* He directed the newspaper's coverage of any event of sufficient aesthetic merit—ballet, opera, art show, symphony concert, foreign films, even the opening of a gourmet restaurant—to escape the net of Popular Culture editor Lee Stamz. (Stamz and his staff covered the lowbrow end of the entertainment world: rock concerts, Hollywood movies, TV programs, nightclub acts, and so on.)

Besides, Xavier had a sense of mission. If he could reach

even one percent of the *Salonika Urbanite*'s weekend circulation of two million (most of whom would dismiss any article about Beethoven or Buñuel as "boring"), he and his staff would be influencing—*for the better*—about twenty thousand people, unveiling for them a panorama of Beauty and Truth heretofore eclipsed by the ubiquitous contemporary smog of bad books, stupid movies, atrocious music, and second-rate visual art.

"I am a railing alongside the torrent," thought Xavier, echoing an epigram of Nietzsche's. "Whoever is able to grasp me may grasp me! Your crutch, however, I am not."

For Xavier viewed himself as a quasi-disciple of Friedrich Nietzsche, as Nietzsche revealed himself in *Thus Spake Zarathustra, Beyond Good and Evil,* and *Ecce Homo.* However, he didn't regard himself as the fabled end product of Nietzsche's yearnings, the Superman. Instead, he was a modern hero *bridging* the chasm between today's bipedal beast-men and tomorrow's transcendent *Übermensch.* In his role as Fine Arts editor, he daily exposed the unwashed masses of Salonika to the highest artistic achievements of humanity.

I'm championing what I believe in, Xavier would sometimes tell himself: I'm acting on my convictions.

"Why keep trying to raise the rabble's taste?" Walter Grantham, the *Urbanite*'s Metro/State editor, once asked Xavier.

"Because it *needs* raising."

"But wouldn't Nietzsche say, 'Abandon the poisonous flies'?"

"Probably," Xavier conceded. " 'It is not thy lot to be a fly-flap,' he writes in *Zarathustra.* "

"But you hang on here, anyway."

"I'm an idealist, Walt. I continue to think there's something I can do. Even for the, pardon me, 'rabble.' "

"Nietzsche'd puke."

"Maybe. He'd say I should love the nonflies enough to quit this job and write the kind of philosophical-poetic criticism that *they* could draw sustenance from."

"So here on the *Urbanite,* Xavier, you *are* a sort of fly-flap, aren't you? Swatting at the buzzing multitudes."

"I guess. But I'm not trying to swat them dead, I'm trying to swat them awake."

About three weeks later, Walt Grantham and the three

members of Xavier's Fine Arts staff—Donel Lassiter (music), Pippa Wiedmeyer (art), and Cliff Todd (drama)—presented him a flyswatter for his birthday. Everyone laughed, including Xavier.

Then Pippa gave him a second gift. Unwrapped, it turned out to be a copy of the latest issue of *Superman*. Xavier guffawed again. As soon as everyone had left, though, Xavier trash-canned the comic book. Emphatically.

2

Aye, and Salonika

Salonika is a city of five million people in the southeastern United States. Its name comes from that of the ancient Macedonian port city best known today for a pair of New Testament epistles—First and Second Thessalonians—written by Saint Paul in A.D. 51 to its struggling Christians. These letters contain seminal teachings on the second coming of Christ.

Present-day American Salonika isn't much concerned with this matter. Its people are too busy. As the capital of the state of Oconee, Salonika is the economic, political, and entertainment hub of the New South. Even though it lies three hundred miles inland from the Atlantic, it functions, like its Macedonian namesake, as a port. This is because it straddles the Chattahoochee River, which divides Salonika into two distinct halves and flows virtually unimpeded from the Phosphor Fog Mountains on the Tennessee-Oconee border south to the Gulf of Mexico.

In 198—, the *Salonika Urbanite* hired Xavier Thaxton away from the *Atlanta Journal-Constitution.* He moved from Georgia, his home state, to Oconee, the Sun Belt's heart, soul, and nerve center, as a bachelor in his early thirties.

He had heard of Salonika all his life, but he had never visited it, not even as a reporter on the Atlanta papers. The moment that he first laid eyes on its flamboyant buildings, lofty "skybridges," landscaped parks, and shamefully nasty river piers, he was startled to discover that he felt vaguely *unreal*—like a character set in motion to carry out a series of dot-to-dot plot machinations. In a few months, this feeling passed. Xavier began to learn the city. Salonika had theaters, bookstores, art galleries, concert halls, libraries, the world-renowned Upshaw Museum, and a choice of fine restaurants that made even Atlanta's admirable array of eateries seem provincial.

EleRail rapid transit and several fleets of dependable private cabs made it easy to go wherever he wanted to without owning a car. Owning one struck him as a real mental and financial drain. Free of that burden, he delighted in Salonika's user-friendliness and began to explore it.

He found that, in addition to bookstores and concert halls, the city had pornography outlets and all-nude bistros, rock clubs and X-rated theaters, baseball-card collection centers and tacky import emporia, comic-book shops and junk-food franchises, floating flea markets and brothels. It had poke-weed dens, speaksleazies, crack houses, dilapidated hangouts for the homeless, and so many whores, addicts, sots, grifters, hoods, and hoboes that Salonika seemed to rival Sodom, Gomorrah, Babylon, and Alabama's once-fabled Phoenix City all rolled into one.

Most of this "sin" was concentrated in an enclave of tenements northwest of the Chattahoochee popularly known as Satan's Cellar, but there were pockets of depravity all over, some of them even in lovely Le Grande Park, the "urban wilderness"—twelve acres of neat grass, Japanese bridges, dogwoods, azaleas, topiary hedges, Cherokee-marble gazebos, and artificial waterfalls—visible from Xavier's twenty-second-story high-rise apartment. On almost any evening, he could look down and watch sinister human shadows sprint from grotto to glade in the park, preying on one another.

Satan's Cellar lay across the river, but the city's criminals could deliver it to you almost anywhere. Early on, Xavier suffered twinges of despair over the prospects of his contriving to turn the city's population from stinging flies into travelers on the bridge to the *Übermensch*. It was folly, thinking that writing about a film by Satyajit Ray or the string quartets of Bartók could uplift the masses. In fact, hoping for his writing to *amuse,* much less *improve,* a single person was also folly.

Quixotic nincompoopishness.

"What a fool I am!" Xavier said (to himself, he thought) a week after his promotion to Fine Arts editor.

"Buck up," Donel Lassiter, his music reviewer, said, startling him. "A buddy and I are going out tonight. Come with us."

"Where?"

"A surprise. Come on, Mr. Thaxton, even though you're my boss man, it'll be our treat."

Pippa Wiedmeyer, the art reporter, sidled up behind them. "You could eat Mexican," she said. She lifted her arms like a flamenco dancer, swayed her hips, and began to croon a jingle that Xavier had heard twice—two times too many—on his favorite classical music station:

"If you want a taco,
Don't drive to Waco.
Go straight to Ricardo's downtown.

"For a big, hot burrito,
It's definitely neat-o
To visit rakish Ricardo's downtown.

"Taste the Holy of Holies,
Our refried frijoles—
At roguish Ricardo's downtown.

"For an elite enchilada,
Don't be persona non grata.
Come to Ri—"

"Pippa," Xavier cried, "why're you repeating that garbage?"

Abashed looks descended on both Pippa's and Donel's faces. If anyone in the day room had committed a faux pas, Xavier realized, it was he, their tight-assed editor.

"Just trying to loosen things up, Mr. Thaxton," Pippa said, not without dignity. "It appeared you could use it."

"That was mimicry," Donel added, "not slavish imitation."

"Okay, okay," Xavier said. "Sorry."

"Proof your work's been getting to you," Donel said. "Bryan and I'll pick you up at seven, sir. Be ready."

Maybe he did need some intraurban R and R. He was losing his grip, going off half-cocked. He couldn't maintain a decent working relationship with his staff if he let the seeming hopelessness of transforming Salonikan society sabotage the attitudes of those who were supposed to help effect that transformation.

Xavier sat behind Donel and his friend Bryan in the latter's fire-engine-red Porsche. After crossing the Chattahoochee Bridge into Satan's Cellar, they drove straight to a girlie joint called Salome's, where the girls strutted down a runway in nothing but heels and feather boas and the jukebox boomed raunchy 1950s-style rhythm and blues. It struck Xavier as an out-of-character choice for both his companions, and before forking over the cover charge, he balked, refusing to enter. Not, he stressed, because he had moral objections, but because these were bottom-drawer amusements, unworthy of their time and attention. He couldn't help remembering a quote from *Thus Spake Zarathustra:* "Thy silent pride is always counter to their taste; they rejoice if once thou be humble enough to be frivolous."

"Listen, Mr. Thaxton—" Donel began.

"Xavier. Outside the office, call me Xavier."

But Donel couldn't. "The whole point of our night out is to do something *different* from what we have to do at work."

"Not this."

"What, then?" said Bryan. "What?"

Donel suggested crossing back into Salonika proper to see the Cherokees play the St. Louis Cardinals in the city's brand-new multibillion-dollar domed stadium, the Hemisphere. The Cherokees were one of three major professional sports franchises in the city, and all Xavier knew about them was that they played baseball badly enough to finish last in the National League eastern division every year. The city's other pro teams were the Spirits (basketball) and the Grays (football), equally inept franchises.

The collective failure of these three teams ate at the souls of thousands of Salonikans (who could talk of little else during their respective seasons), but didn't bug Xavier at all. He didn't like baseball. He saw basketball as so much higgledy-piggledy galloping about. He loathed football. Competitive sports of almost any kind—excepting handball, swimming, and chess—afflicted him with a profound existential nausea.

"Awwl RIIIGHT!" Bryan said. "The Great American Pastime! Good clean country fun!"

"Suthren fun!" Donel said.

"Suthren fun!" Bryan concurred. (Never mind that the New York Yankees had a record that the Cherokees couldn't hope to equal for another century or so.)

"Okay," Xavier reluctantly agreed.

He hated to go, but he didn't want to be a party pooper again. Besides, some intellectuals seemed to find baseball stimulating. The odd geometries of the ball parks, the situational complexity spurring each managerial move, gave them an almost erotic kick. All Xavier could see was grown men rubbing their plastic codpieces and dribbling tobacco juice.

The air-conditioned Hemisphere was cold. The beer that Donel bought him was as warm as the samples lined up for drug testing in the general manager's office. Fans behind them were smoking cigars or making crude remarks about the ball girls. No one scored a run, despite several walks and a host of errors, until the bottom of the sixth. Xavier couldn't remember when he'd been so bored.

In the top of the ninth, it looked as if the Cherokees might win. A Cardinals batter fouled a pitch down the third-base line. Donel and Bryan sat heedless of the ball's flight, but Xavier saw that it would hit Bryan—with the full force of a hard liner—if he didn't act.

He shoved Donel aside and caught the ball in the palm of his left hand an instant before it would have shattered Bryan's cheekbone. The stinging impact of the drive staggered him. He had to clutch a seat back to keep from falling on Bryan, who had spilled beer on his trousers but who was otherwise unhurt.

"Sign him up!" a few fans screamed. The PA announcer boomed that a representative from the Cherokees' front office would wade into the stands to offer him a contract.

"Wow," Donel said. "Who'd've thunk it?"

"Thank you," Bryan said. "Thank you. I mean, *thank you.*"

"Don't carry on as if I were the Wuss of the Western World," Xavier said. "Did my catch seem *that* miraculous?"

They said, No, no, it didn't—but Xavier could tell that they saw his split-second grab, and the fact that he'd managed not only to keep the ball from hitting Bryan but to catch it bare-

handed, as a fluke. Of course, he'd never played handball with
either of them before—a game at which he was very good—
and neither of them knew that while at Vanderbilt he had won
the five-hundred-meter butterfly at the annual SEC swim
meet. Hell, even Nietzsche knew that the best physiological
condition for those striving toward the *type* of the Superman
is "great healthiness." He was also a hiker and camper. It was
group sports that held no attraction for him.

The Cherokees won the game by two runs.

On the way out to the parking lot, a young man in a ribbed
tank top and sneakers shoved Xavier in the back, picked up
the baseball he'd caught, and darted off between the parked
cars like a rabbit doing an evasive slalom through a vegetable
patch.

"Hey!" Donel shouted. "Hey! Come back!"

"Never mind," Xavier said. "No great loss." He knew that
if the baseball had meant anything to him, he'd've chased the
thief. And despite Donel and Bryan's evident assumption that
a man of his sedentary profession and finnikin tastes must be
as uncoordinated as a newborn colt, he'd've run the punk to
ground and taken back the stolen ball. But the ball meant
nothing to him, and the effort would've been . . . well, wasted.

At Bryan's elegant little red Porsche, it pained Xavier, almost as much as it pained Bryan, to discover that a vandal had
torn off the rearview mirror and bludgeoned the hood and
fenders with a tire iron, confirming Xavier in his opinion that
anyone who owned a car in the city was courting both headache and heartbreak.

"Oh, shit!" Bryan cried. "Why? *Why?*"

Because we're in Salonika, Xavier thought, and Salonika,
like every other big city, is a dung heap that attracts, and then
feeds, millions of poisonous flies.

Aloud, he said, "This would've never happened if we'd gone
to the flute recital at Sycamore First Presbyterian."

"You've got insurance, don't you?" Donel said. Bryan admitted that he did. "Buck up, then. Mr. Thaxton just saved
you from reconstructive plastic surgery, and the Cherokees
flummoxed the Cardinals. Don't let a couple of dents in a
piece of machinery—a material object, for heaven's sake—put
you in a funk. Buck up, buck up."

Xavier was surprised—astonished—that this admonition

actually worked. Bryan's mood improved, and they concluded their evening by driving to the Oconee Plaza Hotel and listening to an adept black pianist in its well-appointed lounge play Gershwin, Cole Porter, and Duke Ellington.

3

A Dream of Plant VanMeter

Every July in the small Oconee township of Placer Creek, in the mirage-blue mountains ninety miles northeast of Salonika, Phosphor Fog Community College sponsors its annual George Bernard Shaw Drama Festival & County Crafts Fair. This event began in 1975, and it has been so successful, drawing visitors from many foreign lands and nearly every state in the Union, that its organizers believe it will be held forever.

The crafts fair isn't remarkable, particularly in Dixie, where such fairs take place nearly every summer weekend. What sets apart the Phosphor Fog Festival & Fair is not the rosin potatoes bubbling in tarry kettles, the scrimshawed jewelry and the antique furniture on sale, or the bluegrass music carrying through the oak groves—but the performances of five or six different G. B. Shaw plays over a six-week stretch beginning on the Fourth of July and continuing into August.

Performances take place in the Phosphor Fog Community College Fine Arts Auditorium or at the Oconee Mountain Amphitheater, in a natural bowl between two small hills. One new American play is produced each summer along with the obligatory, but hugely popular, Shavian fare—mostly to counter the charge that putting on only the works of a dead socialist Brit is unfair to Southern American playwrights. The actors are always professionals or accomplished collegiate drama students selected for the honor by famous Broadway or London directors. Securing tickets to the festival has become an exciting in-thing hassle not only in the Southeast, but also in New York City and Los Angeles.

Four years after snagging the lined foul ball and about a year before the main events of this story, Xavier went to the G. B. Shaw Drama Festival & Country Crafts Fair in Placer Creek.

As drama critic on his Fine Arts staff, Ivie Nakai had expected to go. Ivie, a bright Japanese-American, had joined the *Urbanite* right out of the University of Georgia—to replace the retiring Cliff Todd. Although still a novice, she was hurt that Xavier had picked off this plum assignment for himself. Two years ago, she'd acted in the GBS Festival, then written a prize-winning story about it for the student newspaper, *The Red and Black.*

"Can't we both go?" she asked Xavier. "They double-track the plays up there. It'll cut your reviewing load in half if you take me with you."

"The *Urbanite* would have to foot the bill for two hotel rooms and two different reporters' meals, Ivie."

"The Parker-Cranston Syndicate makes kaboodles. My going to Placer Creek wouldn't squeeze them at all!"

Most novices weren't so persistent. But Ivie had passion to go along with her credentials, and Xavier was reminded, inevitably, of a passage from *Thus Spake Zarathustra:* "I tell you: one must still have chaos in one, to give birth to a dancing star. I tell you: you have still chaos in you."

But so did he, and seniority counted for something.

"Listen, Ivie, it's not the money. The week I'll be off to the Shaw Festival, two new productions of classic plays will be opening here in Salonika."

Ivie studied him warily. "What are they?"

"Our Hearts Were Young and Gay by the Proscenium Players and *Arsenic and Old Lace* at Under Southern Stars."

"Aaaaaiiii!" shouted Ivie Nakai. "Aaaaaiiii!"

In Placer Creek, Xavier forgot Ms. Nakai's anguish and enjoyed himself at excellent stagings of *Major Barbara, Back to Methusela, The Devil's Disciple, Saint Joan, Mrs. Warren's Profession,* and *Pygmalion.* The new American play was a (superbly acted) turkey about machine intelligence, a crippled French space station, and an aging hippie activist trying to recover the star-creating inner chaos of his youth. As bad as this play was, it couldn't taint the pleasure Xavier took from the vintage dramas by Shaw.

Between plays, Xavier hiked some of the Phosphor Fog Trail and rummaged through the first editions in the antique shops on Placer Creek's main street. He ate vegetarian meals at Pamela's Boarding House, panned for gold in a stream next to one of the hills forming the Oconee Mountain Amphitheater, and lay in bed one evening—a four-poster feather bed, with a calico canopy—listening to the summer thunder and watching fantastic zigzags light up not only the hilltops beyond the boarding house but also the abstract arabesques of the wallpaper.

Nietzsche had been sick much of his life—a man for whom the ideal of "great healthiness" had been a fleeting will-o'-the-wisp, but he had also had moments like this, moments of exaltation that redeemed the brain-racking agony of his work.

SIZZLE! CRACK! BOOM!

This is how the Life Force flows, Xavier thought, wriggling his toes under the sheet—this is how it renews us. He thought then not of another passage from *Zarathustra* but of some telling lines from the poetry of Dylan Thomas: "The force that drives the water through the rocks / Drives my red blood."

After the festival, Xavier got into his rented car (he hated to drive, but you couldn't hail a cab in the Phosphor Fogs) and headed not toward Salonika—with its inescapable air of disintegrating civilization—but deeper into the mountains. He wanted to find a Nietzschean solitude that would heal his neglected Life Force.

Grantham wasn't looking for him until late the next afternoon, and Pamela—of Pamela's Boarding House—had told him how to get to a clear-water spring seldom visited by tourists. He might be able to indulge in a moonlight swim there without disturbing anyone or being disturbed.

By seven that evening, he had found the spot, a limestone sink at the base of a wooded cliff well back from the highway. An old mill had stood downstream from the pool into which this icy spring emptied, but the mill hadn't operated for years.

Now, it was only weathered timbers and the rotten paddles that had once given torque to its wheel: a picturesque ruin.

Xavier parked above the mill, carried a picnic basket down a path tangled with blackberry vines, and ate his dinner on a rock ledge over the spring, nibbling Gouda cheese and sourdough bread while sipping a good but inexpensive Chardonnay.

There was a nylon tent in his rented car, the sort that can be pitched by snapping out its aluminum supports into a miniature Hemisphere. Xavier decided to swim, camp on the rock ledge, and take another swim in the morning. Then he'd get his gear and begin the two-hour drive back to Salonika. He'd have an entire day to recuperate at home before returning to the day room. There was no rush. The GBS Drama Festival was small potatoes, journalistically speaking, ranking well below a sex scandal featuring either a public official or a televangelist.

Later, tipsy from the wine, Xavier went skinnydipping. The water was clear as glass and almost as sharp. Swimming in it was like drinking white lightning chilled in dry ice. Going under the spring's surface was like closing your mouth on a stick of licorice and opening it on total vacuum. Bubbles rippled over Xavier's body like fresh 7UP, astonished minnows fled from him like glassy-blue match flames, and a languidly coiling eel hung before him as if trapped in gelatin. It was a weird eel, uncannily long, with eye spots as red as poppies and a violet dorsal fin that seemed almost feathery.

Xavier broke the surface. Were electric eels ever a variety of freshwater fauna? Nope. The eel might bite him, but it wouldn't discharge thousands of volts into his helpless body. Hell, *it* must be scared of *him*. A little healthy thrashing about would frighten it away and get his own sluggish blood moving.

He began butterflying across the spring, dolphin-kicking as his arms looped in and out of the water. Soon, he had neutralized the cold and driven off the eel.

"The force that drives the water through the rocks / Drives my red blood."

Xavier rolled to his back and saw the oblate moon shining down, silvering the pool. The moon was a radioactive skull— possibly Nietzsche's. Nietzsche envied him both this lovely experience and his "great healthiness."

Out of the water, Xavier put on a pair of shorts and set up

his tent. Crouched beside it, he heard a splash from the rock
pool: a very loud splash. He grabbed his flashlight and shone
it on the water. Immediately, there was another splash, just as
loud, and this time he thought he saw some kind of creature
leap from the bank to the pool. A muskrat? Xavier crossed the
ledge and peered down into the weeds growing out of the
jumble of rocks next to the water.

His flashlight's beam picked out a shape that experience and
memory told him was that of . . . well, a frog. A bullfrog. An
enormous bullfrog. As big as a well-fed house cat. He had
heard of an African variety of frog that grew even larger than
these frogs had grown, but he'd never seen one in the States,
and the appearance of this *beast,* glistening a faint emerald-
grey in the flashlight's cone and the eerie wash of the moonlight, gave Xavier the shivers. He stared and stared. At last,
the third, and last, bullfrog plunged into the water, throwing
up spray and disappearing into the dark mirror of the pool. A
dream? Xavier went back to his tent and lay down.

He soon fell asleep, on the still warm slab of the rock ledge.
Owls hooted, bats twittered, treefrogs chuckled. Eventually,
even Tarzan could not have been more at home in the jungle
than Xavier was here in the Phosphor Fogs.

Then, he began to dream. His dream had the stark su-
prareality that cleverly made horror movies sometimes have,
and he woke from it uncertain whether he were awake—Friedrich, I am *not* a sleeper—or still under the spell of his sub-
conscious.

He crawled out of his tent in his shorts, looked up at the sky,
now moonless, and saw that under the stars hung an imperceptibly glowing membrane, a thin airy scarf occupying that
part of the sky directly above the rotting mill, the hidden
spring, and some of the nearby forest.

Besides this glow, Xavier noticed a prickling of his scalp and
skin, as if microscopic mites had hopped onto his body and
started feasting on him. It didn't hurt, this prickling, but it
burned a little.

An imaginary sensation? The Phosphor Fogs were notorious for causing unsuspecting tourists to hallucinate.

July or no, it was too cold to swim. Xavier put on his boots,
pulled on a shirt, and found some stepping stones in the
stream. On the other side, guided by the shimmer overhead, he
climbed through a maze of blackberry vines and trees to a dirt

roadway. He hiked it, two ruts in an open-topped tunnel, until the sky-glow led him to an overlook above eight concrete towers resembling huge termitaria.

The light staining the sky here, sending its tendrils into the adjacent Phosphor Fogs on plumes of steam, was urine-colored, a sickly yellow, the product of hundreds of smoky arc lamps. It was nothing like the glow Xavier had seen earlier, but it came from the *same place* where that other bleak shimmering had originated, i.e., here at this half-hidden power station.

The "termitaria" were cooling towers for the nuclear reactors. Xavier was gazing down on Plant VanMeter, the facility built by Consolidated Tri-State to serve major parts of Tennessee, Georgia, and Oconee. Despite protests, the plant had come on line, as scheduled, the same spring Xavier joined the *Salonika Urbanite*. Here, on the edge of Phosphor Fog National Park, it had run efficiently ever since.

The plant was walled, fenced, moated. Tonight, it looked like a set from a horror film about the crematoria in Hades. In fact, Xavier could see an army of figures in white masks, caps, and suits swarming around the hourglass towers. A helicopter treaded air above them. A man leaned out and shouted instructions through a megaphone at the swarming workers. But Xavier could hear no cries, no rotors. Had cold spring water rendered him deaf?

Along with the plant's eerie yellow glow, its dreamlike silence unnerved him. He gripped his elbows, scratching his upper arms in an effort to ease the prickling-tingling-burning there. He *wasn't* deaf. He could hear his fingernails scraping skin, his own ragged breathing, and the forest's night noises. He also heard a man on the ridgetop fifty yards away.

"Hey, dude, what're you doing up here?"

Nothing, Xavier thought. Just gawping. Just wondering about my selective deafness. Still, he *felt* guilty. And when this man, a helmeted security worker, yelled again, Xavier bolted.

He darted back into the trees and, from their cover, followed the roadway until he could hear the creek. Winded, he knelt, scratched and bleeding, among blackberry vines until certain that nobody was coming.

Then he forded the stream and scrambled back to the ledge on which he'd set up camp. There, he removed his shirt, moistened it, dabbed at his wounds, and crept back into his tent. He no longer cared about the oddball shimmering just under the stars.

The sting of his cuts had replaced the weird tingling that had earlier mystified him. He lay down on the rock and slept hard until morning.

When he awoke, Xavier couldn't shake the feeling that something very odd had happened. On the other hand, he didn't know if he had dreamed his trek to Plant VanMeter or if he had really gone there—only to be run off by a guard and his own needless guilt. The cuts that had seemed so bad last night looked, now, like ordinary scratches. Perhaps he had gotten them hiking between the mill and this spring.

Light began to fill the Phosphor Fogs. Xavier had no desire to go swimming again. He felt sure that people would soon be along, either tourists or a forest ranger or some local hillbillies or—if he hadn't dreamed the whole episode—a few inquisitive guards from the power plant.

"Light I am: ah, that I were night! But it is my lonesomeness to be begirt with light!" (Nietzsche again.)

Last night, Nietzsche had smiled down from the moon, but now he was lost in sunlight, and these words from "The Night-Song" seemed to be advising Xavier to run to darkness again.

He gathered up his gear and drove nonstop from the mountains of north Oconee to his high rise in Salonika. He made this trip in less than two hours. Then he sat in a wing chair, curtains drawn, listening again and again to a recording of Gustav Mahler's Symphony No. 7 in E Minor.

4

Consolidated Tri-State Meets the Press

The pretty guys from the networks will be down here en masse," Walt Grantham was saying when Xavier entered the day room. "And Consolidated Tri-State's doing its utmost to stonewall *every*body."

A kind of controlled chaos seethed from floor to floor through the Ralph McGill Building. Telephones rang, reporters zigzagged between desks, a TV monitor high on a support column sustained a small crowd of journalists with no direct involvement in the story that had just broken.

"What's going on?"

"Later," Walt Grantham said. "Glad you're back—but later, Xavier, later."

Lee Stamz grabbed Xavier by the elbow and maneuvered him into a partitioned area given over to the staffs of the Entertainment and the Fine Art divisions of the *Urbanite*. Stamz was a black man in his late forties who'd played middle linebacker on the last Oconee State University football team to win the national championship. It was impossible to resist him when he *leaned* you whichever way he wanted you to go.

Stamz had a transitive *lean* that was irresistible. Bodyguards, bouncers, Secret Service men, and professional boxers would have paid small fortunes to attend a seminar on how to develop a *lean* as authoritative as the former All-American's.

"You really don't know what's going down?" Stamz said, *leaning* Xavier into a swivel chair.

"Con-Tri's just had its own Chernobyl?"

"It ain't that bad."

"Three Mile Island, then?"

"Despite the hoohah here, it don't seem to me it's even a patch on *that* one. Hard to say, though. Con-Tri's bigwigs are trying to contain things—more than the hot stuff from an auxiliary cooling tank that's overflowed."

"When did this happen?"

"A stranger in Placer County says yesterday morning, but she didn't pick up on it until late yesterday evening. Grantham didn't find out about it until she phoned him around four A.M. The dinks at WSSX learned of it before we did and sent a van to Placer Creek around one or so. If you'd been awake, you could've watched their live on-site ex-po-*zay* just when Grantham was groping for the phone and finding out we'd been scooped by the vacuum tubes."

Over the day, it became clear that an accident of some kind *had* occurred at Plant VanMeter. At a news conference telecast live at 6:30 P.M., officials of Consolidated Tri-State admitted it, but said that operator error had had "nothing to do" with the release of an "acceptable level" of radionuclides from Reactor No. 4. The failure had been a relief valve's in the core-cooling system, but neither negligence nor faulty maintenance had led to the accident.

Well, what had? everyone demanded.

The engineer who'd supervised the construction of the reactors took the mike and explained that the valve in question—yes, the physical artifact itself—had given way of its own accord, had cracked in spite of its alleged long-term invulnerability to such behavior, and that some instances of metal fatigue were completely unpredictable.

This explanation made no one happy, least of all the *Urbanite*'s Metro/State reporters. The next several questions snapped off at the Con-Tri representatives bristled with scorn.

"How much radiation was vented?"

Not much. About four curies, about a quarter of that released at Three Mile Island. And everyone should note that in the 1986 disaster at Chernobyl, about fifty *mega*curies of radionuclides as pernicious as cesium 137 and iodine 131 had escaped. By *that* standard, the Plant VanMeter "event" was a trifling thing—hardly any reason to evacuate the surrounding areas or to demand the total closure of the facility.

"What's the operational state of Reactor Number Four right now?" a network correspondent asked.

Operators at the plant were working steadily and professionally to achieve cold shutdown, a "scram" state they would bring about within the next few hours. Decontamination procedures and repair work would then begin.

Because of design modifications effected as a direct result of the Three Mile Island accident, the reactor would probably return to full operational capacity in less than six months— nothing at all like the seven years necessary to put the damaged reactor at the Susquehanna facility back on line. It would cost, of course, and cost quite a lot, but Con-Tri, accepting full responsibility for the gremlinish valve failure, was prepared to bear this expense without imposing a rate increase. Moreover, members of the Nuclear Regulatory Commission were being kept abreast of developments, as were those of the Institute of Nuclear Power Operations, and the President himself would soon visit the plant to show that there was no substantial danger now and never really had been.

"We've come a long way in handling out-of-the-blue breakdowns resulting neither from negligence nor operator error," said Plant VanMeter's spokesman. "The public should applaud the speed with which we detected the breakdown and the efficiency with which we're remedying it."

"*Any* breakdown is unacceptable!" a reporter said.

"Hey," said another, "how can the public applaud the idea that some breakdowns are random? That there's no way to prevent them? That all that remains is to cope with this unpreventable crap *after* it's happened?"

"That's *not* what we're saying," the engineer said. "It's just that omniscience in any complex mechanical-technological enterprise isn't to be had. We're not gods."

"Then what gives Con-Tri the right to play God with us and our children's lives?"

Another correspondent said, "Letting a kid juggle marshmallows is one thing, giving him a boxful of live grenades is another."

"The public can take confidence," the sweating spokesman said, eyeing the press distastefully, "from the fact that we *don't* claim infallibility. If we thought we were infallible, we wouldn't be as vigilant in our monitoring procedures."

"Look," said the engineer, "every important human activity has risks. You can sit in a padded room doing nothing, or you can go climb a mountain. You may fall into an abyss, or you may gut it on out to the summit and find out how big the world is. But you won't end up with upholstery sores on your fanny."

"Hear, hear," a reporter said sarcastically.

After the news conference, Ivie Nakai buttonholed Xavier in the corridor. "You were up there. Placer Creek's only about fifteen miles from Plant VanMeter. Can you point to anything that might've tipped you off to the accident?"

"No."

"You didn't see or hear anything?"

"Are you bucking for an investigative reporter's job?"

"No, sir. I'm just interested. I mean, it's hard for me to be blasé about anything nuclear. I had family at Nagasaki."

"Okay. I understand. But the accident took place yesterday morning. At least, the *recognition* of the problem occurred then, and by that time I was on my way home. I couldn't have had a clue to what was going on over there because even the folks at Con-Tri didn't know what was happening yet."

Xavier rode EleRail home. He was convinced that his adventure above the power station, his near-capture by a security guard while spying on those antlike workers and that soundless helicopter, had taken place only in dream. A vivid dream (he could still see the urinous sheen enveloping the facility and the huge termite cones of the cooling towers), but still a dream.

After all, Consolidated Tri-State wasn't playing cover-up; they had released all the facts at their disposal. Now, the President would visit the plant to reassure the nation that nuclear power was still the safest, most economical, most practical sort of energy-generation available to the American people.

This visit duly took place. Plant VanMeter remained open, and Reactor No. 4, which achieved cold shutdown as predicted and stayed off line for 167 days while decontamination procedures and repairs were accomplished, was brought back to full operational capacity at the end of December. Radiation studies authorized by the NRC and INPO found that only five *curies* of radiation had escaped into the atmosphere—only slightly more than the figure acknowledged by Con-Tri. The accident wasn't a "disaster." Genuine disaster would have

been to shut down the entire facility, depriving the people in
three progressive Southern states of a safe, cost-effective
source of electrical power.

Xavier agreed with these conclusions. By September's end,
he had ceased to think about his . . . dream.

It was opera season. Salonika's young but accomplished
company had scheduled works by Bizet, Handel, Verdi, and
Wagner. Because Ivie Nakal had spent her summer covering
hoary farces and musicals, Xavier told her that she and Donel
could divide the opera openings between them. This was his
way of apologizing for shutting her out of the Shaw festival.

"Hot damn!" Ivie cried, banging her fist on the desktop.
"Hot damn!"

5

Bari Carlisle

That same September, Xavier met Bari Carlisle. He met her on one of the polished hardwood ramps curving around the skylighted atrium of the Upshaw Museum.

Today, this ramp was housing a traveling exhibit of African masks, statuary, and carvings, and Bari stood there on it with two photographers and three long-legged models. The models resembled Giacomettian parodies of human females.

None of these women, to Xavier's eye, was as beautiful as their employer, for Bari Carlisle was a young fashion designer whose line had won acclaim not merely in the U.S., but also in London, Milan, Tokyo, and Paris.

Bari's of Salonika was her logo, and Xavier could approve on practical as well as aesthetic grounds almost every garment bearing this eponym. The women modeling Bari's creations might look like shaved giraffes, but the fashions themselves were attractive, functional, even elegant. Her cleanly made sportswear would not have been out of place at a formal dinner or a chic society soirée, for she knew how to make sailcloth look like acetate and denim like satin—well, not to *look* like those fabrics, maybe, but to drape a woman's body so strikingly that even "common" fabrics acquired a classy sheen.

In the Upshaw, Bari recognized Xavier because his photo ran in the *Urbanite* beside his column, "Thus Saith Xavier

Thaxton," and Xavier recognized Bari not only because she was such a high-profile figure in Salonika but because he'd once attended a fashion show in her atelier, a remodeled textile mill on the Chattahoochee. Today, she was busy directing her models and her photographers, working to assemble a catalogue of her fall-winter line for a Dallas retail house. Xavier, meanwhile, was studying the Senegambian artifacts for his next column.

"You can't be here now," Bari told him as he ambled by.

"Pardon?"

"The museum staff told me I'd have sole access to this exhibit from four o'clock until closing."

"It told me, a month ago, I'd have sole access on the afternoon of," consulting his watch, "yes, fourteen September."

"That's today," Bari said. "Obviously a scheduling error. Why don't you go downstairs and have them make you another appointment, Mr. Thaxton?"

"Sorry, Ms. Carlisle, but I have a deadline."

"And I've got my models and photographers to pay. Even here in the gracious old state of Oconee, they don't come cheap."

Xavier understood that Bari's investment in the situation was indeed greater than his own. "All right. I'll withdraw my claim. But I'd like to set two conditions."

"You would?"

"First, that you let me watch the entire shoot. I want a look at what Salonika's finest couturière has been doing lately."

Bari said neither yes nor nyet. She was waiting for Xavier to state his second condition.

He obliged: "I'd like the chance to take you to dinner as soon as you've finished here."

After hesitating briefly, Bari agreed.

Xavier was surprised. His photo appeared in the paper a few times each month, sure, but he didn't make the money in a year that Bari's of Salonika took in every fortnight (if not every day); and he was such a minor celebrity that it embarrassed him—made him feel like an imposter—if anyone approached him to thank him for a column or to request an autograph. But Bari was willing to go to dinner with him. Did she know what she was doing?

But she *had* agreed, and although the shoot required five hours and dozens of costume changes, she said goodbye to her models and left the Upshaw with him at 9:17 P.M. After a twenty-minute wait, they got a table at Lesegne's and dined on blackened pompano with a bottle of Meursault white burgundy. They made each other laugh, enjoyed each other's talk, and rubbed noses good-night on an ornate little drawbridge in front of Bari's red-brick atelier, which stood in a remodeled rivershore neighborhood thick with elms, sycamores, and willows.

This could be the start of something big, Xavier thought in the taxi on his way home, humming and snapping his fingers.

It *was* the start of something big, this sporadically conducted romance. Its sporadicity resulted not from their lukewarm feelings about each other, but instead from Bari's work, which took her out of Salonika at least once a month. She knew several famous designers, including Kawakubo in Tokyo and Alaïa in Paris, and to sell her lines to retailers abroad and to renew her contacts with her mentor-peers, she had to fly off to see them.

Everyone in the business advised Bari to leave Salonika, to set up a studio in New York, if not in London or Paris; but one of her goals—as quixotic as it seemed, even to Xavier—was to turn her city into a respected international capital of fashion. This goal made Bari seem to him not merely an intelligent woman but a kind of soul mate, for just as he hoped to elevate the tastes of the masses, she hoped to show the sachems of haute couture that a city in the southeastern state of Oconee could waltz, gracefully, with the elite.

Chances to date Bari occasionally arose, and it was these dates that kept Xavier from regarding their relationship as doomed. For example, after attending a performance of *Twilight of the Gods* by Salonika's Rivershore Opera Works— Donel Lassiter had praised the orchestra; Ivie Nakai had criticized the singers' acting—he and Bari had a martini together and took a cab to her studio.

Inside, he found that the old mill housed not only an immense second-story work area, but also quarters downstairs for seven of her firm's twenty employees. The other thirteen men and women had their own homes or apartments.

Bari lived in the loft and slept on a mattress under a drafting table. She'd learned this time-saving procedure from the Tunisian, Alaïa, who had also encouraged her to secure her workers' loyalty by showing concern for their welfare, eating with them, and taking every available chance to talk to them. Consequently, she had a kitchen on the studio floor, and she and her employees prepared a communal meal at noonday: a monstrous chef's salad, three or four baked chickens, or a host of cucumber-and-pâté sandwiches.

Xavier admired this setup on one level, but found that having seven workers on the premises at all hours sabotaged not only his peace of mind but also his libido. So he often tried to persuade Bari to come to his place. When she did, they enjoyed themselves in every way that two people possibly can. He appreciated her body, the breadth of her learning, the near-flawlessness of her tastes. And, knowing so little about haute couture, he asked her to teach him about it.

Bari declined. He hadn't had to tutor her in the rudiments of contemporary art, music, and literature—so if he wanted to learn about her profession, he could burn the midnight oil. After-hours shoptalk wasn't Bari's idea of a stimulating evening. Xavier was her sole refuge from fashion, and she didn't want to give it up by conducting an off-duty tutorial.

Understanding each other in these ways, they became a couple, and Xavier accommodated himself to her hours, her flights away from Salonika, and the fact that she was far better known locally than he, no matter how often his picture appeared in the *Urbanite*. But he was glad to make these adjustments. He had fallen, chapeau over cordovans, in love.

6

''For Love Designed''

A couple of things did bother Xavier about Bari. Minor things, sure, but he had to work to keep them in perspective.

First, it was Bari's daily habit to tape a monstrously dreckish soap opera called "For Love Designed" and to watch it every evening on her outsized TV before crawling under her drafting table and going to sleep. Once, she used the master remote to turn on the VCR just as Xavier was about to kiss her goodnight. He stood there bemused, until she pulled him down into a pile of pillows and made him watch the program with her.

The soap opera, as he soon learned, dealt with two sisters who at birth had been Siamese twins joined at the spine. Fortunately, their wealthy father, the head of a multinational corporation, had been able to hire a renowned French surgeon to separate them. The girls then had relatively normal childhoods, growing up beautiful and much desired.

Because the sisters had been dizygotic (nonidentical) Siamese twins, one was dark and one fair—each with a personality and a character metaphorically at odds with her coloring. In short, the fair sister hated the dark sister, while the dark sister was in a constant struggle to *keep from* hating the fair one. After going to private schools in Switzerland, the twins began careers as fashion designers. Competition between them accelerated, not only in their work but in their romances.

And so the title, "For Love Designed," which also had something sinister to do with the operations performed upon the sisters as infants. In the episode he watched with Bari, the French surgeon had just reappeared in their lives, a Byronic figure of mystery and menace.

"This stinks," Xavier said. "I swear to God, Bari, it's so bad it makes my teeth hurt."

"Of course. For the past fifteen minutes, you've been grinding them."

"I'm not kidding, Bari. Why waste good tape to preserve it?"

"It's so bad it's amusing."

"It's so bad it's abominable."

"Hey, this is what I do to wind down. What's the problem? You think I'm an airhead for watching a soap opera?"

Xavier said nothing, having already showed his hand.

"You're always tossing Nietzschean bons mots at me. Let me turn the tables. Who said 'The more complex the mind, the greater its need for simple play'?"

"Oscar Wilde, I think. But *that* isn't simple play, Bari, it's a schlocky crime against humanity. As with currency, bad drives out good. By watching such shameless crapola, you're an accomplice to the debasement of taste. You, of all people."

Bari began to laugh.

"This isn't funny. It's a matter of real consequence."

" 'A reviewer who expresses rage and loathing' for a work of the imagination," Bari quoted and paraphrased, " 'is like a person who has put on full armor and attacked a hot fudge sundae or a banana split.' Kurt Vonnegut."

Xavier waved an arm at the soap opera. "That isn't a work of the imagination, Bari. It's the vapid dramaturgical excreta of a script-writing committee."

Bari patted Xavier on the knee. "Why don't you go home and let me finish debasing the American taste by myself?"

Xavier did, aware that he'd behaved like an asshole, but still convinced that "For Love Designed" stank. It deserved permanent encasement in an iron cassette cartridge and immediate deep-sixing in the Chattahoochee.

Why would Bari "wind down" with such stuff? You could wind down with a flute concerto by Bach or an essay chapter from *Tom Jones* or *Moby Dick*. Resorting to a soap opera was evidence of a lack of seriousness about life's earnestness or of a submerged lack of respect for oneself.

Even if Bari was the most poised and self-reliant woman he'd ever met.

Xavier put Bach's "Sheep May Safely Graze" on his stereo. Such beautifully soothing music. But only a few seconds later he had a humdinger migraine. He resisted taking an aspirin, but, as the music unraveled, the pain intensified.

Xavier staggered to the bathroom, fumbled at the cotton in the neck of an aspirin bottle. His face, there in the medicine-cabinet mirror, bore an odd resemblance to that of the actor who played the French surgeon in "For Love Designed." His mind went prowling back over the lurid episode he'd watched with Bari.

Lord! He was *dwelling on* a stupid soap opera. Disgusted with himself, he dug furiously at the stubborn plug of cotton, knowing that he would go quietly berserk if he didn't extract and take an aspirin soon.

But, remembering a melodramatic scene in which the fair sister had confronted the dark sister in a swank restaurant, he realized that his headache was gone. He felt fine. There was no need to take an aspirin. None. He stuffed the cotton plug back into the bottle and returned to the living room.

"Sheep May Safely Graze" had concluded. Xavier put on another CD, this one a Pergolesi composition. Less than a minute into it, his headache came raging back, worse than before. Xavier removed the CD, struggled back to the medicine cabinet, popped an aspirin, and waited for it to do its stuff.

And waited.

And waited.

When it did *not* take effect, he turned off all the lights and lay down on his bed wondering about Bari's untoward fondness for a soap opera. Eventually, his pain eased a little, and he was able to sleep.

A second thing that upset Xavier about Bari was her spontaneity—often to the point of impropriety—in erotic matters. Many men would have found this trait in so elegant a woman an exciting plus, but Xavier considered it out of character, as her fascination with "For Love Designed" was out of character.

An example?

While Bari was home from a trip to San Francisco and getting ready for another to Toronto, he took her to Lesegne's again. Turbot, sole, and salmon in a delicate tomato sauce, with baby vegetables and succulent pieces of crayfish. Poached oysters with whites of leeks. Finally, an after-dinner digestif, from Château Grillet at the northern end of the Rhône Valley.

During dinner, Bari kicked off one of her high heels and placed her stockinged foot on Xavier's instep, then slid it up his calf to the inside of his thigh. Only the heavy linen table-cloth allowed her to carry out this maneuver in public, but Xavier could tell by the way that a patron at another table was staring at them that he had caught on to Bari's foot play, and maybe even envied Xavier his abashed status as its object.

All Xavier could think of was the scene in the film *Tom Jones* where Tom and a buxom flame-haired wench turn a shared meal into the prelude to some energetic lovemaking. And, on the taxi ride home, Bari practically crawled into his clothes. Her lips were like migrating decals on his temple, face, neck. Whenever Xavier could sneak a glance into the rearview mirror, he saw the cabbie's startled eyes drinking everything in.

"Bari," Xavier whispered. "Bari, we can't do this here."

She drew back and looked at him. "It *is* physically possible, you know."

"It's also—here, anyway—animalish and rude." He nodded at the mirror.

"You're right," Bari said, sitting up and placing her hands in her lap. "You're absolutely right."

And the rest of the way to her atelier, she sat beside Xavier as chaste as a prioress. Once in Bari's loft, though, they locked the door and at his insistence moved a table in front of it. Then they made love. Bari was wild as a cougar. They wrestled each other so vehemently that it was more like warfare than love-making. Xavier kept expecting a concerned worker to arrive with a battering ram. Although pleasantly sated at the end of these exertions, he felt like a man who has just taken part in his first house-clearing brawl.

"A little slower next time," he said. "With Debussy on the CD player and your mattress somewhere nearby."

"Sure," Bari said. "We'll trade off. The only civilized thing to do."

And they did. In fact, their affair, despite Xavier's doubts about his own worthiness and Bari's recurrent need to travel on business, prospered. The world would have been a wholly delightful place, Xavier decided, if not for the headaches that continued, at the oddest times, to afflict him.

If not for the headaches, that is, and an unexpected telephone call from his older sister, Lydia Menaker.

7

"Uncle Xave"

Lydia and her husband Philip were physicians. A refugee-relief agency headquartered in London had asked them to go to Pakistan to oversee the medical facilities at a refugee camp near the Afghan border. Although the Menakers had been working with the urban poor in Southern California, mostly illegal aliens from Mexico, they'd decided to accept this challenge and fly to Peshawar. Lydia told Xavier her plans over the telephone.

"Congratulations," he said dubiously. "When will you and Phil be leaving?"

"In a month," Lydia said. "But there's a problem."

"I'd surely have a problem," he said, thinking of Peshawar's crowded streets and the frightening squalor.

"The problem's Mikhail," Lydia said.

Ah, yes. Mikhail Geoffrey Menaker, Xavier's fifteen-year-old nephew. It shamed him to think that he had forgotten to ask about the boy. It had been almost four years since he'd seen Mikhail; he still pictured him as a befreckled eleven-year-old, not as a gawky, acne-afflicted teenager.

"What kind of problem is Mikhail, Lydia?"

"He doesn't want to go. Given conditions over there, we're not all that keen on his coming with us, anyway."

"Being named Mikhail might not stand him in such great stead, either." (The Menakers had named their son after one of Philip's swashbuckling great-uncles.)

"His name's not an issue. For the past year or so, he's had us call him 'Mick' when talking to him and *'the* Mick' if referring to him in the third person."

" 'The Mick'? As in *themic,* short for *thematic?"*

"Phil and I know it's a phase he's going through. We humor him in it. Anyway, Xavier, he doesn't want to go. Nor does he want to stay here in Chula Vista."

More and more wary, Xavier said, "What *does* he want, Lydia?"

"He'd like to come live with you. You're his favorite uncle."

"I'm his *only* uncle."

"Salonika fascinates him because that's where the company that makes his favorite comic books is."

"Comic books?"

"He's a fan and collector. Uncommon Comics, UC Comics—their headquarters are right there in your state capital."

"A sound educational reason to come here, all right."

"Phil and I checked into a school near you. Ephebus Academy—across Le Grande Park from your condo—gets very high marks."

"Ephebus Academy?"

"We'll pay tuition. They've already agreed to enroll him."

"Lydia, you *do* recall there was a mishap at Plant VanMeter this past summer, don't you?"

"Yes. But the radiation hazard was said to be minimal, and the damaged reactor is already back on line, isn't it?"

"True," Xavier said. "But the effects of radiation exposure on young people aren't very well understood."

"Xavier, if you don't want the Mick to come, say so."

"It's not that," Xavier lied. "I haven't been feeling too well lately." (Which *wasn't* a lie.)

"Symptoms?"

"Little things. I'm embarrassed to state them. A headache, an instant of fatigue. They come and go, but usually strike while I'm on assignment."

"Maybe you're working too hard."

"It's not *always* on the job, Sis. I'll get an eye tic reading Céline. Or the hiccups watching TV—once while the Sankai Juku dance company was performing on PBS."

"Go for a checkup. My long-distance diagnosis, though, is that you're suffering from tension. Simple nerves."

Whose nerves are simple? Xavier thought. And won't taking in a fifteen-year-old apartment guest do a wonderful job of calming them and easing my mind?

"This seems to be a bad time for you," Lydia said. "Forgive me for asking." She mumbled something, then spoke aloud: "Mikhail—the Mick, I mean—wants to say something, Xavier."

"Hello, Uncle Xave." The boy's voice went up and down like a roller-coaster car: the teenager's identifying squawk.

"Hello, Mikhail."

"I'd try not to be a drag on you. I mean, you know, I'd, like, behave myself."

Lydia came back on. "He means it. He's not a, huh—he's not a bad kid. He's bright. He even knows how to cook."

Ultimately, Xavier agreed to shelter Mikhail and to act as his guardian during the Menakers' eighteen-month stay in Pakistan. He owed Lydia and Phil that much—and he would not have been able to live with himself if they'd had to enroll their son in a military academy or to pay complete strangers to take him in.

Once off the phone, Xavier saw that his hands were trembling.

"Uncle Xave?" he said. "Dear God, I'm an *Uncle Xave.*"

8

The Mick

Mikhail Geoffrey Menaker flew into Sidney Lanier International Airport two weeks later. Bari, who was between business trips, rode out to the airport with Xavier on an EleRail train to provide moral support when he met the boy.

"What does he look like?" she asked when they sat down at the appropriate gate on the concourse.

"A long-haired Tom Sawyerish kid with freckles and a toothless grin. Last time I saw him, that is."

Xavier had no trouble recognizing the boy once passengers began to disembark. Most of the flight's passengers were adults, and Mikhail emerged through the birth canal of the docking tunnel as if he were a unique type of humanity, either a devolved specimen or a futuristic model still in the throes of becoming. Actually, it wasn't that Xavier had never before seen anyone who looked and dressed like his nephew, it was instead that he had not expected the Tom Sawyer clone of recent memory to appear to him in such a guise.

"Ah," said Bari, more interested than appalled. "A retropunk."

"Pardon?" said Xavier, more appalled than interested.

"Retropunk. You know, it's just started coming *back* in."

"Yeah?"

"Yeah. I saw a lot of it again last month in Tokyo."

Xavier gawped at Mikhail, who stood just inside the passenger gate surveying the crowd. He wasn't much taller than he'd been four years ago. He was wearing faded jeans, a sleeveless leather jacket embossed under one pocket with a thumbtacked skull or robot face (it was hard to say which), old motorcycle boots, and a spiked wristlet hinting at recent imprisonment in a Roman galley.

Mikhail's hair bristled on top. It was skinned clean at the temples. It flowed from his nape in a braid that was mint-green and magenta. He had an arrowhead on one earlobe, black circles under his eyes, and high on one cheek a grease-painted atom with orbiting electrons.

"A real fashion plate," Xavier said.

"More imaginative than ninety percent of the people who got off the flight with him."

Xavier said, "About as imaginative as combining a terry-cloth toga, a baseball cap, and loggers' boots."

"At least he isn't a geek in a grey flannel suit, Xavier."

They moved toward the boy, who had a duffel bag and an armload of comic books.

The comic books featured on their covers a host of costumed superheroes. So many that if there were *really* superheroes, they could more easily set themselves apart from their umpity-ump fellow vigilantes by abandoning the lookalike tights, capes, and hoods and wearing, say, khaki slacks and T-shirts.

Xavier introduced Bari, put the comics in the boy's duffel bag, and shouldered the bag himself. Then he said, "They won't let you into Ephebus Academy with that haircut, Mikhail."

"I can have my head shaved, can't I?"

"And the clothes—you won't be able to wear them at Ephebus. They have a uniform."

"Yeah, I know. Navy pants. Ash-grey shirts. A throat-gag of a school tie. And a fucking *escutcheon.*"

"You going to have trouble with any of that?"

"From nine to three every day? No sweat, Uncle Xave. It'll keep my real rags"—he meant the outfit he had on—"from going downhill so god-awlmighty fast."

Bari and Xavier looked at each other. There was no doubt that Mikhail—"Call me the Mick," he said—lived and breathed at a remove of several generations. He wasn't just younger: he hailed from another tribe, another country, maybe another *planet.* He was like an exchange student from Uranus.

As soon as they reached Xavier's apartment, the Mick found the TV set (no easy feat since it was hidden behind a pair of louvered cabinet doors) and snapped it on. Insanely, "For Love Designed" smoodged into fuzzy focus.

The fair (evil) sister was informing Dr. Merleau that the dark (good) sister had been trying to have him deported to Paris as an undesirable alien and that the only way he could prevent her (the dark sibling) was to feign a marriage with her (the fair sibling). Meanwhile, she would tell one of her *ouvrières* to telephone a bomb threat to the dark's sister design studio.

"I love this fucking show," the Mick said. "It's a hoot."

Gak, thought Xavier. But after stepping into his tastefully decorated condo again, his eyes had gone a little out of focus, blurring everything within his view. Just a few minutes of watching "By Love Designed," however, seemed, unaccountably, to have restored his vision to its normal acuity.

Bari sat down beside the Mick on the sofa, dropping an arm over his shoulder like a loving big sister.

A loving *blond* big sister, Xavier reflected. In the context of this development, their shared affinity for a hokey sudser, Bari's blondness made a statement as clear as that of the show's fair-haired sister.

Like V. S. Naipaul, Xavier felt intuitively that "vulgar people have vulgar interests; common minds have common excitement." And he was dismayed to think that the woman he loved was a soap-opera addict and that his nephew was likewise a fan.

How was he going to survive the next eighteen months?

9

(Don't) Paint It Black

The Mick had brought only the clothes on his back and the stuff in his duffel: toiletry gear, a few more clothes, some paperback books, a selection of CDs, and not much else.

Two days later, a moving van dropped off several boxes that Xavier and the Mick pushed into the elevator and toted down the hall to Uncle Xave's twenty-second-story apartment. They found room for the boxes in the study that Xavier had given the boy for a bedroom. Five long white cardboard boxes held Mikhail's comic-book collection, more than a thousand titles. Another pair of cartons contained his CD collection, the illustrated inserts of which all seemed to feature fuzzy-maned band members with protruding tongues, bugged-out eyes, and garishly painted faces.

The truck had also brought a CD player, a small TV set and its stand (casters included), a portable tapeplayer/radio or "boom box," a 768 personal computer, and some portable plastic files for cassettes and diskettes. Xavier began to realize that the Mick was with him not simply for a weekend pajama party, but for a time with . . . well, the likely subjective duration of the afterlife.

Oddly, for a while after Mikhail's arrival, Xavier ceased to suffer the minor physical upsets that had begun to plague him in September. At work, his colleagues remarked on his improved mood (translation: Lately, you've been a real bear), and he was able to enjoy the art work, dramas, films, symphonies, and dance recitals that it fell to him to cover. Maybe it all had something to do with the fact that the Mick was trying, here at the outset of their relationship, not to be too much trouble. Emphasis on *trying*.

For example, he had his hair cut, took the arrowhead earring off his ear, and scrubbed away the atom symbol on his cheek and the corpselike half-circles under his eyes. Each morning, he left for Ephebus Academy dressed in the required uniform. He hated it, but he suppressed the urge to rebel and waited until after school to put on duds more accurately reflecting his tribal allegiance. He griped a lot, muttering under his breath if not actually cursing aloud—but he hadn't yet brought drugs to the dinner table or purchased a submachine-gun.

And, as Lydia had promised, Mikhail cooked—scrambled eggs, hot dogs, cheeseburgers, tomato soup, chili. He didn't cook *well*, but after a long day traipsing from EleRail station to EleRail station, Xavier was glad enough to eat what the Mick had prepared. Sometimes, though, he bullied the Mick into presentable clothes and took him out for an expensive dinner.

Bari occasionally went too. Although the Mick used four-letter words as if they meant "great" or "Oh, rats," he had a quick mind and plunged head-first into any conversation that didn't depend on a knowledge of topics yet unstudied. The out-of-left-field quality of some of his insights was compensation, almost, for the crudity of his tongue. Bari enjoyed these outings, and Xavier relaxed in the realization that playing uncle to the Mick wouldn't necessarily put a disabling crimp in their romance.

Early on, though, he and the Mick had a major clash, and it was the Mick who found the subterfuge that kept it from escalating into a permanent feud. Almost.

"I want to paint my room," he said.

"Fine. What color?"

"Black. I need a funky cramped feeling, sort of a black hole of Calcutta twenty stories up."

"You're kidding."

"Why do you think that, Uncle Xave?"

"It sounds hideous. And if you do a halfway decent job of it, it'll be almost impossible to paint over later."

"So I can't do it?"

"No, you can't."

"I'm a refugee in your backyard, right? Not like your *real* flesh-and-blood kin but a sort of nonperson gook squatter."

Xavier sighed. "No, Mikhail. But this is still my place. I'll have to live here even after you've left, and I simply don't want a 'black hole of Calcutta' here in my apartment."

"Boy, you're a proprietarial bastard, Uncle Xave. You could be a fucking fatcat landowner in Central America."

"I'm the fucking fatcat landowner only of my home, and you're not going to paint any part of it black."

"Whoa. Sorry I ripped your cord."

A week later, the Mick invited Xavier into his room, and Xavier was taken aback to find—even in the deliberate gloom—that the walls were all black. Plutonian black. Stygian black. Atop this black were black-light posters of rock stars, four-color posters of comic-book superheroes, and signs proclaiming NO SMOKING UNLESS YOUR SOUL'S ON FIRE, DARE TO EAT A PEACH, and I SEE UC, YOU SEE UC, WE ALL SEE UC, & THE UC WE SEE IS GOOD. All Xavier could really see, though, was the black walls behind these cryptic tape-ups. He grabbed the Mick's skinny arm.

"Hold your fucking ponies, Uncle Xave! Take a look, okay?"

Xavier looked. Mikhail had draped every wall with black linen, every one. He had bought king-sized white sheets, carried them across the river to a dyer's shop, and had them stained the color of anthracite. All for less than three hundred bucks. Wasn't that a bargain for totally redecorating a bedroom?

"What's that smell?" Xavier said.

"The dye. My joss sticks. It'll go away. No big deal."

Xavier, sniffing, looked around. How to respond? Finally, he hugged his nephew. "Thank you, Mikhail," he said.

"For what?"

"For respecting my feelings in this. It's amazing. A sign of a nobler sensibility than I expected."

"You think I'm a punk who'd like sniff dog vomit?"

Xavier waved at the walls. "In a sense, you have. Just look at what passes with you for interior design."

"I do. All the time. That's what I taped it all up for. If you don't like it, beat it for a while."

Later, Xavier realized that the Mick had run him off for insulting his values. Still, the Mick had found a way to do the room to his own standards without breaking Xavier's rule against painting it black: a small cause for celebration.

Except that it wasn't. The smell in the room wasn't dye or incense, it was a more familiar smell. One day while the Mick was at school, it drew Xavier in. He lifted the black linen drapery just inside the door. Behind it was more blackness. A harder blackness. And the smell of fresh paint.

The Mick *had* painted the walls black. Then he'd disguised his misdeed by hanging black sheets over the proof of his contempt for Xavier's rules. A closer look showed Xavier that two of the room's four walls were no longer draped in black at all. The Mick had put these sheets on his bed and rigged a swag-bellied black canopy from the ceiling with the remaining dyed linen. The Mick had played him for a sucker. Had lied. Had laughed him to scorn.

"Why?" Xavier raged when the Mick got home from Ephebus. "Why would you go to so much trouble to deceive me?"

"No trouble," the Mick said. "Had me a blast."

"You disobeyed me. Stabbed me in the back. Why?"

"This is my room. *I* live in it, not you. And I wanted black walls, okay? Issat a fucking crime?"

"If I say so, it's—"

"If you say so, unc, it's GIGO: garbage in, garbage out. Hey, relax. It'll grow on you. That's why I did it this way. So you wouldn't have nine heart attacks getting over your fuddy-duddyism and cadging how to skate the nool." *Nool,* Xavier had learned since the Mick's arrival, was a slangy collocation of *new* and *cool.*

Fearful of a firecrackerish sequence of heart attacks, Xavier backed out of the Mick's room, slammed the door, and stalked to the kitchen for a double shot of scotch.

The Mick made few friends at Ephebus Academy. He talked about school only if Xavier pumped him. When he did talk, he offered few details and seemed indifferent about the school. If pressed, he would say "It's boring." Or: "The kids're stuck-up nerds, and the teachers're tofu-eating yuppies."

Mikhail's inability, or refusal, to make friends at Ephebus did not seem to bother him. Once home, he put on his funky

duds and diddled with the graphics on his computer. Or he
flopped on the bed to read his *Decimator* and *Scarab* comic
books, admitting that although most retropunks despised superheroes, he thought they were " 'lutely nool." Sometimes he
plugged into his CD player to listen to hoodluminati bands
like Mace, Rectal Exam, Cold Grease on Cary, and Smite
Them Hip & Thigh. He never seemed to do any homework,
but he somehow passed his classes. Every essay and test paper
that he brought home had earned him at least a C−.

About six weeks along, the Mick sauntered up to Xavier,
then relaxing in a wing chair, and handed over a note from his
English teacher. The note said there were certain assignments
Mikhail adamantly *refused* to do, an attitude that wanted
correction.

"What assignments do you refuse to do?"

"Anything that bores me. If it bores me, I *can't* do it."

"What's the latest thing you haven't been able to do?"

"Read *Moby Dick.*"

"*Moby Dick,* the great American novel, bores you?"

"It drags, Uncle Xave. No juice, no jazz, no pizzazz."

"Mikhail, you're simply missing it."

"It ain't there."

"From the teeming wisdom of your fifteen years, you're
telling me *Moby Dick*'s a bore?"

"It and *Nostromo* and *Portrait of the Artist as a Young Man*
and *The Sound and The Fury* and *Women in Love.* Yawnsville,
all of 'em."

"Who do you like, Mikhail?"

"Jim Thompson. Philip K. Dick. Stephen King. Frank
Miller. Elmore Leonard. John Shirley. Those guys."

"Nobody else?"

"Stuff they won't even let in the door at Ephebus. Private-
eye stories. Sci-fi. Horror. Comic-book superheroes."

Xavier stared at the Mick as if at some incomprehensible
sci-fi alien. Mahler, Melville, and Monet bored him. His idols
were punk rockers, horror novelists, comic-book artists.
Xavier's heroes were elitist stiffs who'd lasted as long as they
had only because nerdy academic types had taken up their
overclever crap as the best route to gassier egos and longer
careers.

What could Xavier say? That he loved what the Mick dismissed? That he found in the strivings of even the most diffi-

cult artists a heroic affirmation of intellect as well as heart? That symmetrical complexity can be as beautiful as stark simplicity?

Sure, those would be good things to stress. But he could also say that anyone may learn to appreciate *both* kinds of beauty if not repeatedly warned away from the former by philistines and from the latter by snobs.

Maybe, in rendering certain judgments, he came on like a . . . a snob? Damn, he didn't like to think so. You couldn't praise the bad just because it was accessible. Or put down the praiseworthy simply because it failed to excite the masses. Unless, of course, you didn't give a damn about the truth. Xavier didn't think he was an elitist. He believed in the Keatsian doctrine "Beauty is truth, truth beauty," and he didn't like people to mistake pewter for platinum.

Out of this reverie, Xavier found that the Mick had retreated to his bedroom. He followed him to his door.

"Mikhail, do you think I'm a snob?"

The Mick, cross-legged on his bed, sat under a poster of the hoodluminati band Smite Them Hip & Thigh: five teenagers of three distinct racial phenotypes and six different hair colors. Linked by an electronic umbilical to his music, Mikhail unplugged.

Xavier, irritated, repeated his question.

"You'd know better'n me, Uncle Xave."

"Let me rephrase. Do I *seem* to you a snob?"

"Let me ask *you* a question." The Mick smiled cryptically. "Do you think I'm a fucking yahoo?"

"You're unfinished. And too quick to label boring what you don't yet understand. But you're no yahoo. You're too smart."

The Mick considered this. "You're unfinished, too," he said. "You in your high-art way, me in my kipple-packed hoodluminati rat hole. Your way could be worse."

Xavier would have liked to argue this, but he had to pick up Bari at the Salonika Trade Mart, and their discussion came to an indeterminate end. Even so, he went out thinking that it might be a worthwhile experiment to sit down—when he had more time—and listen to the irritating hoodluminati yahoos known as . . . Smite Them Hip & Thigh. Maybe.

10

Critical Mass

One morning, Xavier took Bari and the Mick to mass at Christ's Episcopal Church in downtown Salonika, a lovely white edifice in the classic Greek style. Mikhail hadn't wanted to go—he'd never gone with Xavier to church before—but when he learned that Bari was also going, he reconsidered.

On the walk from Franklin Court to Jackson Square, he slouched along behind Xavier and Bari, wearing blue jeans, sneakers, and a clean white T-shirt with his Ephebus Academy tie. Xavier had been about to forbid him to come, if he dressed with so little respect, but Bari, a vision in mockingbird-grey and eggshell-white, had urged Xavier to relax his standards— not to demean the scheduled high communion, but to make it easier for Mikhail to go with them.

"What's more important, Xave, that he look like a little earl or that he take part in the Eucharist?"

Even Xavier knew the answer to that question; and in the wide, cool sanctuary of Christ's Episcopal, as the choir on the mezzanine sang cheerfully to guitar and flute accompaniment, the issue of the kid's dress ceased to matter. Xavier felt uplifted by his presence in the church and exalted by the music. Nietzsche would puke, of course, but Xavier was religious not merely by childhood upbringing but on tested philosophical-aesthetic grounds. Preparing for high communion, he felt almost exactly as he did when strolling past a superb exhibition in the Upshaw or seeing Aeschylus well performed at the state theater.

So what if the Mick had schlepped into God's house clad like a retropunk haphazardly whirled through a men's shop? So what if Xavier's head still throbbed from too much wine at Lesegne's? So what if Bari had come along more to keep him company than to take the elements? And so what if his nephew was thumbing through the Book of Common Prayer as if it were an out-of-date volume of *Comic Buyer's Guide?* What mattered now was this sublime striving toward Godhead. A sublime striving—as scandalous as the notion would seem to most priests—spiritually *akin to* the Nietzschean urge to obtain to the *Übermensch.*

"Are you all right?" Bari suddenly asked Xavier.

"Fine," he whispered, half surprised to find himself still in an earthly building in latter-day Salonika.

The robed priest had finished his homily. He was calling his parishioners to the altar to receive the wafer and to drink from a silver goblet. Ushers were gesturing pew occupants to their feet and nodding them into a shuffling double queue. The huge painting of Christ behind the altar, a fresco in which the Son of God looked like either a Dante Gabriel Rossetti longhair or a superannuated hippie used-car salesman, seemed to lend the Savior's own blessing to this steady procession. Xavier grabbed the seat back in front of him to get to his feet.

WHOOSH! his sinuses roared open. He pulled out a hand-kerchief, blew his nose, dabbed his upper lip and chin.

But Xavier was the victim of an untimely allergy. Not only did his nose run, but his eyes gushed, his lips discharged a colorless sebum, and his ears drained a waxy amber goo.

"Fucking gross," yucked the Mick.

Xavier was disoriented; he felt as if a very large person—Lee Stamz, say—had seized his noggin and plunged it into a zinc bucket of acidic vanilla extract and melted crayons.

"Xavier, you're ill," Bari said, taking his arm.

"I'm all right!"

"You can't go up, Uncle Xave," the Mick whispered urgently. "They're using a fucking common cup."

An usher—a watery ghost in a three-piece suit—said, "The boy's right. Things being what they are nowadays, we can't let you go up with everyone else."

Had Xavier insisted on that privilege, there might well have been a scene in Christ's Episcopal. But Xavier didn't insist. Balloon-headed, he offered no protest when the usher led him and his companions to the vestibule.

Asked the usher, "Like me to see if there's a doctor among our worshipers this morning, Mr. Thaxton?"

"No, thank you."

Xavier, Bari, and the Mick walked home. Or, as it seemed to him, swam home, dog-paddling through the bizarre mists generated by his own inner weathers.

Yuck. (The only word adequate to the situation.)

Later, laid out on the sofa in his apartment's living room, a towel protecting the pillow under his head, Xavier began trying to compute the chances of drowning while unsubmerged.

"We should call a doctor or take you to the emergency room at Salonika General," Bari said.

"Uh-uh. I'll be all right."

Squatting, the Mick opened the louvered doors hiding the TV.

"Not now, Mikhail," Bari pleaded.

"Uncle Xave didn't get decently churched. Watch this."

Dwight "Happy" McElroy's "Great Gospel Giveaway" flickered into view. Wide-angle pans of the Televangelism Temple in Rehoboth, Louisiana, revealed several thousand jubilant worshipers. McElroy was dunning both them and his video audience for money, currently with a performance by twelve poodles dressed in robes: McElroy's Dixie Dog Disciples. The poodles danced around the evangelist as a two-hundred member choir sang: "Giving your all, / O yes, your all, / Yes, giving your all / For JEEEEEE-suhss."

"What a fucking trip," said the Mick.

"Spare me," Xavier said, squinting at this spectacle between his stockinged feet. "Mikhail, spare me."

"Come on, Mick," Bari said.

"Just want ol' Uncle Xave to get his weekly minimum allotment of religion, Bari-Bari."

"That's not religion, Mikhail. That's an abominable conflation of sideshow hucksterism and pious razzmatazz." Xavier sat up and pointed at the screen. " 'Great Gospel Giveaway' has about as much to do with the cultivation of faith as astrology with the acquisition of knowledge about the heavens. A hypocritical sham. It makes me sick. Sick to my soul."

"That may be. But," Bari said, "you seem to be doing a little better physically."

Xavier was surprised to find this true. Strange fluids had ceased flowing from his eyes, ears, and nose. His mucous membranes had dried out, he was witnessing McElroy's vaudevillian tom-foolery with mist-free eyes. "Gospel Giveaway" offended him spiritually, but he couldn't deny that he was otherwise in the pink of health.

How thoroughly he'd recovered from his untoward allergy attack during high communion!

"Turn that off, Mikhail. Now."

The Mick, picking up something implacable in his uncle's tone, obeyed.

11

Chad, Di Pasqua, and the Therac 4-J

Teri-Jo Roving's two-year-old son, Chad, stood on the carpeted speaker's platform in an auditorium of the Miriam Finesse Cancer Clinic. Dr. Witcover, a visiting oncologist, had just given a lecture on recent advances in detection-and-diagnostic procedures, and, Chad, podium mike in hand, was doing a dead-on and very funny baby-talk impersonation of the departed lecturer.

Dr. Di Pasqua heard the noise and came back into the auditorium from the corridor. He had been so busy dispensing hospitality and local color to Dr. Witcover that Teri-Jo hadn't yet had a chance to talk with him. Well, that chance seemed imminent. . . .

"I'm sure you all have things to do," Dr. Di Pasqua told Teri-Jo and the others watching Chad.

"Yessir," everybody said, obediently beginning to leave. Chad stayed on stage, beside the podium, swaying in knock-kneed spasms and carrying on a conversation with the microphone that was nothing but amplified popping.

"Is that your grandson?" Dr. Di Pasqua asked Teri-Jo, who was trying to halt the toddler's performance.

"No, Dr. Di Pasqua, this is my firstborn."

"Sorry," Dr. Di Pasqua said. "Of course."

Teri-Jo carried Chad down from the platform to Dr. Di Pasqua. During her pregnancy, he had been on a research sabbatical; as a result, he had forgotten, or had never learned, that her labor had been hard and her recovery slow.

"Chaddie's here because my husband's sick. Our regular day-care providers are remodeling their building."

"Never mind. So long as he isn't burlesquing a distinguished guest, I don't object to his being here."

"Mamma," Chad said, a low murmur. He placed both hands on her face and pushed his button nose into her hair.

"Come, Nurse Roving," Dr. Di Pasqua said. "I've got something to show you."

They left the lecture hall. When Dr. Di Pasqua thought better of Chad's accompanying them, Teri-Jo took him to Bonnie Gainsboro, a secretary, who seemed even less thrilled by this arrangement than did Chaddie. His heartbroken wails were audible all the way to the service elevator to the basement.

Downstairs, Dr. Di Pasqua led her into the tunnel connecting the cancer clinic with Salonika General. "A custodian found this yesterday," he said, "but Dr. Witcover's visit kept me from trying to deal with the problem until now." They stopped short of the tunnel's midway point, in the mouth of a bleak tributary corridor that Teri-Jo had never really noticed before.

Kept *me* from trying to deal with the problem, she amended her boss's words. That's what you really mean.

"This is an auxiliary storage area." Dr. Di Pasqua opened the door with a tarnished key. "The custodian came in here yesterday to inventory cleaning equipment, but ended up"—escorting Teri-Jo past a tall metal rack of disinfectants and paper products—"ended up finding something rather alarming."

Briefly, Teri-Jo imagined the janitor stumbling upon a corpse, maybe even Dr. Wayman Huguley's. Which was absurd. She had gone to the old man's funeral.

"There," Dr. Di Pasqua said, pulling a frayed light string to reveal the inanimate cause of his alarm: *"That."*

Teri-Jo gaped. It was a cancer-therapy device, an antiquated machine whose type the clinic no longer used and a working example of which she hadn't seen in over fifteen years. Radiation therapy was still a relatively young science, but in the presence of this obsolete treatment machine, Teri-Jo felt as a contemporary sports-car enthusiast might feel in the presence of a Stanley Steamer.

"What I'd like to know," Dr. Di Pasqua said, "is if this thing has been radiation-decommissioned."

"Desourced?"

"Yes. This must have been one of Dr. Huguley's purchases. If so, there's no telling how long it's been moldering in here."

Despite the easy and Scrooge-like slur on Dr. Huguley, her boss might be right. If he were right, he'd shown damnably bad judgment allowing them both to walk in here as if the therapy machine were as benign as any old Wurlitzer. They should have worn vest shields and carried a dose-rate meter. On the other hand, if any of the janitors had been mopping the halls with radioactive disinfectants, the clinic's weekly checks would have told them so long ago.

Teri-Jo knelt beside the machine. Its markings—and her own memory, belatedly kicking in—identified it as a Therac 4-J, a device once manufactured by the EarthRay-Schenck Corporation of Danby, Ohio. Teri-Jo examined the machine carefully.

"It looks to me as if its source is intact, Dr. Di Pasqua. The cylinder holding the cesium cake is right here, just where it would be if the device worked. However, it's possible there's no cesium in the can." She wrote down the machine's serial number and date of manufacture.

"How possible?"

"Not very, really. If somebody's going to decommission a source—empty out its heat—why would they shove the empty cylinder back into the machine? We'd probably be smart to regard the Therac 4-J as alive."

"All right. We will. Which means we may have another disposal problem on our hands. If so, I'm charging you to get rid of this therapy machine without a drawn-out search for a disposal site. We don't have the room, and I don't have the patience." Dr. Di Pasqua directed Teri-Jo back out into the main tunnel.

Tell me something I don't know, Teri-Jo thought. Aloud, she said, "At least I've got a telephone number this time. A lead. If they haven't changed it. If they're still in business."

Dr. Di Pasqua locked the door, and he and Teri-Jo returned to the clinic, where she rescued Bonnie Gainsboro from Chad (and vice versa, probably) and carried him into her own office to scan the computer files for the radiation-disposal invoice and to flip past all her dog-eared Rolodex entries looking for the telephone number of . . . Environomics Unlimited. Ah, there.

"We're in business, Chaddie."

On the floor with a box of facial tissues, Chad pulled them out and tossed them away like a magician releasing doves with clipped wings.

That afternoon, Milton Copperud, the NCR physicist assigned to the cancer clinic, dropped by to tell Teri-Jo that, just as she had surmised, the Therac 4-J was still "loaded." It had not only its source cylinder, but, within that cylinder, a hefty complement of the radioactive stuff that had once made it a moderately effective therapy instrument. *Moderately effective* because this model of the machine had always had some design problems.

"Its last resupply from EarthRay-Schenck was two years before Dr. Huguley hired me," she told Copperud, consulting a file folder that no one had ever troubled to log onto computer disk. "Cesium 137's half-life is thirty years. That means there's still a goodly mess of curies clicking away in there."

"Well, Teri-Jo, they're safely pent—the emission level's not even measurable yet. But the sooner the Therac's gone the better."

"You talking public health, Milt, or my job security?"

Copperud laughed, gave her a two-fingered salute, and took off for another part of the clinic. Chad snoozed in a nest of carpet shag, snoring in a high-pitched, eerie impersonation of his daddy's sleep sounds. Teri-Jo smiled at him and punched out the old number for Environomics Unlimited.

Blessedly, it rang.

12

Variations on an Unknown Malady

In the next month, nothing similar to, or quite similar to, the episode at Christ's Episcopal befell Xavier. He told himself that an allergy had been to blame. When this theory failed to quell his doubts, he posited such causes as diet, stress, a rampant virus, or an extreme reaction to exhaust fumes or other pollutants.

Damn it all, Xavier's body had begun to betray him in strange ways. Nothing like the sinus problems—"head leakage," Mikhail had dubbed that whole complex of symptoms—suffered at communion, but stuff just as hard to account for and to deal with. In fact, Xavier accounted for and dealt with it all by refusing to think about it.

If he thought about it, he would have to take steps—write out a list of his episodes, visit a doctor. And visiting a doctor was out of the question. He didn't want to know what the doctor might find. Cancer. Muscular dystrophy. AIDS. Alzheimer's. Nothing but a clean bill of health would relieve his anxiety, and he was afraid he couldn't get one. So he never thought about his illness except recurrently through the day and continuously through the night. In "The Night-Song" from *Thus Spake Zarathustra,* the prophet says, "But I live in my own light, I drink again into myself the flames that break forth from me." Xavier was living in his own darkness and drinking again into himself every potentially enlightening tongue of flame. Maybe those flames would flicker out if he ignored them. . . .

The Mick weaseled his way through his classes at Ephebus, bringing home a D− in English for refusing to let Melville, Conrad, Joyce, and Faulkner "bore" him. This attitude enraged Xavier, who saw it as an excuse for avoiding the unfamiliar and for dismissing big chunks of humanity's past as irrelevant and unworthy of study.

During Ephebus's Christmas break, the Mick hunted different means of getting through the days while Xavier was at work. He read (comic books), eyed the tube (soaps and game shows), fiddled with his computer (interactive video games), and listened to his tapes and CDs (especially those of Cold Grease on Cary and Smite Them Hip & Thigh). What he *didn't* do, Xavier noted, was throw the football in Le Grande Park, lift weights at the Y, take walks, or join a youth basketball league.

"You've got to get some exercise," Xavier told him. "You can't just sit up here and vegetate."

So the Mick rummaged up his skateboard, purchased knee and elbow pads, a pair of high-topped athletic shoes, and a helmet, and began spending his days "thrashing" the sloped concrete walls at Skateboard City on Battery Place.

He did this both in the morning and the afternoon. He did it wearing his court gear and a pair of loose dove-grey sweats—so that when he got home in the evening, he had the parboiled look of a lobster and the reek of a well-worked dray horse. His shins, forearms, and palms bore the bruises and hamburgery scrapes that he had acquired playing "war" against other skateboard jockeys, and at dinner Xavier felt lucky if Mikhail didn't nod off with his fork almost to his lips.

"You've got to take it easy," Xavier said. "You can't try to wear your skateboard out before the New Year."

So the Mick stayed home the next day, and that evening Xavier asked him to play some chess. It took a while to convince Mikhail that this was a good idea, his own preferred sports being televised women's roller derby and the rough sort of concrete surfing favored at Skateboard City, but at last he fetched the chessmen and laid out the board. This, thought Xavier, is what Mikhail needs. His skateboarding was a sport on a par with such déclassé recreational amusements as pro wrestling, jai alai, and drag racing. Chess, on the other hand, was a hallowed variety of intellectual combat.

The game began. The two traded pawns and erected defenses even as they engineered wily lines of attack. Xavier was enjoying the game, and the Mick seemed equally absorbed. Abruptly, Xavier's nose began to bleed. He'd never had a nosebleed in his life, and the sight of so much crimson splashing the chess pieces—*"The Red Sea!"*, to quote Cyrano— unnerved him. He feared the hemorrhage implied a fatal cancer. Both hands over his nose, he recoiled from the board as if from blazing coals.

"Caramba!" the Mick cried. "Looky there, unc—you've done a *Friday the Thirteenth* sequel on your whole damned army!"

Nearly every piece on Xavier's side of the board resembled the gore-covered victims in a slasher film. Seeing the bloody carven knights, bishops, rooks, and royalty . . . well, it made him recall every rotten horror film that he'd stumbled into accidentally or whose plot he'd heard numbingly detailed by one of the *Urbanite*'s Popular Culture staff.

Abruptly—as abruptly as it had begun—Xavier's nosebleed was staunched. Mysteriously staunched.

"You okay?" the Mick asked.

"I think so," Xavier said, wiping his face and hands with a tissue.

"Here." The Mick picked up the entire board. "I'll clean the bloody little fuckers up.

"Go ahead, but there's no way I'm going to touch one of those pieces again. None."

The Mick considered the crimson flood an interlude in their play, not an emphatic period, but Xavier would not continue. He retreated to the bathroom for a washcloth and peered at himself in the mirror with bemused and haunted eyes.

That same December, a few of the actors scheduled to take part in the next George Bernard Shaw Drama Festival in Placer Creek came to Salonika's Oconee State Theater to do a staged reading of "Don Juan in Hell" from *Man and Superman.* This reading was a preview of the festival itself and a sop to those city officials who felt that Phosphor Fog Community College was too small an institution, in too remote a spot, to host such a prestigious event.

Xavier, now recognizing Ivie Nakai's passion for all things Shavian, took her with him. Because she would be attending the GBS Drama Festival & Country Crafts Fair as the *Urbanite*'s Fine Arts reporter, he wanted her to have a head start on the out-of-state competition. He'd outperformed the *New York Times, Washington Post,* and *Atlanta Journal-Constitution* reporters who'd come to Oconee last July. Ivie would too.

The first reading was a private affair for the mayor and a few media people. The actors dressed casually and moved about the bare stage as if their playbooks were superfluous. Xavier was impressed by their preparation and the ease with which the actors playing Don Juan and the Devil spieled Shaw's witty speeches.

Suddenly, Xavier found himself resisting an urgent pressure in his lower colon. Ivie Nakai, enraptured by the performance, was unaware of his problem. How to dam this intestinal tide? Should he run to the john to keep the Life Force within him from arranging his public embarrassment?

Near the end of the piece, as the Devil was advising, "Beware of the pursuit of the Superhuman: it leads to an indiscriminate contempt for the Human," Xavier had no choice. Standing, he said, "Forgive me, Ivie. This is . . . urgent."

It was, too, but he made it. In the john, he tried to recall if he'd eaten or drunk anything that would have affected him this way. Out of disgust for its radio ads, he avoided Ricardo's, and he'd never been big on martinis or kraut dogs. But even as empty as an unused wineskin, his stomach continued to knot and unknot. Xavier crept back into the theater and eased down in his seat just as the actors were taking their final bows.

"God," Ivie said. "You're as white as a slug, sir."

Xavier left the theater and caught a taxi back to the Ralph McGill Building. He had work to do, and the cramps he was still having were no immediate threat to his sanity. They'd surely stop soon. (Wouldn't they?)

In the lobby, Donel Lassiter saw Xavier and waved a supermarket tabloid called the *Instigator* at him. "See this rag. A classic, a bona fide classic."

"Garbage, Donel. Garbage pure and simple."

"How can you say that, sir? This story"—slapping the front

page—"is Pulitzer Prize material." He thrust the *Instigator* into Xavier's hands. "See for yourself."

"Wait a sec—!" But Donel was off, waving cheerfully over one shoulder as he exited onto the street.

Xavier, his gut aching, carried the paper to his office and sat down in his swivel chair. 84-YEAR-OLD WOMAN GIVES BIRTH TO FROG! declared the headline of the story that Donel had cited as Pulitzer Prize material.

Other headlines?

TEENAGE SEX SLAVE'S FAVORITE SNICKERDOODLE RECIPE.

JESUS'S UFO TWIN ADDRESSES ISRAELI KNESSET WITH GHOST OF JOHN LENNON.

DANNY DEVITO AND JACKIE O. TALK ABOUT THEIR FORBIDDEN LOVE.

Xavier, incredulously agog, perused the stories beneath these headlines. In a while, his wrenching intestinal spasms ceased, and he felt himself again.

An evening later, Xavier was attending a performance of the Salonika Symphony Orchestra. The airier his spirit, however, the heavier his body. As the tenor horn sounded soulfully in a late movement of Mahler's Seventh Symphony, his knees began to tremble, his eyes to tear, his arms to depend like dead-weight salamis. Not again, he thought.

He had to stay conscious. If he fainted, he'd halt the winter concert, embarrass himself, and miss the fifth movement's stirring *Kapellmeistermusik* parody, a rondo that never failed to tickle and revive him. How terrible, to succumb again to the perverse ailment that had plagued him off and on ever since . . . but never mind his fateful camping trip in the Phosphor Fogs.

What barbarous times, he thought, still trying hard to focus on the fourth movement's lovely *Nachtmusik*. A barbarism that includes various nuclear hazards, global terrorism, the galloping debasement of popular tastes—and the soul-destroying physical and emotional fallout from these horrors. Xavier envied the *civilized* romantic angst of Mahler, who'd composed this movement in 1904 at Maiernigg in the Tyrolean Alps. Even in those transitional times, one could fall into existential nausea. But in 1904, at least, it was still possible to shape, without embarrassment or apology, sublime works of art, passionate expressions of the human soul that could change one's life and redeem the age.

The harp and the tenor horn lifted Xavier's spirit ever higher, but his body seemed to be filling with sludge.

"Xavier," said the beauty sitting beside him in the *Urbanite*'s reserved box. "Xavier, what's wrong?"

Bari Carlisle, a world-famed couturière. The woman he planned to marry. He could not answer her. He pulled himself up by the balcony rail and stared down on the audience. Closing his watery eyes, he reached toward the musicians so brilliantly rendering the Seventh. Gravity seized him, and he began to topple.

"Xavier!" Bari cried.

Later, he heard people conferring above him.

"An honest-to-God swoon," a disembodied male voice was saying. "You rarely see that anymore."

"Better to call it a 'swoon dive,' " said a woman.

"If Ms. Carlisle hadn't grabbed him by the cumberbund."

"Otherwise," the woman replied, "he'd've swoon-dived right into three or four concertgoers."

"Who is he, Tess?"

"The Fine Arts editor on the *Urbanite*. Anyway, he favors that highbrow idiot's picture."

"Idiot or no, he brought this Mahler marathon to an end. I'm forever in his debt."

"Then," said Bari, kneeling beside Xavier, "why not give the 'highbrow idiot' a little air?"

"Why?" said the woman called Tess. "I mean, he's always giving himself airs, isn't he?"

Holding a moist towel to Xavier's forehead, Bari glared at the bitch. Disconcerted, Tess and her escort slunk off via the stairs, and the orchestra belatedly launched the bravura fifth movement of *Song of the Night*.

"Thanks," Xavier managed, opening his eyes and reaching up for Bari's hand. He still felt weak, but getting out of their balcony seats had restored a modicum of his vitality. Unfortunately, the wonderful music swelling anew in the concert hall had already begun to erode it again.

"We're leaving," Bari said.

"I *can't* leave. Concert's not over. I've got a review to do."

"Haven't you liked what you've heard so far?"

"Of course. This is a definitive Seventh, Bari."

"Then the fifth movement won't be a letdown, either." Bari helped Xavier stand. "Write what you've told me and your review's as good as in the system."

"That'd be cheating, Bari. That'd be—"

"—surviving, lover, and that's all we're going to say about the matter. Here, anyway. Come on."

She helped him down the stairs and out of the concert hall.

13

At First Stringers

A counterman at First Stringers cried, "Walk two mutts through the mud! Coupla spudboats 'n' a pair of dopes, make 'em beanless!"

Xavier couldn't believe he was in this trilevel fast-food emporium, the greasiest greasy spoon in all Salonika. He hated hot dogs, French fries, onion rings, soft drinks, all the garbage urban masochists indiscriminately devoured in their search for what he could only assume was Perpetual Dyspepsia. That Bari'd brought him here, thirty minutes after he'd swooned at a Mahler concert, flouted all logic.

"He means two chili dogs, two orders of fries, and a couple of decaf Cokes."

"I know what he means, Bari. The appalling part's that we're actually ordering these culinary offscourings."

"Pretend it's caviar, coq au vin, and Napoleon brandy."

"If I could do that, I'd quit my job to write novels."

He looked around. Of all places to end up, First Stringers was the nadir. Its patrons were pimply vo-tek students, Oconee State undergraduates, acne-afflicted ladies of the night, possibly even pimply pimps. Sometimes, a few tony uptown types would come in slumming, but they were worse than the locals who had nowhere else to beg or buy their next assembly-line burger.

Bari, carrying their tray as if he were either minor royalty or an invalid, led him into a cavelike first-level TV-cum-dining room, on one wall of which was mounted a concave video screen now showing an ancient episode of "Gilligan's Island"; Xavier took the tray and placed it on the writing surface of one of the old-fashioned school desks that served as tables, then watched with numb incredulity as Gilligan and the Skipper played hot potato with a prodigious crab. Around the room, six or seven zombied-out customers bovinely chewed and bovinely watched.

"Bari, what're we doing here?"

"Squelch that, okay? How do you feel?"

Oddly, he felt pretty good. The bone-deep physical ennui that had overcome him at the concert hall had fled. Even the pervasive reek of grease and stale streetwalker perfume hadn't yet reversed or noticeably slowed his recovery. He told Bari as much, braved a sip of his syrupy cola, and marveled that he should be "dining" in this egregious travesty of a "restaurant." Next to it, McDonald's was another Antoine's.

"Say what you like about First Stringers, Xavier. It seems to be one of the cures for your peculiar malady."

"What 'peculiar malady'? I passed out at a performance of the Salonika Symphony. Now I'm fine again."

"Don't give me that. You've been having spells like this for weeks."

"No, I haven't. . . . I mean, they're nothing, brief moments of weakness. I work hard, hit my deadlines. It takes a toll."

Bari wasn't buying this. She asked him to remember their most recent outing together:

"Last week, at the Upshaw, we were standing in front of that magnificent Vermeer. What happened? After maybe ten minutes of devout silence, you went down on your knees, in what seemed to me an *excess* of admiration."

"A flukish episode. As soon as I'd sat down for a while, I was okay again."

"You sat down on the marble bench in the viewing room, but you didn't start feeling better until I told you to turn and look out the window facing Sycamore. The buses going by with ad panels for Uncommon Comics, 'Schlock Theater,' and the tristate tractor-pull finals—that's what got you back up on your feet. Literally. Five minutes of drecky ad panels was all it took to replenish your vim, lover."

Xavier eyeballed Bari skeptically.

"Deny it," she said. "You can't, though. It's true."

"It's nonsense, Bari. I *recovered,* that's all. I had a dizzy spell from standing so long."

Bari wouldn't concede the point. "Look, we left the Up-shaw. You were fine again. We caught a taxi to the Bergman revival at Screen Dreams. Where, please recall, you were able to *sit,* not stand, for ninety-plus minutes for an exclusive showing of *Smiles of a Summer Night.* Tell me what happened there."

"Nothing. Or nothing much. I fell asleep."

"You *never* fall asleep at a Bergman flick, Xavier. You're the only man I know who could happily watch *The Silence* three times in a row. But you zonked out during maybe the most charming film the Infallible Ingmar ever made. A *romantic comedy!*"

Xavier glanced at the big curved screen. Gilligan was standing on a rock imitating a crippled albatross. "I was tired. It's that simple, Bari: I was tired."

"Not *that* tired. Ray and I practically had to give you CPR to bring you round. We were afraid you'd had a heart attack. Once we'd got you awake, Ray made you gobble jelly beans— for energy, he said. Then he sprocketed up that old Mighty Mouse cartoon, and you were fine again. Again."

"What's your point, Bari?"

"That you're refusing to draw the inevitable conclusion."

"This is absurd."

"Absurd or not, the inevitable conclusion grows more and more obvious. Doesn't it?"

Xavier took another reluctant bite of his chili dog. By almost any standard, it was execrable food, and yet he felt . . . well, *fortified* by the chemically suspect weiner and the too spicy chili, sufficiently fortified to face the issue:

"You're saying that although I esteem high art, the kind that stretches our God-given capabilities to the limit, the products of high art have begun to destroy me physically."

"Partly. What else?"

"Shoddy, inferior work *replaces* the vigor leached from me by my appreciation of Quality. Uncompromising artists weakeneth me, but dreckmeisters restoreth my strength, if *not* my soul."

"Bull's-eye."

Although alert and able-bodied, Xavier was demoralized by this analysis of the problem. "What am I going to do?"

"See a doctor."

"A nonsense syndrome. I must be its only victim."

"Remember when you were a kid and thought every food that was good for you had to taste bad? Liver, spinach, Brussels sprouts? For you, Xavier, it's happening again—but in a way that violates your carefully cultivated *grown-up* tastes."

Xavier was unable to refute Bari's reasoning. He was thriving here on assembly-line garbage, from which his taste buds recoiled, and on sitcom fare that offended his sensibilities in the same way that child molestation offended most well-adjusted Western adults. Short of complete annihilation of the species, he couldn't imagine a worse waking nightmare.

14

The Philistine Syndrome

When he came back to his apartment from First Stringers, Xavier tried to come to grips with what had just
happened. In a nutshell, Bari had diagnosed him. She had
taken circumstantial evidence and built from it a formidable
case for his affliction by a malady that you could call . . . the
Philistine Syndrome.

That did the trick. It perfectly defined the ailment that had
come upon him—ever so slowly—in the wake of his midnight
trek to that ridge in the Phosphor Fogs overlooking Plant
VanMeter. It informed him that fine art, no matter how much
he might appreciate it on an intellectual and spiritual level,
made him sick, while its antithesis—dreck, schlock, trash—
gave him back his physical health while raping his aesthetic
sensibilities and depressing his mood.

I'm the *Urbanite*'s Fine Arts editor, Xavier reminded himself, leaning against his door and surveying the framed opera
posters, lithographs, and original watercolors decorating his
living room. If listening to Weber, or appreciating a Pollock,
or reading Barth turns me into a bizarre variety of invalid,
well, I'm finished as a reviewer. Hell, I'm finished as a *person*.

The door to Mikhail's room was shut. Xavier checked to see
if his nephew had gone to bed. He had.

In bed himself, Xavier realized that Bari's, not to mention
his own repressed, diagnosis of his "peculiar malady" was

right on the money. All Bari had had to go on was his reactions to (1) a mass in Christ's Episcopal, (2) a stunning Vermeer, (3) a lovely Bergman comedy, and (4) a Mahler symphony that unperceptive critics wrote off as "disjointed" when he had always heard in it the transfigured suffering that made all five movements a unity.

In any event, it was amazing that, from these four cases, Bari had figured out his problem. Even though he'd had more to go on—headaches, nosebleeds, sudden attacks of diarrhea—it had taken him longer. And only Bari's relentless pursuit of the matter had made him acknowledge, aloud, the validity of her insight.

Xavier thought back. The high communion at Christ's Episcopal had occasioned his first major attack of the Philistine Syndrome. Why? Possibly, the exalted dignity and solemnity of that mass had qualified at some level of his consciousness as a work of art. In so doing, it had triggered the untoward physical reactions that had prompted the usher to deny them a place at the altar with all the other communicants. Back at home, the tackiness of Dwight "Happy" McElroy's "Great Gospel Giveaway" had "cured" him—at least for a time.

Then there'd been those two episodes of which Bari was still blessedly ignorant, namely, the interrupted chess game with Mikhail and the dash to the restroom at the Oconee State Theater during the reading of "Don Juan in Hell."

Coincidence, Xavier thought, his hands folded before him on the coverlet. He didn't really believe this wishful hypothesis, but he decided to test it. He took from his headboard shelf a volume of Proust's *Remembrance of Things Past.* Defiantly, he began to read. He read for a half hour with perfect comprehension and with total enjoyment. At the back of his mind, meanwhile, lurked an uneasy awareness that, generally, no symptoms of the "Philistine Syndrome" overcame him until he was well into the sublime activity at hand.

Blam!

Less than fifty pages into *Cities of the Plain,* the syndrome struck. Xavier lost his grip on the book, which fell into his lap and cartwheeled from there to the floor. He had no power to pick it up. Except for his eyes, nostrils, and mouth, he seemed to be paralyzed. He could glance around, breathe, and grind his teeth, but he was unable to twitch a finger or wiggle a toe. Panic fell on him like an embroidered shroud.

"Anything but paralysis," he whispered.

His voice startled him. He could speak! At once, he began to shout, *"Mikhail!"* Meanwhile, he prayed that the Mick hadn't gone to bed with Smite Them Hip & Thigh or Tough Grease on Cary rapping in his headphones. *"For God's sake, Mick!"*

Mikhail, ghastly pale, came running in dressed in gym pants and a denim vest festooned with old campaign buttons and phony military medals: his outré substitute for pajamas.

With forced calm, Xavier explained about his sudden paralysis and the strong likelihood that his late-night reading of Proust had triggered it. The Mick looked down at the guilty novel.

"I coulda warned you, Uncle Xave. I really coulda."

Xavier was still too scared to register annoyance. He went on to outline his and Bari's theory that acknowledged masterworks had recently begun to impact him negatively on a physical level, but that artifacts of inferior quality or aim would eventually overturn these ill effects.

"That's crazy," said the Mick. "I'd better call a doctor."

"Don't. Just bring me a few of your *Mantisman* comic books and hold them where I can see them."

"Screw you." Mikhail kicked the Proust.

"Wait!" Xavier cried. "Don't be so all-fired sensitive! Don't abandon me like this!"

The Mick pondered briefly, then left. He came back pushing a TV stand on casters. He attached the wire from the cable outlet and switched the set on. "Weekend Schlock Theatre" was running on Channel 87. Now showing—Mikhail'd already checked the guide—was *Mesa of Lost Women* with Jackie Coogan as the wicked Dr. Aranya and a clutch of nighty-clad quasi-starlets as zombie spider women. A few scenes of this movie reversed Xavier's paralysis.

He crawled from bed.

Weeping with relief and gratitude, he hugged the Mick, hanging from his neck like an outsized crucifix.

15

Captive to Kitsch

Two days later, Xavier sat fully clothed on an examination table in Dr. Nesheim's office. Bari had accompanied him, leaving her atelier in the keeping of her second-in-command, a businesslike middle-aged woman named Marilyn Olvera. Bari was sitting on a low divan near the door.

"At first," Dr. Nesheim said, "I thought you needed a shrink. Work-related stress. The plays, paintings, concerts, and novels your job asks you to review had started to make you ill, even when they were fine examples of their kind. My initial opinion was that the culprit, Mr. Thaxton, was a sub-conscious psychological defense mechanism, one causing a rare sort of hypochondria whose subliminal 'purpose' was to get you relieved of your duties."

"Dr. Nesheim, I *love* my job."

"Stress can overtake people even in jobs they love."

Bari said, "Xavier takes all the best assignments. The rest of his staff review the things that don't appeal to him."

"But there's still the responsibility of field-marshaling the whole enterprise, Ms. Carlisle."

"That's not stressful," Xavier said. "That's fun. Besides, my staff and I get along fine."

In a chair near the examination table, Dr. Nesheim steepled his fingers and frowned. "What I'm trying to say—not well, I fear—is that I *agree* with you. Your condition, your syndrome, isn't a somatic manifestation of a psychological maladjustment.

Stress has nothing to do with it. I believe that your dismaying somatic responses to fine art have an underlying physical cause. In other words, Mr. Thaxton, you aren't crazy."

"What's the underlying physical cause?" Bari asked.

"The first indications of the tests we took on Monday are that Xavier's syndrome may be, well, radiation-induced. He tests out as having absorbed a dosage of six millirems or so."

"What?" Xavier said. "You're kidding."

"No. No, I'm not. About six millirems."

"That should put me at risk for cancer," Xavier said, "not for diarrhea attacks at readings of 'Don Juan in Hell.'"

"Right," Dr. Nesheim said. "You should be dying. Instead, you seem to have such strong psychoemotional reactions to fine art that they alter your body chemistry. Blood-sugar, hormone, electrolyte, enzyme production are all affected. Usually, your system adjusts itself homeostatically as soon as you leave the concert hall or set aside the disturbing novel. But the millirems your body appears to have absorbed are disrupting the readjustment process. Now, the only way you can regain biochemical equilibrium is to put yourself in the way of inferior works of, um, 'art.'"

Xavier looked at Bari. Bari looked at Xavier.

"Dr. Nesheim," Bari said, "that sounds like a lot of jive."

"What can I say, Ms. Carlisle? Much of what I've just told you lies outside the range of a layman's comprehension. I've done my best to simplify it, but radiation remains an unplumbed mystery and so do many of its effects." He turned to Xavier. "Have you had any X-rays recently? Have you visited any contaminated sites? The Marshall Islands? Chernobyl?"

"I was camping out in the Phosphor Fogs when the accident at Plant VanMeter occurred," Xavier said, remembering the glow in the sky and the eerie look of the cooling towers. "From an overlook, I saw workers at the facility trying to cope with it." Was that it? Was that the cause of his syndrome? Xavier found himself thinking of 1950s sci-fi films in which ants, tarantulas, or locusts attained menacing proportions because of radioactivity. And of comic-book stalwarts who had come by their powers as the result of radiation exposure. He, though, was the *victim,* not the beneficiary, of the unplumbed radionuclides. "Are you trying to tell me that I'm the way I am because of that Plant VanMeter business?"

"That's suspicious, all right," Dr. Nesheim said, "but most

of the radionuclides released from the Plant VanMeter mishap
drifted eastward to the sea. I really don't think that's the
source of the radioactivity you've absorbed, Mr. Thaxton."

"Really? Why not? You on their board of directors?"

"Come on, Mr. Thaxton," Dr. Nesheim said with dignity.
"It's just that the accident there, though by no means negligi-
ble, was a minor one. The radioactivity released was minimal.
Only one Con-Tri worker had to be removed from duty at that
site to stay within government-specified exposure limits. You
didn't venture into the reactor building itself, did you?"

"Of course not."

"Then I think the source of your radioactive-poisoning
must lie elsewhere. Despite the very real suspiciousness of your
being near the plant at the time of the accident."

"Dr. Nesheim, Plant VanMeter's the obvious culprit."

"Right. And if it *were* the culprit, people in Placer Creek
and other communities up there—as well as a bunch of plant
employees—would be suffering observable effects. I've stayed
abreast of the situation, Mr. Thaxton, and they simply aren't
suffering such effects."

"Not yet."

"Granted, not yet. But I'd also point out that there's no one
else, in my knowledge, suffering anything remotely similar to
your 'Philistine Syndrome.' No one. You're the only victim.
So there must be another source of exposure, something
you've forgotten or aren't yet aware of."

"Could it be ongoing, then?" Xavier said. "Cesium 137 in
the walls of my apartment building? A radiation-emitting
video-display terminal at the *Urbanite?*"

Dr. Nesheim hesitated. "It could be. But unless you know
of anyone else in your condo, or at work, suffering a really
peculiar malady, probably not."

"What can Xavier do?" Bari asked. "What's the cure?"

"The cure's innate in the syndrome," Dr. Nesheim said.
"Every time a Bach fugue creates a systemic imbalance, he
should put on an album by a retropunk band. The antidote for
too much Tolstoy would be a paragraph of Sidney Sheldon.
For too much Chagall, a matador portrait on black velvet.
And for too much—"

"That just enslaves me to my syndrome," Xavier said, "it
really doesn't cure me of it."

"Besides," Bari said, "couldn't the repeated triggering of

such odd responses, none of them predictable, prove dangerous? Couldn't they lead to a stroke or a heart attack?"

"Sure," Dr. Nesheim said. "But I just don't know enough
about this business to prescribe effective treatment. I'd appreciate the chance to study Xavier on a day-to-day basis, but I'd
assume he'd prefer to go on living as normally as possible,
even though he'll have to make adjustments."

"Adjustments!" Xavier said. "Dr. Nesheim, I'm going to
have to cultivate a tolerance for that which I hate—in short,
every sort of self-expressive abomination spun out by our
species!"

Dr. Nesheim studied his hands. "I'm afraid so."

"There must be an alternative," Bari said. "He could retire
for extended periods to a sensory-deprivation chamber. A
closed room with no art, books, or music. Which would short-
circuit the syndrome by depriving it of . . . *fuel.*"

"It would short-circuit *me.* And destroy my career."

"Maybe three or four hours a day would be long enough to
calm you biochemically and to keep the syndrome from kicking in."

"And maybe it wouldn't," Xavier said. "And even if it
would, I wouldn't want to live that way."

"Which is wholly your choice," Dr. Nesheim said. "I'm
sorry I don't have better news."

"Maybe I could sue the folks who built Plant VanMeter."

"That again," Dr. Nesheim said dismissively. "I'm afraid
you have no proof of their culpability."

"I have a suspicion, though. The memory of a weird prickling all over my body. The knowledge that a guard at the plant
didn't want me around."

"They seldom want civilians around, Mr. Thaxton, and
with good reason, don't you think?"

"I don't know."

"Allow me to keep you under observation. I'd treat you free
of charge."

"Forget that."

"Xavier!" Bari said.

"I'm not a lab rat. If I'm not dying, I'm not dying. I don't
plan to will my living body to the medical profession."

"Your choice," said Dr. Nesheim.

To his secretary in the outer office, he spoke a single word
over the intercom, *"Next."*

16

"For Me There Is No Vulgarity"

That evening, Bari came to Xavier's apartment for a candlelight dinner, some dancing, and a little tension-defusing love play. The Mick was on an overnight field trip with a metropolitan chapter of the Smite Them Hip & Thigh fan club, which had booked seven rows at a concert in Montgomery. And Dr. Nesheim had told Bari and Xavier that, if they took their standard precautions, there was no reason Xavier's elevated radioactivity level should keep them from making love.

Bari was wearing one of her own creations, a skintight acetate gown of emerald-green with sinuous cutouts and a helically winding zipper. Only a self-possessed woman as well built as Bari, Xavier understood, could wear such a dress, for on a shy, a lean, or even a vaguely chunky female, the same outfit would have looked crass, either the cry for attention of an insecure deb or the come-hither smirk of a streetwalker. On Bari, though, the gown was as apt as a white fur in Stockholm.

"Whoo-ee," Xavier said, taking her hands. "You're ravishing."

"'Whoo-ee'?"

"What a dress. It's . . . *unique.*"

"It owes a lot to Azzedine Alaïa," Bari said. "I love the way that man defies bourgeois expectations without stooping to avant-garde silliness." She turned for him, showing the dress, not her body. "A design my mama would've approved. But not one she'd've ever imagined herself."

"*I* couldn't have imagined it." Xavier felt lust insinuating itself into his abstract admiration.

Bari shed her shearling gloves, dropped them on the sofa arm, sashayed into the kitchen. "That's why you're a reviewer, right?" She started palm-fronding carrots, heedless of the incongruity of wielding a vegetable grater in such upscale garb.

Xavier tried to envision Pippa Wiedmeyer and Ivie Nakai, both of whom were attractive young women, in this wolf-whistle dress—they could get away with wearing it only if they acted tough rather than demure. Bari's gown sported leather grommets on the knee-high hem, and the V-shaped strap lifting the sexy bodice was made of a green swatch of sailcloth. Grommets, canvas, a toothlike metal zipper—how could these sartorial doodads lend a down-and-dirty eroticism to so refined a female?

"Gak," he implored, touching Bari's naked shoulder.

"Know what Azzedine once told me?" she said, as if privy to his bemused speculations. " 'For me, there is no vulgarity, and the street is never in bad taste.' Or do you think the street's *always* in bad taste?"

"Of course there's vulgarity," nuzzling her, "and what you've got on tonight definitely isn't 'of the street.' "

"But it is. It's simply that I've taken street materials and transfigured them by reimagining, and then reinventing, them."

"I'm reimagining you, minus the dress."

"No vulgarity," Bari said. " 'There are women who can mouth the worst obscenities,' Azzedine told me, 'and they can go around naked and still be elegant.' He says that such women have 'the superior quality of being able to invent themselves.' We fashion designers make our livings by tempting insecure people with money to believe that they can buy, and then magically assume, that valuable *je ne sais quoi.*"

Xavier looked up. "No vulgarity? Even your rationale for your work sounds cynically vulgar, Bari."

"Maybe. The secret's not to *do* it cynically. Vulgarity is a part of us not always to be despised."

"What?" Xavier didn't agree.

"No arguments," Bari said, gesturing with the grater. "I'm not in the mood. What else are we having?"

"Broiled blue fish, stuffed crab, and steamed asparagus. The wine's an iced Sauvignon Blanc."

"Good," Bari said. "Good."

While they were waiting for the oven to do its work, Xavier and Bari swayed in their stocking feet to Duke Ellington's orchestra's recordings of "Mood Indigo," "Sophisticated Lady," a dozen other Swing Era numbers. As they danced, Xavier told Bari in some detail about his midnight adventure, nearly a year ago, in the Phosphor Fogs.

"You witnessed the accident," Bari said. "You saw them trying to contain it. Despite what Dr. Nesheim said, that could be how you got the radiation that's reacted—synergistically, I guess—with your metabolism and body chemistry. *Voilà,* your syndrome."

"I don't know, Bari. I thought I'd dreamt the whole episode."

"Who am I to say? Perhaps you did."

Xavier demurred again. "Con-Tri told us the accident took place the following morning, Bari. Perhaps my dream was a premonition of what was to happen a few hours later."

"Are you given to premonitions, Xave?"

"Not usually. I never had a clue that you and I'd happen. I certainly didn't foresee Mikhail coming to live with me."

"Then maybe what you *think* you saw, you saw. Which would mean that Con-Tri was lying."

"And why would they do that?"

"You're the newspaperman, Xave. No guesses?"

"It hardly matters now. The NRC investigation cleared Plant VanMeter's staff of negligence, and the damaged reactor's been back on line over a month now. Let's forget it."

Bari gave him a puzzled look, then shrugged.

They swayed to the syncopated Ellington. Despite the incessant air-conditioning, they warmed in each other's arms.

"Popular music," Bari said a few moments later, halting him and nodding at the stereo.

"Meaning?"

"Ellington was a jazzman. Jazz is an American invention, born in whorehouses and gaming casinos. It surprises me that you find it listenable. After all, it's a bastard child of'"— wrinkling her nose in a fetching parody of high-minded distaste—"*pop culture.*"

"Sure, I can approve it. Much of it, anyway. To what

should we be dancing? Gregorian chant? Bach? Wagner?" He smiled. The notion that a man of his education and taste could appreciate only concerti and sonatas was absurd.

"Then you think this stuff, our grandparents' pop music, is good?"

"Some of it. Ellington, almost always."

"Then isn't it possible that the Mick's favorite music—some of it, at least—could also be good?"

Xavier laughed. "You've turned Socratic on me, Bari. I guess it could. Why don't we find out for ourselves?"

"How?"

"By replacing the Duke with one of young Menaker's hood-luminati bands."

An inspired notion. Xavier went into the Mick's room, riffled through his collection, and returned with a copy of the CD *Subways* by a group called Up Periscope.

Off the turntable came "Mood Indigo"; then, out of the player next to it, came a raucous love song called "Tickling the Man in the Boat," followed by "Dangler's Fandango," "My Bleeding Beauty," and "Sexual Secrets of the Higher Primates," this last featuring the refrain "Hugga-mugga, hugga-mugga, / I always did think / I'd be in the pink / If I gave her a banana tonight."

Xavier didn't know if Up Periscope was a favorite of Mikhail's, but scratches on the CD case suggested that the disk received a lot of play.

"Enough," Bari pleaded.

"You see," Xavier said, removing *Subways* and putting the Duke's sophisticated swing back on, "despite what Alaïa claims, there *is* vulgarity, demoralizing vulgarity, and these unregenerate yahoos"—waving the CD's play list—"typify it."

"Try another of Mikhail's favorites, Xavier."

"Another?"

"Try one by that band whose concert he's gone to. It has to be better than"—nodding at the Up Periscope disc—*"that."*

"It's all gangsterish garbage, Bari. Why waste any more of our time with it?"

Acting wholly on principle, he returned *Subways* to his nephew's room and pointedly closed the door on it.

Then, sitting on the carpet beside his coffee table, he and Bari ate. The candlelight dancing in Bari's eyes flickered to the

rhythms of "Solitude," "Satin Doll," and "I Got It Bad and
That Ain't Good." It seemed to Xavier that they'd outwitted
vulgarity, that the woman with him was an Eve without flaw,
that the world was well-ordered and serene.

"Marry me, Bari," said Xavier. His heart was pounding like
the timpani section in an overture by Tchaikovsky. How
would she respond? Despite the perfection of the evening thus
far, he quite sensibly did not expect either a straight yes or an
outright no. Bari was not a predictable quantity. Her unpredictability was part of the reason that he'd fallen in love with
her, but the part, yes, that most troubled, sometimes even
dismayed, him.

"Why?" She put her plate into the dishwasher and looked
at him with eyes as large as Andalusian olives.

He took her hand and led her back to the sofa.

There, he used all the time-honored formulae for winning
over a coy mistress, not forgetting heartfelt avowals of undy-
ing love and crafty updatings of the carpe diem snowjobs of
Marvell, Lovelace, and Suckling.

"Xavier, Xavier," Bari said. "We've already 'sported' us
while we may and are 'like' to do so again."

Xavier was glad to hear it, but assured her that it wasn't
only the immediate slaking of his lust that mattered, but the
forging of a permanent bond with the legal imprimatur of the
state.

"Why?" she asked again.

Love, he began. Love, he continued. Love, he concluded.
(Her questions were confusing him.)

"Look," she said, putting her hands on his collarbones.
"I've got this hunch that you see yourself as, well, a superior
specimen of Salonika's maledom and me as your local female
counterpart. The First Man and First Lady, so to speak, of the
Oconee intelligentsia cum Beautiful People."

"Bari—"

"Never mind that not some would regard 'Oconee intelligentsia' as an oxymoron."

"That's *not* how I see us," Xavier said. "I want you to
marry me because of the exaltation I feel when I'm with you.
But even if I did see us a well-matched pair of superior specimens, what would be wrong with that? Maybe we are."

Bari went to the antique secretary in Xavier's living room

and picked up his well-thumped copy of Nietzsche. "D'you want me to be your partner in some egotistical eugenics experiment?"

"My partner in what?"

Opening the book and paging quickly through it, Bari said, "To quote your favorite German philosopher—or, that is, to take the words right out of his Persian mouthpiece's mouth: 'Every woman is a riddle, and everything in woman hath one solution—it is called pregnancy.' "

"Gak," Xavier protested.

"Do you believe that?"

"Nietzsche was a brave and uncompromising man, Bari, but he had some blind spots, his atheism being one, his attitude toward women another." The evening, along with the likelihood that Bari would say yes, seemed to be slipping away from him.

"Unfortunately, Xavier, there are too many times when you come on like that Nazi's ass-kissing acolyte."

"He *wasn't* a Nazi. He hated Wagner for his anti-Semitism. And I'm no fawning devotee of every line he wrote."

"No?" Bari was smiling. She returned his copy of *Zarathustra* to its spot next to a leather-bound Bible.

"No. Most emphatically not. How could I be? He disparaged my profession. Listen: 'Just see these superfluous ones; they vomit their bile and call it a newspaper.' And I don't buy the ideas of the death of God, the inferiority of women, or the tawdriness and inconsequentiality of journalism. No, I assuredly don't. What I do buy is Nietzsche's arguments that although we're nearly always less than what we should be, we always have the capacity to become *Übermensch.*"

"*Übermensch.* Overman." Bari ran her hands through Xavier's hair. "You're the man I'd like over me."

Later, the evening's perfection restored, Xavier was unloosing the strap on Bari's gown (with the same finesse with which he would dismember an imported artichoke) when his scalp began to writhe and an itch unlike any he had ever known assailed the soles of his feet and the insides of his thighs.

Horrified, he staggered away from Bari, alternately clutching his head and raking his manicured nails down the inseams of his Italian slacks. He hopped up and down on his burning feet. Dimly, he understood that his body chemistry, addled by his absorption of the untoward radiation that Dr. Nesheim had posited, was betraying him again.

"I know what's happening," Bari said, trying to keep him from unsocketing an arm or throwing his hip out of joint. "We've been pretty stupid, actually."

Xavier kept jiggling, flailing, twisting. He couldn't think at all. His various itches were so excruciating they'd reduced him to a spastic automaton.

After pinning his arms, Bari pushed him down onto the sectional sofa. "The dinner, the music, your silken approach to eroticism—they've rekindled your private Philistine Syndrome."

"Bari, help me!" He'd yanked off his socks and trousers and was pivoting on the sofa cushion on the top of his head, struggling to halt the writhing of his scalp.

"We should have had sardines and crackers. We should have done the Freddy, the fish, or the funky chicken. We should have ripped each other's clothes off, greased up with Crisco, and committed two dozen cheap unspeakable acts in as many minutes."

"Bari!"

"My God, Xavier, we've been a pair of absolute goofballs!"

"BARI!"

Quickly, Bari gathered several silk ties, along with a twenty-five-foot extension cord, and bound him half-naked to a chair.

Xavier gradually calmed, meanwhile recollecting that Bari had done this to keep him from injuring himself and that animality in sexual relations had always struck him as dé-classé. He continued to think so, but tonight he had reasons to forsake his Apollonian standards and to let Dionysus romp. In two dozen minutes, in fact, the itching had ceased.

But only the physical itching.

"Bari," he said worriedly, "am I going to have to move into a cold-water tenement flat? Is that what's indicated?"

"I don't know, lover. But you may have to redecorate."

17

Pickup and Disposal

Environomics Unlimited took longer than Teri-Jo had expected to come after the Therac 4-J that she wanted removed from the cancer clinic. The delay, according to the company's telephone rep, was the result of taking care of vehicle maintenance here in Oconee and a raft of backlog contracts in other parts of the country.

Anyway, a pair of men in khaki coveralls eventually showed up, one evening between eleven and midnight, to carry away the obsolete treatment machine. One of the crew was Will, whom Terri-Jo recalled from the radium-waste pickup that had saved her reputation with her boss and thus her job. The other man was a young Chicano, "Gooz," who worked with speed, efficiency, and care, as if to make up for Will's sluggish approach. Will looked bad, sallow and exhausted, and he was touchier than he'd been before—not with Terri-Jo, but with the world in general.

Will's irritability was no less puzzling than the truck that he and Gooz showed up in. It wasn't a trailer truck, a van, or even a panel truck. It was a candy-apple-red pickup with a rollbar and enameled gunwales. It lacked markings identifying it as an EU vehicle. It lacked even a REGULATED MEDICAL WASTE sticker.

"Awl our company trucks tied up in this big toxic-waste job over by Jurja," Will said. "This un's th' boss's."

With Gooz doing most of the lifting and steering, the two
men accomplished the removal of the Therac 4-J as if it were
an upright piano or a deep-freeze. Neither man wore the
butyl-rubber suits that had so boggled Teri-Jo on EU's last
pickup.

"Two thousand 'Merican greenbacks," Will said on the
loading dock behind the clinic. Gooz, meanwhile, was tying
the Therac 4-J into the load bed. "Payable awl at wunst."

Teri-Jo already had the check in hand. She passed it to Will.
"Three thousand less expensive this time."

"Less work," he said. "More likely praafit."

"What, exactly, is your company going to do with it?"

"We'll pull th' source canister and send it to a low-level rad
dump. Simple. Th' rest of thatere thing'll be checked real close
for any signs o' leftover radioactivity, and what can't be
used'll jes' be scrapt."

Gooz shouted, "Le'z go!" He leapt down from the load bed
and climbed into the truck's passenger seat.

"G'night, ma'am," Will said.

As Teri-Jo watched the truck turn out of the clinic's delivery
area, she suddenly felt that the check she'd given Will was
either too much or too little for the service just performed. She
was glad to be so quickly rid of the obsolete and potentially
hazardous Therac 4-J, but also vaguely dissatisfied with the
paperwork given to her to sign—it seemed perfunctory, in-
complete—and with her niggling suspicion that Environomics
Unlimited stood to realize a healthy profit on the discarded
therapy machine, a profit unrelated to the flat $2,000 fee to
remove it.

Over the remodeled bridge near the Hemisphere, Will drove
Gooz and him straight to Satan's Cellar, where he bumped
them through a maze of cobblestone alleys that eventually
debouched on a red-brick warehouse on the Cellar's western
outskirts. Oconee countryside was close enough that you
could smell the clayey loam of farms and hear the occasional
eerie wailing of screech owls. The warehouse's narrow windows, just under its eaves, were painted white or grey, or else
crudely plywooded.

Gooz had dialed the truck's radio to a Spanish-language
station broadcasting from New Orleans. The station was playing Andalusian flamenco music: pounding guitars and scale-

running Gypsy cries that made your neck hair prickle, the whole musical sheebang coated with an overlay of static. When they stopped in front of the warehouse, Will had an episode of nausea that had been growing on him for the past twenty minutes. He hopped out of the truck, stumbled to the warehouse, and retched into the weeds and broken glass edging its cracked foundations. Gooz hurried over.

"Weel," he said, "jou hokay?"

Will wiped his mouth with his sleeve. "Turn that pritty music arf, would jur?" Flamenco strains floated into the night: lovely, haunting, unbearable.

Gooz returned to the truck and clicked off the radio. Rotating one hand, Will told him to slip behind the steering wheel and shine the pickup's headlamps on the building's huge swinging doors. Gooz obeyed. Will, still shaky, stood in the overlapping cones of moted light and keyed open the doors' padlocks.

The warehouse contained a shadowy mountain of burlap-scented soft goods and oily machinery. Gooz drove the pickup in, and the two men undid the Therac 4-J's bindings and manhandled it out of the load bed onto the clay-dirt floor, where it crumpled with a muffled crash—almost a crunching sound—that lifted acrid dust and sent a platoon of rats or mice scurrying through the stacked-up crates, gunny sacks, building supplies, and machine parts.

Gooz eased the pickup out of the warehouse, back into the owl-haunted night on Satan Cellar's edge. Will wrestled the warehouse doors shut and climbed in on the passenger's side.

"Coupla poke dens still open," he said. "How 'bout a faceful, Gooz? Lemme stand you to some salad gas."

"Nossir. I am myself takin home."

"Drop me off, then. 'T ain't far from here."

"Gonna haffa get jou own ride home, Weel. I ain't waitin."

"Shore. I don't want jur to."

Gooz bumped the pickup back toward the river through a maze of alleys to a neon-lit enclave of pokeweed clubs. On the sidewalk in front of one of these bistros, Will waved at Gooz as he headed down another alley to his wife and daughter.

18

Flamingos

Over the next few months, Xavier tried *not* to review all the concerts, dance recitals, art-exhibit openings, theater events, and novels that, ordinarily, he would have killed to attend. He traded off with Lee Stamz, the Pop Culture editor, so that he could take assignments that, once, he would have avoided as if they were rabid chihuahuas.

He reviewed disease-of-the-week TV reruns, the latest volumes of "Garfield" and "Heathcliff" cartoons, paperback reissues of the works of Robert E. Howard, three different lounge-lizard singers at three different lounge-lizard nightspots, an Edward D. Wood, Jr., film festival at Ray Kleiner's theater, all the laughable stand-up comics booked into Hooter's during this period, and a variety of other tacky amusements: the finals of the tristate tractor pull, a designer-sleaze cyberpunk sf novel, the Brother Rutherford Q. Weems Municipal Tent Revival & Stock Market Symposium, mud wrestling at Orton's DiscoTech, and the menus of two new (unspeakably loathsome) fast-food franchises.

Back from these outings, he wrote vitriolic, revulsion-drenched notices that hiccupped with contempt and hummed with outrage, that reviled and chastised. They also provoked so much angry mail that Walter Grantham, his immediate boss at the *Urbanite,* congratulated him on waking up the masses. He even encouraged him "to keep on trucking." Circulation was up, primarily from newsstand sales and coin-operated vending machines.

"I can't keep doing this," Xavier said.

"Sure you can. Even if everybody hates you, they love the way you zap them for their lowest-common-denominator tastes."

"It's killing me, Walt."

"You *look* great. Your cheeks're rosy, your step's light, even your hair seems thicker."

"Inside, I'm a hand grenade with the pin pulled."

"Impossible. A nervous fella, an uncertain man, couldn't write with such indignant authority."

"I want to listen to Berg again, look at the lovely Rodins at the Upshaw, reread *Middlemarch.*"

"Sorry, but you can't. I thought you and Stamz were crazy when you pulled this switch, but it's working so well you guys look like journalistic geniuses."

Gak, thought Xavier, mentally machine-gunning his unhappiness: Gak, gak, gak, gak, gak.

It was August. Bari was in Italy, showing her winter line to international buyers at the Milan Fair. Her designer friend Romeo Gigli had invited her to the show, and she would not be back until early September. Because she'd repeatedly tabled Xavier's marriage proposal, some of his current funk, he realized, had its seeds in the fact that it was still hanging fire.

The Mick was passing their long, hot summer in ways that Xavier couldn't help seeing as unhealthy: slope-wall surfing at Skateboard City, playing computer games, listening to CDs, and reading, if you could call it that, comic books. The same old diversions that had occupied him since the conclusion of school. Impatience welled in Xavier, an impatience tinged with contempt.

"Why don't you go to the library?" he demanded.

"I'm on my holiday, Uncle Xave. What do you want me to read? Henrietta James? Fucking Scott Fitzgerald?"

"Sure. Why not? You're smart enough."

"You bet I am. Too smart to do it. Now that we're down to it, though, why don't *you* go to the library?"

Xavier stalked out of Mikhail's sanctum. He *couldn't* go to the library. He couldn't visit the Upshaw or put a Beethoven string quartet on the CD player. If he did, he reacted. And Mikhail *knew* he reacted. His question had been a variety of taunt, and Xavier resented it just to the degree that it manifested the Mick's lack of compassion.

Hurt, he retreated to the living room and began paging through a copy of the *Instigator:*

LONG AFTER CRASH,
RECOVERED AMNESIAC FIGHTER PILOT
SAYS, "ETHER ALIENS TO BLAME!"

SPEECH ANALYSIS PROVES NEW JERSEY SENATOR IS
"CHANNEL" FOR SUMERIAN PRIESTESS DEAD 3,000 YEARS

REVOLUTIONARY ZEN MASSAGE FROM ORIENT
GUARANTEED TO CURE INFERTILITY, IMPOTENCE

The Mick appeared before Xavier looking about as repentant as a would-be hoodluminatus was able. "Sorry, Uncle Xave."

"Forget it."

"I get deep-down fucking bored. Makes me testy."

"I was trying to help ease your boredom, Mikhail. I get bored too." He thought a moment. "Actually, working Stamz's beat, I'm more likely to be psychically tormented than bored—but suffering that psychic torment spares me physical pain."

He folded the *Instigator* and laid it on the floor. Reading the execrable rag made him feel spiritually polluted, as if he had just lied to a nun or kicked a puppy, but at least he had no headaches, nosebleeds, or crazy-making itches.

The Mick picked up one of the pink plastic flamingos that Bari had given Xavier to help keep his Philistine Syndrome in check; he collapsed into the bean-bag chair that she had sent over at about the same time. Xavier hated the flamingos— there was one in every corner—but he hated even more the painting of dogs playing poker that hung in the place where once had hung a brush-stroke reproduction of an Auvers- period Van Gogh. He was beginning to see how poor Vincent could have killed himself.

Embracing the flamingo, Mikhail said, "What if you found some, well, some lowbrow art—TV sitcoms, comics, belly dancing—that also just happened to be, like, *good.*"

"Oconee intelligentsia," Xavier murmured.

"Sir?" (That was a first: Mikhail never said sir.)

"Nothing. Just my private code phrase for a contradiction in terms. Don't fret it."

The Mick didn't. "What I was thinking," he said, "is that if you could expose yourself to a *second-rate* kind of art that had a few *first-rate* examples, maybe you could balance off your problem, like, and get back to a fucking seminormal existence."

"As, for instance, the world's most meticulous manufacturer of plaster-of-Paris flamingos?"

"Yeah. Or the world's best ventriloquist, or the world's best cartoonist, or the world's best kazoo player."

"Argh."

"Worth a zap." The Mick rocked his flamingo as if it were an infant. Meanwhile, his bean-bag chair emitted crepitating melodies that only a gastrointestinal specialist could love.

The next morning, by either destiny or coincidence, Grantham informed Xavier that he wanted him to attend a press conference at Salonika Towers. That afternoon, the editor-in-chief of Uncommon Comics, the New South's independent answer to Marvel and DC, would be there, along with several of the fledgling company's artists, to make an important announcement.

"That's one I'd like to cover," Lee Stamz groused.

"Would that you could," Xavier said.

"No dice," Grantham said. "Things are snapping along nicely as they are."

Xavier telephoned Mikhail, comic aficionado par excellence, and advised him to meet him at Salonika Towers at two o'clock. "Take a taxi," he said. "On me."

19

Stalwart in Salonika

Xavier met Mikhail on the sidewalk outside Salonika Plaza, an elaborate shopping complex not far from the Ralph McGill Building.

Ginkgo trees graced the immense stonework patio in front of the galleried towers, a band was playing Dixieland on a raised redwood deck to one side of the smoke-colored doors, and bright awnings and sail-sized advertising banners flapped languidly all the way up the face of the three chockablock towers containing the Salonika Plaza Mall and its chic, scurrying patrons.

"Decadent fucking bourgeois capitalism run fucking amok."

"Yes, I know. Which store would you like to go to?"

"Goldfinger's," the Mick said.

"You're in luck. That's where we're going."

Goldfinger's was the official bookstore, souvenir gallery, and comic-book emporium owned and operated by the backers of Uncommon Comics. It was UC's premier retail outlet in Oconee, if not the Southeast.

It was also, unquestionably, an even more flagrant example of "decadent fucking bourgeois capitalism run fucking amok" than the department stores, boutiques, jewelry stores, health-food bistros, exotic restaurants, and chichi import houses occupying the rest of the high-rent floor space in Salonika Plaza.

The Mick ignored this fact, for Goldfinger's allowed him to conspicuously consume comic books in plush surroundings. It provided reading rooms and free soft drinks to patrons who could validate a five-dollar, or larger, purchase within the past week.

"But why're *you* going to Goldfinger's?" Mikhail asked.

"I take it you haven't been listening to the radio or reading the ads in your, ah, illustrated trade journals."

"Is that your smart-ass fucking euphemism for comic books?"

"Actually, it's my clever-fanny sexual-intercoursing euphemism for comic books."

This riposte went right by the Mick. "Then today's the day!" he exclaimed. "Today's the day UC introduces three new characters and updates its Stalwarts for Truth series!"

"I'd forgotten that you came to Salonika only because UC has its headquarters here."

"Forget that. Let's move our butts, Uncle Xave."

They entered Salonika Plaza's right-hand tower. Goldfinger's dominated the lofty glass-and-plastic, aluminum-and-copper court at its heart. Fountains plashed, cool air wafted, and exotic palms and multicolored orchids imparted the aura of a sanitized jungle to this section of the mall.

Goldfinger's had three floors on the central court. From its highest wrought-iron balcony hung a computer scroll, decorated with dozens of UC characters in action poses. It screamed:

> I See UC, You See UC, We All See UC,
> And What We All See Is
> *FAN-TABULOUS!!!*

On the second balcony, a red-haired man in blue jeans and a pullover stood with three costumed figures, all more or less human in appearance. Xavier assumed them to be living stand-ins for the two-dimensional superheroes that kept the creative and managerial "talents" behind Uncommon Comics in either bread money or filet mignon. (Blessed with both insight and experience, Xavier had long since figured out who got which. Why, he was still working on.)

"Who're those three fools supposed to be?" he asked Mikhail.

"The Decimator, Mantisman, Saint Torque. They've all got their own monthly books. Together they were like, you know, the founding superheroes of 'Stalwarts for Truth.' *Stalwarts* has its own comic and six or seven alternate superheroes, depending on who's doing the writing and penciling."

"Don't be shy, ladies and gentleman, boys and girls," said the red-haired man on the balcony, the occasion's de facto emcee. His voice boomed through the lofty plaza.

"You know who that is?" the Mick said excitedly. "It's Bowman himself, unc! Tim Bowman the Great! *Jesus!*"

Apparently the Mick had been looking so intently at the idiots in their superhero gear that he hadn't immediately recognized his hero, the man who had created them. Now that he had he was as bug-eyed as if he were wearing goggles.

"Step right into Goldfinger's," said Bowman, from the balcony. "We're giving away sample copies of *The Decimator, Mantisman, Snow Leopard, Scarab, Saint Torque,* and *Ladysilk* while they last. One to a customer, please. The stalwarts here with me"—succinctly, Bowman introduced them—"will be happy to autograph their titles for you between three and four this afternoon."

"After which," he continued, "we'll bring out—*in person,* as their own stalwartly selves—the three newest Uncommon Comics' superheroes. You'll want to follow the adventures of these latest Unique Continuum stalwarts every month."

Under his breath, Xavier said, "So that *we,* kiddos, can grab off another hunk of your allowances."

"Come on in, folks. No need to worry about muggers and such while you're in Goldfinger's. Guys like that wouldn't *dare* show their faces while Mantisman, Saint Torque, and the Decimator are here on the premises to defend you."

As if to punctuate this assurance in the most swashbuckling way possible, Bowman grabbed a cable (disguised as a vine) hanging down from a lofty ceiling girder and swung himself out over the plaza's crowd in a Douglas Fairbanksian maneuver that startled Xavier with its suddenness. Bowman passed overhead, pedaling air, and pushed off the elevator tube opposite Goldfinger's with his tennis shoes. In addition to his casual clothes, he wore a scarlet Uncommon Comics cape for dash and publicity, and when he struck the escalator tube, he vented a bloodcurdling Tarzan yell. Swinging back to the stalwarts on the balcony, he twisted in midair and banged his knees into the railing. Saint Torque and the Decimator had to catch him and pull him over the bar to safety.

"I'm all right!" Bowman shouted breathlessly, holding his leg. "Come in and see what's goin' down!"

"My God," Xavier said, "the man's a fruitcake."

"He's an or-what genius," the Mick countered.

Bowman and the stalwarts retired from the balcony.

Inside, Goldfinger's was pandemonium. Three quarters of the teenagers in the place were male, most of them outfitted more like Ephebus Academy preppies than like the Mick, whose hoodluminati, retropunk garb drew both hostile stares and sarcastically lifted eyebrows. The grownups on hand seemed to be either keepers of the kids' money or employees, while the line for complimentary comics snaked among the display racks and souvenir shelves for what Xavier estimated was a hundred miles.

Mikhail got lost, quickly and deliberately. The nubile ingénue impersonating Saint Torque showed up beside Xavier to escort him to an interior office where the red-haired editor in chief of Uncommon Comics, seated and unselfconsciously rubbing his knee, was already briefing the press about the "updating of our Unique Continuum." There were press releases. There were comic books. There were illustrated guides to the characters whose "distinctive likenesses" were trademarks of UC, Inc. There were letters of testimonial from movie stars, TV personalities, and other well-known connoisseurs of "illustrated storytelling."

Xavier took no notes. He saw no need. Instead, he spent most of his time discreetly ogling the healthy young female— sixteen? seventeen?—in the Saint Torque costume.

From a handout, he learned that, while a child, her character had been struck by a ricocheting bullet during a bank robbery and paralyzed. The bullet had lodged, inoperably, at the base of her spine. With the onset of puberty, though, Samantha Pershing—the stalwart-to-be's real name—had recovered from her paralysis to find that the residual spin from the bullet still in her back had given her a most unusual superpower:

She was able, whenever adrenalized by an innocent person's fear and helplessness, to fly through the air like a missile, or through the water like a torpedo, or through the earth's crust like a drill bit, and so to rescue that endangered person.

"What rubbish," Xavier said aloud.

"I beg your pardon," said Tim Bowman, and Xavier saw that everyone in the room—artists, reporters, ersatz superheroes—was looking at him as if he'd belched during a recitation of the Lord's Prayer.

It was astonishing how devoted to, and jealous of, the nonsense that supported them these people were. They were zealots, True Believers, hallowing the origin and exploits of Saint Torque, and every other UC "stalwart," like hagiographers hallowing the lives of the great Catholic saints.

"Nothing," Xavier said sheepishly. "Go on."

Tim Bowman began to talk again, the reporters from the trades to ask more questions, and superhero lookalikes—Mantisman, the Terrier, Ladysilk, and so on—to wander in and out as autograph sessions and other publicity maneuvers demanded.

Mantisman was the oddest-looking impersonator on hand, an actor costumed in a long, green, insectoid exoskeleton. He was the lone Stalwart for Truth (according to the *Official Guide to the Unique Continuum of UC Comics*) who operated not in Salonika itself, which the comics always referred to, transparently, as Nick City, but out in the Oconee countryside. In fact, Mantisman's identifying shtick was that he was almost wholly a *rural* superhero, defending farmers from livestock and equipment theft, ponds and streams from everyone who would pollute them, Afro-Americans and other ethnics from the vigilante activities of Ku Klux Klansmen, and deer and other game animals from poachers.

Xavier couldn't quite fathom Mantisman's *modus operandi*—his exoskeleton contained a mysterious power source permitting him both to hover and to jet—but he mostly relied on surprise, along with the fear that his appearance evoked, to overcome his adversaries. In "real life" (avowed the *Official Guide*), he was an entomologist named Grady Rupp employed by the state Department of Agriculture in a county extension-service office in the small town of Hothlepoya, Oconee. No one but the governor, who'd been in office for decades, knew of Rupp's secret identity as a flying insect.

"Acch," said Xavier.

Everyone was looking at him again. He put a hand to his throat as if he had involuntarily reingested part of his lunch. Go on, he signaled the others with a nod: Don't mind me.

The Mick had come into the office with a stack of free comics. How had he avoided the lines, stolen past the security people, and squeezed under Xavier's arm? Now he was waiting for Bowman to wow everybody with UC's latest marketing ploy.

Said Bowman, "Here to introduce the three Unique Continuum stalwarts who'll be debuting this week is America's most admired superhero . . . *the Decimator!*"

Xavier could feel Mikhail's excitement. This claptrap was just about the highest creative endeavor he could imagine. He would probably feel like Michelangelo if Bowman asked him to submit some drawings to one of their projects.

As for me, Xavier mused, I'm bored past boredom. But at least I'm not bleeding from the nose or trying to outlast the trots. I'm suffering this mental agony from a physical posture of—Nietzsche be praised—"great healthiness."

Physically, Xavier was as stalwart in Salonika as the imaginary Stalwarts for Truth. Psychically, he was a conflicted mess.

The actor impersonating the Decimator swaggered into the packed manager's office of Goldfinger's. His uniform was a streamlined parody of a Roman centurion's: a tight-fitting hard-plastic helmet, a form-fitting breast plate, a pleated skirt, and sandals that were a minimalist variety of athletic shoe.

The Decimator was the monarch of the UC line, the superhero par excellence, known around the world (and even to Xavier Thaxton, an avowed debunker of the "popular arts") from the trio of films based on his heroics, his animated TV ads for Dwoskyn Pest Control, and a syndicated strip featured in at least twelve papers overseas. What *Superman* was to DC and *Spiderman* to Marvel, *Decimator* was to the Unique Continuum of Uncommon Comics—"ever stalwart in his battle against the crime lords of Nick City."

In "real life," according to the *Official Guide* and the famous first issue of his eponymous title (a comic book now worth, in mint condition, $500), the Decimator was a former Green Beret. Before Vietnam, he had been a military-history major. After the fall of Saigon, he'd lived for three years in Rome, journeying around the Mediterranean to assess that region's best responses to terroristic acts and to brainstorm ways to use these responses in U.S. cities. He was independently wealthy, of course, but worked off and on with the Army Corps of Engineers as a consultant. His "real" name was Grant Mayhew. Like Bruce Wayne (Batman), he had no superpowers, but was strong, wily, and resourceful.

Mayhew had acquired his name the Decimator by taking hostage a tenth of the total membership of each of the major crime syndicates in Salonika. He held the thugs in solitary in the Catacombs under Nick City, using them as leverage against the capos who worked out of Satan's Cellar but who sought to extort tribute from merchants in tonier parts of town.

(Once, shortly after the Mick had moved in, Xavier had argued with him the credibility of this scenario:

"It's asinine, Mikhail. If a self-appointed vigilante were to kidnap the members of crime families and demand they quit doing evil, they'd take hostages of their own—innocent people with no connection to the mobsters' crass activities—and the potential for loss of life would widen, not narrow."

"The hoods'd fucking surrender, Uncle Xave. The Decimator hits 'em where they live."

"Pure juvenile fantasy, Mick. In *real* real life, the violence would escalate, people would die, and Mayhew would agonize guiltily over the victims of his macho confrontation ethic."

Mikhail had said, "It's only fucking *stories,* Uncle Xave."

"Right. Bad stories. Prevarications."

"Interesting ones. *Amusing* ones. More so than the artsy-fartsy crap *you* want me to read." Whereupon he'd retreated to his sanctum and slammed the door.)

The actor-model playing the Decimator looked about twenty-six, hardly old enough to be either a Vietnam veteran or an expert in counterterrorist procedures. Nor did he closely resemble the actor who'd played the Decimator in the three films licensed by Uncommon Comics. He was merely a handsome would-be heartthrob who lifted weights and who probably sent photos of himself to *Playgirl* hoping to acquire a staple through his umbilicus.

"The three newcomers to our Unique Continuum are ready to meet you guys," he said, making no effort to keep up the illusion of stalwartliness. "They'll come out one by one, as I say their names and, like, present 'em to you all for interviews and pix. Okay?"

"You and that guy have the same speech teacher?" Xavier asked the Mick, sotto voce.

"Ha ha," said the Mick, mildly.

"Okay, here's the first one. We call him the DeeJay."

And so the character dubbed the DeeJay came bopping into the room. Xavier squinted at this young man, studied a handout, and quickly discovered that the DeeJay—his costume was a retropunk zoot suit—owned a portable radio station from which he broadcast warnings to hoodlums and tips to the police. Also, in his daily strolls through Le Grande Park, the DeeJay chased any bad guys he happened to see. Usually, he was able to apprehend them by taking old 45 RPM records from the tote bag he carried and hurling them like Frisbees. The 45s would strike the hoodlums in the crook of the knee and invariably bring them down. There was more about the DeeJay, but Xavier, who'd already overdosed on stalwartly nonsense, tuned it out. The Mick, though, kept paging through the free comic devoted to the DeeJay's first adventure.

The Decimator then announced the name of a new female stalwart, Gator Maid. Half listening, Xavier learned that this character—her impersonator wore a simulated alligator-skin bodysuit—was a female counterpart of Mantisman; that is, another rural superhero. As herself, Alice Gatlin was a marine biologist with a doctorate from the University of Miami; she worked for the federal government in the Choctawhatchee Swamp near the Oconee coastline on the Gulf of Mexico. Unlike Mantisman, Gator Maid sometimes entered Salonika to battle *urban* crime, for she was good at navigating Nick City's sewers. She helped the Decimator kidnap bad-guy hostages and guard the Catacombs against sabotage and attempted escapes.

"Neat," breathed the Mick.

20

Introducing Count Geiger

At last, the Decimator introduced the final brand-new stalwart, a character called Count Geiger. Xavier looked up at the first mention of this vaguely askew monicker, pricked by something both familiar and disturbing in it.

The actor-model doing Count Geiger strode in on panther's feet, and a profound hush fell not only on the Uncommon Comics personnel, but also on the media people. Count Geiger wore what looked to be a micron-thin aluminum-mesh suit with an "energy counter" set just beneath his rib cage. His shoes were silver-lamé slippers, and his helmet, hood, or cowl was really a burn mask.

This mask gave the stalwart a more forbidding appearance than that possessed by either the DeeJay or Gator Maid, and for a moment Xavier feared that the person essaying the part was a crook who had chosen this disguise as a way to get inside and steal Goldfinger's ready cash.

The Mick was even more enthralled, if that were possible, than he'd been by the previous two superheroes. He shifted his comic books and waited for either the phony Decimator or editor in chief Bowman to provide details.

What were the origins of this new superhero? What powers did he have? How would he fit into the Stalwarts for Truth team now comprising the Decimator, Mantisman, Saint Torque, Ladysilk, and so on? Would he have his own TV show? newspaper strip? feature-length film? Who would write and illustrate his stories? But, breaking the pattern already established, "Count Geiger" handled his own presentation:

"I am the stalwart known as Count Geiger," he said in an accent convincingly East European. "My real name is Wladyslaw Leshowitz. I am a Polish nuclear scientist once affiliated with the Kurchatov Institute of Atomic Energy in Moscow. My great-grandfather was a titled Polish nobleman who fought to secure freedom for all ranks and classes of his countrymen.

"As for me, in the immediate aftermath of the disaster at the Chernobyl nuclear power plant, I worked for weeks near the stricken reactor. I was heedless of the risk that my proximity to so much radiation posed, and eventually, falling ill, I was returned to a hospital in my native land—specifically, the city of Gdansk. My Soviet colleagues wished to keep me at a facility in Moscow, but I exercised my rights as both scientist and acknowledged hero of the battle to entomb reactor four and flew home for treatment. For a while, though, I was near death.

"In about sixty days, a turning point in my radiation poisoning occurred. Instead of deteriorating further, I began to experience strange augmentations of my body's capabilities. Cuts that would ordinarily require a week or more to heal now healed in only a day or two. I could see better in the dark, almost as if equipped with a natural variety of ultraviolet or infrared imaging. I could live with no distress or loss of strength on, yes, merely an apple or a slice of melon every few days.

"And, from the people around me, I could now pick up spiritual emanations identifying them as friendly or hostile. Indeed, I soon became aware that this capability allowed me to distinguish degrees of spiritual and moral integrity among all those with whom I came in contact.

"In my hospital lurked a Soviet KGB agent posing as an orderly, and this person deduced what was happening to me just as I intuited *his* real identity. He, I saw, wanted to take me back to Moscow to be schooled in espionage. The KGB would then engineer a situation making me look like a defector to the West, when, in fact, I would be a Soviet pawn using my radiation-augmented powers to spy for the Kremlin. Therefore, I sneaked out of the hospital, stowed away on a merchant ship at the Gdansk docks, and voyaged all the way from Poland to the Gulf of Mexico, Choctawhatchee Bay, and up Sidney Lanier's river to the inland port of Salonika.

"In your great city, I acquired forged papers presenting me to the world as the stevedore Wallace Lester. After meeting Grant Mayhew in my work as a dock employee and after plumbing his secret identity as the Decimator, I confessed my wish to become another Stalwart for Truth and gained my place in this exclusive fellowship by demonstrating for him the full range of my powers as . . . *Count Geiger!*"

Almost imperceptibly, the Count bowed. Prompted by Bowman and the two other superhero impersonators, everyone in the office began to applaud—even the reporters from the local TV stations who prided themselves on a sardonic insusceptibility to hype.

Xavier refused to join in. "Come on, Mick, let's get out of here," he said loudly.

"Why? It's not over yet."

"Because it's bullshit, that's why. Because these people don't even quail at exploiting an historic disaster like Chernobyl. They know nothing, but they pretend to know everything. They impute the acquisition of superpowers to an accident that killed people and to a phenomenon, radiation, that threatens to destroy even more. They lie to seduce the immature imaginations of kids like you, Mick, and to separate you from as much money as you'll let them!"

"You intend to write that, Mr. Thaxton?" Bowman said. "That we're exploiters? That our additions to the Stalwarts for Truth team are cynical lies?"

"I'll write what's required," Xavier said. "And I won't lie." He looked at his nephew. "Come on, Mikhail."

"You've got a poker up your ass, Uncle Xave. You think life's all one thing. You think you've got a lock on what it really is because you're so fucking high-minded."

"Life is earnest. So is art. What we choose to extol in the way of art ramifies into our lives." Xavier could not believe that he was carrying on like this *in Goldfinger's,* the top retail outlet of UC Comics, Inc. That he was fighting to uphold the sanctity of high art in this bastion of commercial kitsch. "Come on," he said again. "Let's get out of here."

"You're going to dump on these folks, aren't you? Like you've done to every other thing you've reviewed lately."

"Mick—"

"What you dump on *ramifies* into people's lives, too, doesn't it? You look like a genius prince and everybody else like blind filthy peasants!"

The Uncommon Comics staff, including the impersonators in their costumes, applauded the Mick. When a photographer from one of the comics trade publications snapped Xavier's picture, he thought, I'm outnumbered here, an owl among sparrows.

Outraged and embarrassed, he turned on his heel and strode from Goldfinger's with no backward glance or any thought as to what the Mick's next move might be.

He wasn't sure, but he thought that as he exited, Tim Bowman stood up and twirled his stupid Uncommon Comics cape around his shoulders like a bullfighter performing a contemptuous veronica. Once again, the crowd in the room applauded.

21

Volleys

A week later, Xavier was playing racquetball with Lee Stamz in one of the sweltering courts at the Oconee Tech field house. He was wearing the ex-linebacker down, stroking shots that zoomed past Stamz or dropped so tantalizingly from the wall that Stamz, walking on his knees to reach them, ended up with the barrel of his torso applying a sweaty lacquer to the hardwood.

"You're one mean sonuvabitch today, Xave," Stamz said, rising from the floor. "Let's quit—you done whipped my ass."

A moment later, racquets at their feet, they sat next to each other, backs against the rear wall. The echoes of smashes and ricochets came to them from adjacent cubicles, and, for the first time in days, Xavier was semirelaxed.

"What's happening?" Stamz asked. "You only play like that when you've got a hard-on for somebody."

"What? When I'm erotically aroused?"

"Shit, no," Stamz said, giving him a funny look. "When you're angry-mad." He narrowed his eyes. "Who're you angry at?"

"I'm not angry at, or with, anybody. It's the Mick who's angry at—with—me."

"Yeah. I thought that might be it."

Xavier explained that his column on UC, Inc., and its three new campy stalwarts had upset—*alienated*—his nephew. In fact, he hadn't been home since the press conference, at which the Mick and he had engaged in a ludicrous public argument about art and popular culture.

"Hasn't been home? You called the police?"

"I would have, Lee, but he telephones and leaves messages on my answering machine."

"Messages?"

"He says," 'Uncle Xave, I'm not lost or missing. I'm hiding out. I'll come back when I'm finished being pissed.' Every day I get something like that on my answering machine. Which means I can't tell the police he's run off or been kidnapped. All I can do is wait for him."

"You trashed his heroes. You can't trash a kid's stalwarts and expect him to love you."

Nobody loved Xavier for his jeremiad against the shoddiness, the dishonesty, and the discouraging derivativeness of Salonika's home-grown comics industry.

Letters to the editor had arrived in fat olive-drab mail bags. Only a few were in agreement with Xavier's arguments. Most laid into him for (1) snobbery, (2) the sin of reverse provincialism (in which one always ranks the foreign over the domestic, no matter how superior the local product to the exotic import), (3) a passion for arbitrary deconstructive pronouncements, (4) treason against the best economic interests of the city, (5) a disproportionately harsh assessment of a minor but always legitimate, and often magical, art form, and/or (6) sheer wrongheadedness.

Dear Jerks [*wrote one disgruntled* Urbanite *reader*],

Get somebody else to write about UC and the three bitching new additions to Tim Bowman's trailblazing list of stalwarts. Thaxton doesn't know comics, he doesn't like them, and he doesn't bring any objectivity to their criticism. Let him go back to reviewing books whose first sentence is a wraparound of the last one and to wetting his pants every time Screen Dreams shows *Citizen Kane* again.

I've read the first numbers of all three new comics, which are quantum leaps over the stuff churned out by the dolts in New York. *The DeeJay* reveals the impact of our high-tech entertainment and news media on contem-

porary urban life, while *Gator Maid* spotlights environmental concerns with a nonsexist portrayal of a female
heroine [*sic*] with brains, heart, and sex appeal.

And then there's *Count Geiger,* the most revolutionary
title in the entire Unique Continuum. It uses the hard-
hitting vocabularies of street talk, MTV images, and
computer jargon to give us the Word that xenophobia is
a sickness, that agitprop is agitprop no matter who's laying it down, and that a single dude, one *stalwart* person,
can make a difference.

But Thaxton dismisses these ideas out of hand. Why?
Because the artists at UC have had the unmitigated creative gall to present them in accessible, but socially dis-
reputable, comic-book format. (*Gasp*, *cough*,
choke.)

Well, my advice to Thaxton is to buy himself a one-
way ticket to James Joyce's grave and to sit on it until
the *aginbite of inwit* drives him sufficiently bonkers that
none of the rest of us have to wear hip boots to wade
through his holier-than-thou drivel again.

[Signed] Noah Ward

That was one typical, if stylistically startling, response to
Xavier's review, and one whose (relative) literacy had disconcerted him. Bemusedly, he carried a clipping of it in his wallet
to show his friends, a clipping that, there in the Oconee Tech
field house, Lee Stamz was now intently reading.

"Saw this when it came out," Stamz said, returning it.

"And?"

"Sounds to me like the Mick, like he's coming back at you."

Xavier had suspected as much. Noah Ward was clearly a
nom de plume—for Xavier deserved, please note the sardoni-
cism, *no award* for his bigoted opinions.

"Do you think he's right?"

"He scores a point or two. More'n I scored out here today."

"What point, Lee? Three bogus concepts—a vigilante
deejay, a half-croc'd marine biologist, and a Polish nuclear
scientist who survives Chernobyl to become a stalwart in
Salonika. Three bogus additions to the threadbare superhero
format. So what point does this smartalecky kid score, Lee?"

"This one: you're looking so far down your nose at the

format you can't see if anything good's being done with the medium. Maybe that disqualifies you as a critic whose ravings have any merit, at least to folks who've adopted the medium and who like that format."

"Medium? Format?"

"Poetry's a medium, the sonnet's a format. Comic-book art's a medium, the superhero convention's just a format."

"A bankrupt one."

"Maybe. But you think poetry and sonnets are legitimate kinds of art, and you'd be delighted to praise a poet who goosed a little juice into the sonnet form."

"What're you saying, Lee?"

"If you hate eggplant, and if you hate it fried, stewed, or au gratin, how the hell can you pass a useful judgment on an eggplant soufflé that eggplant connoisseurs are doing cartwheels over?"

"You might as well say there're levels of aesthetic achievement among snuff flicks, Lee."

"Bullshit. Snuff flicks are immoral. Unless the cook puts in some strychnine, I doubt there's an immoral eggplant recipe—just good and bad ones."

"But comics—"

"Same goes for comic-book art. It can be good or bad, if you care about it. And the times when it's immoral—okay, maybe there are some—you'd have to fault the character of the artist, not his draftsmanship."

"Isn't that what I've done? I've faulted the character of the people who try to pass off these five-bit superhero fantasies as worthwhile responses to the complexities of reality."

"Yeah, but you don't like the comics—so you're training your bazooka on a swarm of gnats."

Xavier was reminded again of the quote about a reviewer who evinces deep-seated hatred for a novel being like someone who puts on battle gear to demolish a banana split. He believed there was a good deal more to it.

Even a second-rate work of the imagination can have a powerful impact on its audience, and if it glorifies a glittering lie, that lie may prompt some to regard the world in dehumanizing, selfish, or unrealistic ways. Only if would-be works of art acted solely as pain- or time-killers did they forfeit the privilege of occasioning a reviewer's lavish praise or heated disgust, and, Xavier thought, those were the works that had no real significance at all. Thus, by attacking the artists and writers of UC, Xavier was granting them what many of their tribe had long ago claimed for themselves, namely, significance.

Awkwardly, he tried to explain all this to Lee Stamz, who shook his head and said, "Heavy stuff, Xave baby. Heavy."

"It is. But so was having a President whose entire concept of international relations was grounded in World War Two combat films and the narcissistic heroics of Sylvester Stallone. What if some ten-year-old collector of *Decimator* grows up with an interest in politics? What if he runs for President? What if he's elected?"

Lee Stamz stared at Xavier, hard. Then he broke into laughter, which rolled through the racquetball courts like thunder.

"You're a pip," he said, finally. "And you know what I think, Xave baby?"

"No, what?"

"It's time we traded back. I'm tired of woodwind recitals and you're dragged out on tractor pulls and stand-up comics. So let's tell Grantham, okay?"

"Fine by me."

But if he returned to the Fine Arts beat, would he again fall victim to bunions, hangnails, halitosis, a whole variety of gonzo mix-and-match ailments? He'd tested positive for the Philistine Syndrome, and only daily exposure to kitsch kept him symptom-free.

He also had Mikhail to worry about. Where was the kid staying, and who was feeding him, and was he well?

22

Pokeweed and Water Uzis

This long-distance connection was one of the worst Xavier had ever had. Lydia seemed to be burbling at him from the floor of the Marianas Trench, through a six-mile-long breathing tube.

"... ward to ... ZZZZZZWHR ... break from the agon . . . SQQQQQWRRRRHHH . . . nesday . . . KRRRRXXXXXXX."

"You're taking some R and R?" Xavier shouted. "Is that it? I should expect you soon?"

"SQQQQQQQXXXXX ... the MicKKKKKK?"

"Speak to Mikhail? He's just stepped out, Lydia."

". . . kay . . . KRRRZZK . . . uv ya . . . SQQRRZZZZXXXXX."

Off the phone, Xavier understood that Lydia, although not Phil, would be coming back to the States for two weeks, to see the Mick and visit friends in California. She was flying into Sidney Lanier International Airport on Thursday. That gave him two days to find the boy and reinstall him in his ebony sanctum. To complicate the issue, Bari would be coming back from Europe on the same afternoon, and Xavier had to meet both flights.

"No wonder Zarathustra lived apart from the world," he told the most sympathetic-looking plaster flamingo.

The next morning, Donel Lassiter came up to Xavier's desk

and leaned toward him with a friendly confidentiality missing
from his behavior ever since Xavier and Lee Stamz had
swapped assignments.

"I saw Mikhail last night, Xavier." (It had taken Donel
years to call him Xavier, but he still said it as if syllabling
aloud the Tetragrammaton.)

"Where?" Xavier's eagerness was palpable.

"At this poke house in Satan's Cellar. Bryan and I were
there, messing around. Mikhail was toking some steam in a
side room with a passel of hard-trade types."

A poke house was a bistro offering alcoholic drinks and
tawdry entertainment, but it was also a front for peddling
"salad gas"—the street term for the high imparted by eating
chemically treated pokeweed (an ingestible substance now illegal) or by inhaling the fumes rising from a bowl of hot poke
(a practice possible only in the weed's presence and so illegal
too).

Getting poked up, or salad-gassed, was now the substance-
abuse pastime of choice among Salonika's urban poor, specifically those northwest of the river. It hurt Xavier to think that
by expressing his honest reaction to the falsehood of *Count
Geiger* and company, he had driven the Mick into the arms of
poke pushers and salad-gas impresarios. It was too late to help
that, but maybe not too late to rescue his nephew.

"A poke house? My God. Did you talk to Mikhail? Did you
try to get him out of there?"

"Nope," Donel said. "The company he was with was too
rough for us. Besides, the Mick was so poked up he wasn't
aware of much but the vapor fuming off his bowl."

"Take me there tonight."

"Maybe Bryan can find it again. I'm not sure I remember
how to get there."

"Donel, you guys meet me at the EleRail station in Le
Grande Park at eight o'clock," Xavier said. "In the Cellar,
we'll catch a cab. *Don't* tell me you can't remember the way."

That evening, Donel and Bryan—lovers who had only recently abandoned their public impersonations of straights—
met him at the EleRail in Le Grande Park and rode with him
across the river to a nightclub in Satan's Cellar. The place was
called P.S. Annie's. It was on a street in an area so bombed-
out-looking that some of its denizens called it Pearl Harbor.

P.S. Annie's had only a small cover and no minimum—but if you stayed too long without buying into some of the action, either at the card tables or in the poke dens off the main cabaret, a bouncer would ask you to leave.

Donel and Bryan stayed in the front room. Xavier made his way into a side room redolent of the characteristic reek of salad gas. He'd read about poke for months, but this was the first time he'd come face to face with any of the pathetic human specimens addicted to it. Although the authorities had tried to confine the epidemic to the Southeast, habitual substance abusers in New York, Chicago, and California had fallen prey to the "redneck allure" of salad gas—partly in response to the high costs of better-known drugs after the wholesale bombing of Central and South America's coca fields, and partly in reaction to the heightened visibility, and coolth, of all things Salonikan.

The Instigator called getting poked the "white-trash high." It hinted that celebrities like Emmalyn Pugh, R. Haliburton, and Graig Goudray were growing pokeweed in windowboxes or on secluded areas of their estates. To proffer your guests the white-trash high was chic, even if an instant's rational thought told you that doing so was like substituting crawdad for lobster at a formal dinner. But no spoiled celebrity had ever visited a poke house in Salonika or beheld in person the degradation and hopelessness of habitual users who scarfed the stuff not because it was trendy but because it was dead-dirt cheap.

Xavier found the stench in the poke den nauseous. The addicts hunched over warm bowls or Sterno-heated chafing pots were as frail as ghosts. The steam coiling dreamily about them gave them an aura of insubstantiality, of weightlessness, of eerie semiexistence. If he could keep down the contents of his stomach, it wouldn't be hard to drag one of these haints outside. A pokeweed junkie would have neither the strength nor the moxy to resist him.

Xavier moved from table to table, looking at the specters bent over their habits. The faces that pivoted toward him were those of human gargoyles: greenish-grey Halloween masks, haggard mugs from lamely colorized film noirs. Shuddering, Xavier squinted into the choking fog, asked if anybody'd seen a kid nicknamed the Mick, and, getting no reply, stumbled deeper into the poke den's maw.

"You're thatere Xavier Thaxton," a slurred Good Old Boy

voice, mostly baritone, accused him. "Thatere snooty Fine Orts feller on th' *Urbanite.*"

"No," Xavier said, his wrist encircled by a fat red hand.

"Yaah, you are. Don' give me thatere false-modesty crap. Your pitcher's in th' paper awl th' time."

Xavier found himself sitting next to this poked-up character, a crewcut, ruddy-faced boar of a man who introduced himself as Wilbon T. Stickney. Stickney informed him—over Xavier's protests of no time, no time, he was looking for a lost child—that, once upon a time, he, Stickney, had been a "true cunnersewer of th' fine orts: old Brother Dave Gordner comedy records, all thirteen *Nightmare on Elm Street* flicks, them'ere crafty sports paintings by Leroy Whatz-his-face, and th' orticles on censorship in *Playboy, Penthouse,* and *Hustler.*"

"Mr. Stickney, I've got to—"

"Shut up, Thaxton. I'm trying to tell you somepin."

"Then get on with it, please."

"It's jes' this. A few months back, it turned where I couldn't listen to Brother Dave, or Jerry Clower, or Minnie Pearl, or any of them'ere comedy people 'thout coming down with a bellyache, a case of dizzies, or a pesky little blip sore on my tongue. Same 'ith my favorite slasher vids and trucker paintings on nappy black velvet. Same 'ith my reruns of 'Petticoat Junction' and th' orticles in my cutie books. Somepin'd happen every time I tried to eddicate or amuse myse'f—upset stomach, eyebrow tic, a wort sorter sprouting out on my thumb. You know."

"You're kidding," Xavier said.

"Naaw. Why would I? I mean, it was sorter like I wuddun meant to enjoy th' fine orts anymore. Like my body was trying to tell me to give 'em up. 'At ever happen to you, Mr. Thaxton? I mean, what 'ith your snooty-hooty jaab and awl?"

"No," Xavier said.

" 'At's why I'm a pokeweed junkie—not 'cause I *like* th' high everybody brags on. Hell, no. It's only 'cause it gives me *relief* from awl my aches, pains, and whatnots after I've jes' done somepin sorter classy." Stickney put the squeeze on Xavier's wrist. "You get me, don' jur, Mr. Thaxton?"

"I don't know."

"It ain't complicated. Before I got so low as to toot poke, I found other things that'd help—for a while. I wish they *still* did me some good, I shorely do."

Xavier's wrist hurt. "What kinds of things?"

"It's embarrassing, Mr. Thaxton. I had to get *real* low to do myse'f any good. When Brother Dave records made me sick, I storted calling Dial-a-Breather every udder night or so. When *Nightmare on Elm Street* broke me out in hives, well, I storted renting videos of old forts jocking off to 'cordion music.' They 'uz lousy—I mean, really lousy—but my hives'd go away. And when my favorite works of ort made my hair fawl, or my knees smell like rank cheese, or my elbows blister, I'd head downtown, straight for th' men's room in a bus station, and spend a little time looking at th' ort work in th' restroom stawls. Binger! Cured again."

"Let go of me," Xavier said.

Stickney obliged. "Today, none of that lowdown stuff works for me anymore. For reliable relief, I'm down to jes' two things. One of 'em's thisere putrid pokeweed." Stickney nodded at his chafing pot. "Damn it awl to hell."

"What's the other?" said Xavier, massaging his wrist. Stickney had mesmerized him, he'd've heard him out even if unforced—once, that is, Stickney got rolling. "Tell me the other."

"Boxing," Stickney said. " 'Fie can wortch a fight on TV— you know, even two old forts clutching and rubbing their laces in each udder's eyes—uh, I'm fine for a day or two. Thonk Awlmighty God for boxing. It jes' ain't on orfun enough."

Stickney, Xavier realized, had what he had, a peculiar variety of the Philistine Syndrome. A *lower-order* variety of the syndrome, maybe. Radioactivity of some kind—from Plant VanMeter?—had affected Stickney's metabolism just as it had affected his. The only difference was that Stickney's concept of the "fine orts" had been several rungs down from Xavier's. Thus the discrepancy in degree between the higher arts triggering Stickney's ailments and those triggering his. Thus the discrepancy in degree between the debased arts affording each of them temporary relief.

P.S. Annie's was noisy. Bottles clinked, little tins of Sterno whooshed and puttered, people sang, snuffling noises punctuated any ebbing of the general hullabaloo, and, from a side room to Xavier's left, hand-clapping, cries, and foot-stomping bounced off the walls and ceiling.

A minor riot, thirty or forty feet away.

Stickney's red nostrils spasmed. He was still trying to talk to Xavier when Donel materialized behind him out of the salad-gas fumes.

"We think we just saw him, sir," Donel said. "But when he saw us, he skedaddled."

Xavier stood, knocking his chair over. "The Mick? You saw the Mick? For God's sake, let's go after him!"

"Bryan's already chasing him, sir."

"Call me Xavier, Donel, not sir. We're not in the office, this is Satan's Cellar." He made as if to go through P.S. Annie's main room to the street—but two young men in powder-blue jumpsuits emerged from the fog and trained on them a pair of snaky-looking automatic rifles: Uzis, if he knew anything at all about assault weapons.

Amateur white yakuza in their late twenties or early thirties. One was sandy-haired and hollow-eyed, the other very well muscled and blue-jowled with stubble. Their jumpsuits—leisure garb, not work clothes—bore big ameoboid stains slightly darker than the surrounding fabric.

"Hands up," the blue-jowled gunman said, raising the drawbridge of one eyebrow. "Both of you."

"Shee-it," Stickney said, inhaling a puff of poke gas. "C'mon, Trey. C'mon, Lamar. Lay off theezere fellers."

"Keep a-whoofing, Pops," Trey, the blue-stubbled gunman, said. "And stay out of our bidnuz."

"Up!" said Lamar, the sandy-haired gunman, using his Uzi barrel by way of illustration.

"All I've got on me is credit cards," Xavier said, reaching for his wallet. "But you can have them."

"Uh-uh," Trey said. "We don't give a hobbled he-goat for your credit cards. Keep 'em."

"Shee-it," said Stickney, thrusting his face into his poke-weed steam and withdrawing from the matter.

The gunmen paraded Xavier and Donel at Uzi-point through the poke den's smothering fog. Their destination was a side room—a bar, as it happened, with a runway upon which two young women in high heels and G-strings were cocking their hips and showing their headlamps on high beam. This was the same room from which all the shouting, hand-clapping, and foot-stomping had issued as Xavier talked with Stickney.

The noise from this room hadn't subsided at all. Men continued to howl, chortle, clap, wolf-whistle, cheer, gibe, tramp in place. The B-girls exposed on the catwalk, a discolored mirror on the wall behind them, looked bedraggled, defeated, violated.

They *weren't* cocking their hips or showing their headlamps on high beam, Xavier saw. No, not really. They were enduring what P.S. Annie's customers were paying for them to endure, taking what had to be taken—not with high spirits and good grace, but with repressed anger and true bemusement.

Their bodies glistened, shining under the colored spots, while their hair clung to their skulls in sticky strands. They were soaked, Xavier suddenly realized, their near-nude bodies streaming with . . . *beer.* That was it, that was the smell. The women in this room had been drenched in warm lager. In fact, the drenching hadn't stopped, it was continuing. The target-shooters' Uzis and AK-47s were plastic water rifles.

My God, Xavier thought.

For the Good Old Boys in Annie's were drilling streams of beer from authentic-looking weapons at the two young women struggling to stay upright on the catwalk. They were shooting each woman in the face, in the stomach, and (to the raucous cheers of those urging them to "nail the bitches!") in the sequin-shielded V of her pubic zone.

The gunman named Trey took his Uzi off Xavier and pointed it at the bent-kneed woman on the right. Over and over, he squeezed its trigger, sending narrow rays of beer ricocheting in splashes off her thighs, belly, chest, and spangled crotch. A bearded yahoo at the bar's other end caught this same woman in an amber crossfire. She turned from side to side in her heels, seeking safety where there was none, increasing the likelihood that she'd slip and crack her head.

"Stop!" Xavier shouted. "You damned animals!"

Trey and Lamar laughed. They grabbed Xavier and Donel, pushed them through the cheering crowd to the catwalk, shoved their fake Uzis into Xavier's and Donel's hands, and commanded them to "take you some target practice"—a boon not granted to many fellas who weren't P.S. Annie's regulars, they pointed out.

After all, they'd rented the guns, bought the beer serving for ammunition, and picked out Xavier and Donel because they looked "in outright need of a happy little cunt hunt," being newspaper dudes with deadlines, late hours, and plenty of other stressful shee-it, right?

"Shoot!" Trey said. "It'll melt thatere poker you got running straight up your back from your ass!"

Xavier held Trey's Uzi, Donel held Lamar's. Too many blotchy-faced men hemmed them in to be able to swing about and drench Trey and Lamar—but the idea crossed Xavier's mind and, he believed, maybe even Donel's. No way was he going to abase himself or these young women by obeying the beetle-browed louts encouraging them to do just that.

"Shoot!" Trey shouted again.

"No," Xavier said.

" 'N' why not?" Trey wondered. "You're the hotshot who's always quoting Nee-chee, aren't you?" He sounded, to Xavier's surprise, almost literate.

"What's Nietzsche got to do with it?" he shouted into the roar ballooning up from the men as the girl on the left (a heart-faced kid hardly out of her teens, with half-moons under her eyes and a cranberry birthmark on one haunch) slipped and put both hands on the bar to prevent a worse fall.

"Jes' this!" Trey shouted. "I read in a old column of yours, *'Man shall be trained for war, and woman for the recreation of the warrior: all else is folly.'* I guess old Nee-chee said a mouthful there. So go on, Thaxton—pot 'er in th' mouse!"

"No, I can't."

Trey got behind him, applied a half-nelson with his forearm, dug his radius into Xavier's Adam's apple. "Shoot her, Thaxton! Shoot her, you highbrow wuss!"

Aching from this excruciating pressure, Xavier took off-balance aim at the woman on his right, the elder of the two dancers. She saw him. Her eyes were brown, the glazed brown of a roast turkey. With his own eyes, he tried to tell her that he couldn't help doing this, that another stream of stale beer couldn't hurt her much more than the previous barrages. She caught what he was trying to tell her, but she no longer gave a damn, the game was too far gone, and when the stream from his fake Uzi hit her thigh, splattering like urine and dripping golden down her legs, she sucked in her cheeks, a signal of either acquiescence or contempt.

Laughter—appreciative laughter—from the Good Old Boys in camouflage fatigues, grease-stained khakis, bib overalls and string ties, white shirts and Levi's. Yucks from the jumpsuited bullies cheerleading Donel and him. In fact, so happy with his reluctant marksmanship was this crew that once Donel had squeezed off a token stream at the kneeling dancer, they grabbed back their water Uzis, flung Xavier and Donel aside, and even more fiercely renewed their own B-girl shoot.

Xavier and Donel, trading looks of wary disbelief, cut through P.S. Annie's labyrinth of dens to the street.

Outside, Bryan was waiting for them. He gestured breathlessly down the bricked defile into the recesses of Satan's Cellar.

"I lost him. . . . A guy could get killed in there."

"Mikhail too," Xavier reminded Bryan.

They stood at P.S. Annie's weather-stained brick façade, near a pawnshop and hole-in-the-wall Vietnamese restaurant, waiting for a cabby with spunk to drive up.

Donel had his arms crossed. "Why would you quote Nietzsche to the effect that men are warriors and women their toys?"

"I didn't do it approvingly," Xavier said. "I was reviewing an exhibit of martial art at the Upshaw."

"Whatever you meant, you gave those redneck creeps intellectual justification for their vulgar game."

"I can't believe that idiot read my piece," Xavier said. "It's even harder to believe he *remembered* it well enough to toss a quote from 'Nee-chee' back at me."

"A redneck philsopher," Donel said disgustedly.

"On some level, I'm being read," Xavier noted. "On some weird level, I'm having an impact."

"Right," Donel said. "Your words are being used to justify the public humiliation of young women dependent on bar work to earn a living. How does that feel?"

"Terrible," Xavier said. "But I'm . . . *being read.*"

"People still read the Bible," Bryan said. "Some of them wear sheets. Some of them bomb abortion clinics."

"That's a misapplication of what they've read," Xavier said. "My work's being misapplied, too, but at least it's getting through to some of the yahoos."

"In a twisted way," Bryan said.

Donel said, "Somebody quoted you to those guys. Quoted

you quoting Nietzsche, I mean. There's no way they read your column themselves. No way."

A cab finally came. They rode it, minus Mikhail, back over the cobblestone bridge into Salonika proper.

23

Mikhail, Come Home

S orry, Lee. Sorry, Xave. But I don't want you to switch back to your old beats yet."

"Walt," Lee Stamz implored.

"Walt," Xavier wheedled, echoing Stamz.

"I'm doing you a favor, Xave," Walt Grantham said. "I'm going to help you get Mikhail home before your sis flies in from Peshawar or your lovely Ms. Carlisle from the Continent."

"Yeah? How?" Xavier was thinking how lousily their jaunt into Satan's Cellar had gone. Donel had emerged from it blaming him for the recreational perversities of lower-middle-class Suthren males. Bryan, traumatized by unrealized dangers, hadn't showed up for work this morning. And Mikhail . . . Mikhail had fled.

"Actually, I've already done it," Grantham said. "For the past two days, I've run an item for you in the *Urbanite*'s want ads." He picked up a newspaper, shook it open, and pointed out to Xavier his miniature masterpiece:

> Mick, chill out & phone home. I have 2
> tckts for Frdy's STH&T gig at Grotto. If
> back by Thrs, we go f'sure. Truce, X.

"Ess, Tee, Aitch, and Tee?" Xavier said. "What's that?"

"An acronym. Meaning Smite Them Hip and Thigh, whom the Mick, I hear tell, nigh-on to wets his pants over."

Lee Stamz *leaned* into Grantham. "You're sending Xave, the acme of *un*hipness, to a Smite 'Em gig? Meanwhile, Mister Walt, what 'm *I* s'posed to do?"

"The *Turandot* preview at the opera house. You see, the pop stuff Xave's banging on, well, *that's* selling papers." Grantham thought better of this all-out stroking. "I mean, along with our sex-lives-of-school-superintendents series and Duplantier's daily 'Computer Cannibals' strip."

"*Turandot!* Jesus, Walt."

"I'd never write something like 'we go f'sure,' " Xavier said, eyeballing the ad copy. "Never."

Stamz said, "It's amazing a dude who's gotta sign his name with an 'X' can write anything at all."

"And he won't phone me, either." Xavier pursed his lips.

Grantham handed him a pair of tickets. "These'll bring him—bet you money. Who cares if he phones, s'long's you get him home again, huh?"

"Giving Thaxton those tickets is like giving a blind guy a paint-by-numbers kit. A man with no feet, shoes. A snake, a catcher's mitt. Jesus, Walt."

"A fisherman, a foolproof lure—'at's more like it," Grantham said. "Hey, Lee, where's your philanthropic spirit?"

"Blown clear at my last bassoon recital."

"And who's to say he'll even look at the ads section?" Xavier fretted. "Seems a long shot to me."

"The *Urbanite*'s full o' concert hype, the Mick's a Smite 'Em fan, the ads're a popular ticket-exchange. Trust me, Xave, he'll *see* the damned thing."

That evening, exiting the elevator on floor 22, Xavier felt the carpet and the walls thrumming with inaudible, bone-conducted bass notes. The purr of a dentist's drill could make your body tingle with a throb similar to that buzzing in the corridor. Feeling it, Xavier knew that Grantham's ploy had worked, that the prodigal had returned, and that, hallelujah, he wouldn't have to tell Lydia he'd chased her only child from the security of his apartment into the sin dens of Salonika's worst neighborhoods. For what he felt was music: music cranked out at jet-engine decibels from Mikhail's CD player and conducted through the building's girders as vibration rather than sound.

Ah, the retropunk brat had come home.

When Xavier pushed open the bedroom door, the Mick was sprawled on his bed in filthy clothes tapping a pen on his knee in time to the deafening music.

Turn that down, Xavier waved. The Mick merely stared at him. Xavier went to the CD player and turned it down himself. He ceased to quake so crazily; it would take a while for the floor to vibrate him back into the hall.

"About time," he said. "Past time, I'd say."

"Don't rev up, okay? Just don't rev up."

"You're presuming to tell *me* how to conduct myself?"

The Mick said nothing.

"If you hate me, Mikhail, what pulled you in out of the cold?"

"Your ad. The tickets. I've like come to get 'em."

Xavier produced them from an inside jacket pocket. "Think I'd lie? Why think that? I don't lie, Mikhail. Not-lying's what did me in with a certain person who'd've rather I sold out my standards than tell the truth as I saw it. Right?"

"Truth's relative, unc. You should know that by now."

"You're relative, too, nephew. In fact, that's the only reason you got into my life to begin with."

Mikhail yogi'd around on his mattress and punched his CD player all the way off. Silence. Motionlessness. "Don't start, Uncle Xave. You're s'posed to slay the fatted calf and throw me a killer wingding. That'd be the classy way to welcome me home."

"Would it? Well, your wingding's Friday night, at the Grotto. Just like the ad promised."

"Promises, promises."

Xavier strode all the way into Mikhail's sanctum. There was no uncluttered place to perch, except the end of the bed, and even it hosted a pair of capsized tennis shoes, their fat, quilted tongues lolling out. He'd have to pace. Fine. He *needed* to pace.

"Look, I've got a right to be angry. I was—"

"—worried sick," Mikhail preempted him.

"Sure. And why not? Donel Lassiter and Bryan Cline saw you in P.S. Annie's two nights ago hanging over a bowl of pokeweed. A hot one. Inhaling."

"No they didn't."

"Don't bullshit me. You were there again *last night.* Bryan tried to catch you."

"Whoa. Whoa there, okay?"

Xavier didn't want to let the kid fabricate an off-putting lie, but his refusal to shut up until Xavier shut up made it hard not to hear him out. His story was simple. He'd been hungry. So with a stevedoric assgrabber three times his age, he'd ventured into P.S. Annie's for some crackers and a bowl of hot chicken stock. He was supposed to repay this guy in illegal tender of a type that Xavier could easily deduce for himself.

"You weren't doing salad gas?"

"Naw. I was spooning soup. Oliver Twist-style." This was a lie. Xavier would bet money on it.

"Afterward, did you . . . pony up?"

"You kidding? I scrammed from that fudge-packer. Flim-flammed him. But so it goes for AC-DCs, right?"

"What about last night? Why'd you run from Bryan?"

"Hadn't seen your ad yet. Wasn't ready to go home. Knew I'd have trouble cadging a meal while you and your swishy buddies were nosing around."

"Don't talk like a little bigot. You hungry now?"

"Uh-uh. Mopped up on the leftovers in the fridge. Sorry."

"I'll bet. Consider it your fatted calf."

Xavier peered sidelong at the Mick. A mixed blessing, at best, having him back in the apartment. Would the kid light out every time one of his reviews offended him? Would Xavier have to pretend to like what he hated, or to hate what he liked, to keep his status as the Mick's narrowly tolerated proxy dad? Xavier asked these questions aloud.

"You worried about writing up the Smite 'Em concert? 'Fraid I'll hightail it if you dis 'em?"

"Yeah. Yes, I am."

"Hey, you're prejudiced against Smite 'Em. And you've never even listened to one of their albums."

"The bongoing I've heard seeping out of your headphones doesn't sound too promising."

"Well, if they're as bad as you think, at least you'll suck up a health-preserving energy rush." Mikhail dared Xavier to prepare for the concert by listening to several Smite 'Em CDs. That would offer a yardstick by which to measure the band's musicianship on stage. Xavier, the Mick said, was a know-

nothing about rock 'n' roll. He knew even less about retropunks. So any preparation at all would be helpful. It might
even allow him to get off on a set that had the rest of the crowd
communion-juking.

Xavier doubted that listening to STH&T before its concert
would acculturate him to its idiosyncratic tribal sounds or its
on-stage choreographies, but, working on the proposition that
he would never attend an art exhibit without previewing the
artists or a new stage play without first trying to read its script,
he spent the next two evenings immersed in a gonzo rhythmic
discord that violated most of his notions of what music was,
how it was supposed to mean, and the way it should caress the
ear.

"Just remember McGudgeon's Law, Uncle Xave."

Imprisoned between the Mick's headphones, Xavier said,
"What're you talking about?" ("McGudgeon's Law" sounded
like the title of a TV cop show.)

"From Gregor McGudgeon," Mikhail said. "Smite 'Em's
front man, keyboard player, and lead guitarist. He's also
heavy into computer graphics, vitriform carving, and sci-fi
poetry."

"Right," Xavier said. "A Renaissance man."

"McGudgeon's Law is personal, but it has universal application: 'Only five percent / Of what I do / Is deathless art. /
The rest is meant / To buy us stew / Or ease my heart.' Can
you glom that?"

"Probably not. I'm not a very good glommer."

Mikhail grimaced. "No, you ain't. Maybe it's got something to do with your wussy Philistine Syndrome."

Xavier, angry, made a series of shooing gestures with the
back of his hand.

Actually, recently, he'd been doing better, working Stamz's
beat—until his dutiful homework on the anarchic music of
Smite Them Hip & Thigh. Now, he felt unsettled, vaguely
queasy, on the edge of the flu. What did *that* mean?

He tried not to think about it.

24

Lydia Dearest

On Thursday, Lydia and Bari whooshed into Lanier International Airport on separate flights. Their wide-bodied jumbo jets landed only twenty minutes apart on Concourse D. Xavier had Mikhail stay in the waiting area of the gate where his mother would disembark. He stood at the panoramic plate glass of a waiting area five gates nearer the main terminal. Lydia would want some time to talk to her son alone, and this arrangement would give her that even before they got to Xavier's. Xavier, in turn, was looking forward to his reunion with Bari.

Who, unfortunately, came off the plane utterly dragged out, in a charcoal-colored Dolce & Gabbana dress pleated with an array of weirdly spaced clasps that reminded Xavier of aluminum locust. The dress was from a decade-old collection. Had Bari worn it to mirror her morose mood and listlessness, or had the gloomy dress triggered those conditions?

Who knew? Bari was "really glad"—she claimed—to see him, but, although usually immune to the depredations of jet lag, today she didn't want to meet Lydia, or come by his apartment, or make a date of any kind until next week. All she wanted was to return to her atelier, crawl onto the mattress under her cutting table, and sleep, sleep, sleep.

To Xavier's surprise, Bari insisted on taking a cab home. He could help by collecting her luggage—she gave him the tickets—and bringing it to her later.

Presto! she hurried off.

Xavier walked back toward the gate where he'd left Mikhail to meet his mother. Most of the flight's disembarked passengers had already cleared the area, but Lydia and the Mick were standing in the concourse arguing, going at it like sparring partners. Xavier grimaced and hung back.

The only good thing about this development was that Lydia was too engrossed in her spat to be either disappointed or annoyed that Bari—the famous Bari of Salonika—had left the airport without saying hello to her. It hadn't been a snub, not a deliberate one, anyway, and now Lydia wouldn't be able to regard it in that light. Xavier would tell her that Bari had *wanted* an introduction, but had been too embarrassed by her argument with the Mick to intrude. He steeled himself and strolled toward the pair.

"You have to come to San Diego with me," Lydia was telling her son. "You have no choice."

Xavier heard in her tone an echo of his manner of dealing with staffers when he'd had a bad day. This was both a startling and a depressing insight.

"I don't have to do nuthin' you tell me," the Mick said, his nose a tissue's width from Lydia's. "You abandoned me in Salonika, shunted me off on a cubic geezer who can't even play chess without catching a nosebleed."

"Your uncle? Are you talking about your uncle?"

"Uncle? He's a fucking know-it-all parole officer."

"Hello, Lydia," Xavier said. Because she didn't even bother to turn his way, he kissed her lightly on the temple. She brushed at the spot as if a fly were trying to land on it. "Lydia, I'm here," Xavier said, gingerly stepping back.

"Parole officer? Well, he sure hasn't done much to clean up your language. And what do you mean, 'abandoned' you here? You *wanted* to come to Salonika."

"What I really wanted, Ma, was *not* to go to Pakistan."

"You wanted," Lydia repeated, "to live with Xavier, to explore a new part of the country."

"Sheeesh," the Mick said, with a disbelieving sneer.

"What's going on?" Xavier said.

Lydia finally faced him. "Philip and I have been transferred from Pakistan to Bangladesh. We're going to be helping three UN agencies and some people from the Ford Foundation with the medical side of flood relief there."

"How wonderful," Xavier said.

"We'd like Mikhail to join us there, but Mikhail emphatically doesn't want to."

Xavier wondered *why* they'd want Mikhail to join them. At this point, he'd've done almost anything, short of hiring a hit man, to be shut of the willful brat.

"A guy'd have to be a masochist or a monsoon freak to pack up and move to Bangladesh," the Mick said.

"Is that how you regard your father and me? As masochists? As monsoon freaks?"

"No, ma'am," the Mick said. "As bleeding-heart libsters with first-degree delusions of sainthood."

"Mick!"

"Mama!" the Mick shot back.

"You're flying to San Diego with me tomorrow, young man. No ifs, ands, or buts. Well, the only if is this: If, after a week with me, you still don't want to join us in Dacca, you can return to Salonika, none the worse for wear—assuming, that is, Xavier will take you back."

"A big ass oooming," Mikhail said.

A very big ass oooming, Xavier thought. Mikhail had disrupted his life. His motor mouth, retropunk attitude, and recent moronic defection to Satan's Cellar had disillusioned Xavier, who sometimes wondered if the Mick's presence hadn't aggravated the effects of his Philistine Syndrome.

Lydia turned to Xavier and began picking with big-sister-knows-best impunity at his clothes. She straightened his tie knot, undid and renotched his belt-buckle prong, and darted a finger around his collar to check for fraying. "I know you thought I'd have a few days to visit with you, Xavier, but I don't. This new mission's an urgent one, and I've got some stuff to do in Chula Vista to prepare for it. Would it hurt you terribly if I kidnapped Mikhail? If he keeps refusing to join Philip and me in Bangladesh, I'll send him back to you next week."

"I ain't going to Bangladesh *or* to San Diego," the Mick said. "No way, either one."

"To San Diego at least," Lydia said. "For some QT—quality time, I mean—before I have to fly out again."

"QT, huh? On the qt, Ma, your QT usually ain't."

Feeling trapped and persnickety, Xavier said, "If you're flying out of here tomorrow, Lydia, there's another reason the Mick's not anxious to go with you."

"C'mon," the Mick warned. "Keep it on the qt, unc."

"There's a Smite Them Hip and Thigh concert tomorrow night, I'm covering it, and my boss gave me an extra ticket."

"Ah," Lydia said. "Outgunned again." She looked at Mikhail. "Didn't you see that tribe of yodeling banshees in Birmingham last year? Do you have to see them again?"

"Every show's dif. And I got to make sure your *'iddle brutha* gets righteously culture-briefed, don't I?"

Lydia handed Mikhail a baggage-claims ticket. "Go see that my suitcase hasn't been stolen. I need to talk to Xavier."

After snatching the ticket, Mikhail swaggered toward the escalator to do what he'd been told to do. He looked grateful for the excuse to absent himself.

"Philip and I haven't been able to do anything with him for I don't know how long. Please let him go on staying with you. It's clear his mind's made up against returning with me."

"Lydia, I can't do a helluva lot with him either. He ran away for a week. He only showed up again last night as the result of an outright bribe. I was afraid you'd get here without his having come back yet. I could imagine your wrath, Lydia. I'd've deserved every reproach, every bitter word."

"But he did come back. You're doing wonderfully well. Better than Phil and I did."

"Then you lied to me when you foisted the little bugger off on me last fall."

"It would have been a very difficult foist if I'd told you the truth. Wouldn't it?"

"We do semiokay sometimes, sis. We haven't done even semiokay for a good while, though. The Mick's headstrong and tetchy. He's . . . impossible."

"You're a steadying influence, Xavier."

"His performance at Ephebus got worse each grading period. If that trend continues this year, they'll suspend or expel him. And I won't be around all day to keep him from doing salad gas, tuning in the Pornucopia Channel, or computer-cracking the secret formula of Diet Coke. Who's to say I could stop him even if I *were* around all day? Not me."

" 'Not *I,*' " Lydia corrected him. "You're a man, though. You're providing him an accessible masculine role model."

"What's Phil, then? An inaccessible hermaphrodite?"

"The 'inaccessible' part's on target. And, um, I'm"—Lydia sighed poignantly—"not much better, I guess."

Gak, thought Xavier. The noose was tightening.

"We'll pay you, Phil and I will. We'll up Mikhail's allowance, we'll stand you your rent and utilities, we'll—"

"No. Definitely not."

A concourse cart carrying a handicapped person beeped at them, and Xavier pulled Lydia out of its way. "He ran away from us too," said Lydia, heedless of the cart's passage. "Once, he stayed gone a month and a half. We had him declared a missing person. When he came home, we locked him in his room." Xavier gave her a quizzical look. "It was a suite, actually. With a bathroom."

Lydia badgered, harangued, and cajoled as they strolled to the escalator, as they rode the train to the baggage carousels in the main terminal. By the time they reached the claim area, Xavier had agreed to let the Mick stay another year with him. The first one hadn't been all azaleas, but neither had it been an utter disaster, and perhaps attending a Smite Them Hip & Thigh concert with the boy would do something to effect a rapprochement.

Even if it didn't, Xavier believed that Lydia had given him her forgiveness, in advance, if the Mick cut out again, OD'd on salad gas, or came down with a fatal disease. Not that he wanted any of these things to happen, God knows, but that if something unforeseen and terrible did occur, he wouldn't have to walk about the rest of his life under an ugly guilt-lined cloud. The Mick did have a way with words, and he did sometimes cook, and Bari didn't regard him as an unrehabilitable yahoo. . . .

When Xavier got home from work on Friday, his sister was gone. Mikhail said that she'd taken EleRail back to the airport all by herself, since he hadn't wanted to go with her, to catch her flight to San Diego. Meanwhile, the Mick had dressed for that evening's concert at the Grotto East.

The Mick *looked* ready. He was sporting a reprise-punk outfit (black denim as gloomy as Bari's locust-clasp D & G number), with face paint, shaved temples, a spiked collar, and ankle-high boots. As an obvious peace offering, he'd also prepared dinner—hot dogs with chili, oven-ready French fries, and, for dessert, microwaved apples.

"This almost looks edible," Xavier said. "But I don't think I can eat."

"Yeah. I'm pretty excited too."

The fact that Mikhail might not see his mother again for a year or even two didn't appear to distress him much. But, hell, he was *used* to not seeing his parents. Even in Chula Vista, Lydia and Philip had been upwardly mobile workaholics. The Mick had had to become . . . well, exactly what he'd become.

Namely, the Mick.

"Look," Xavier said. "Could we declare a sort of moratorium on feuding? Would that be possible?"

" 'S nool. Your ad said 'Truce,' remember? I didn't come back only for the Smite 'Em tickets. Mostly, but not only."

Xavier didn't remember that his ad had said "Truce," just that it had offered a bribe—but, of course, Grantham had written the ad, he hadn't, and he was inclined to think that the bribe had had more to do with Mikhail's return than had the doubtful extension of an olive branch.

25

"Count Geiger's Blues"

They sat front-row-center in the Grotto East. On the Mick's recommendation, Xavier had worn blue jeans (*designer* blue jeans, to the kid's disgust), a white shirt, a pair of high-tech tennis shoes, and a navy-blue windbreaker. He didn't look retropunk, not at all, but he didn't look like some old fogey either. Earlier, Bari had told the Mick that such dress would probably get his uncle through the show without bringing down catcalls or a thrashing with bicycle chains.

Unless, that is, someone at the Grotto East recognized Xavier. As a precaution, then, he'd also worn a pair of granny glasses with cola-colored lenses.

To Xavier, the warm-up band for Smite Them Hip & Thigh sounded like twelve people continuously breaking glass in an empty swimming pool. They were called either The Indictments or The Incitements, but Xavier didn't see that their antiestablishment monicker made an iota's difference, either way, and refused to set down in his notes the titles of their "songs." Aesthetically, it was a mercy and a relief when the I-worders finished their set and departed the stage basketing their crotches, wiggling their outthrust tongues, and blessing the delirious crowd with upraised, cheerily pogo-sticking middle fingers.

"Homey touch," Xavier told the Mick amid the hubbub. "Staining their bird fingers blue."

The Mick was in too good a mood to rebut either this sarcasm or Xavier's observation that *any* band following these guys would sound like "melodic troubadours."

And, in fact, Smite Them Hip & Thigh did come across, when they seized the stage, as melodic troubadours. But only by comparison. Its three women all played percussion instruments—drums, sticks, tambourine, xylophone—while Gregor McGudgeon, on either a guitar shaped like a futuristic post-hole digger or an upright synthesizer on chrome-plated casters, and the white-haired bassist Kanji Urabe laid down melodies counterpointed by the computer-generated images flashing on two huge screens at the back of the stage.

Xavier had never heard music that sounded quite like this. It had Oriental, African, and Polynesian flavors; it bristled with an electricity that was more than simply amplified sexual energy. And if he listened hard, Xavier could make out the mocking but literate poetry that McGudgeon had set to this music.

Except, he thought, maybe "superimposed on" was a more accurate way to put it than "set to."

Whatever, the lyrics were as much a part of Smite Them's appeal as the grab-bag quality of their music or as the contrast between the women's robotic footwork and the men's fierce immobility. The Mick sat transfixed watching them, a zircon of spittle at the edge of his mouth, while the rest of the audience either swayed in place to the weirdly infectious rhythms or tried to lip-synch McGudgeon's rapid-fire lyrics as he expressionlessly talked/sang them over each number's accompaniment.

It was undoubtedly blasphemy to make such a comparison, even in his head, but Gregor McGudgeon reminded Xavier of Rex Harrison as 'Enry 'Iggins in *My Fair Lady*. A young, lean, *angry* 'Enry 'Iggins, with lots of hair, fiery eyes, and a wardrobe incongruously patched together from Salvation Army castoffs and the most expensive items in a swank New York leather shop. McGudgeon was that self-assured, haughty, and charismatic. His Broadway *savoir-faire* kept rubbing the nap off his au courant disdain for the zombied-out mindlessness of the pop world's regard.

At one point, Xavier was certain that McGudgeon was staring at *him,* gazing down from behind his keyboard with a look that drilled to the crux of his hypocrisies and presumptions. You're irrelevant to the universe that my band is re-creating from the present chaos, McGudgeon's look said. You're a tottering anachronism. The fact that McGudgeon was machine-gunning the words of "Nowhere Man Redux" only heightened Xavier's discomfort.

"Whaddaya think, Uncle Xave?"

"I don't know."

"You don't know? What's not to fucking know?"

"Listen, Mikhail, I'm trying to take everything in, okay?"

"Sure. Suck it all up, unc. Suck it all up."

The kids around them were swaying, although *not* dancing, to the band's weird music. As song succeeded song ("Game, Set, & Match to Jill," "Pope-a-Dope Shuffle," "The Bush Man's Got a Nerve to Brag," "O, You Vulgar Boatmen," "The Utes in Their Utopia," etc.), Xavier grew more, not less, confused. He recalled some of the lyrics to a cryptic old Bob Dylan song—"Something's going on here, / But you don't know what it is, / Do you, Mr. Jones?"—and he thought that Smite Them was making that statement to him while talking around him to their clued-in fans. Was what they were laying down good or bad? Deathless art or smarmy dreck?

McGudgeon introduced a new number. "This un's in honor of your city, Salonika, metrop of the hustle, home of UC's stalwarts. Git sit, sibs—'Count Geiger's Blues'!"

He gave his band a downbeat, and Urabe, Matison, Suarez, and Kambo launched into a ditty that was a true toe-tapper, even though its lyrics included lines like "Lost her forever / Near the Pripyat River" and "Old Man Meter's a red-cell eater. / Don't he make you wanna / Call yourself a goner?"

Now, at last, the group's fans—collectively, the Mick said, known as Smittens—started to boogie, gyrating in front of their thirty-buck seats. Xavier, smitten by—well, *something*—began to move too. He moved with so much energy and enthusiasm that the Mick gave him a smile and flailed even harder himself. The entire Grotto East was rocking, the computer screens behind the band were flashing up multiple images of Count Geiger in his silver suit and ghastly burn mask, and Xavier was knee-twitching and elbow-jerking with the most frenzied of them.

Only Xavier understood that the Philistine Syndrome had struck again. He wasn't dancing. He was reacting on a perverse physical level to the sheer Quality of Smite Them Hip &

Thigh's unique brand of art. A kind of palsy had seized him. He *looked* to be enjoying himself, but he was suffering. With his hands at shoulder height, he couldn't keep from thwapping himself in the face. He was doing a Saint Vitus jig, in thrall to such a madcap chorea that his limbs and torso shook, his facial muscles spasmed, his internal organs jounced. He liked what Gregor McGudgeon's band had showed him, he considered their act worthy of praise, but he was in hell, a sinner in the hands of an angry God.

"Get it!" the Mick cried. "Go, Uncle Xave!"

Before "Count Geiger's Blues" ended, Xavier lurched toward the stage, staggered, and, toppling, struck his head on the edge of the platform. As at Mahler's Seventh some time ago, he was out, really out, and for exactly the same reason.

The review that Xavier later wrote, scribbling it out in pencil while propped up in his bed, had this lead:

Five percent of Gregor McGudgeon's work is "deathless art," and Smite Them Hip & Thigh brought only that 5 percent to their brilliant show in the Grotto East on Friday night.

26

A Run to SatyrFernalia

Over the telephone, Grantham said, "It says you've lost your edge, that's what your Smite Them Hip and Thigh rave-up says to me, Thaxton."

Thaxton. Not Xave or Xavier. A bad sign. "But McGudgeon's band is good," Xavier said. "Mikhail was right about them. Dead on the money."

"Thanks," said the Mick, sotto voce. He was sitting on a red stool across the living room while Bari, alarmed to learn that her lover had suffered another fainting spell at a concert, had come to Franklin Court to see about him. She lounged beside Xavier on the sofa, a hand on his arm.

"Uh-huh," Grantham said through Xavier's handset. "Now what're you gonna give the kid for Christmas?"

"Unfair, Walt. I called that concert as I saw it. As I *heard* it. Smite Them are very good at what they do."

"Yeah. And at what they did, Hitler and Company were very good too. Would you give *them* a four-star write-up?"

"Walt, that's a cheap shot. A *bigoted* cheap shot."

"Maybe, maybe not."

"You weren't there—"

"Thank God for major mercies."

"—but I was, Walt, and I gave them a review in keeping with the respect their performance earned."

"Hey, you've been under the weather. You tripped and hit

your head on the stage. Now, you're selling out your values. Maybe, to rehone your edge, you should go back to the 'really good stuff.' I want you and Stamz to return to your old positions."

"That'll make Lee happy."

"You're not cut out to do pop entertainment, Xavier." (Calling him Xavier was supposed to soften the rebuke.) "And the last thing I want from you in the coming week is a hallelujah chorus for some potty-mouthed comedian at Hooter's or a round of sloppy kudos for a slasher flick."

"I wouldn't give those things—"

"Xavier, who knows what you'll do? That nephew of yours's got your artsy-fartsy head screwed on backward."

"The spectrum of what I'm able to appreciate has been expanded, Walt. That's all. I'm delighted that it has."

"Listen, 'Thus Saith Xavier Thaxton' should be withering stuff, not nosegays and pulled punches—at least when you're covering the crap Lee and his gang usually do. Get well, okay?" Grantham abruptly hung up.

"I'm reassigned to my Fine Arts post," Xavier announced.

"Your first love," Bari said.

"Yeah," the Mick said, picking his nose, "but, hey, he's got an *expanded septum of appreciation.*"

"Spectrum. Meaning I'm further away from licking my Philistine Syndrome. In fact, Mahler and McGudgeon are now equally capable of making me sick."

"Awl riiight!" the Mick said, ironically raising a fist.

Xavier ignored him. "But reassigned to my Fine Arts desk, I'll be fair game for temporary blindness, falling hair, or involuntary echolalia every time I encounter something good."

"After reviling junk for so many weeks," Bari said, "maybe just getting back to the good stuff will stabilize you."

"I don't know," Mikhail demurred. "Uncle Xave liked Smite 'Em's show, but lookit—liking it put a fucking walnut over his eye."

Xavier touched the bandage on his forehead. "Much more of this and I may just lie back and sip my hemlock."

"What you need," Bari speculated, "is a talisman, something you can keep with you even at a gallery opening or a ballet."

"A talisman?"

"Something to override your syndrome so that you could cover an entire event without any ill effects."

"A kind of phylactery? An asafoetida bag?"

"Sort of. Something that's the product of either superstition or the popular imagination. You'd have to be able to keep it close to your body, so close it was almost a part of you."

The Mick hopped off the bar stool. "I've got an idea. Not a bag of garlic or anything like that—but something that could be a whole heckuva lot fucking better."

"What?" Xavier and Bari said together.

"Got to call this dude," Mikhail said. "After which it could maybe mean going on a little run."

"Who?" Xavier said. "Who'd have to go on this . . . run?"

"You and me," the Mick said. "Bari, if she wants to, but you'd definitely have to come with, unc."

Great, thought Xavier. A "little run" at nine o'clock on a hot September night in Salonika. A *Saturday* night. With his forehead gauze-wrapped and his body still subliminally twitching from Smite Them's "septum"-expanding show, Xavier could think of many things that he'd rather do tonight than go out on a "little run"—but, scooting obligingly aside, he let Mikhail punch out a code on the telephone.

In Satan's Cellar, not far from P.S. Annie's, the Mick led them through scrap-strewn streets, under the switchbacking cages of fire escapes, and past the wino-blockaded foyers of fleabag hotels to a cobblestone alley lit by unreliable fluorescents and teeming with people so far removed from the plebian mainstream that you couldn't even label them hoi polloi.

A few tuxedoed or evening-gowned slummers had wandered into the Cellar, but even they were wasted-looking, poked up, strung out on alcohol or technodrugs. Xavier saw that Bari and he, imperturbably guided by the Mick, must look to this crowd like Tory tourists on a walkabout among the urban damned.

He wished that Donel and Bryan—or, better, Lee Stamz— were along to afford their expedition some muscle, for these alleys were Salonika's stews. He was almost grateful for the bandage on his head. It made him look a little tougher than he was, a lot tougher than he felt; it caused some of the hard-trade types they ran into face-on to glance aside, to sidle away.

This section of the Cellar was like something out of Hugo or Dickens. Or an old comic book.

"Mick, where the hell're you taking us?"

The Mick plunged on through the crowd, checking occasionally to make sure he hadn't outrun them. Eventually, he turned into a side street with less light, fewer people, and a heavy, disabling reek. The stench seemed to be a combination of grease paint, stale roses, and anonymous pharmaceuticals, but Xavier was guessing, he couldn't focus his suspicions about the place or determine a point of origin for all the overlapping odors.

"Here," the Mick said. "Through and up." He ducked into a three- or four-story building—collapsing, like all the others in the area. It had an almost elegant neon logo above its entrance: SatyrFernalia. This winked on and off, its shaped tubes flickering crimson and violet. Briefly, the Mick reappeared in the doorway. "Come on. It's okay."

Hesitating only a moment, Xavier and Bari followed him up the steps and into the disintegrating shell. The Mick waited on the landing of a cockeyed stairway; each step in its creaking scaffold seemed on the brink of giving way to midnight and empty air. From the landing, the Mick beckoned them impatiently.

Despite the stairs' sorry condition, they rail-walked to a loft room constituting at least half the third story. They crossed this echoey space into a vast bay where a balding man in pleated pants and an outsize houndstooth jacket hunched behind a counter reading the *Urbanite* in the spots cast by the flashlights mounted on three greasy iron poles. On one page of his newspaper sat a rodentlike beast—a gerbil, Xavier supposed—busily shelling a small pile of sunflower seeds.

"Do for you?" the gerbil keeper said.

"Yo, slick, I called."

The man looked Mikhail up and down. Xavier, meanwhile, noted with some pleasure that he'd been reading his review of the Smite Them Hip & Thigh concert. Or, maybe, the story just under it about the variable fortunes of a dog track in Alabama. Xavier, as the gerbil cracked another sunflower seed, suspended judgment about the man and which article he'd been reading.

"Shake out the cobs," the Mick said. "I did call."

"Okay," the man said. "My name's Griff. What you want's

back there. Somewheres. Go ahead and look." He waved
brusquely at the shadowy racks behind him, acres and acres of
clothes, as if the bay were a quartermaster's barracks or an
all-night laundry.

"How are we supposed to see?" Bari asked.

"Take you a coupla beamers," rasped Griff, nodding at the
poles supporting his flashlight lamps. At the bottom of each
pole was an iron plate on casters—Xavier, looking over the
counter, realized that they were supposed to maneuver these
unwieldy devices into the bay, like patients on IV drips walking their bottled glucose down a hospital corridor. Sort of.

Griff lifted a counter section to let them through. Guiding
their flashlight poles into the bay's warehouse, Xavier, Bari,
and the Mick soon learned that SatyrFernalia specialized in
mechanical sexual aids and sartorial aphrodisiacs. The costumes racked here were meant to stimulate the imaginations of
their renters. (Were kinky trysts occurring in hidden warrens
around the building?) He had glimpses of waxed leather, polished brass, delicate lace, and intricate ivory or plastic devices.
There were also capes, hoods, tights, belts, scarves, and less
identifiable garments.

"Mikhail," he said, halting his nephew, "how do you even
happen to *know* about this place?"

"You guys buying or renting?" Griff called out.

"They're buying," the Mick said over his shoulder.

"Mikhail!"

"Stow it, Uncle Xave," the Mick whispered. "It's the super-
hero garb I skate on. They've got Scarab, the Snow Leopard,
Ladysilk, the Decimator, Mantisman, Saint Torque, the
Deejay, Gator Maid, Yellowhammer, Warwoman, MC^2—"

"Damn it, Mikhail, that's plenty!"

"Shhhh," said Bari. "Can't you see why he's brought us
here?" She turned her flashlight pole so that its beam white-
washed a rack of costumes. Motes swam blurrily. Braidwork,
piping, and strange medallions glittered.

"Frankly, no. None of this epic tackiness makes a *soupçon*
of sense to me, Bari."

"Your talisman's not exactly a talisman, Xavier. Instead,
it's a costume, a stalwart's outfit. Pick one out."

"That's crazy."

"We didn't come all this way, in the seediest part of

Salonika, to have you nix the Mick's idea without a trial, Xavier. I mean it, pick one out."

Xavier realized that he couldn't win here, that Bari and the Mick were allied against him. They'd brook no lengthy or energetic defiance. The Mick was his ward for who knew how long, and Bari was . . . the woman he loved. A fact that gave her leverage. He felt like a small boy resisting his mother's insistence that he try on new clothes for Easter: doomed. His talisman wasn't a talisman—no amulet, no coin, no magic feather—but an entire *costume*. Would that work? Would that afford relief from the absurd horror of the Philistine Syndrome?

On a nearby rack, Xavier rummaged through the gaudy costumes, squinting at an emerald-green leotard, a cape made to resemble a fanlike spiderweb, an ermine sheath with a cat's face and gloves clawed with tortoiseshell plectra. His fingers finally came to rest on, felt, and extracted a suit shining like hammered tinfoil. He handed this costume out to Bari.

The Mick took one of its sleeves. "Count Geiger! That's it, Uncle Xave. *That's it!*"

Bari also fingered the material. "I'm not sure what it's made of, but it's light enough—porous enough—to wear under a suit without bulking you up too much or giving you heatstroke."

"Under a suit?"

"You could wear this *instead of* a suit, but you'd catch some ribbing at work. Better to wear a suit over it—the way Clark Kent wears his Brooks Brothers over his superheroic BVDs."

"Heatstroke be damned," Xavier said. "I'm more likely to come down with the everlasting Count Geiger's Blues."

"Or everlasting relief from your problem," Bari said. "We just don't know, do we?"

"Stop bitching," the Mick snarled. "You're getting the fucking suit." He swallowed the snarl. "Aren't you?"

Back at the counter, Griff spread the silver bodysuit out, then folded it as if it were a handkerchief. (Griff's gerbil was in the pocket of his houndstooth jacket, its paws hooked over the lip and its beady eyes glittering. It looked at Xavier with the same kind of contained derision that McGudgeon had fixed on him at the Grotto East.) Griff lifted the folded bodysuit and placed it in a box not much larger than a man's billfold.

"Great choice," he said. "Lightweight. Portable. Stylish. That'll be one grand in greens."

Xavier imitated apoplexy. *"One grand!"*

"A bargain," Griff said. "We clear that much in a week renting out thisere Count Gargle outfit." He tweezered a sunflower seed off the newspaper pile and handed it to his gerbil—"Here, little Spudsy"—which accepted the seed daintily and ducked out of view to crack it.

"If it's so profitable, why sell it?" Xavier said.

"We got three others just like it out now. Makes good sense to underwrite another coupla costumes with a straight-up sale or two. Occasionally, anyway."

"If you don't get it after I've gone to all this trouble," the Mick said, "I just might hotfoot it again, unc."

"Don't tempt me, boy-o."

They bought the costume, Xavier sharing the cost with Bari, who threatened to boycott their relationship if he didn't allow her to help him buy it. Call it blackmail; a tender—indeed, a *sweet*—sort of blackmail.

"Sorry I've done boxed it up," Griff said. "Hope you weren't planning to wear it home."

27

The Suit

From that peculiar evening forward, Xavier began to develop a secret relationship with his Count Geiger suit. Wearing it every day (although it put him in mind of the "garments," officially blessed underclothes, that some Mormons wore, believing them charms against speeding bullets, car-crash injuries, animal bites, etc.), he had to admit that the suit had more or less worked for him. He went back to editing the *Urbanite*'s Fine Arts section, labors he could now perform without feeding plum assignments to Ivie Nakai, Donel Lassiter, or Pippa Wiedmeyer.

Secreting the Count Geiger costume under his everyday clothes, Clark Kent-style, did create some minor problems. Its lightness, flexibility, and micromolecular thinness aside, it still contrived to make Xavier sweat. The fact that September and October were a little cooler than usual mitigated this tendency, but Walt Grantham insisted on maintaining a year-round work-environment temperature of seventy degrees Fahrenheit. Sometimes, encased like a laminated cheese slice in his stalwartly long johns, Xavier tried to imagine that a cooling blizzard had swept through Salonika, that soothing snows were drifting through its late-autumn asphalt canyons and its tarry culs-de-sac. Already, he'd begun to dread next summer, still seven months away.

Every night, Xavier hand-washed his costume. It dripped

dry in an hour, then he'd spray it with a commercial fixative obtained by his nephew for an exorbitant fee at SatyrFernalia. The fixative dried on contact, but, usually, Xavier sat in his bedroom, naked, luxuriating in his brief evening respite from the suit's tyranny. Eventually, he'd put it back on, for if he dawdled too long without wearing it, a snatch of Beethoven's Ninth, even a snatch overheard in a corridor, had the power to trip a pernicious somatic response—Xavier never knew what sort or how crippling it would be—and to threaten his livelihood.

Naturally, he was careful. Dressed in the suit, he was able to enjoy historic recordings by Gluck, Gershwin, and, yes, even Gregor McGudgeon. Without penalty, he was able to read all that he most admired, to see all the films and artwork deserving his attention, to listen to all that he deemed meritorious. For Xavier, this was freedom—even if imprisonment in, and subtle manipulation by, the Count Geiger suit was freedom's despotic price.

The suit had other disadvantages, some of them too personal or intimate to record. (But let's relate one anyway.) In brief, like a bundling board, the suit literally got in the way of Xavier and Bari's evolving physical relationship.

Although he could roll its tinfoilish-appearing sheath onto his naked person with speed and precision (mentally, he compared it to a body-sized prophylactic), the costume was damned hard to skin out of. On those evenings when the Mick wasn't home—finally, he'd made a friend or two at Ephebus— it was frustrating for Xavier to discover that he couldn't unzip, unpleat, unholster, or disencondom himself fast enough to address the urgency of either his or Bari's passion.

Bari still hadn't agreed to his marriage proposal, noting that the fashion products of Bari's of Salonika were now so popular that she'd be unable to fulfill the vows that he, as a Suthren male of old-timey values, would expect her to meet. On the other hand, in the Mick's absences, when her work didn't call, she still liked to "do the deed" (her words), and it drove Xavier crazy—crazier—to have to wage all-out war on his Reynolds Wrap skivvies to take advantage of her randy moods.

"Don't rush," Bari'd whisper. "Please don't rush."

But generally he did, pinching the porous, pliant foil, digging at it with his fingernails, struggling doltfully to prise apart the invisible seam bisecting it into vertical body halves, making so many unseemly noises—grunts, moans, curses—that Bari would often end up laughing, albeit with a flushed face and visibly erect nipples. It wasn't quite so bad as being victimized daily by the Philistine Syndrome, but almost.

Things would have gone better, Xavier knew, if he'd just asked Bari over *after* struggling free of his Count Geiger duds; then he could've met her at the door in a dressing gown. But that approach was so clinical it sabotaged the element of romance essential to a fulfilling erotic encounter. For, as Bari understood, spontaneity was a crucial part of the mix, and Xavier didn't want to assume too much, on any given evening, about Bari's desires. If she'd had an especially grueling day, for example, all she wanted was a shoulder to cling to, and he was more than happy to oblige. Meeting her at the door in his dressing gown would have been like placing a bowl of condoms on his coffee table or slapping an X-rated cassette into the VCR as soon as they'd finished dinner.

One evening, the Mick out taking an acoustic-guitar lesson in a neighborhood called Sinatro Heights, Bari showed up in a state of diffident rut. The Suit (as they now apostrophized it, subjecting its tyrannical traits to glum upper-case mockery) had thwarted them at least twice before.

But this evening was different—Bari had brought two small packages, neither bigger than a man's wallet, wrapped in silver, gold, and ebony foil. "Excuse me a sec," she said, retreating to Mikhail's room but reappearing, moments later, in a sexy Saint Torque costume, rented, as it turned out, from the gerbily Griff Sienko at SatyrFernalia.

Xavier, smiling, "You look—"

"Don't say it. I know."

"*Scrumptious* was the word I had in mind."

"Beats the one that was surfacing through my vocabulary—it's hard to be positive about the couturier's design approach."

Xavier nodded toward the Mick's room. "So what's in the other little box?"

"Later. If this"—lifting her arms, doing a quarter pirouette—"does anything for you now."

"Oh, yeah."

And, in fact, it *helped* to find his heart's first lady clad in a costume as corny and kitsch-freighted as the Suit that, there in his living room, he speedily stripped to. It helped *a lot*. Xavier

found a seam of tenderness in himself that he hadn't explored
in a long time. Beside it, so to speak, he located a hidden seam
in his Count Geiger costume that let him explore this tenderness with Bari at pleasurable length.

Eventually, Bari dragged herself off to the Mick's room only
to show up again, revitalized, in the outfit of a modern Ama-
zon known to UC-comic readers as Warwoman. To Xavier's
amazement, additional hanky-panky ensued. His strength was
renewed, tried, depleted, and renewed again. The mechanism
of this renewal—minus the fumbling and frustration that the
Suit ordinarily inflicted on him—seemed to be the synergistic
effects spawned by two SatyrFernalia costumes interfacing in
easy lubricious cahoots.

So there *was* a way to sidestep at least one of the Suit's
major shortcomings, and, through this method, Xavier knew
several welcome kinds of relief.

After these diversions, he Suited himself again and carried
Bari a cold glass of pink-grapefruit drink. In the lotus position
on his sofa, she sat sinuously brushing her hair.

"We could be married at Christmas," he said, handing her
the glass. "The festiveness, the color, the . . . the *anticipation.*"

"Oh, yeah. Whose?"

"Mine," Xavier said. He was afraid—to himself, at least, he
had to admit this—that if he didn't put a band on her finger and
an official state imprimatur on their relationship, she would
break it off and turn to another. You could also escape from a
marriage, of course, just as you could be faithless within it, but
Bari was in many respects still an orthodox Suthren girl, and if
he took her to the altar, he'd have her. Really have her.

"We've danced all over this topic," said Bari, sipping her
pink-grapefruit drink in the minimalist costume that the First
Couturier had unimprovably fashioned for her. "Not tonight
too."

"Christmas would give us plenty of time to plan."

"Only if we substituted a Saint Torque or a Warwoman
outfit for my wedding gown, lover."

"I'd have no objection."

"I bet you wouldn't. Would you stand up in the Suit?"

"Well, I'd—"

"Look, I'm trying to assemble my line for the February
couture in Paris. That's occupying all"—glancing down at

herself—"well, not quite *all,* of my energies at present, and if
I agreed to marry you at Christmas, it wouldn't be fair to you
as my new husband to put you on hold for the next two
months. I was lucky to be able to get away tonight. Designing
an entire new collection's like laying out strategy for a global
war. How many times do I have to explain this to you?"

"Every night would be fine, if you'd do it in person."

Bari set her glass on a coaster and drew the multicolored
shawl draping the sofa back around her shoulders. She patted
the cushion next to her. "Sit down, Xave." He sat. "Don't
doubt me, okay? I hate being doubted, and preemptively possessed, and jerked around by somebody else's insecurities.
You should be more worried about how you and the Mick
stand than about how you and I are doing. You and I are
doing"—reassuring smile—"fine."

"Is Mikhail the reason, I mean, is he the—"

"The Mick's got nothing to do with my determination to
hold off a while. Is that what you're trying to ask?"

"I guess it is."

"What rot. What paranoid rot. Sure, I'd like to see you guys
hitting it off like frat brothers, but that's not a condition that
has to be met before I'll marry you."

Xavier stared at his glittery thighs. "Right now, Bari, we're
into mutual tolerance. School's started, he's back at Ephebus,
and although he's still doing crappy, I don't ride him as much
and we can sit down for breakfast together without throwing
Pop Tarts at each other."

"Commendable."

"Know what's helped?"

"Probably knowing that you're all he's got here in the
States. His protector and food source."

"Maybe. What else?"

"Your rave for Smite Them Hip and Thigh."

"Yeah, there's that, I guess. What else?"

"Your expanded septum of appreciation."

"And?"

"I don't know, lover. What?"

"This Suit. He's proud of himself for getting us to buy it.
He's proud that it's helped me. But mostly, Bari, he's proud
that he has a blood relative running around in aluminum-foil
long johns in secret impersonation of a comic-book stalwart."

"Well, sure," said Bari, laughing. "Well, of course."

28

Shaker Design, Shaken Faith

Early in November, Xavier noticed—or thought he noticed—that the Suit's effectiveness against the Philistine Syndrome had begun, just maybe, to taper off.

He wore the Count Geiger costume, under his sports clothes and minus the stalwart's hood, to an exhibit at the Upshaw called "Shaker Design." The Mick went with him because his history class was studying Early America Utopianism; the hand-crafted objects on display—wheelbarrows, cupboards, spinning wheels, baskets, and dry-goods dippers, among other items—spoke eloquently of the artful practicality of these "radical idealists," as a typed label beside one of their toy milk buckets characterized the Shakers.

One section of the exhibit, under the watchful eye of a museum guard, allowed visitors to touch some of the goods. Mikhail took up an ax handle. Xavier ran his fingers over a pyramid of drawers in a cherrywood cabinet. Although the idea was heresy to the kid, maybe the past did have something to teach the present.

"Well"—Xavier turning smugly to the Mick—"how does this hoary old stuff stand up to today's VCRs and PCs?"

"It's all right," the Mick conceded. "I mean, it's technology too. An earlier technology. And it's art because it's so . . . so spiffily framed."

"But *primitive* technology, right?"

"Naw. Shit, no. I mean, for the period these holy rollers crafted 'em, it was state-o'-th'-art gear."

"*Interim* technology. That's what you're implying, isn't it?" Because Mikhail was contemptuous of any human enterprise antedating Smite Them Hip & Thigh, and because Xavier felt pinched by his Suit, his job, and the retropunk lodger in his apartment. It had been a lousy day. Although this Shaker stuff was weirdly soothing, a kernel of irritability gritted somewhere inside his clandestine underarmor.

The Mick returned fire: "Hey, *all* technology's interim, unc. That's what technology is: one step from Back There to Up Here, forever. A technology that *ain't* interim is end-o'-th'-world. Unless it holds out hope for some add-on tomorrows, who'd like give a fuck about it anyway?"

"Easy, Mikhail. Didn't mean to . . . uh, rip your cord."

"Right. What's the *problema?* You about ready to stick me on a flight to Bangladeath?"

"Mikhail, I *am* sorry." He was. "It's the Suit, it's Grantham, it's Bari's refusal to marry me."

"You mean it's me putting the kabosh on your at-home adult entertainment."

"No. No, I don't."

"Yeah you do. So look at it this way—you don't exactly light up my social calendar either."

The guard strolled over, as if sensing that these two visitors were about to go at it. Gently, he took the ax handle from Mikhail and laid it back on its display case, a priest returning a saint's bleached ulna to its reliquary.

The guard's name was Addams, it was impressed on a hard plastic tag above his heartside pocket. Addams apologized for liberating the ax handle from the Mick. Ax handles, even Shaker ones, made him nervous. In Atlanta, once upon a time, his great-uncle had been bum-rushed out of Lester Maddox's Pickrick restaurant by a group of white men brandishing ax handles, "nigger knockers" in their fey lingo. Thus his tendency to go bug-eyed at any whitey so equipped, even if with a 175-year-old Shaker forerunner of the bigots' weapon of choice. This explanation made, Addams launched into a by-the-numbers spiel about the Shaker exhibit.

"Mother Ann Lee of Manchester, England, was the primary Shaker mover, so to speak—a working-class lady who arrived in New York City with eight disciples. Her followers eventually established communes over here from Maine to Kentucky. . . ."

The Mick, incredibly, was *listening* to Addams's spiel, at one point even recording his remarks on a Japanese unit that looked more like a Day-Glo clothespin than a tape machine. Could the Mick be getting into . . . history? He was pretty much a blank slate, a void between the ears. Ordinarily, his interests were limited to the newest retropunk CD, "chix" with "to-die-for bods," the next local thrasher challenge, and *Soap Opera Digest*'s rundown of the latest doings on "By Love Designed."

"One of Mother Lee's most distinctive precepts—it says a lot about every item you see here—explains the Shakers' tendency to turn their handicrafts into art: 'Do all your work as though you had a thousand years to live, and as you would if you knew you must die tomorrow.' Deep, huh?"

"Yeah, deep," the Mick agreed. Addams picked up and passed back to him for another reverent feel the Shaker ax handle. Xavier heard the footsteps in other galleries and on the Upshaw's swooping atrium ramps as a soft drumming, a nonintrusive beat for the music of reconciliation. The burr in his underarmor ceased to chafe. He was serene amidst the beveled smoothness of all the Shaker spinning wheels, chairs, benches, plows.

Later, on the street with Mikhail, Xavier felt nausea flying moth circles in his gut. Had the sublimity of a certain kind of art—today, Shaker spirituality bodied forth in fine household goods and farm tools—gnawed through the metabolic/ psychological shield afforded by the Suit? Or had lunch at First Stringers—a steamed pimiento-cheese burger, flaccid fries, and a cup of coffee not even an old beat cop could have stomached—been the culprit? Hard to say.

Lunch had been hours ago. Before the trip to SatyrFernalia, attacks of his syndrome had always come *during,* not after, a fine-arts experience. So lunch seemed the likelier of his two choices—though it may've taken a while for the sublimity of the Shaker Design exhibit to counteract the beneficial whammy of his weakening costume. Maybe.

Xavier, an arm over Mikhail's shoulder, limped back to Franklin Court uncertain and apprehensive.

29

"Say Yes to Droogs"

n Satan's Cellar, the Droogs needed Christmas bread, and two Droog eyemen, Qwarq and Shai Shiv-T, had had a warehouse under heavy vid for three days. That night, a prop cop in a go-truck stopped at the warehouse, checked it out, and shuttled on.

"He be gone," Qwarq said. "Let's hit it." Qwarq was amazing. With more tools on his whip-thin person than a hardware store, he magicked a filament pick out of his coat.

Qwarq and Shai Shiv-T ran in a crouch toward the warehouse, and Qwarq popped the padlock. Each of them took a door half and jammed it back so that they could squeeze inside. Suddenly, they were standing in a lumpy blackness, smelling goods rank with mildew and dust.

At first, they stumbled around filching penny-ante junk, some of which would fence and some of which was so rat-gummed that a guy would have to be lidded-out just to consider boosting it. Finally, though, Shai Shiv-T bumped against some kind of crumpled machine. The Droogs' penlights frisked and tickled it. It had a nameplate, an ID tag: *Therac 4-J.*

"Therac 4-J," Shai Shiv-T said. " 'At be some vandal handle."

The warehouse doors began to rattle. The prop cop who'd left a minute ago was standing inside them with a beamer. He flicked its light about like the hot ash of a cigar. His face was as broad and flat as a frying pan's. He couldn't see Qwarq or Shai Shiv-T and didn't really seem to expect to, either.

Shai Shiv-T threw a quarter at him. It banged against one door's tin liner and ricocheted away. Qwarq, lithe and pantherine, closed the twenty steps between the Therac 4-J and the startled cop, clothes-lining him with a jacket arm. The prop cop flopped. Almost as quick as Qwarq, Shai Shiv-T was on him, a knee on either side of his bug-eyed face.

"Ice him," Qwarq hissed. *"Ice him!"*

In a creamy blade of alley light, Shai Shiv-T watched the prop cop's irises roll like marbles under his brow.

"Do it!" Qwarq said. "Come on, Shaister—*do it!*"

"Don't sound me with that Shaister shit."

Qwarq backed off. Shai Shiv-T was a brother Droog, entitled, and the prop cop did look to be surfing a totally trampled brain wave. He probably hadn't even scoped them.

"All reet," Qwarq said. "Let's rack him somewhere safe." He dug into his hardware inventory, closing the prop cop's mouth with a strip of duct tape and blinding him from earhole to earhole with another silvery strip.

"When that tape come off, this fuzz ain't got him no eyebrows anymore," Shai Shiv-T said.

Qwarq and Shai Shiv-T stowed the prop cop in a closet in the back of the warehouse.

"Take the go-truck and roust the brothers," Qwarq said. "Then hustle your butt back. I be here to overwatch the trove."

Hustling, Shai Shiv-T drove the stolen go-truck through Satan's Cellar to the Droogs' basement HQ. On one wall hung a poster with a photo of five homeboy gangbangers: SAY YES TO DROOGS. The slogan was Hi-Quince's invention.

Tonight, Hi-Quince wasn't around, but Anthony and Papa Mel Mel were playing slash card at the basement's only table. They heard Shai Shiv-T out and came along. Anthony rode up front with Shai Shiv-T in the doorless cab, but Papa Mel Mel hunkered in the cargo bed among rolling soda cans and crumpled cigarette packs.

At the warehouse again, Qwarq said, "Most of this stuff ain't for shit, but Bro' Therac might be worth a ride."

Grunting and wheezing, the Droogs lifted the Therac 4-J over the go-truck's drop-gate, shoved it into the load bed, and blocked it up against the cab. After kicking soda cans and coffin-nail packages out of the truck, they hooked the machine into place with a leftover bungee cord.

Hello, Cracker Land, Shai Shiv-T thought. Here we come. . . .

Qwarq and Shai Shiv-T dropped off Anthony and Papa Mel Mel two blocks from the warehouse. Then Qwarq ran the truck at fifty mph out Highway 42 toward Silvanus County and its bohunky county seat, Philippi. With its doors chopped, the truck was a wind tunnel, and side-of-beef cold. Shai Shiv-T's teeth chattered the fifty-odd miles between Salonika and the piny edge of Philippi. Qwarq kept waiting for an Oconee Highway Patrol car to come wailing up, but it never did. Sheer luck.

Cherokee Junque & Auto Parts Reservation dawdled across about a quarter mile of highway on Philippi's eastern outskirts. All Shai Shiv-T could see of it was starlit hulks among the scrub brush, and dying kudzu vines strangling the midget trees growing in the shadow waste: stove-in sedan tops, wheelless limos, an up-and-down row of lookalike jalopy husks.

Driveway gates popped up at uneven lengths along the blacktop, and eventually Shai Shiv-T saw a two-story gas station and office shack slotted back from one gate. Studying the place, he felt like he'd been smoked and shipped to some ratty hell planet.

"Too early to crash the man," Qwarq said. "Better park and let 'er cool." He drove the truck up to the gas pumps. A metal sign, visible beyond the last pump, said CHEROKEE JUNQUE & AUTO PARTS RESERVATION / *Gas Oil Hot Sandwiches Worms / Tune-ups Fishing Licenses Videos*. A yellow bulb in the downstairs office winked on, and Juitt, a long-haired cracker in a suit of tree-bark camouflage, kicked open the inner door. Squinting, he slapped the screen wide and limped toward the driver's side of the go-truck.

"You two niggers mighty brave to ride into Silvanus County in a stolen vehicle this time o' the moon," he said.

"You mighty brave to talk that honky dis shit," Qwarq said.

Juitt eyed the go-truck. "You brung me this? Larry Glenn'll have to repaint the sucker."

"Naw, not this," Qwarq said, nodding tailward. "That gleamer piece of hospital 'quipment."

Juitt sidled away to assess it. "To do what with, pray tell?"

"Cut 'er down." Qwarq followed him to the load bed. He rubbed the machine's nameplate. "Looky here. It be a Therac 4-J."

"Give you twenty-five for your broken Brother Therac," Juitt said. "And three C's, cash, for thisere truck."

"Three hunnerd!" Qwarq said. "That be cockroach scale!"

"I got overhead. I got, already, cop trouble. I got paint to buy. 'Sides, Larry Glenn's gonna taxi you back to the Cellar."

"Praise de Lawd," Shai Shiv-T said. Juitt looked at him as if a ventriloquist's dummy had come alive.

In the end, the Droogs took the deal, and Larry Glenn Wilkins, Juitt's flunkie, drove them back to Salonika, gut-scared the whole trip that they'd roll and ditch him. They didn't though. They were three hundred heavier in their pockets than they'd been before tying up the prop cop and boosting the Therac 4-J.

At a pay phone in Satan's Cellar, Shai Shiv-T dropped a quarter and called police central. "Prop cop down but not dirt-napping in a Satan Cellar warehouse. Put a thermometer in the pig." His duty done, Shai Shiv-T hung up.

30

Bad Time at the Parataj

Tchaikovsky proved to Xavier that doubt and fear were rational responses to his hunch that the Suit was losing its powers.

A month after the Shaker art exhibit, Salonika's shiny towers reduced to dullness by December mist and Chatahoochee fog, Xavier took in one of the Metropolitan Ballet's annual performances of *The Nutcracker* at the Parataj Theater.

Houselights down, the inner dome of the Parataj glowed purple. On the worn upholstery of their seats, kids fidgeted beneath this off-world planetarium show, some awestruck, some bored.

Gratingly, the orchestra tuned its instruments. And when *The Nutcracker* actually began, Xavier got deeply into it, for this production was in every respect superior to last year's. He'd say so in print, for the Metropolitan Ballet relied heavily on yuletide revenues to make up for its less popular offerings.

A pair of ten-year-old boys next to Xavier were studying him with disgust. He recalled that at one crescendo in Tchaikovsky's score a painful twinge had rippled across his knuckles. His hands, arranged on his knees like two pale tarantulas, were exuding pus from between his fingers. The smell was cheesy-sharp. While their female guardian beamed at the doings on-stage, the two boys pinched their noses and mouthed "yuck" and "phieuw" at him.

The stench got worse. Xavier's trousers were blotched. He had to spread his fingers to make room for the pus oozing out. Worse, he had to reach into a hip pocket, further smearing his clothes, to retrieve a handkerchief with which to stifle both the ooze and the smell. The brats beside him looked vilely green-gilled.

"RrrUPPH!" went one kid, actually letting go of a half-digested slaw dog and the unabsorbed remains of a soda.

The boys' guardian—mama? aunt? nannie?—saw this substance crawling between her feet. She said, "Oh, Spencer," rose halfway from her cushion to help him get his face out of his own duodenal overboil, and immediately caught Xavier's eye. Xavier, unmindful of those behind him, stood, nodded coldly, and began easing himself out of the row.

"Oh, believe me, sir," the woman said, "Spencer's sorry."

But, his handkerchief wrapped around his joined hands, Xavier backpedaled away. In the aisle, he pivoted and strode toward the lobby. He left the Parataj without looking back or regretting at all his deception of the woman.

What did she know about real suffering, anyway?

"The Suit's not working the way it's supposed to," Xavier told the Mick later, once safely back at Franklin Court.

"Hey, nobody feels tiptop all the time. Forget it."

"It's not 'all the time' that worries me. It's during, or soon after, an aesthetically rich experience when, by rights, I ought to feel great, and instead I feel . . . really crappy." Xavier sat in a recliner with his handkerchief-bandaged hands deep in the pockets of his robe. He slowly withdrew and clumsily started to unwrap his hands. *"The Nutcracker* was great," he said, "but see what happened during the dance of the Sugarplum Fairies." He raised his hands and spread his fingers reveal-ingly.

"Yuck," said the Mick. "Phieuw."

"It's starting again. The Philistine Syndrome. What it means is . . . doom, I think. *My* doom."

"Be glad it was your hands. Think what else could've hap-pened at a performance of, you know, *The Nutcracker.* "

Xavier continued to display his hands as if they'd been mangled by a sleep-starved intern with an unoiled chain saw. Eventually, the Mick decided to show Xavier some low-grade celluloid art with the VCR, a stratagem he fulfilled by locating a bootlegged video of Ray Dennis Steckler's *The Incredibly Strange Creatures Who Stopped Living and Became Mixed-Up Zombies,* shot in the early 1960s in a process dubbed by Steckler "Hallucinogenic Hypnovision." Once this video started rolling, the cracks between Xavier's fingers began to heal and his hands to drop toward the thighs of his Fred Flintstone pajamas. His look of wary fascination hinted that in a numbed-out way he was *enjoying* the movie. . . .

31

A Rival?

Two nights later—luckily, it was the weekend and he could send his staff members out on assignment—Xavier caught a cab to the riverside neighborhood where Bari had her atelier. In his Sam Spade trench coat, he stalked up and down the tree-lined avenue in front of it. (The trees stood ribby and frail beside the greasy water, inmates of winter's concentration camp.) His breath was visible, each puff a dialogue balloon in a Unique Continuum comic book featuring the DeeJay, say, or the Decimator, or, that stalwart of stalwarts, Count Geiger.

In this godawful weather, Xavier was glad for his pseudo-mesh long johns, but not for their right-next-to-the-skin reminder of his unshakable syndrome.

Bari seemed to be avoiding him. Whenever he telephoned, an answering machine intercepted his call. A voice—not Bari's, but an employee's—asked that he leave a message at the sound of the bleeping beep. The insecurity of his teenage quasi-nerdhood rising from his past like a fumigatory cloud, he feared that she'd grown bored with him, that in Tokyo, Milan, or London she'd succumbed to the big-shouldered charm of some jet-setting moneybags, the sort of hunk she'd belonged with from the get-go, the incongruity of her fling with a bush-league critic finally striking even her as . . . ah, well, incongruous.

Across the avenue from the drawbridge into her fashion

factory, Xavier saw a light in one of the half-shuttered windows on its second story. At one o'clock on Sunday morning, she was still at it, or else she was finally relaxing after a long day sketching, cutting cloth, draping dummies, and starting over when the results proved either cockeyed or clichéd.

An industrious gal, this illustrious Bari person.

The door beyond the drawbridge, a broad mahogany plank screened by a portcullis, boomed as if taking a jolt from a battering ram. The portcullis ratcheted up, the door groaned open, and a man in a pea jacket left the atelier and began to cross the bridge linking the old mill to the barren winter street: a young, virile-looking guy with shoulder-length hair, a despicable December tan, and blue eyes that sparkled like chiseled diamonds.

My cuckolder, thought Xavier. Probably a millionaire playboy from Aruba, Majorca, or Saint-Tropez. In short, a jerk.

Xavier accosted the jerk as he came clomping heelwise down this side of the bridge. The man's eyes overflowed with panic, his chin began tick-tocking in search of a beat cop or a taxicab, and his gloved hands fisted at his chest in a reflex that may've been more face-saving than menacing.

"Who the hell are you?" Xavier huffed. "And what're you doing here at this hour?"

The guy started sputtering, hurling saliva from his lip corners like Sylvester the Cat. "St-st-st-stop," he told Xavier. "Don't s-s-sock me."

He grabbed the lapels of his own pea jacket and pulled it open with the swift disdainful anxiety of a flasher. What Xavier saw then was a costume, the mottled frost-and-charcoal bodyshirt of the Snow Leopard, a UC stalwart.

Well, that was a hot meringue in the kisser. Had Bari come to such a pass, erotically speaking, that she'd developed a fetish for guys gussied up in superhero drag? (Holy roentgens.)

"Give me one good reason why I shouldn't—*shove you into the river,*" Xavier improvised.

"I'm a r-r-registered trademark of Uncommon C-Comics," said his leotarded rival. "You m-m-might get s-sued."

Then the retrohippie in Snow Leopard garb slammed Xavier in the chest and went galumping off at a Quasimodo-ish clip bewilderingly out of synch with his svelte physique.

Xavier picked himself off the sidewalk, found a grease stain on the tail of his trench coat, and, mutedly cursing, seized a handful of gravel from the planter beside the drawbridge.

Because the seven staffers living downstairs made crossing that bridge and rattling her portcullis an unhappy option (someone would intercept and deflect him, someone other than Bari), Xavier stepped back and hurled his gravel at the second-story window. He was scooping up another round when someone came to the window, squinted out into the street, and, seeing him, struggled to lift the sash. (Ah, Bari herself!) She raised it high enough to talk sideways through the crack, asking him who the holy hell he was and why he'd rained pebbles on her window.

"Bari," Xavier pleaded.

"Xave? *Xave?* God, lover, haven't you got the feeble motherwit you were born with?"

The balcony business from *Romeo and Juliet* or *Cyrano,* achingly bittersweet. But when Xavier only stood there mute, Bari vanished and showed up a moment later at the downstairs entrance. She then led him into the meat-locker-cold foyer as if he were a foundling in need of adoption.

"Who was that guy? What was he doing here?"

"Hold your ponies. Come upstairs."

The foyer had an elevator, a cage with a full-length mirror, two dented metal stools, and an old cherrywood hat-tree on which various off-the-wall accessories hung—hats, gloves, scarves. The cage creaked upward, Bari meanwhile slipping a sheepskin vest from the hat-tree over a jumpsuit in which Xavier knew she often worked. She wasn't, thank God, in a French peignoir or a leather teddy with revelatory-cutout options.

"His name's Howard, Xave. Howie Littleton. He's both a model and a couturier. We were working."

Bari's studio, as they entered it, floored Xavier. He almost literally staggered back from the sight of her in-progress designs—surrealistically airy skirts, Technicolor blouses, decal-covered leggings, copper-lamé capes, flocked jerseys—which Bari and her assistants had placed about the studio on wire armatures, or hung like parachutes from ceiling beams, or fanned out against the umber bricks like street-rad tapestries.

But there was more happening here than hue and dye, fabric and stitchery. Xavier recognized the clothes—or at least the style that had dictated their patterns and color schemes—as a homage to the garish costumes of the characters in the Unique Continuum of Uncommon Comics: gangsters and palookas, stalwarts and sidekicks, baby-faced kids and scar-faced psychos.

"My spring line," Bari said. "The motif is—"

"—Nick City camp. Don't tell me what it is. It's lifted, it's secondhand. Bari's of Salonika will have to change its name to . . . to Bari's of SatyrFernalia."

"Easy, Thaxton."

"You did a deal with the child abusers at Uncommon Comics. You bought a franchise. UC's going to make as much money from this as you are. Maybe more."

"That's none of your business. If our line sells, everyone'll do okay, though. What's wrong with that?"

"Gak."

"Gak yourself. In fact, I wish you would. You've got no right to be jealous of Howie or contemptuous of our work. There's some real avant-garde creativity on display here, and the fact that it's also silly, colorful *fun* . . . hey, that's a plus, not an excuse to turn blue and badmouth us."

Xavier calmed down. He took off his trench coat, hung it over a torso frame already sporting an outfit inspired by Saint Torque's sexy getup, and wandered aimlessly about the studio looking at the clothes patterned on the costumes of other UC stalwarts. He felt as he had felt in the gloomy clothing bay of SatyrFernalia, like a character in an animated cartoon. A light fixture could've fallen from the ceiling, compressing his body to the size of a Campbell's soup can, and he'd've gone on waddling about the room, balancing on first one side of his bottom rim and then the other, coldly sizing up the work of the woman with whom his uncompacted, real-life self was in major-league love.

What a drag. What a kick. What a testament to the multifaceted unpredictability of life.

"A pox on Howie," Xavier grumbled, sitting down crosslegged on the mound of cushions strewn over the floor of Bari's entertainment nook. "A pestilential pox."

Bari, her hands inside her vest, did not sit down. "It was our visit to SatyrFernalia that inspired all this. Plus Mikhail's hots for UC-oriented designs. You might be interested to know, Thaxton, that—"

"Hey, call me Xave. Or"—plaintively—"lover."

"—it was Howard Littleton, the gentleman you're poxing, who designed the Count Geiger costume that's saving your ass from . . . well, whatever it's saving it from. *Thaxton.*"

"It may not be saving it from anything." He filled Bari in on recent events, including his bad time at the Parataj, a carnival of pus, upchuck, and embarrassment.

"Oh, Xave, I'm sorry."

Better. *Better.* He complained that he was doomed, that he'd missed her the way the eunuched Abelard had pined for Héloise, that his life was virtually meaningless; his syndrome, and her refusal to marry him, had deprived it of all joy.

She, in turn, mentioned his duty to the Mick, tweaked him for surrendering so easily, pointed out that the Suit had given him a magical reprieve. Its potency might still not be exhausted, and, even if it were, some as-yet-undiscovered talisman might give him permanent immunity.

"What sort of talisman?" Xavier edgily wondered.

Bari sat on the cushion beside him, hooked a finger over his shirt collar, and rubbed his stalwartly BVDs. "Who knows? A medicinal nape patch, maybe. A daily cup of Postum. Occasional handjobs from a lady using a first baseman's mitt."

"I'm doomed."

"Then I'd be an *idiot* to marry you."

"I have insurance. I bought it before my syndrome even'd begun to develop. Bari, you're my primary beneficiary."

"What about the Mick?"

"He's a contingency recipient. Lydia and Phil'll take care of him—that's not a concern."

"I don't covet your insurance. I don't *need* it. And I'm not about to marry a man in chain-mail skivvies who whines about being, ah, *doomed.* Tell me something *good* about being the only man in the world with this weird-ass ailment."

"You're kidding."

"Uh-uh, I'm not. Give me upbeat. Give me positive."

"How about this? I may not *be* the 'only man in the world with this weird-ass ailment.' "

He told Bari about Wilbon T. Stickney, the man in P.S. Annie's who couldn't listen to Jerry Clower albums anymore, or look at his favorite truckstop artwork, without getting a bellyache or a thumb wart. Stickney, to ease the symptoms of his lower-case philistine syndrome, resorted to reading rest-

room graffiti and watching boxing matches on TV. That didn't
strike Xavier as an upbeat gloss on his ailment, but it proved,
at least, that he wasn't the oddest duck on the planet.

"Was this man—Stickney?—exposed to radioactivity too?
He must've been." Bari thought. "Well, knowing you're not
alone's a big step toward coming to terms with your problem."

"I don't want to 'come to terms with my problem.' I want
to be well. Cured."

"Maybe you could start a support group," Bari said.
" 'Calling all PS sufferers, sign up now for group therapy
sessions designed to calm your fears and bolster your self-
image.' " She framed this announcement with her hands, pan-
tomimed rolling it onto a billboard or an alley wall.

"A support group of two," Xavier mused. "Me and ol'
Wilbon T. Stickney. Now, *that's* uplifting."

"There could be others. A public announcement would
spotlight their existence and draw them into the open."

"And if there aren't any more, maybe ol' Wilbon T. and I
could bribe a few lepers or AIDS patients to sit in with us."

"Hold the simpering sarcasms, okay?"

Xavier said, "Most folks'll think PS stands for poke salad.
Ol' Wilbon T. and I're goin' t'end up dialoguing, if that's at
all possible, with salad-gas snorters."

"Forget I said anything. Drown in self-pity."

Xavier said, "You *like* this Howie Littleton, a.k.a. the Snow
Leopard, character?"

Bari rose from the floor, switched on CNN, and returned to
the cushions next to Xavier's as if he were a stranger on an
EleRail platform and there was nowhere else to sit. She hadn't
thrown him out, but she wasn't going to talk unless he deduced the nature of his offense and hurried to clean it up.
Living with this lady was an unlikely goal, marriage as incon-
ceivable as persuading a mullah to take communion.

The news sequenced past in a montage of video clips and
talking heads. Another unbelievable week:

Without renouncing his office or excommunicating himself,
the Pope had married a divorced Irish countess with six children. In a display of ecumenical bonhomie, Jimmy Swaggart,
Makarios IV, the Archbishop of Canterbury, and an unnamed
Catholic chaplain from the U.S. Sixth Fleet had officiated at
the nuptials.

Meanwhile, Arizona was seceding from the U.S., declaring itself an overseas satrapy of the United Arab Emirates, and inviting all qualified widows and orphans from Abu Dhabi to homestead parcels of the Papago Indian Reservation west of Tucson. This secession owed something to the black-market price of kachina dolls and something to the intention of the Phoenix Suns to play a yearly home-and-away series with the Riyadh Sheiks.

A man in Listre, North Carolina, had invented a lighter whose flame burned downward so that pipe smokers could light up without singeing their eyebrows or straining unduly on the insuck. At the National Institutes of Science, an irate spokesperson claimed that such an invention defied the laws of physics.

According to archeologists at work in Thule, Greenland, Santa Claus had been "a real human being," probably an altruistic Viking with a taste for metheglin (i.e., mead) and female reindeer. The archeologists had the bog-embalmed corpse, complete with desiccated organs, both internal and external, to support this claim. One of the body's discoverers held up for the camera the rotted scraps of a cardboardy red suit.

Alternative President J. Danforth Quayle had officially opened his Alternative Republican White House in South Bend, Indiana, near the University of Notre Dame. He was now screening applicants for speech therapist, first press secretary, spin-control team, second press secretary, and an articulate ophthalmalogist to swear that his deer-in-the-high-beams gaze was really a steely Stare of Command. Further, a Hollywood producer had just signed Quayle to play Robert Redford's part in a remake of *The Candidate.* To minimize costly retakes, the Alternative Prez would lip-synch Redford's dialogue from the original 1972 soundtrack.

Xavier glanced over at Bari. She aimed her chin like a rifle at the nose of every talking head. Each of CNN's reports seemed to have her transfixed.

"This just in," said a female reader. "A farmer in Placer County has raised a six-legged horse. Named Cockroach, the animal was recently sold to Hallelujah Stables in Raceland, Tennessee. 'I know Cockroach's going to win his new owner money,' Deke Hazelton said yesterday. 'He doesn't quite run, he more like scuttles, but whatever you call it, he does it *fast.* '

Hazleton thinks his farm's proximity to Plant VanMeter may have had something to do with his horse's six-leggedness. He fears that pregnant women in the county may also deliver, quote, 'monsters,' unquote. Con-Tri officials reject the idea that emissions from their plant caused Cockroach's abnormality. Radiation levels around the facility, they argue, are well within NRC regulations."

Another talking head, male, reported that Gregor McGudgeon of the hoodluminati band Smite Them Hip & Thigh had enrolled at the Graham School of Theology at Skye University in Salonika, on full scholarship, to take, among other offerings, "Modern Theological Interpretations of 'Upon This Rock . . .' (Matthew 16:18) and 'Who Shall Roll . . . ? (Mark 16:3)." McGudgeon was happy to abandon touring for a while, but the fact that all his fellow band members had enrolled with him meant that Smite 'Em would continue to write songs, rehearse, and perform together.

"Rewind the six-legged-colt bit," Xavier said. It had touched something in him. A nerve. Or maybe a memory.

"I can't," Bari said, surprised. "That was live."

"Oh, yeah, of course." Xavier aimed a kiss at Bari's earlobe, elbowed himself up, grabbed his coat, and walked backward to the door. "Good night, Bari."

"Xavier, what is it?"

"Nothing. I'd better see about Mikhail. Everything's upbeat, though. Tiptop. Don't worry about me." With a jaunty Errol Flynn flourish, he bowed and let himself out.

32

Double Exposure

The next morning, Xavier saw the Mick off to Ephebus Academy and telephoned Grantham to say that he didn't feel well. Then he took a cab to Sidney Lanier Airport, found a car-rental agency in the main terminal, and rented a car with radar-eluding add-ons that enabled him, without fear of detection by either the Oconee State Patrol or the fuzz in a dozen intervening hamlets, to zip at 125 miles per hour into the Phosphor Fogs. Once there, he cruised the streets of Placer Creek, rubbernecking the sky for any sign of a telltale addledness.

But it was day. The sky would better reveal any disquieting sheen, if it had one, at night.

When Xavier saw a man in overalls limping along a sidewalk on Major Barbara Avenue, he pulled abreast and got directions to the Hazelton farm.

"Above Frye's Mill," the man said. "Near Plant VanMeter."

Why this sudden need to talk to Deke Hazelton? Well, it had something to do with the Suit's decreasing ability to counteract his syndrome, something to do with Bari's workaholic devotion to her comic-book fashions, and something to do with Hazelton's belief that Plant VanMeter posed a health threat to the county. (Never mind that he'd reaped a large profit from a six-legged thoroughbred "engineered" by that threat.)

Deep in the Phosphor Fogs, Xavier found Hazelton's place. A brick wall and a metal gate blocked the long drive leading to the secluded house. Xavier got out of his car and pushed a button on the gate's speaker unit.

"Who is it?" a thin female voice asked. "Environmentalist or another Con-Tri stooge?"

"I'm a newspaperman."

"Which paper, please? And why should I let you in to bother my daddy?"

"The *Urbanite,* miss. I'd like to talk to your father about the mutations among your farm animals."

"That darned CNN report. Everybody's picked up on it. Phone's been jangling since five this morning."

Xavier glanced around. Loblollies, red mulberries, and yellow poplars, all but the pines more or less leafless, edged the highway fronting the farm. "But I'm the first one up here, aren't I? That should count for something."

After a brief pause, the voice said, "You Alex Meisel?"

Alex Meisel was a young reporter covering Metro/State affairs for the *Urbanite.* "Yes," Xavier said. (At least he and Alex each had an *x* in his Christian name.)

The gate's lock clicked open. "You're awfully early, but drive on in. Close the gate behind you, please."

At the house, a two-story hodgepodge with wood-shake shingles, five gables, coping-sawed curlicues about the eaves, widows' walks, and a screened-in L-shaped porch, Xavier met Ailene Hazelton, a pale sixteen-year-old with rough-cut bangs and eyes as moist as a bush baby's.

Ailene led Xavier to the sunroom, where her father was at work in a leather chair, tapping the deck of a laptop computer. He set the computer aside and offered Xavier—Mr. Meisel—a glass of orange juice. Xavier declined. A fake Christmas tree stood in one corner. Ceramic wise men, shepherds, camels, and sheep were arrayed on the green felt tree skirt.

"Kept Cockroach a secret for over a year," Hazelton said. "But now all hell's breaking loose."

"After selling him, sir," Xavier said, "you accused Con-Tri of causing the mutation."

"What else could've done it?"

"Why did you wait so long before making that charge? Isn't a delay like that"—briefly hesitating—"unconscionable?"

"Ailie and I got attached to the critter. We were afraid the government would take him away from us."

"But you sold him yourself. To a stable in Tennessee."

"For a *lot* of money," Ailene said. The chunky-kneed girl was sitting on an upholstered bench next to some sliding glass doors. Through them, Xavier could see the shallow end of a heated swimming pool enclosed by an inflatable dome of lime-green plastic. "Now we can afford to move, Mr. Meisel, even if nobody shows up to buy our contaminated farm."

"The government ought to buy it," Hazelton said. "They bought the land Plant VanMeter's on. Bought the county commissioners off by building us a school—Placer County High—that looks half like a museum and half like a parliament building. Niiice. Real niiice." He didn't sound pleased. "It's pritty, that school, but it was a big fat bribe for taking the nooklur plant."

"But you sold Cockroach to Hallelujah Stables?" Xavier said, trying to imagine the creature under a professional jockey.

"Sport o' kings," Hazelton said. "Time he's a three-year-old, Cockroach'll win the Derby."

"There's no rule against an animal with two extra limbs running in the Derby?"

"I don't think anyone ever considered the possibility," Ailene said. Her hands were folded in her lap. On one finger, she wore a white-gold ring with a deep red stone.

Xavier sat down on the bottom step of the steps just inside the sunroom. Get to the point, he advised himself. Did Cockroach's dam get irradiated from Plant VanMeter the same night of that valve failure in Reactor No. 4? The night *I* was exposed? The upshot for me was a bad case of the Philistine Syndrome. The upshot for the Hazeltons was a valuable mutant colt.

"Have you or Ailene suffered any obvious ill effects from your farm's nearness to Plant VanMeter?"

"Headaches," Hazelton said. "Worry." He glowered at Xavier. "That's enough, don't you think?"

"If your horse is your only real evidence for a local release of radiation, it's not much."

"It's not our only evidence," Hazelton said.

"Another six-legged horse? A two-headed chicken? Let me

see the places on your land where your animals were irradiated."

"Why? You crazy?"

"No. But I'd like to help you establish Plant VanMeter's
role in causing these abnormalities."

In another room, a telephone rang mutedly. Ailene pressed
her lips together and brushed a strand of frizzy hair back into
place over her ear. After three rings, the telephone fell silent.
It was undoubtedly attached to an answering machine. Xavier
got the idea that the answering machine had received a grueling workout in the wake of last night's CNN report.

"You want a *scoop*," Hazelton said. The word, the way he
said it, sounded feces-stained. " 'S all you care about."

"Daddy," Ailene said.

"Scoops, as you call them, keep the public informed,"
Xavier said. "The public, if knowledgeable, works to safe-
guard its own welfare. Reporters like me"—*well, like Alex
Meisel*—"are instruments of enlightenment. You can't assume—"

"Argh," Hazelton said. "No lectures about the noble
press."

"Then let me see your evidence. So I can spread the word.
So Con-Tri can either defend itself or take the blame for its
betrayal of the public's trust."

"The spring above Frye's Mill," Hazelton said. "That's
where you need to go. Some damned fishy varmints in there."

"May I go out there?" Xavier felt that a lost puzzle piece
had perhaps come to hand.

Hazelton groaned. "Let me get my coat."

"Just tell me the way. I'd be glad to go alone."

Once again, the telephone was ringing. Ailene turned her
eyes to the ceiling and drummed her fingers on her knees.

Following Hazelton's directions, Xavier drove into the
woods to the spring near the old mill to which Pamela, of
Pamela's Boarding House, had pointed him over a year and a
half ago. This approach was from a different starting place,
though, and it was too cold to go for a swim. The site drew
him, anyway. The Hazeltons might be right about Plant
VanMeter's contribution to the mutant condition of both
Cockroach and the unspecified creatures in the spring. If so,
the public should be informed.

Xavier had another motive for revisiting the site of his first exposure to radiation. A selfish motive. He wanted to reexpose himself to the radiation that had altered the eel and the frogs he'd seen in or near the spring on his last visit to the Phosphor Fogs. Reexposure might reverse the effects of a syndrome that, imperfectly diagnosed and countered, had become unbearable. Or it might kill him outright. For death was the only unequivocal and lasting cure. And, as Nietzsche put it, "That which does not kill us makes us stronger."

It wasn't yet noon. The millrace with its cold, languid pools seemed different from Xavier's recollection of it. Sweetgum trees stood leafless. The ground cover of pigwort, moss, and blackberry shrubs had a vaguely scorched look. But there was no mistaking the limestone ledge on which he'd camped or the glassiness of the water across which he'd paddled, frightening all the see-through minnows and that bloody-eyed eel.

Xavier jumped from the limestone shelf to a narrow section of the bank where a piece of stovepipe—no, a dark gray trash can—no, a tube of unexploded ordnance—glinted near the quiet, almost frozen water. He hunkered beside the object. It had been drilled and replugged by a material just like that comprising the cylinder itself. He pushed against it, but it wouldn't budge. The cylinder was wedged into the slick mud beside the spring. Standing, Xavier peered into the water. Down deep—so deep that they rippled and broke, re-formed and broke again—lay a jumble of cylinders like the one he'd just examined.

Probably, a sleazeball auto mechanic or dairy farmer had dumped his trash in the pool. Oxygen canisters from a welding operation? Ancient milk tins? What? No telling. Sometimes, though, a string of bubbles would rise through the water and pop on the surface like cellophane beads.

Xavier was torn between two options. He could hike across the streambed near the pool and then up a naked hillside to the service road to Plant VanMeter, where a security guard would probably catch him. Or he could strip to his Suit, dive into the pool, and drop lazily to the cylinders sending up their jukebox bubbles. So what if it was December? It still wasn't as cold as it was in New York when members of the Polar Bear Club went for an ass-freezing winter dip. Besides, the shock to his coddled system might bring about a remission of his syndrome.

Finally, Xavier decided. He shed his clothes, except for the mesh leotard of his Count Geiger costume, which he also hoped would benefit from immersion, and did a racing dive into the pool before either the cold or his native good sense could prevent him. Water shattered under him like plastic, raking his limbs and splintering all around him as he plummeted toward the strange tins. There was shock, all right. He was disintegrating, like a shoat thrown to piranhas. As his lungs collapsed, his eyes ballooned to the size of streetlamp globes.

I'm a dead man, he thought.

Then he saw the trash cans, or milk tins, or torpedo casings, shimmering in their underwater jumble, and his body, aided perhaps by his Suit, miraculously reassembled itself. Destructive cold yielded to a bathlike warmth. Soft, heat-tinged waves massaged his face, chest, stomach, legs. Xavier dolphined into this glowing upflow, hovered over the dreamily bubbling canisters, bathed in their near-silent white noise.

Right next to these canisters wallowed a glowing, three-eyed, emerald-green catfish with filamentous whiskers that corkscrewed out from its gigantic head like antennae. The catfish's central eye indifferently beheld Xavier swimming down to it.

If the cry of his oxygen-depleted bloodstream had not begun to reach him, he would have stayed. He would have wrapped his arms around the giant catfish and clung there like a barnacle. But the cry of his air-hungry body did reach him, and he came up through liquid crystal to temperatures only a few degrees above freezing. Out of the water, crazily enough, he was not reduced to helpless shivering. He dried his Suit thoroughly with his dress shirt and pulled on the rest of his clothes.

Half-dazed by this encounter, Xavier hiked back to his renter, climbed in, and slapped it into gear. He got back to his apartment before Mikhail arrived home from school.

33

Tim Bowman Purged, The Mick Irate

anuary flew by. February came. Xavier saw to his duties at the *Urbanite* with alacrity and wit. The Suit seemed to be working again. Or, to rephrase, the instances of pain and/or embarrassment attendant upon his experience of the fine arts were so brief and mild that he *believed* it to be working again.

With Marilyn Olvera, Howie Littleton, and a band of mascaraed, anorexic giraffes (i.e., high-priced models), Bari had soared off to Paris for the February couture. She'd taken with her the flash and filigree of her upscale Uncommon Comics styles, about which she was decidedly jittery—even though her ready-to-wear versions of these same fashions were virtually guaranteed best-sellers here in the States. Xavier hadn't bothered Bari during the pressure-cooker period leading up to her departure, and now he was almost relieved that she was gone. In her absence, he could ponder the wisdom of staying involved with her.

Discretion was important. Self-protection was important. For these reasons, in fact, Xavier had told no one of his visit to the Hazeltons' place in the Phosphor Fogs, or of the revivifying hot springs in the stream above Frye's Mill, or of the giant three-eyed catfish in that stream.

First, after the CNN report of Cockroach's sale and Hazelton's charge that Plant VanMeter was a community health hazard, the NRC had found no evidence of heightened levels of radioactivity at the plant. Nor had it found any hint of malfunctioning equipment or a willful disregard of mandated safety procedures.

Second, Alex Meisel had been covering this very story for the *Urbanite,* and Xavier couldn't bring himself to admit publicly that he had impersonated Meisel at the Hazeltons'. Meisel, now fully aware that *someone* had done so, was trying hard to figure out the culprit's identity and angle. Although nervous and ashamed, Xavier could not persuade himself that confessing would work to either his or anyone else's advantage.

Certainly not mine, he thought. To suppress his anxiety and his shame, he put himself wholly into his job and found escape in the arts. So, it seemed, did the Mick, who often seemed to miss Bari more than Xavier did.

However, where Xavier took comfort from opera, drama, symphony performances, ballet, and painting, Mikhail gravitated to rock 'n' roll, movies, and comics. Better a long session with Up Periscope, Spike Lee, or the DeeJay, he clearly felt, than with the politicos jawboning on C-Span.

In fact, what most exercised the Mick in late February was a power struggle in the headquarters of Uncommon Comics. Apparently, UC's publisher, F. Deane Finesse, had fired Bowman. A story about this firing, by Lee Stamz, dominated a front page otherwise devoted to a gruesome pokeweed murder.

"They've canned him," Mikhail said when Xavier came through the door that evening. "The greatest fucking innovator in the history of comic books, superhero subdivision. A wild man, I grant you, a nutzo—but still a fucking genius."

"What?" Xavier had been to a print exhibition at a gallery in Sinatro Heights. All he wanted was to peel off his Reynolds Wrap undergarment and marinate in soapsuds.

"The fucking führer at Uncommon Comics has purged Tim Bowman," the Mick raved on. "They've run him off."

"Really?"

"You're wearing silver long johns that Tim Bowman designed, and all you can say is 'Really?' Jeez, that stinks."

"I thought Howie Littleton, couturier-model-and-professional-pain-in-the-rear, designed my Suit."

"Littleton designed your costume from one he saw in the first Stalwarts-for-Truth comic, and Bowman was responsible for that—just like he deserves credit for every other stalwartly costume in UC's books."

Mikhail thrust Stamz's story into Xavier's hand, demanding that he read it. Xavier did. From it, he learned that Bowman had lost his grip on the Unique Continuum by making heady financial demands of Mr. Finesse, viz., paying his artists and writers wages akin to those of their counterparts in New York, and urging Mr. Finesse to endow several Southern art colleges with UC "Special Achievement" scholarships. He'd alienated some of his own employees by closely overseeing their projects and allegedly refusing to compromise even on obvious nits. Two other factors prompting Finesse's decision to sack Bowman, said Stamz, were the broken negotiations between UC and Blackguard Pictures for a *Yellowhammer* movie, and recent issues of *Mantisman* accusing Plant VanMeter of causing mutations among Placer County's livestock and wildlife. Just as provocatively, a recent issue of *Gator Maid* had caricatured Finesse himself as a baboon in a seersucker suit and a Panama hat.

"Mmmm," Xavier mmm'd.

"Finesse is a greedy old fart with a Yahweh complex," the Mick said. "He's also Bowman's boss. You'd think that'd've been enough to make Bowman cut the verminy old tightwad some slack. Uh-uh. He went after him like the Orkin Man."

"Not smart, Mick."

"Maybe not. Classy, though. Heads up, heart out. *Now* what's he going to do?"

"Bowman? He'll sign on with another comic company."

"One way or another, he's trashed them all. Parodied them in UC's books. Badmouthed them in, like, interviews."

"Maybe he could host a late-night talk-radio program."

"I mean, UC was Bowman's life. He created three quarters of the characters. He got UC off the ground."

"Residuals," Xavier said, bored with the topic. "He's got all his financial problems hacked, sounds to me. He can do anything he wants."

"Can he fly? Or jump tall buildings? Or take on the fat-cat powermongers at Con-Tri?"

"He'll survive," Xavier said, massaging the Mick's shoulders. "Settle down."

But the Mick kept growsing, indignant that such an injustice could have occurred. It was as if the members of Smite

Them Hip & Thigh had drummed Gregor McGudgeon out of their group rather than following him into seminary. The Mick's compassion for Bowman was profound. Never mind that Xavier himself didn't give a bullhead's whisker for Bowman's fate.

"Forget it," he said. "There's nothing you can do. And there are better things to stew about: ozone loss, the Greenhouse Effect, the silverfish population in your bedroom."

"Radioactive drift?"

"Sure. That too."

"At Ephebus, Uncle Xave, I'm worrying about it. I'm building a radiation detector in my physical science class."

"A Geiger counter?" The Mick was building a Geiger counter at school? Gee. Had the comics and his own involuntary impersonation of Count Geiger, the UC stalwart, inspired his nephew to undertake an honest-to-God science project?

"It's actually called a Geiger-*Müller* counter, but just about everybody forgets old Müller."

"Well," Xavier said uneasily, "I hope you'll let me see it when you're finished."

"I'm going to write this Finesse turkey," the Mick said, going back to the upheaval at UC. "In words of one fucking syllable. To tell him where he can . . ." And so on.

Xavier slipped away to skin out of his Bowman-Littleton BVDs and to wrinkle pleasantly in a hot bath.

34

A Garage Party in Philippi

For over two months, the stolen go-truck that Elrod Juitt had bought from a pair of junglebunny gangbangers out of Satan's Cellar had stewed in his garage at the Auto Parts Reservation outside of Philippi. Juitt hadn't yet painted the truck or torn down the Therac 4-J in its loadbed for scrap.

Every three or four days, Juitt would have Larry Glenn Wilkins throw back the tarp covering the truck and start up its engine—just to exercise it. Mostly, though, Juitt ignored the vehicle and the medical machine in its loadbed.

One afternoon in early March, Larry Glenn roared up from town on a beat-up Harley—he'd totaled his Camaro—and found Juitt cradling the telephone receiver in his tobacco-scented office.

Juitt said, "What the hell is it, Larry Glenn?"

Larry Glenn waited for Juitt to hang up. "They's a couple of Salonika cops, plainclothes types, at the Philippi Inn, Elrod. Jim Percy"—the inn's owner—"says they've come to investigate a stolen security-cop truck and 'll likely be out here first thing tomorry. Spent the whole day axing about you, pumping folks."

Juitt blinked. "You sure they ain't coming out today?"

"Not according to old Jim Percy. Who knows, Elrod?"

"We better get humping. Come on." Juitt led the way back and through an auto-parts aisle toward the garage. "Fisher," he yelled at one of his employees, "keep an eye on things here! Me and Larry Glenn got work to do."

In the garage, they unveiled the truck and set to work, sanding off security-firm logos and filing off the vehicle identity numbers on the engine block and chassis. They filled and sanded. Wearing goggles, plastic caps, and stained coveralls, they spray-painted the truck a glossy candy-apple red—every part of it, in fact, but the loadbed and the Therac 4-J.

"What you gonna do wi' thatere whatzit?" Larry Glenn gesturing at the Therac 4-J.

"Nothing right now. It's no bigger a worry than the truck. We got to finish up and get 'em both out."

The garage stank like a turpentine factory or a fume-strangled dope den, so badly that Larry Glenn couldn't even drink a beer for the reek. Finally, though, the truck was like new. Larry Glenn, with his Camaro totaled forever, wished that it was his. He could take his Harley to dirt-track races in it; haul pine straw or new potatoes or horse manure; make some extra money.

"Here," Juitt called, tossing him the keys. "Park the sucker behind the smokehouse on your place. Hide 'er. When we sell 'er, I'll give you a third of whatever she brings."

"Jeez, Elrod. Thanks." A wish come true.

Larry Glenn drove the go-truck down a narrow country road to the half acre he'd inherited from Daddy Wilkins last October. He had family living there, his wife Missy and their daughter Callie-Lisbeth, a four-year-old going on forty, but they probably wouldn't be waiting up for him at six A.M. He wouldn't've wanted them to be waiting up either.

It was soothing, somehow, to stand out behind the collapsing smokehouse, sixty feet from the used doublewide where Daddy Wilkins had had his stroke—soothing to be doting on the candy-apple-red truck that might one day be his.

Eventually, he covered it with canvas. He cut some evergreen branches and laid them over the canvas as camouflage. Inside the trailer, he lay down on Daddy Wilkins's bed, so as not to disturb either Missy or Callie-Lisbeth, and slept until almost noon.

35

Big Mister Sinister

Tim Bowman had been incognito ever since his firing. Like a villain in a *Decimator* comic book, he had gone underground. There actually were mephitic-smelling, interconnected sewers, dank and intricately bricked, under the crowded alleys of Satan's Cellar. On the day after his firing, Bowman prised up a manhole cover not far from P.S. Annie's, lowered himself into the opening, pulled the manhole cover clankingly back into place, and worked his way rung by rung into the dripping caverns of the undercity.

The sewer was surprisingly like the sewers Bowman had drawn as a comics-infatuated kid: echoey, wet, claustrophobia-inducing, rat-haunted. With a flashlight beam, he carved a path along a concrete ledge on the main tunnel's inner wall. Ahead of him lay catacombs, grottoes, tributary tunnels, stopes, niche-in-the-bricks hideouts: safe places for drug smugglers, pokeweed addicts, and gangsters of the notorious Nick City crime cartel. You could also probably find madmen, losers, and failed suicides down here. Bowman, psychically aseethe, had come below to think about his meteoric descent into a category encompassing all three types.

First, he had no family now that F. Deane Finesse had cut him loose. A foster child through his thirteenth year, he had fled a poultry farm near Tuscaloosa to make his way to Salonika, where, for three years, he had survived squeegeeing, for extorted pay, the windshields of cars stalled in traffic. He had also sold hubcaps, boosted office supplies, and slept in the pews of unlocked churches from Sinatro Heights to Chattahoochee Park.

While a vagrant, Bowman had taught himself to draw, copying the figures in shoplifted comics, on humorous billboards, even from the photographs and funny papers of wind-tumbled pages of the Salonika *Urbanite*. Without a tutor, he'd served the apprenticeship that one day brought him to the notice of F. Deane Finesse, who, at Bowman's urging, incorporated and funded the home-grown enterprise known as Uncommon Comics.

Now, hiking a sewer ledge or wading in the slop crawling like blackstrap molasses about his ankles, Bowman was on his own again. He knew how to cope, he'd learned as a kid. But the image of what he'd achieved, and the full-color grandeur of what he'd lost, rode him like stones. He thought seriously of submerging himself in the underground sludge and deliberately inhaling it. Why not? He was the world's—well, at least this city's—redheaded stepchild, and he saw no future for himself apart from the wonder and security of UC's Unique Continuum.

Hours, maybe days, passed as Bowman vacillated on the crucial issue of self-extinguishment. Pondering, he threw a brick fragment at a water rat the size of a Pekinese. At the intersection of two tunnels, he stole the soggy French fries of a snockered bum asleep there. He scarfed the dregs of a bottle of Strawberry Street Wine that he'd found in a rusty grocery cart capsized in a tunnel under Satan Cellar's trolley terminus. He kept his eyes open for victims to roll, rodents to stone, and organized human predators to dodge. He brooded on his options.

Don't off *yourself,* a voice advised him. Get the creep who did this to you.

F. Deane Finesse?

Hell no. He lifted you out of poverty. If you've fallen back into it, it's because circumstances beyond your control—beyond even old F. Deane's control—worked to pull you down.

What circumstances? Who?

Think, Bowman. Tuck your carroty hair up under your thinking cap and . . . THINK!

He did, and it came to him—namely, the exact Who responsible for his descent into the smelly depths. His memory of the
event that had sabotaged him, that had made everything go
blooie, set him moving again, slogging through Satan Cellar's
syrupy muck toward a ladder up and a manhole out.

Bowman emerged in an alley. A stray dog fled, ki-yi-yi-ing
as if he'd kicked it. A whore, in laddered black hose and a skirt
not much larger than a dish towel, gasped and ducked into a
doorway. Bowman trudged past her, shedding oily ropes of
decaying tissue and braided waste matter, like a three-dimen-
sional replica of the Mulch Creature from issues 47–54 of
Mantisman.

He met other people in the midnight alleys, but not one of
them tried to mess with him. They all employed the avoidance
strategies of the yelping stray or the startled hooker.

There was an all-night gun shop in a cul-de-sac just off West
Bush Street. Bowman schlepped down this alley and caromed
into the shop like a mud-plastered tackling dummy. The faces
of the wizened owner and his three patrons, one in full Klan
gear, revolved toward him with expressions ranging from
doubt to unabashed admiration. Bowman approached the
owner, whose crease-lined mouth reminded him of a ventriloquist's dummy's.

"I need a pistol."

"How many?" the owner said hopefully.

"One. A small one I can hide on my person."

"I've got a two-for-one special tonight. Or buy three makes
of different caliber and get twenty percent off a twelve-piece
Syrian assault rifle in a carrying case that makes it look like a
laptop computer."

"A pistol. One pistol."

The owner showed Bowman stub-barreled, silver-plated,
pearl-handled, double-hammered, and half-cocked pistols.
Bowman chose the smallest, and cheapest, Saturday-night lethal. He also bought a box of bullets, opened it, and loaded the
pistol right there on the premises.

"Twenty-seven ninety-eight," said the owner. "Plus tax."

"Shit," Bowman said, spinning the dented handgun's chambers.

"Well, you look like a decent sort. I'll knock off five. And
you can forget the tax."

"Way to go, Sleezer," the Klan goon said. " 'At a way to go." The other two guys slapped each other's backs.

Bowman pulled out his wallet. Sleezer and his friends recoiled from this unrecognizable object, but the sight of the limp bills in Bowman's hand immediately calmed them. Pocketing his new pistol, he nodded a curt thanks and went out.

Next stop: SatyrFernalia.

Griff Sienko and his pet gerbil, Spudsy, were on duty in the upper-story costume bay, Griff watching the Pornucopia Channel on a TV the size of a wrist corsage, the gerbil sitting paws-up on the checkerboard on which Griff had arranged a handful of sunflower seeds, a pile of Hartz Munchy O's, and a tiny playground of toilet-paper tubes and empty matchbooks.

"That any good?" Bowman asked, nodding at the tiny TV.

"Hard to say," admitted Griff, squinting. "It's sort of like watching finger puppets across a football field. What can I do you for, Mr. Bowman? You look a little grimy."

Bowman said nothing. There was a bathhouse behind the costume bay, a good-sized facility with polished wooden slats crisscrossing the shower-room floor. After dumping his clothes into a trash chute, Bowman stood for an hour under a spray that began semihot, trickled quickly to lukewarm, and finished as cold as a Phospor Fog waterfall. So what? He was washing away the past, preparing for his collision with the lout who'd destroyed his career. The water leaking from the showerhead wasn't a patch on the deafening seethe of the storm inside him.

Griff helped Bowman dress, bringing him the zoot suit that Howie Littleton had designed from Bowman's drawings of Big Mister Sinister, the crime cartel overlord from the *Decimator* series. Wide, striped, pleated trousers bulging at the hips and tapering toward the ankles. A jacket that hung so far below Bowman's butt that it was almost a dressing gown. A hat that Zorro would have loved (except, maybe, for the lavender band).

"Costume party?" Griff asked. "Hot date?" He seemed to have no idea that Finesse had let him go.

"Sure," Bowman said. He located his freshly scrubbed wallet, tipped Griff, slid his pistol into one of the jacket pockets, and sat down on a shower-room bench to think.

According to Griff, it was almost dawn. Soon the city—not just Satan's Cellar, but Salonika proper—would be alive again, and Bowman would have work to do.

At nine o'clock, he presented himself to the receptionist at the desk in the lobby of the Ralph McGill Building. A security guard appraised him as if he'd fallen off a wardrobe truck from the touring company of a *Guys and Dolls* revival.

"Yes?" said the receptionist.

"Somebody wants to interview me."

"Who? Do you have an appointment?"

"Somebody. Anybody. Lee Stamz, probably."

"Your name?"

"Big Mister Sinister."

"I beg your pardon."

"Tell them—tell Lee Stamz—that Tim Bowman is here dressed like a character from a *Decimator* film."

"Is this a publicity stunt?"

Bowman nodded at the switchboard, the front brim of his hat an insistent edge. The receptionist punched up Lee Stamz and relayed Bowman's message. Stamz said, audibly even to Bowman, "Say what?" and, when the receptionist repeated herself, replied, "Well, glory be. Get some ID and send the joker up."

Of course. At the height of the shakeup at Uncommon Comics, Bowman had refused Stamz's every request for an interview. This change of heart was gratifying.

On the newsroom floor, Bowman watched Stamz do a comic boggle, mostly intentional, at the sight of him. Then Stamz took Bowman into the day room, where everyone not already hard at work gave him a gander. Yeah, he was hard to miss. Did they know his character from the first two *Decimator* movies? Or was he something amusing to gawk at on an otherwise humdrum morning?

"Wanna come into my cubicle?" Stamz said, *leaning* Bowman almost instinctively in that direction.

"Not yet."

"No? What, then? You got an agenda? I'd be happy to show you around, if that's your druthers."

Bowman nodded, a tilt of his Zorro brim, and Stamz escorted him here and there among the thocking keyboards and half-walled offices of the day room, introducing him to every drudge—faces, Bowman saw, with almost nothing drawn on them—as "Big Mister Sinister, heh heh heh," as if the spontaneous tag of his giggle were, say, a college degree.

"And this is a colleague of mine in the entertainment section," Stamz said. "Xavier Th—"

"Thaxton," Bowman said. "I know." He pulled his handgun from his pocket and fired three quick shots into Xavier's gut:

Bang! bang! bang!

36

"Adios, Superman"

Xavier heard the reports as if they were widely spaced notes in a symphony of three movements, each movement a year in length. The impact of each bullet was a one-note crescendo.

Why was a man outfitted like a 1940s barrio hipster trying to deprive him of a good morning at the keyboard? With the exception of Ricardo's Mexican Restaurant's radio ads, he loved all things Mexican. He found the talents of Orozco, Paz, and Valenzuela *muy simpático*. Some days, he could even tolerate mariachi music. Why was a son of that noble culture shooting him?

"Eat this, you s.o.b.!" the man cried. "And *this!* And *this!*" Or had cried. Time was out of joint for Xavier. Events no longer had a reliable sequence.

He was lying on the floor. Everything happening above him was happening in blurred slow motion. This wasn't just a murder. It was an assassination. He was being removed for murky ideological reasons. His views, as expressed in "Thus Saith Xavier Thaxton," had led this assassin, who sure looked like Big Mister Sinister in a *Decimator* movie, to walk in and shoot him.

"You don't know comics!" the man was shouting. "You don't like them! You bring no objectivity to their criticism!"

Comics? thought Xavier, mouthing the word.

Lee Stamz karate-chopped the pistol from Big Mister Sinister's hand, grabbed him, flung him to the floor. "Call nine-one-one!" he shouted at the day room.

On the floor, his face less than six feet from Xavier's, Big Mister Sinister raged: "Go back to reviewing artsy-fartsy books whose last sentence wraps around to their first one!"

Pardon, Xavier mouthed, as surprised by this vaguely familiar verbal attack as by the shooting.

"Go back to wetting your pants every time Screen Dreams shows *Citizen Kane!*"

Xavier gaped sidelong at Big Mister Sinister.

"If you survive, hie yourself to James Joyce's grave and sit on the slab till your ass freezes to it!"

As if on cue, Stamz sat on Bowman to keep him from rising. He urged Ivie Nakai, who'd just hurried up, to kick the smoking pistol farther out of Big Mister Sinister's reach. She did, as if playing a desperate variety of shuffleboard.

"Aginbite of inwit!" Big Mister Sinister shouted red-faced at Xavier. "May it drive you bonkers!"

"Shut up!" Stamz shouted at him. "Shut your fucking mouth!"

"Only if he dies. Then we'll never have to pull on hip boots to wade through his holier-than-thou drivel again."

"Who is that?" Xavier managed. It was past time that he should have passed out from shock, blood loss, maybe even his first wonky intimations of death. Why hadn't he?

"It's Bowman," Stamz said. "The bastard who wouldn't give me an interview when Finesse fired his ass."

"He wrote the letter," Xavier said. "Bowman . . . wrote it."

"What letter?" Stamz said.

Urbanite employees had surrounded Xavier's desk. They milled around like spectators at a car wreck. Someone had called 911. Someone else—Donel Lassiter, bless his heart—was struggling to loosen Xavier's tie.

"Give Mr. Thaxton some air," Donel said. "Stand back, you all, give him room."

It was a relief to know—although he couldn't say just why—the Mick had not written that letter. (If the Mick had written it, he might have been able to raise his grade in English.) A hostile letter to the editor was more public, and thus more shameful to its recipient, than a mugging. Whoa. What skewed logic. Good thing he hadn't voiced that argument out loud. Sticks and stones and all that . . .

Xavier looked over at Bowman. "I like your costume," he said. "Rakish . . . getup."

A portion of Bowman's hat's brim was caught under his neck, but it was still recognizably a hat. Bowman was nonplussed. He stared bemusedly at Xavier.

"But it's too much like the DeeJay's," Xavier said. "The Zoot Suit Look. The DeeJay's a . . . stalwart. Big Mister Sinister's a . . . cr-crime lord. That confuses . . . the k-kids."

"Save your breath, Mr. Thaxton." Donel's smile was kindly.

"I prefer Count Geiger's costume," Xavier said. "It's a . . . um, true classic."

Bowman seemed confused. Was Xavier an enemy of the comic-book business, or an astute critic of its shortcomings and excesses and thus a variety of friend? Had Bowman walked into the Ralph McGill Building and unwittingly shot an ally?

At that moment, the police arrived. Stamz got off the gunman, and a cop much smaller than Stamz yanked Bowman up and handcuffed him. A female cop disinterestedly Mirandized him.

"If he just took three bullets," the male cop said, pointing at Xavier, "why ain't he dead?"

Xavier lifted his head off the floor. "Bulletproof vest," he said. Donel was trying to unbutton his top shirt button. Xavier brushed Donel's hand away. He didn't want everyone to know that he was wearing tinfoil skivvies. Had his Count Geiger gear kept him from dying? So it seemed.

"Bulletproof vest?" the cop said. "That standard issue around here? Y'all that afraid of your readers?"

"He is," Stamz said.

"An elementary precaution," Xavier said, getting to his feet with no help from Donel and only a little from the edge of his desk. Two paramedics came rushing into the day room with bandages, drugs, resuscitation equipment, a canvas litter.

"Shit," Bowman said, looking at Xavier. "You didn't die."

"Sorry," Xavier said. (Actually, he wasn't.)

The female cop led Bowman, hangdog and surly, away.

* * *

The paramedics wanted to examine Xavier. According to both Stamz's testimony and the confession of Big Mister Sinister, he'd absorbed three bullets at close range. Smart people didn't try to walk around with three slugs in their guts, a paramedic said. They asked to have the bullets removed and their wounds treated.

"Don't touch me," Xavier warned. "I don't want you to remove the bullets. I don't want you fiddling with me."

He could see tomorrow's headlines: FINE ARTS COLUMNIST XAVIER THAXTON SHOT BY VICTIM OF UC PURGE / *Undergarments reveal Thaxton as secret admirer of his assailant's work.*

No way.

"What the hell's the matter wi' you?" Stamz said. "You *want* to get gangrene? You *want* to die?"

"I'll be okay. Donel, help me to the restroom, please."

Donel helped him to the restroom. Xavier refused to let Donel come inside with him, arguing that he wanted to put some cold water on his face, examine his wounds himself, and try to get emotionally centered.

"Mr. Thaxton—Xavier—you need medical attention. You've been shot."

"All in a day's work," Xavier said. Knees wobbly, brow sweat-beaded, he went into the restroom, locked the door behind him, and draped his jacket on a hook in the central toilet stall. Off came every single conventional wardrobe item that he'd worn to the Ralph McGill Building that morning.

In front of the room's long mirror, he observed that his Count Geiger costume had *not* deflected the slugs from Bowman's pistol. Three craters pocked the foil, in a lopsided constellation across his abdomen. Ouch.

Standing there, he began to concentrate on the highest of the three slugs, the one under his left ribs. Using the hypochondriac muscles in that region (their scientific name, as he knew from the medical books he'd purchased soon after his first P.S. attacks), he managed to expel the slug. It emerged, dented and bloody, through the mesh of the Suit, dropping with a plink and a rattle into the washbasin. The mesh instantly sealed itself, as if he hadn't been shot at all. Then Xavier worked on the other two bullets, rippling the muscles around his navel and in the epigastric region. These slugs soon popped out, too, as if flipped by a strong and accurate, if ghostly, index finger.

Plink, rattle. Plink, rattle.

The mesh around each miniature crater drew together. The torso of his Count Geiger costume was whole again. Well, that was his Suit. What about the wounds in his gut? Were they healing as fast as the rents in the Suit?

Xavier fingered his three wounds. With no external evidence to go by and no tender places under the unbroken mesh to offer a clue, he couldn't even find the bullet holes.

This doesn't have much to do with the Suit, Xavier thought. A little, but not all. How, then, had he acquired the power to pop out pistol slugs and to effect a psychosomatic cure of his wounds? It scared him, the comic-book inspecificity of his trip to instant health, but why gripe? If he had to choose between being disabled by bullets and improving by means of a tacky supernaturalism, the choice was a no-brainer.

Hallelujah, I'm alive. Hallelujah, I'm not dead.

He put his everyday clothes back on, even his bloody Van Heusen shirt. He deposited the slugs in a paper cup already on the mirror ledge and returned to the day room with the cup.

"Go home, Xavier," Walt Grantham said. "Go home and get some rest. You're entitled."

The male cop, still questioning staffers, accepted the cup from Xavier and bagged the slugs for forensic analysis.

"How'd you salvage these?" he asked.

"They got hung between my bulletproof vest and my shirt. It was a snap, finding them."

The cop asked Xavier if he were okay ("Fine," Xavier said) and if he had any idea why Bowman had tried to kill him ("He thinks I hate the comics," Xavier said). Then Xavier told Grantham that he still had work to do and felt just fine, thank you.

"Damn it," Grantham growled. "I said, Go home!"

Oddly, the boss had allies. Lee Stamz, Donel Lassiter, Ivie Nakai, the cop—everyone in the day room—urged Xavier to take the rest of the day off.

"I appreciate your concern," Xavier said, "but I'm okay. You all're blowing this incident out of proportion."

"I'm *ordering* you home," Grantham said. "I'm not the kind of brute who makes wounded employees punch a time clock."

"If you like," Xavier said, "I'll sign a statement swearing I stayed out of sheer muleheadedness."

Everyone around Xavier's desk looked incredulously at everyone else.

"He must think he's Superman," said the cop with the slugs in the paper cup, heading for the elevator. "Thanks for cooperating, folks. Adios, Superman."

37

Mikhail Menaker for the Defense

Even at staid Ephebus Academy, a bastion of upper-middle-class rectitude, the Nick had his sources. Before his last class was over, he heard from his friend Truitt Gustavson, who'd heard from Juliana Coniglio, who'd caught the story from an afternoon report on WPNK, ROK RADIO, that Tim Bowman, ex-editor in chief of Uncommon Comics, had seriously wounded *Urbanite* critic Xavier Thaxton in an early-morning shooting incident.

"Holy fuck!" The Mick was in his sixth-period physical science lab, at a work station with fluorescent lights and a generous array of electronic equipment.

"Mikhail," Mr. Hulet said. "Show some restraint, okay? Some respect for—"

"Stuff that, Mr. Hulet! Gotta go!" He grabbed the radiation-detection device that he'd assembled under Mr. Hulet's supervision and bolted from the lab: down the tiled hall, out the glass doors, along West Azalea Avenue, dodging alarmed or heedless pedestrians, to the condominium on Franklin Court. Tim Bowman had *shot* Uncle Xave? What a deep skidder that was. It was like . . . well, like learning that your best friend has just run over the fucking family dog. On purpose.

Lugging his Geiger counter, the Mick burst into the apartment to find Uncle Xave sitting in his bathrobe in front of—

this was a real boggler—an episode of "For Love Designed."
He had taped it, no doubt. He was alive, no jive.

"You're alive, Uncle Xave!"

"You're home early." Uncle Xave checked his watch. "By
ten minutes." He used the remote to click off both the TV and
the VCR. "Caught me, didn't you?"

"Bowman shot you."

"Three times."

"Why?" The Mick was confused. About two completely
unrelated matters. "Why"—nodding at the TV—"were you
scanning that? You hate laundry dramas."

"I tape them for Bari, Mikhail. Sometimes I'll watch a
couple just to, I don't know, reestablish contact."

The Mick sat down. What if Uncle Xave had been dead or
even critically wounded? In either case, the apartment would
have been empty after the Mick's panicky dash from Ephebus.
He would have opened the door on a nauseating silence. Why,
his own common sense would have asked him, didn't you peep
your uncle's condition and whereabouts *before* dashing
through the city for answers unavailable in a vacant condo
flat?

"Why aren't you dirt-dead, unc? Worm waffles?"

"My would-be killer's bullets took a coffee break about an
inch away from my intestines. They couldn't go the distance."

Leaving his Geiger counter on the floor, the Mick stood up
and paced. "Why?" He shook both fists like maracas. *"Why?"*

"Why couldn't they go the distance?"

"Why'd this have to happen? Why'd old Tim Bowman try
to desoul you? How'd you manage to rip his cord?"

"The same views that ran you into Salonika's stews"—
guiltily examining his hands—"displeased Mr. Bowman. His
response to them, as I'd expressed them in 'Thus Saith Xavier
Thaxton,' had a longer lead time, though."

The Mick considered. He remembered. His uncle's column
on the "cynicism" inherent in the monthly presentation of
UC's stalwarts—particularly such newcomers as the DeeJay,
Gator Maid, and Count Geiger—had been just about the
snootiest criticism the Mick'd ever had the thrashed-out luck
to fume over. No wonder the great but unpredictable T.B. had
shot his uncle Xave. On the other hand, that had been weeks
ago. *Months.*

"It was Finesse who canned Bowman," the Mick said with

as much diplomacy as he could muster. "Why didn't T.B. shoot that stingy codge instead?"

"No offense, Mikhail, but I'm afraid some of Mr. Bowman's logic circuits aren't reliably wired."

"Yeah. Maybe. But if I'd've been anywhere around when your sappy head-dreck 'bout UC's brand-new stalwarts came out, *I*'d've shot you. No gas."

"Good thing for me you'd already run off."

"Bet on it." Suddenly dispirited, the Mick sat down again. "Where's Bowman now? What'd they do to him?"

"The Salonika city hoosegow. DA's going to indict him for attempted murder."

"You're not pressing charges, are you? I mean, he *didn't* desoul you. His head's on cattywampus from all the stress."

"I don't *have* to press charges. There was a cloud of witnesses to the shooting. Murder, even attempted murder, is a crime against the state. It's almost always prosecuted. The fact that I didn't die—no thanks to your zoot-suited friend—along with the fact that he was deeply agitated when he came gunning for me, *could* help him around sentencing time. Maybe."

"You plan to testify against him?"

"If called to the stand, I'll truthfully answer all questions put to me."

"Sheesh!" The Mick thought hard. "The Suit!" he cried. "The Suit saved your life!" He got up and started pacing again, like a hotshot TV defense attorney unexpectedly stricken with a wonderful courtroom ploy. "It *wasn't* attempted murder, Uncle Xave! I mean, you were wearing the Count Geiger costume, and T.B.—this is what trucks it—*designed* that costume! Shooting you was just a way to act out, really vividly, see, just how p.o.'d your fucking column'd made him. It wasn't actually attempted murder because he'd already slipped you one raver of an antidote for the gunshots. I mean, the Suit's the key to—"

"Mikhail."

"What? *What?*"

"Unless one or both of you betrayed my secret, the only people who know I wear the Suit are you and Bari."

The Mick made a noise like a blatting game-show buzzer. "No, sir, Uncle Xave. No, sir. Griff Sienko knows too. And it's like an upper degree of probability that old Griff tracked that news on to T.B. So Bowman'd know too. Which means the only—"

"Mikhail, I was polite to Mr. Bowman even after he'd shot me. I complimented him on his Big Mister Sinister getup. He looked at me and said, 'Shit. You didn't die.' "

That stopped the Mick. Uncle Xave occasionally talked like a Thomas Fuckington Macaulay essay, but, so far as the Mick knew, he didn't lie, at least not to him, and if T.B. had really said that, well, that suggested . . . ?

"Part of the show," the Mick ventured. "To make his dummy hit look, you know, dirt-dead googol-real."

"Come on, Mikhail. He could have used blanks. He didn't. He tried real hard to perforate my abdomen. If he'd aimed at my face, I wouldn't be here. Sometimes, I'm afraid, even our most beloved stalwarts fail us. This is known as Real Life. People who face it and go on anyway are called adults."

"Or BOFs," the Mick said.

"BOFs?"

"Boring Old Farts." But the sarcasm didn't lift his morale. He sat down again with his hands hanging between his knees. Slump-shouldered and morose, he studied Uncle Xave: the smooth V of skin visible at the throat of his robe, the paleness of his legs, which he'd propped on an ottoman and crossed at the ankles. "The Suit?" the Mick said. "Where is it? Is it full of holes? Can you still wear it?"

"It's hanging from the shower spigot. I sprayed a little of Mr. Sienko's Stay-Brite on it. It's—"

The Mick ran to the bathroom, yanked back the shower curtain, and grabbed the Suit between his thumb and forefinger. It looked . . . what was the word? *immaculate?* It looked immaculate, slick and unpocked as a brand-new robot. The Mick squinted. Well, there was one subtle puckering in the mesh. And a second. And a final one. Three in all. These irregularities reminded him of sweater snags repaired by hooking the yarn-snag back through the face of the garment. You'd've never guessed that three bullets had lodged in the costume's midsection.

The Mick went back to the living room. Uncle Xave was sitting in another chair with the radiation detector in his lap.

"Your Geiger counter," he said. "You've brought it home. Is it finished, then?"

"Yeah."

"Does it work?"

The Mick took a small, jagged piece of low-grade uranium out of his pocket and placed it on the coffee table. He picked the Geiger counter out of Uncle Xave's lap, lugged it to the coffee table, and tested the uranium specimen for radioactivity. A series of clicks, hesitant telegraphy, rattled faintly from the homemade contraption, certifying the uranium sample's feeble pedigree. The Mick raised and lowered the counter to demonstrate both its method of operation and its performance at varying distances.

"It works," Uncle Xave said. "May I try?"

The Mick carried the device to him, leaving it on to show Uncle Xave that it could also record harmless background radiation. It failed to click, though, until he set it on Uncle Xave's knees, at which time it started energetically rattling again. The Mick and Uncle Xave exchanged looks. The Mick lifted the device from Uncle Xave's knees to his midsection, from his stomach to his chest, and from his chest and arms to the crown of his head. The counter's alarmist sputtering got faster and louder with each repositioning but the last. Only when the Mick stepped away from Uncle Xave did its chaotic telegraphy subside into music reminiscent of a lovesick cricket's song.

"You're radioactive, Uncle Xave."

"Maybe a little. Not that much."

"The fuck you say. Mr. Hulet and I field-tested the clicker yesterday afternoon, and I did some fine-tuning today before coming home." What really puzzled him was that the counter went crazy a half inch from Uncle Xave, but registered only ordinary background radiation at every other remove. No doubt about it, though: Uncle Xave was "hot." The Mick said so.

"I already knew that." He made the Mick turn off the device. "A holdover from my trip to the Phosphor Fogs when Plant VanMeter had its relief-valve failure. Or an increase in my radioactivity level from my most recent trip up there."

"You should see a doctor."

"I've gone that route already, Mikhail, and I feel better— discounting this morning's unpleasantness in the day room— than I have in months." Uncle Xave stood. "Did you happen to notice if the fixative on my Suit had dried?"

"Yeah. It had. Totally."

Uncle Xave, checking his watch, speculated that he'd best get into it again, to prevent even a chance of a "relapse into my old P.S. mode." He came back from the bathroom wearing the Suit, with a ratty jogging outfit that more or less disguised it. The Mick gave Uncle Xave an unannounced Geiger-counter exam, and his device, to their mutual surprise, emitted not a single click. Xavier surmised that the Suit had absorbed and locked in the radiation from Hazelton's spring.

"You're not hot no more."

The Mick felt head-blown: his parents in Bangladesh, Bari a defector to the City of Lights, Tim Bowman in Salonika's catacombs, and Uncle Xave not only a gunshot victim but a walking radioactive cloud. Criminy.

There was a picture in his head: a tattered orphan standing in a bombed-out ruin as a mournful wind whipped snow across the muddy hills surrounding the collapsed building. The Mick knew that he was that orphan.

"I know how you feel," Uncle Xave said.

" 'The check's in the mail.' 'I've never been with anybody but you.' 'Why, of course I'll finish the job if you go ahead and pay me now.' "

Uncle Xave fended off the Mick's attempt to stiff-arm him and wrapped him in a fast, upright hug. "No. I really do. I know how you feel. Exactly. I can remp you."

"Remp?"

"Read you empathetically."

"Like pud you can."

"Listen," Uncle Xave said: "Desolate. Abandoned. Emptied. Forsaken."

For the Mick, each of these words had an unwordlike depth that allowed it to echo inwardly. Each had unwordlike resonances. It was clear to him that Uncle Xave *did* know how he felt; in fact, he knew exactly.

The Mick began to sob. Uncle Xave held him. The shielded radioactivity of Uncle Xave's body warmed and calmed the Mick even as he let himself cry.

Catharsis. Release. Healing.

"I want to visit Bowman," he said. "Everybody's abandoned him. So I'm going. You can't stop me."

"I don't want to. We'll both go."

The Mick broke away. He felt like a beaker of acid into

which someone has poured a neutralizing liquid—but all the acid wasn't gone yet.

Shoulders bent, the Mick slouched to his room. Its blackness was once simply a shrine to his punk nihilism, but now it was a grim objectification of his mood. He lay down in the middle of his bed. For once, Uncle Xave had the grace, and the good sense, not to follow him.

After a while, the Mick remembered the bottles of airplane-model dope in his headboard. He carefully rummaged out these tiny bottles, selected one from the multicolored brigade, and began to paint his fingernails black. In the cones of light raying down from the bedroom's recessed spots, his fingernails shone like ebony buttons, bleak digital bruises.

Forsaken, he thought.

And then, thinking further: *Almost* forsaken.

38

Night Thoughts

That was good, Xavier thought. Mikhail's heartsick. Angry, befuddled, grief-stricken. But we *touched*. . . .

In the kitchen, Xavier tested a hypothesis that had just come into his head. From a wooden knife-holder, he took a small dicing knife with a black handle. He scratched the back of his hand with the tip of its blade. There was pain and blood, but not much. On the contrary, the act gave him a rush—like swatting a roach. He set the knife down, touched the slowly seeping blood, and watched as the blood stopped flowing and the scratches immediately healed over, leaving fresh, pink skin where just seconds ago there'd been evidence of a minor violation.

Incredible, Xavier thought. Incredible . . .

A rapidly healed scratch was nothing compared to three gunshot wounds, which he'd survived without a trip to the emergency room. Well, try something a little more drastic. With the knife, Xavier sliced off the tip of his index finger. Pain and blood again, but, again, nothing unbearable. He picked up the severed finger cap and pushed it against the wound.

I should be faint. I should be sweating. . . .

When he eased the pressure on his finger, the cap remained in place. Like the scratches, this small mutilation had already begun to heal. He examined his hand. The faint line between the finger and its cap was disappearing as they fused. A miracle? Radiation-induced healing?

In the living room, Xavier sat down to think about what was happening to him. It grew dark outside. Traffic noises subsided. The Mick turned off the light in his room.

Eventually, Xavier realized that like a comic-book hero created by freak exposure to "atomic energy," he was acquiring "stalwartly powers." He wasn't yet capable of (1) outrunning the shot pattern of a 12-gauge shotgun, (2) taking the place of an Oconee Southern diesel engine, or (3) leaping any of the towers in Salonika Plaza. And he *knew* that he couldn't fly. Even so, he was no longer—a pulpish phrase occurred to him—"an ordinary mortal." Consider his recovery from Bowman's attempt to kill him. Or, flexing his finger, his demonstrations with the knife. Or the high degree of empathy he'd displayed, and felt, trying to comfort Mikhail. Hey, he had actually remped the kid.

Did he need further proof?

Xavier found that he could hold his breath almost indefinitely without gasping for air. If he pushed himself much past a half hour, though, objects in his vision began to go wonky and out-of-focus on him. Blindfolded, Xavier opened his refrigerator and identified the leftovers in plastic buttertubs by touching the tubs and smelling his greasy fingertips. Without using a tea glass as an amplifier, he put his ear to his neighbor's wall and picked up (1) the scurrying of a solitary silverfish, (2) the faint whine of an ice maker, and (3) the faraway burbling of somebody's unsettled gut.

Xavier removed his blindfold and turned off every lamp in the apartment. Still, he could see into every cranny by Salonika's late-night glow. In fact, he easily negotiated an obstacle course of chairs, pole lamps, *objets d'art,* coffee tables, stools, and plaster flamingoes.

I'm augmented, thought Xavier, looking out his picture window into Le Grande Park. Even at this height and hour, he could see lovers trysting, pokeweed lords conferring, cops on stakeout, a dog in heat leading a panting mixed-breed army. He could smell sweat and salad gas, thermos-bottle coffee and raw doggy lust. The whole park was in his eyes and nostrils.

Go to bed, Xavier advised himself. Forget the day's upsetting events. Sleep.

He realized that he hadn't eaten since breakfast, but that he wasn't hungry. This lack of hunger resulted not from distraction or emotional upset, but from a comfortable satiety. A slice of melon and a bowl of low-calorie cereal had helped him through an entire day, and he felt that he might be able to go another week without eating.

Similarly, he needed sleep no more than he needed food. Sleep might have offered a brief escape from his dawning awareness of his specialness, but why escape that discovery? It was exciting. He wondered if the changes in him had an erotic dimension, if he could shift at will into spectacular Casanovan overdrive?

Slow down, Xavier cautioned himself. Slow down. Walking into those radionuclides from Plant VanMeter almost two summers ago triggered your Philistine Syndrome. But what happened to unleash the powers that you appear to have now?

Bowman's assassination attempt?

No. Not that. That was just a disclosure event. The cause lay somewhere between the relief-valve accident at Plant VanMeter and this morning's shooting.

My trip up to the Hazeltons' farm in December, Xavier thought. The key to the somatic metamorphosis unfolding in him tonight had something to do with the contaminated stream on Hazelton's farm. Cockroach's dam had drunk from that water. That three-eyed catfish had grown from a fingerling there.

Xavier thought of the lead cylinders lying at the rock pool's bottom. What were they? For the first time in two months, he saw them with chilling clarity. For the first time ever, he suspected that the warm bubbles from the pool bottom were proof of Con-Tri's deliberate subterfuge. . . .

The ebb and flow of these thoughts buffeted Xavier, breaking and receding with tidal force. A thought that kept returning, that broke ever further up the shell litter of his worry, was the fear that he was becoming, in the flesh, that which he had always hated, namely, a comic-book trope: an invincible stalwart.

He was becoming Count Geiger.

Nietzsche, even with his exalted championing of the *Übermensch,* would have looked at him and murmured, "That is not what I meant at all. That is not it, at all."

39

Smokehouse

The cops who'd come to Philippi from Salonika inter-
viewed Elrod Juitt around ten on the morning following
Juitt and Larry Glenn's all-night spray-painting party. Juitt
got the feeling that one of them wanted to stroll from wreck
to wreck in his junkyard looking for the stolen truck, but the
size of the yard, and the threat of rattlesnakes waking early to
perforate his ankles, had kept the cop from acting on this
whim. He and his partner left with a reminder to Juitt to "keep
your eyes open."

Of course, the object of the plainclothesmen's search was
three miles away. The truck stayed hidden behind old Daddy
Wilkins's sorry-shingled smokehouse for more than a week
after their return to Salonika, when Juitt drove over from the
Auto Parts Reservation to reclaim it. Larry Glenn offered
Juitt a half interest in his and Missy's doublewide and a release
from the third part in cash that Juitt had promised to give him
for spray-painting the truck. He also offered to throw in a free
week's work every month for six months, to sweeten the deal.

"C'mon, Elrod. I want that truck."

"It still ain't got no doors. Missy won't like that."

"I'll hang some. Reservation's got a pair on it some'eres."

Juitt pointed out that Missy wouldn't want any part of
Juitt's buying a share of their home. Anyway, the doublewide
was useless to him unless he wholly owned it and sold it to
somebody else.

"Damn you," Larry Glenn said. "How 'bout one week a month free for *two years?* Missy ain't ever gonna let me carry her and Carrie-Lisbeth on any Harley." He nodded at the bike leaning against the white-pine deck he'd built behind the doublewide, all by himself, on the third day after his daddy's funeral.

Juitt finally agreed, claiming outright Larry Glenn's totaled '68 Camaro, refusing to talk about the doublewide at all, and extending the one-week-a-month-free clause to cover an extra six months. "You're picking my pocket," he told Larry Glenn, who felt a little that way too.

The day after Juitt and Larry Glenn concluded their deal, Larry Glenn got two teenage boys from Silvanus County High to help him take the Therac 4-J out of the truck and carry it through a gap in the rear wall of the old smokehouse. Juitt had forgotten about the medical machine. Now it was Larry Glenn's. He planned to keep it out of the rain, more or less, until he could peddle its prettiest components to a scrap dealer.

The days warmed. Larry Glenn borrowed a welding torch from the garage at Cherokee Auto Parts and brought it home to cut the Therac 4-J into recyclable pieces. The loveliest thingamajig in the whole mysterious device was a stainless-steel cylinder, about the size of a gallon can of Sears Weatherbeater paint. This cylinder, which Larry Glenn worked free without even using the welding torch, was good to look at and to run your finger along. With some effort, he put it in a wheelbarrow, next to the smokehouse.

"I'm taking that pretty doohickey inside," Missy said.

"Hey, that's what'll most likely bring us a get-back. 'Sides, you can't even lift it."

"I can push it in the wheelbarrow."

Missy pushed the thing, which weighed a *lot* more than an empty paint can, toward the trailer. Like a wind-up doll, Carrie-Lisbeth toddled along behind her through the biting wild onions.

Larry Glenn lowered his welding hood and aimed his torch's thin blue flame at the Therac 4-J. Almost immediately, he had ignited a plank hanging in the back wall's ragged gap. This brand set the smokehouse on fire. Larry Glenn was barely able to rescue Juitt's welding equipment before flames were scouring the walls and leaping skyward like Roman candles. Skin-blistering heat drove him toward the trailer's white-pine deck.

Unable to budge the cylinder in the wheelbarrow, Missy grabbed Carrie-Lisbeth and hurried up the deck's steps. No need to call the Philippi Volunteer Fire Department. It was too late. Missy stood on the deck gazing at the fire. Even at mid-morning, the fire streaked her body with clambering shadows. Carrie-Lisbeth pointed a finger past her daddy, stumbling toward them through the weeds, at the raging source of those shadows.

"Smokehouse," she said, as if understanding the building's name for the first time. "Smokehouse."

40

Through the Gerbil Tube

Bari returned in triumph from showing her UC couture collection in Paris. Her models, as Xavier had seen in a video sent to him by Marilyn Olvera, had strutted the catwalk at the Espace Cardin in a gaudy pageant of acetate, dyed leather, and mirrorlike foil. The inspiration for every outfit was the comic-book costume of a female stalwart: Ladysilk, Saint Torque, Warwoman, or Gator Maid.

The models made catwalk sorties to a synthesized techno-rock beat, or processed about one another to drum-dominated Smite Them Hip & Thigh arabesques. Sometimes they moved so vigorously that they seemed to be fast-breaking. Even the video showed Xavier the pop-eyed awe of the world fashion press and the hip covetousness of the Shiny Set women primed to buy.

Xavier was reminded of an old joke: " 'I hate women, and I want the entire world to know it.' 'All right, then. You must become a fashion designer.' " But Bari didn't hate women; and these clothes, despite their thematic origin in the pages of Salonika's Uncommon Comics, were not subtle sartorial digs at the women who wore them. In fact, the fashions in Bari's collection were cleverly made, with drapings and accessories that flattered rather than mocked. No woman would flaunt them at a backyard barbecue, but none of Bari's outfits would have seemed gauche at a ball or a theater opening: daring, maybe even avant-garde, but hardly vulgar or silly. Such was the skill, style, and wit of their designer.

Still, it was hard not to think that by coopting certain points from the gear of pulpy superheroines, Bari had sold a piece of her soul for both the financial sponsorship of F. Deane Finesse and the market security of a pop-culture logo. Like the teenage boys who collected the comics stateside, the French intelligentsia worshiped all things UC-connected. And Shiny Set women of a dozen different nationalities (the wives and daughters of Arab oil sheiks and Arab import-export merchants being the major exceptions) leapt at these immodestly *déclassé* clothes, to claim for themselves their auras of hipness and heroism.

Both Bari's of Salonika and Uncommon Comics had made a killing overseas. The money would pile up even faster once Bari's ready-to-wear variations on her couture collection premiered in New York and began filtering into boutique and department stores from Maine to Southern California.

One evening soon after Bari's return, Bari was discussing these and related matters with Xavier and Mikhail in the Oaxacan Zapotec Restaurant in the revolving sapphire disk atop the Bridgeboro Tower near the Salonika Hemisphere.

"Hey, Bari, I get off on your UC Look," the Mick said.

"Thanks."

"But it irks me big-time that the dude who really invented it, even if you and Howie Whoever modified it and all, 's been dumped by Finesse. T.B.'s sitting in jail for trying to kill my uncle."

"Of course that bothers you," Bari said.

The waiters in the Zapotec—*waitpersons,* the maître d' called them—wore vinyl loincloths, white war paint, Aztec headdresses, and ocher bodysuits. Despite the tacky overliteralness of these "uniforms," Xavier sympathized with the men. Their pre-Columbian costumes had to be as plaguesome as his own Count Geiger BVDs, with the humiliating disadvantage that *their* outfits were visible.

"What in fuck's *'pollo de Cortés en una manta frita de maíz'?"* The Mick held up a menu the size of a round card at a prizefight.

"A fried chicken burrito," Xavier said. "I think."

"*'Quince dolares,'* " the Mick read. "Sheesh. We could've

all gone to Ricardo's for the price of one fancy cluck-roll here."

"Consider the view," Xavier said. Tonight, the Zapotec's disk was not revolving, but their perimeter table offered a view of the Hemisphere, the glinting surface of the Chatta-hoochee River, and a picturesque enclave of Satan's Cellar, now a-ripple with lights and carved into stark geometries by a salmon-tinted sky sinking toward full darkness. Their waiter—waitperson—took their orders and padded away in his ersatz-deerskin moccasins.

"We thought you'd be home a bit sooner," Xavier said, using the first-person plural to cover his nag. (In some ways, it was a drag having Mikhail along; in others, a godsend. Despite his conviction that Finesse had rudely buggered Tim Bowman, the Mick *loved* Bari.) "I mean, it's the end of *March.*"

"We had dozens of orders. Each buyer had to have individual fittings. One customer had seventeen. Couture fanatics, unlike ready-to-wear customers, regard it as their right to redesign, to *customize,* each ensemble. They also think the designer whose brand they're buying should handle all the alterations. It's a hassle, but I do it to keep the ladies happy. Also, frankly, to make my couture work in the real world. I'd've betrayed both my customers and my vision if I'd left early."

"How does one make the make-believe 'work in the real world'?"

"That's the basic imperative of any art, isn't it? Anyway, I'm one of those who believe that *all* clothes are costumes."

"Amen," said the Mick. He was wearing a silk-screened Smite Them Hip & Thigh T-shirt with a Persian Gulf camou-flage jacket and a string tie with a bucking bronc on its clasp. The jacket and the tie had put the Mick in technical compliance with the restaurant's dress code, even if his galley-slave anklets and black fingernails were wake-up calls to throw him out.

"It's just that some costumes are more low-key, conventional, or unimaginative than others," Bari said.

"Like mine?" Xavier self-consciously pinched a lapel.

"No. Well, yes. Your suit would be perfectly in place, and totally nondescript, almost anywhere."

"Dull?"

"Soporific."

Bari meant this, Xavier could tell, not simply humorously, but judgmentally. It was a put-down and a dare, from a recess of her personality that she'd barricaded from him ever since their chance meeting at the Upshaw. She had loved him once, Xavier decided, in spite of his stodginess in dress, because he'd forcefully attacked orthodoxy and mediocrity on other fronts, but, with the advent of the craven Howie Littleton, via the UC connection, her opinion of him had declined toward tolerant affection. That was the emotion she was broadcasting tonight, amped up a degree or two by the good vibes attendant upon their reunion.

"Boring," the Mick interjected. "BOF City." He crunched a salsa-laden corn chip to punctuate his verdict.

"All right. Presto, change-o." Xavier stood up. He took off his jacket, unknotted his tie, removed his shirt, heeled off his well-polished but outdated oxfords, undid his belt, and stepped out of his pants. While he was aligning their creases and folding the pants over his chair back, their waitperson hurried up to remind him of the Zapotec's dress code. He also noted that Xavier was on the brink of arrest for "forgive me, sir, public indecency."

"I'm wearing more than you are," Xavier said.

"Grunge-all, Uncle Xave!" the Mick cried. "You're giving away your fucking secret identity!"

"Doesn't the Zapotec have a language code?" Xavier asked the waitperson, with a glance at Mikhail.

"That would violate the free-expression provisions of the Bill of Rights, sir."

Xavier was down to his tinfoil long johns. Bari was looking on in amused wonder. The vibes from her were positive. Xavier gave her a smile. He found his protective Count Geiger slippers in the inside pocket of his coat and matter-of-factly pulled them on over his navy-blue dress socks.

"These clothes," he told the waitperson, rummaging about in the coat pocket for the quilted silver hood that completed the costume, "are one of the means by which *I* exercise my First Amendment rights to free expression." He yanked the hood—an eerie aluminum-mesh burn mask—down over his skull, then fiddled with it to get the mouth- and eyeholes lined up. Most of the Zapotec's other patrons were openly gawking.

"You can't wear that mask in here, sir."

"It's really just a hood. It goes with my costume."

"A hood's even worse. The Oconee Supreme Court ruled last May that no one may wear a hood, or any garment both inspiring fear and concealing one's identity, in public."

"That was for Ku Klux Klansmen, wasn't it? And I'm not really concealing my identity. You already know who I am."

"Mr. Thaxton, this isn't Halloween."

Xavier lifted his hooded eyebrows. "I'm aware of that, but it may be that you and your fellow waitpersons aren't."

"And . . . and, uh, you're not wearing a tie," the waitperson defensively noted.

From his chair back, Xavier retrieved his tie, a modestly dear tie with the ever-popular floating-amoeba design. As if fitting a noose, he pulled it on over his head. "There," he said, adjusting the knot. "Please bring our food before I tell the management that you're wearing neither tie nor cumberbund nor cuff links."

The waitperson left off waiting and retreated to the kitchen to fetch their burrito plates.

"Better?" Xavier asked. He knew that his eyes in their cutouts were a pair of gleaming marbles, while his mouth in its oval window was a wet, pink scar. He must look pretty grotesque.

"Better," Bari said. She still might not love him as he loved her, but he'd won a measure of her respect.

After eating, an awkward task in his Count Geiger hood, Xavier folded his trousers and jacket into the Army Surplus backpack that Mikhail had worn to the restaurant and paid the skeptical cashier with a credit card that the Mick also stowed in it. The three of them left the Zapotec, rode an elevator to the Bridgeboro Tower's fourth floor, and strolled side by side side through a skybridge toward the nearest EleRail station. The plan was for the Mick to ride on home alone while Xavier took Bari to her riverside atelier aboard another train. He hoped that this arrangement would prompt Bari to invite him in for a nightcap.

It was late. The skybridge was empty. The streets beneath it were not so pretty at this height. Overcoated drunks slumped in doorways. Discarded paper helicoptered through alleys. Pokeweed junkies huddled on the landings of an ancient parking garage.

"Know what the Cellarites call these things?" the Mick said.
"What things?" Bari said.

"This thing." The Mick stamped his foot. "These bridges over Salonika's fucked-up waters."

Xavier and Bari admitted that they had no idea.

"Gerbil tubes," the Mick said. "Yuppie tunnels."

"Ah," Xavier said. The have-nots' cheap revenge on the haves who walked above them in hermetically sealed cages. So maybe the tubes *were* blatant architectural raspberries to the streets beneath them. Those who couldn't use the skybridges were nothing. Those who could were *Übermensch,* literally. Or gerbils. Overgerbils.

The trio's footsteps echoed in the skybridge, even the whispery schussing of Xavier's slippers. Fifty or so yards from the EleRail court onto which their gerbil tube debouched, they heard a woman's scream, a cry of complex terror. It had high-pitched versicles or parts. In the womb of the skybridge, Xavier perceived each part as a probing needle thrust.

"My God," Bari said. "What's going on?"

"Save her," the Mick said. "Go on, Uncle Xave, help her!"

Help who? Help her what? But Xavier instinctively responded. He broke into a trot. Then he was running. Then he was shooting toward the EleRail court as if drawn by a magnet. To Bari and the Mick, he was suddenly a hammered silver blur retreating from them at an unguessable speed. They could still hear the unseen woman's screams, but what they principally heard was the vacuuming *whooosh!* of Xavier's takeoff and the extended *thwuuup!* of his lightninglike passage through the tube.

Xavier propelled himself into an open space of stucco terraces and fountains fronting the EleRail platform. Stopping, he felt the ghostly afterimages of his own swift progress through the skybridge telescope into his back. The feeling was that of a dreamy double consciousness, one belonging to the self in action, the other to the spectator self looking on in astonished approval. The feeling—if examined, a luxury discouraged by the crisis at hand—was the reverse of that prompted by adventure movies, superhero comics, pulp novels. With those you vicariously assumed the identity of the hero. Here, though, gripped by a demand nearly the opposite of make-believe, Xavier cast back to the safety of a spectator self wholly fictional. Who was he now? Where was he?

Another series of screams scattered his thoughts. He was here, not elsewhere. Just beyond the station's ticketstiles, a woman in blue jeans and a trench coat was holding four black toughs at bay with an aerosol can. Chemical Mace, probably. One man already lay writhing on the platform's stippled concrete. Another, his arm up to shield his face, was yanking at the woman's coat sleeve.

Even as she screamed, she was nimbly allowing the sleeve to be pulled in stages from her arm. A third man, energetically cursing, tap-danced behind the coat grabber. The fourth man on the platform caught sight of Xavier.

"What the fuh," he yelled, pointing a menacing finger. "C'mon, you dumb shih, c'mon 'n' rumber."

The third man, hearing this, stopped tap-dancing and turned aggressively toward Xavier.

Without consciously thinking about them, Xavier reviewed his options. The man who'd just invited him to "rumber" radiated only bluster and uncertainty. If challenged, he'd run. The other man facing Xavier was for real. He'd fight, fully expecting to take out the Reynolds-Wrapped avenger staring at them over the platform, probably with a head slap and a knife swipe.

Xavier dashed forward, hurdled the ticketstiles, simultaneously tripped and shoved in the back the man who wanted to "rumber," and disarmed the self-confident tap-dancer. He used a wrist twist that swept upward into the tough's Adam's apple and knocked him backward into a support column. The man collapsed. After that, it was easy to deal with the only attacker still on his feet and the downed man whom the woman had Mace'd.

With her muggers down, the woman stopped screaming, sidled onto a nearby bench, and began to sob.

"Where the devil's the station cop?" Xavier said.

The woman couldn't answer. Xavier turned back to the four men lying about the platform as if concussed by a bomb blast. There was a utility closet, its door half-open, near the woman's bench, and Xavier dragged an aluminum stepladder out of it. This EleRail platform featured several large, vandalism-proof chandeliers, each with four hooklike globe supports.

Using the stepladder, Xavier hung each gang member five
or six feet off the floor from a separate hook of the same
fixture. The stainless-steel and polystyrene chandelier rocked
back and forth under the men's weight, creaking and coruscat-
ing. So disposed, the men looked a lot like gutted deer car-
casses.

The woman on the bench continued to sob, inconsolably.
Xavier had no idea how to calm or reassure her. In a moment,
though, Bari and the Mick arrived (along with the missing
station cop, who, with extraordinary bad timing, had been
helping a traveler with a broken foot to a taxi stand), and
Xavier retreated into the shadows to let the newcomers take
care of things. It wouldn't do, he realized, to come forward in
his Count Geiger persona. . . .

It was after midnight when Xavier and Bari reached her
atelier; stripped of garments, her second-floor studio was as
bare and cold as . . . well, as an EleRail platform. Bari stopped
to light the space heater, and she and Xavier sat down among
the throw cushions in front of it. Xavier hoped the space
heater would warm Bari's heart faster than it was working on
the frigid air swirling through the loft.

"Please take off that hood."

Xavier had forgotten about it. He pulled it off with a quick
yank, as if it were a gauze pad Velcro'd to a wound. Bari
smoothed his hair back down, less from any tender impulse, it
seemed to him, than from irritation with the way he looked.
Under this touch, he shuddered.

"What's the matter?" he said.

"You think—I mean, you *really* think—you're Superman."

"Count Geiger."

"To hell with the brand name. You think you're a bona fide,
flesh-and-blood stalwart. Don't you?"

"Bari, I have . . . *abilities.* I didn't ask for them, and I didn't
want them, but suddenly I have them. Bowman couldn't kill
me with three shots. Tonight—"

"You rescued a woman under attack. Fine. I can't rebuke
you for that."

"For what, then?"

"For acting like a pulp goon on steroids after you'd disabled her muggers."

Not wanting to, struggling not to, Xavier smiled. A mistake.

Bari scooted back and kicked him in the leg with the side of her foot. The kick didn't hurt. What hurt was the reproachful glint in her eyes.

"Funny, eh? You think hanging those guys up like a bunch of human bananas was clever?

"It impressed the Mick."

"A sixteen-year-old kid with a retropunk sensibility."

"And the station cop was grateful."

"You saved his ass from a neglect-of-duty indictment, possibly a lawsuit. Plus he's going to get credit for making the arrest on those jerks. Of course he's grateful."

"What's wrong, then?"

"That hang-'em-high gambit. Out-and-out grandstanding. Pure comic-book cliché. A by-the-numbers brutality that you think was original and cute."

"Sorry," Xavier said. "They weren't hurt, though. Salonika's finest got them down in respectable shape, all things considered. 'S far as I could see, anyway."

"Tell me this: Is that kind of cheap showboating what you're going to pull every time you warp-shift into superhero mode? Is it? If it is, count me out, Count Geiger. I'm not into adolescent power trips that take off from funny clothes and self-aggrandizing violence."

"Nope," Xavier said. "Funny clothes alone do it for you." He could be as reckless in his speech as she seemed to think he'd just been in his actions. He wanted her to know that.

Bari only stared at him.

"You want me to go?"

"Please. The danger of stalwartly abilities, Xave, the *curse* if you like"—finally sounding almost tender—"is probably that you come to depend on and use them, even when they're not called for. Fillips like that chandelier trick are really pretty despicable. I liked you better when a beautiful tone poem by Debussy gave you the gout."

"It still might," Xavier said. "I don't know what's happening to me. I haven't been myself for nearly two years."

"Good night," Bari said, scooting forward and touching her lips to his temple. "Don't be seduced into shabby exhibitionism by a God-given talent, even if it's a new one."

Going home, hooded again (more to hide his real identity than to strut as Count Geiger), Xavier thought that Bari's

warning—"Don't be seduced into shabby exhibitionism by a
God-given talent"—had a broader application than she knew.
It could apply to Bari herself. Who was more prone to what
she'd warned him against than a fashion designer? Especially
one with a complicated creative and profit-sharing agreement
with a powerhouse comic-book company?

Suddenly, as if from a disregarded nook of his sub-
conscious, up surged a Nietzschean apothegm: "He who fights
with monsters should be careful lest he thereby become a
monster. And if thou gaze long into an abyss, the abyss will
also gaze into thee." The problem wasn't Bari's: the problem
was his.

It dismayed Xavier, once home, to find that the Mick had
waited up for him. Smite Them Hip & Thigh was on the CD
player. The cut programmed to play and replay was "Count
Geiger's Blues." Its beat, melody, and lyrics pounded Xavier
like a brutal aural surf. He begged the Mick to turn the player
off and go to bed. The Mick did both, reluctantly.

Alone again, Xavier sedated himself with a stiff drink.

I have become Count Geiger, he thought. *I have become
Count Geiger.* I HAVE BECOME COUNT GEIGER. . . .

41

"Go Thou and Do Likewise"

A t the Mick's urging, Bari, Howie Littleton, Xavier, and he met one morning at Salonika's main police station to visit Tim Bowman, a prisoner in a basement holding cell of the fortresslike station, a vast, sprawling structure decades old and thus architecturally at odds with the metal-and-mirror towers raised on the wrecking-ball ruins of the recent past.

In the station's echoey lobby, Xavier felt that he had stumbled under the portcullis of a medieval keep. It always surprised him that the cops here spoke Suthren-styled English rather than Breton, Gaelic, or Norman French.

"Y'all can't go in at once to see him," the desk sergeant told them. "One or two at a time's the reg."

Xavier had a painful ambivalence—his gut ached, his hands were cold—about visiting Bowman. It didn't reassure him to have to forfeit the moral support of two other visitors or to send Bari in to talk to Bowman without him.

At a computer as unsuited to this vaulted lobby as a half-track would have been on a Putt-Putt fairway, the desk sergeant tapped in their names and waited for them to make up their minds.

"The Mick and I'll go together," Xavier said.

" 'Kay," the desk sergeant said. "Who's going first? Each set of visitors gets twenty minutes."

"You and Mikhail go ahead," Bari said. "Howie and I have some business to discuss."

I'll bet you do, Xavier thought. He watched the pair sit down on a railway bench near the front desk, then turn toward each other with rapt looks and animated hands.

The Mick tugged Xavier's sleeve, pointing him down a long hall toward a visitors' reception area. A young black police-woman led them. The hall stank of floor wax, bleach, and cigarette butts in sand-filled canisters.

"In you go," the policewoman said, unlocking a door and opening it for them. She locked it behind them.

Unlike in the movies, no upright glass shield divided prison-ers from visitors at the solitary powwow table. Nor would they have to use telephone receivers to talk to Bowman.

Bowman entered under guard through a rear door. He was wearing powder-blue jailhouse garb and cheap low-cut sneak-ers. (No cape, no Big Mister Sinister costume.) His carroty hair had been shaved to burr length, but the barber had left him one boyish forelock, which drooped greasily. He didn't look much like a comic-book hood anymore. He looked like somebody's neglected or abused redheaded stepchild.

"So. You're *still* still alive," Bowman said, sitting down and frowning at Xavier. " 'Bout my damned luck."

"One review," Xavier said. "It didn't get you fired. Trying to kill me was stupid, as close to self-destructive irrationality as an act could be."

"I'm being shrunk by experts," Bowman said. "So spare me your amateur repetitions of the obvious."

The Mick began to unbutton his shirt. The guard behind Bowman, a tall black man with oddly greenish eyes and a name tag imprinted with the word LIVELY, rapped his knuckles on the table.

"Whoa, son, what you doing?"

Xavier was as curious as Officer Lively. It wasn't hot in the visitation room, and surely the Mick hadn't tried to smuggle in a metal file, a pokeweed bag, or a snub-nosed revolver for his hero. The Mick had that much sense. Surely . . .

"It's just a comic," the Mick said. He pulled from his shirt a pristine copy of *Count Geiger,* issue number one, in a clear plastic bag with a white backing board.

"He cain't have no comic," Lively said. " 'T ain't autho-rized."

"I didn't bring it to leave it here," the Mick said, unwrap-ping the comic. "I want him to sign it for me."

"That ain't authorized either. He cain't have a pen 'cept for letter writing and legal documents. And when he's done wi' them allowances, he got to give that pen right back."

The Mick pushed the comic across to Bowman. He gestured at Officer Lively's shirt pocket, which held a dime-store ballpoint in a pocket protector. Lopsidedly smiling, Bowman began riffling the mint-condition copy of *Count Geiger*.

"This'll only take a sec, bro," the Mick said. "Can't he use your pen? It'll only be for letter writing?"

Xavier was amazed that Lively didn't simply seize the comic and warn Mikhail to back off or get sent packing.

"You said a signature," Lively said. "Not no letter writing."

"Yeah," the Mick conceded. "But a signature's letter writing. You know, the letters of a name."

Lively chuckled wanly. Then he reached over Bowman's shoulder and liberated the comic from him. Keeping an eye on Bowman and the Mick, he examined the comic. Eventually, pinching it between thumb and forefinger, he held the comic up by its stapled spine and gave it a careful shake. When nothing dropped or fluttered out—no check, no escape instructions, no map—he returned it to Bowman and grudgingly yielded his ballpoint.

"Sign it for the boy," he said. "And give me back my pen. In thisere push-paper place, a guy got to have his pen."

Surprise: Bowman opened the comic and autographed it neatly on the premier issue's premier story's title page. This act, Xavier realized, automatically increased the issue's resale value at least tenfold. (What sentimental value did it have for the Mick? Xavier was less sure about that.) Bowman returned the pen to the guard and pushed the comic back across the table to the Mick, who opened it to study the autograph.

"Hey, li'l son," Lively said brusquely.

The Mick looked up at him.

"That's it. No mo'. And don't call me bro again either. You lack the credents, hear?" Lively folded his arms and stepped back against the wall in a game attempt to erase himself from the room as thoroughly as would a eunuch in a seraglio. But Xavier had no doubt that if anything else about this meeting struck him as fishy, he'd step in again.

The Mick put a hand on Xavier's arm and leaned forward. "Hey, Tim, that noodlebrain review of his came out months ago. He don't even feel that way now."

" 'Doesn't,' " Xavier said. To Bowman he added, "And I don't."

"Forgive me, kid," Bowman said, ignoring Xavier. "But who the fuck are you, and why should I care?"

For once in his fitful career as a human imposter, the Mick was seriously taken aback. Bowman had challenged him. Why? He was a fan, congenitally nool, an ally with the artist against society's bloats, boxes, and zombies. He might not be Officer Lively's blood kin, but he was unquestionably *Bowman's* bro. Was he going to have to spell that out? Didn't his comic-book smuggling and his smart-ass enchantment of Officer Lively bespeak his noolness? Obviously not. Argh. What a heavy raver of a dis.

"I'm the nephew of the guy you shot," the Mick said. "Mikhail Menaker, better known as the Mick. I was at Goldfinger's—with Uncle Xave—when UC was outing the DeeJay, Gator Maid, and Count Geiger. I popped my unc, so to say, even before you did."

"Oh," Bowman said. He looked at the Mick as if trying to match his features to those of a suspect in a grainy mug shot. *"Oh,"* he said. "Yessir, I *do* remember. Ever ballsy, aren't you? Crusader Kid. My condolences."

"For what?"

"The genetic tragedy that tied you to old Xave the Knave here," nodding at Xavier: "King of the Komix Kickers."

"He's not that way anymore. He's a fan too. Sometimes he even likes—intellectually, he claims—the music and lyrics of Smite Them Hip and Thigh. He's evolved, catch?"

"Imagine that."

"And if Uncle Xave's evolved, there's hope for the globe."

"So you're a fan, eh?" Bowman asked Xavier.

"Didn't I recognize Big Mister Sinister?" Xavier said. "Didn't I bring the Mick to talk to you, my assassin manqué?"

The Mick turned to Xavier and deftly loosened the knot in his tie. "Show him, Uncle Xave." The Mick fumbled at Xavier's collar buttons. "Not only is he a fan," the Mick told Bowman, "he's also a real-life stalwart. Swear to Jesus."

Lively stepped up and rapped the table again. "C'mon, now," he said. "Your uncle didn't sneak a comic in too, did he?"

"It's *not* a comic," the Mick said. "Look," he ordered Bowman. "Lookit here, okay?"

Even Xavier looked. The Mick had exposed, under Xavier's dress shirt, a V of crinkled foil, a porthole on his Count Geiger costume from SatyrFernalia. Xavier brushed the Mick's hands aside, but the disclosure was a fait accompli. Bowman laughed. Lively gave him an angry scowl, as if he were a specimen of human vermin caught in a kiddie-porn investigation.

"Well," Bowman said, "I'd always figured you for a constipated fetishist."

"No more so than an adult male who openly wears a cape," Xavier said. "We all have our reasons."

"At first it was a talisman," the Mick went on. "The Suit, I mean. But now that he's a stalwart, he's wearing it—secretly—for real. Vile-mannered Xavier Thaxton is actually Count Geiger." To Lively, the Mick said, "This is all confidential, though. Can't we get some privacy here?"

"You the dude what conked them rowdies the other night but what let li'l Tyrone Harp take credit?" Lively asked Xavier.

"You've got to sit on that," the Mick said. "That's classified gas. What if every crim in the city found out?"

"You done told *this* one," Lively said, waving at Bowman. "Make up yo' mind. 'Sides, I'm here to keep the visitation-room peace—not to pick up no hush-hush crap to tattle 'round." Looking deeply offended, he retreated to the wall and crossed his arms. "Time's a-ticking," he said. "Best punch it along or this visit'll done be clocked out."

In a guttural whisper, the Mick explained to Bowman how Xavier had been able to expel the bullets fired point-blank into his gut. Breathing hard and zooming his hands, he related in detail Xavier's one-man rescue operation at the EleRail station. Uncle Xave was an honest-to-God living stalwart, whether because of the SatyrFernalia Suit's built-in properties or his unc's exposure to some strength-boosting natural phenomenon, the Mick didn't know, but the stalwart part was definitely proven.

"It's a tribute to you that he is, Tim," Mikhail said. "That's the nifty-weird part."

Wait a minute, Xavier thought. Bowman tried to kill me.

Bowman became excited; agitated, even. He apologized to Xavier for trying to kill him. He laid the blame for his behavior on his own insecurity-driven perfectionism, the jealousy and/or resentment of some of his UC staff, the entrepreneurial timidity of F. Deane Finesse, and the depression and disorientation that had overwhelmed him in the wake of his firing.

A fair-minded person, Bowman argued, would see his descent into Salonika's sewers and his brief rampage in the McGill Building as evidence that he had, well, *snapped.*

"Temporary insanity," the Mick said. "That was it."

"You were a handy scapegoat for a man in my position," Bowman told Xavier. "I'm *glad* you didn't die."

"Me too," Xavier said, feeling edified, stroked, and conned.

"Maybe you could testify for him," the Mick said.

"Easier to do alive than otherwise. If he'd killed me, he'd've blown any hope of my coming in as a friendly witness."

"I'm sorry," Bowman said again. "Really." (Behind him, Lively shifted his weight and sighed audibly.) "A stalwart—a Stalwart for Truth—would do that, though," Bowman pointed out. "Suppress his natural antagonisms to help a persecuted underdog."

"What else would he do?" the Mick prompted Bowman.

"Whatever's noble. Xave—uh, Mr. Thaxton—you're a critic with educated tastes, educated opinions. You're also a man capable of changing his mind. You reassessed Uncommon Comics, your nephew says. Moreover, you've reassessed me. That's admirable. If you actually do have stalwartly powers, use them to promote the general welfare. Shun the dehumanizing adrenaline rush of strong-arm heroics and easy coercion. Eschew violence. Use your gifts to ennoble the masses. Champion the Good, the True, the Beautiful."

Officer Lively startled them all by turning his shoulder to the plaster wall and spitting on the floor.

"That's a positively Nietzschean program," Xavier told Bowman a moment later.

"You may not believe this," Bowman said, "but that program is what I was trying to fulfill in every story I ever wrote or edited for UC. So my plea to you, if you're in fact a bona fide stalwart, is simple. It's this: *Go thou and do likewise.*"

"Amen," the Mick said.

When Mikhail and Xavier had exhausted their twenty minutes with Bowman, Bari and Howie Littleton arrived to visit him. Xavier gave Mikhail cab fare home and strolled back to the McGill Building. No sense in wasting another twenty minutes in the station house just to debrief Bari and her hunky-looking but wussy-souled partner when they returned from their visit. Besides, about the only subject he could imagine the three of them discussing was the coming boom in UC-inspired ready-to-wear, about which, frankly, Xavier didn't give a damn. He and Bari could talk later.

42

Foiled Again

In the next few days, Xavier moved to implement the stalwartly program that Bowman had suggested to him. (He felt great, totally free of the Philistine Syndrome.) He also tried to heed Bari's warnings not to surrender to violence or to the temptation to turn his heroic feats into self-corrupting public spectacles. Sadly, he saw few ways to exploit his secret identity's potential for Doing Good without publicizing the fact that a real-life stalwart, a living proxy of one of the title characters in the UC Universe, was altruistically aprowl in the streets of Salonika.

Much of a stalwart's effectiveness, Xavier reasoned, came from the reputation—maybe even the *celebrity*—of that character. The angel one knows is a more accessible public resource than is an anonymous angel with no known home address and no verifiable track record as a crime fighter. The problem here, Xavier reasoned, was finding a way to trumpet Count Geiger's achievements and potential without (1) turning him into a gaudy media freakshow and (2) wholly disrupting his own private life as Xavier Thaxton.

Xavier shared these thoughts with the Mick, who largely agreed with his assessment, but who believed that public awareness of the real-life Count Geiger would burgeon on its own as Xavier ambushed more thugs and rescued more of their intended victims. Salonika's law-abiding citizens would rejoice; formerly arrogant hooligans and crime lords would quail.

"No more free-lance, make-it-up-as-I-go vigilantism," Xavier told the Mick. "That episode at the EleRail station was a fluke, both in that I happened to be close enough to intervene and in that I crassly manhandled the muggers. Believe me, Mikhail, I'll never do anything like that again."

"Jeez, unc, they were definitely an or-what sight kicking from that chandy. At least you didn't Goetz them."

"At least. Ms. Lebeck was good enough to allow us to let the station cop collect the roses for saving her. That kept my Count Geiger impersonation out of the *Urbanite*. Now, though, we need to find a way to publicize the Count's role without hurting Ms. Lebeck or making Mr. Harp look foolish before his EleRail colleagues and bosses. If we could do that, it would probably work to establish me—Count Geiger, I mean—as a force for good in Salonika. The melodramatic has its uses, after all, and if I don't plan to resort to it again, we'd best cash in on it now."

The upshot of this talk was that the Mick placed an anonymous telephone call to the McGill Building suggesting that a Metro/State reporter interview a citizen named Blanche Lebeck about a mugging recently thwarted at the Bridgeboro EleRail platform. The reporter might also want to examine the activity log at Salonika's central police station to see how city cops had recorded this event. Such a follow-up might prove illuminating.

When Walt Grantham assigned Alex Meisel (whose identity Xavier had borrowed at the Hazelton place) to investigate the Mick's call, Xavier had a retroactive twinge of guilt. Two days later, though, this headline dominated the *Urbanite*'s front page: SILVER AVENGER SAVES WOMAN AT BRIDGEBORO STATION / *Assailants Allegedly Hung Up to Dry, Like Laundry.* Along with the story, Grantham had run a staff artist's sketch of the muggers hanging from the yardarms of the chandelier:

> Blanche Lebeck, a health-food store clerk, claims that on Wednesday night a hooded man in a kind of silver leotard preserved her health—possibly, her life—by single-handedly halting a mugging by four assailants at EleRail's Bridgeboro Station.

"I was terrified," Ms. Lebeck said. "I've studied self-defense techniques, and I'm not usually a 'fraidy cat, but this was four real mean guys. I pulled out my Mace and started screaming. Really screaming."

Ms. Lebeck, 38, says that her screams summoned help in the guise of a silver-suited rescuer whose actions were a purposeful blur. In less than ten seconds, she estimates, he had disabled the three young men still in a condition to threaten her.

"I'd shpritzed one of them pretty good," she said yesterday. "He was already down. Then all four were up. This guy in the aluminum leotard carried them up a ladder and hooked them to a light fixture until the city cops could get there.

"Guess you could say he kind of *foiled* the muggers' plans," Ms. Lebeck said. "That's a joke I thought up later. Things weren't at all funny as they happened, believe me."

Ms. Lebeck's description of the Silver Samaritan, who left just before the city police arrived, makes him sound like a costume-party refugee in the trademarked uniform of a popular Uncommon Comics stalwart known as Count Geiger. But a representative of the Salonika-based comics company claims no knowledge of the man and adds that this stalwart must have been free-lancing.

"Sounds like a wild and crazy guy with a social conscience," the UC spokesperson said. "Unless he tried to go commercial, we're flattered. If he were to get in touch with us and establish his identity as Ms. Lebeck's rescuer, we might be willing to discuss a merchandising and public-relations deal with him."

The story, continued on an inside page, also dealt with other matters: the assailants' names, backgrounds, criminal records, and present condition (satisfactory or better in every case); the brief absence from the station of EleRail security guard, Tyrone Harp; and the police's bafflement about the identity and the quicksilver *modus operandi* of the stalwart's impersonator. But the final line in Alex Meisel's article read, "Salonika can only benefit from the actions of a real-life stalwart like the Silver Samaritan who saved Ms. Lebeck."

Positive citywide reaction was immediate. The sale of both new and back-issue numbers of the *Count Geiger* series skyrocketed. Disc jockeys told jokes about, and made up contests centered on, UC's popular character. Costume companies specializing in comic-book characters—including a shady Satan's Cellar establishment called SatyrFernalia—reported a brisk rental business in tinfoil suits. You could see many of these subsidiary impersonators on street corners selling flowers, hawking steamed bagels, squeegeeing car windows, or even handing out fundamentalist religious tracts. A small army of anonymous nutzos telephoned talk-show radio hosts to "confess" that they were the modest Count Geigers who had saved Ms. Lebeck.

During this hullabaloo, it occurred to Xavier that a real-life stalwart could conceal his true identity either by jumping headlong into a bramble thicket of such frauds or by standing so far away from the ruckus that no one would ever suspect him of caring a jot for such matters. Oddly, in the comic books themselves, superhero impersonators were genuine rarities, as if all the supporting-cast inhabitants of their fictional Gotham or Nick City had attended the same night-school course about the legal and moral indefensibility of trademark infringement. The result—in comic-book stories, that is—was that nobody in town but Batman dressed like Batman, nobody in town but Yellowhammer dressed like Yellowhammer. In the real world, though, stalwartly wannabes crowded the boulevards and side streets of Salonika like so many annoying decoys, too many to count, too many to winnow to get to the genuine article. In such an atmosphere, anyone claiming to be the *real* real Count Geiger was hooted down as a liar or a fruitcake.

So far so good, Xavier thought, when events in the city had come to this pass. Alex Meisel and the *Urbanite* have effectively publicized the coming of Count Geiger, and the joyriders, frauds, and mountebanks in Salonika have provided me a welcome measure of security.

All that's necessary now is . . . *to strike again.*

43

First Stringers Refined

Work for the general weal, Xavier counseled himself. Eschew violence, disdain all nonessential showboating, champion the True and the Beautiful.

Well, he determined, it wasn't only street crime, pokeweed addiction, and various ill-publicized white-collar atrocities that plagued Salonika. It was also self-destructive eating habits, poor hygiene, Neanderthal racial and sexual attitudes, and execrable public taste, broadly speaking, in all those aesthetic areas under the purview of his Fine Arts editorship.

"So what're you gonna do first?" the Mick wanted to know.

"Visit First Stringers," Xavier said.

"But you hate the scuzzy vittles they push there."

"Exactly."

On a busy Saturday afternoon, costumed as Count Geiger but feeling himself as elegantly distinguishable from his brummagen impersonators as the real Santa Claus would be from a department-store brigade of shabby "helpers," Xavier strolled alone to the split-level fast-food factory called First Stringers. All stained tile and murky chrome, this establishment occupied a vast asphalt lot directly across the street from the campus of Oconee Tech, an urban university renowned for producing "agrarian engineers" and NCAA Final Four basketball teams. Today, the lines at the hot-dog and cheese-steak counters were twenty or twenty-five people deep because Tech was hosting a conference-wide gymnastics meet in its nearby field house.

Xavier drew only a few goggle-eyed stares—three or four fellows on line were wearing cheapjack versions of his Count Geiger getup—as he snaked through the impatient, ill-tempered diners to the office of the executive manager, on whose door hung a baseball home plate on which someone had stenciled HARRY BEDICHEK / HERE TO SERVE.

"I'm Count Geiger," Xavier told Bedichek after sweet-talking his way past Bedichek's secretary. "The real one."

"How do I know that?" said Bedichek, annoyed. "Anybody could make such a claim. Did you see all the other Count Geiger doofuses out there?"

"Try to throw me out," Xavier said. "You've got a pretty good physique. Come on. I won't take a swing at you."

"As a matter of fact," Bedichek said, "I'm a body builder. I could accidentally break your arm or something."

Xavier was ready for that. He had wedged a scroll into the belt supporting the "energy counter" at his waist. He removed this scroll, flattened it out on Bedichek's desk, and signed it. "This is a release form," he said. "It holds you blameless, and abjures my right to file a lawsuit, should your best and most concentrated efforts to eject me from First Stringers result in any injury to my person, up to and including loss of consciousness and death. It's prenotarized for your convenience."

Bedichek picked up and read the form. " 'Up to and including loss of consciousness and death,' " he read aloud. "Never seen one of these before, but I guess it's in order."

"It is. Try to throw me out."

Bedichek sashayed around the desk, warily appraised the Count Geiger clone standing squarely before him, and walked around behind Xavier. Although leery of some cunning subterfuge, Xavier held his ground.

"I'd appreciate it if you didn't shoot me or club me over the head," he said. "Your efforts to dislodge me should be confined to orthodox bodily exertions."

"Sure," Bedichek said. "I'm thinking, is all." He slid his arms under Xavier's arms, rapidly lifted them, and locked his hands behind Xavier's head in a wrenching full nelson. " 'S at okay? Can I do that?"

"Sure," Xavier said. "Go ahead."

For three or four minutes, Bedichek tried to frog-march

Xavier out the door. Oofing, bending, and twisting, he pushed
and pushed, but Xavier had resolutely planted his feet, and his
upper body was able to flex against, or to yield to, Bedichek's
exertions without suffering a muscle pull, a ligament injury, or
a cracked bone. He was immovable. Bedichek couldn't budge
him.

"You're a goddamned pile of granite," Bedichek said,
breathing hard. "Or your shoes are magnetized. Something."

When Bedichek let go of him, Xavier took his slippers off
and invited Bedichek to try again. So Bedichek tried. The
results of this new struggle were identical to those of the first,
except that now Bedichek stumbled around his desk and collapsed into his swivel chair. He looked up aggrievedly at
Xavier.

"You'll leave eventually, won't you?"

"Of course. Who'd want to spend the night here? Now, do
you believe that I'm Count Geiger? The real Count Geiger?"

"I suppose so. What's the point?"

"I'd like to use my moral authority to urge your adoption
of some healthful menu changes here at First Stringers."

"Menu changes?"

"Baked chicken breast. Granola bars. Raw vegetable slices.
Fresh fruit juices. Mr. Bedichek, if you're at all amenable to
a full-scale grease-reduction effort, we can discuss this in detail
later."

"A full-scale what?"

"I'm not unaware that both First Stringers' reputation and
its popularity rest on a viscous foundation of grease, but
Suthreners' eating habits are changing rapidly and health consciousness is the new watchword among the well-informed.
I'm sure your profits will actually rise, particularly since you
won't have much retooling to do in your kitchens."

"I don't think—"

"Another thing: It would greatly cosmopolitanize the ambi-
ence of your dining rooms if you kept your mounted TV sets
tuned to fare other than "Gilligan's Island" and "Laverne and
Shirley." You have a host of dining rooms. Keep the set in one
locked on PBS, the set in another on the Nature Channel, the
set in another on, say, CNN. This simple change would harmonize—"

"You've escaped from a psychiatric ward, haven't you?"

"No, Mr. Bedichek. It would harmonize, as I was saying,

your business with the educative mission of Oconee Tech,
from which many of your customers come."

"What a high-handed crock."

"Try phasing in some of my suggestions next week. If profits drop, go back to merchandising animal fat and choles-
terol." Xavier pulled another form from his belt and spread it
out. "By signing, you agree to give my program an honest
try."

"Get out of here."

"I understand: Tradition's a jealous master. Sometimes, it's
hard to change. This time, though, you *must* change."

Bedichek puffed at his own forelock. "Yeah? Why is that?"

"Try to throw me out."

Faced with Count Geiger's intransigence and moral authority, Bedichek signed. What's more, at the Wednesday lunch
hour, First Stringers substituted a baked chicken sandwich for
its pimiento-cheeseburger, and broccoli florets for French
fries. What's more, a VCR in the Bear Bryant room ran episodes of Kenneth Clark's PBS series, *Civilisation.* What's
more, these changes proved not only a public-relations coup
but also a dependable profit-maker.

EAT WHERE COUNT GEIGER EATS, a new signboard in front of
First Stringers read. STALWARTLY FOOD FOR SENSIBLE PEOPLE.

44

Nixing the Cutie Shoot

On Thursday evening, again stripped down to his Suit, Xavier crossed the river into Satan's Cellar on yet another stalwartly mission. A full day in advance of the weekend, the place was explosively teeming.

Xavier saw people in every sort of getup, from tuxedos and evening gowns to bedsheet togas and makeshift sarongs. He saw gods, satyrs, elves, hoplites, Vikings, Crusaders, pirates, cowboys, cops, computer nerds, movie stars, comic-book characters. Here, Xavier was just another mask in the crowd. For the first time in person, he was seeing some of the UC-inspired styles, the costumes of female stalwarts, that Bari had adapted for the States from her February couture collection in Paris.

P.S. Annie's lay in a secluded and dangerous area of Satan's Cellar, an enclave less popular among the slummers than the shops and bars near the river. Xavier's Count Geiger Suit began to look even more splashy and out of place than it had in the alleys near the bridge. Among the bums and hookers here, he stuck out like a sore erection.

The bistro was really shaking. Hoodluminati country music throbbed from a jukebox the height and size of a 4 × 4 truck stood on its tailgate. Waitresses in ruffled miniskirts careened among the tables. The tangs of cigarette smoke and salad gas hung acrid in the indoor fog.

Xavier paid his cover, asked to talk to the owner, and, after assuring a bouncer in a double-breasted suit that he was neither a cop nor a creditor, was ushered to a room off the main bar. Here, studying a tiny computer console, sat D. O. Awtrey, a dapper man who looked oily in spite of a blow-dried haircut and seedy in spite of his tweedy European clothes.

"I'm Count Geiger," Xavier said. "The real one."

"Yeah? And I'm Mister Spock. Awtrey's my *nom de plume.*"

Xavier assumed a posture of nonviolent resistance. "Come on. Try to throw me out."

"I don't do wrestling holds or fisticuffs," Awtrey said. "I *hire* people for that stuff."

Xavier straightened back up. "Without my Suit, I visited you a few months ago. I saw . . . young women being splattered with beer from toy rifles."

"A Party Hearty Cutie Shoot. We still feature it. Don't use beer anymore, though. Makes for too sticky a clean-up."

"Please discontinue that sideshow, Mr. Awtrey."

Awtrey scooted his chair back and stood up. He was shorter than Xavier; shorter, even, than the Mick. "Ask me to stop eating, Count. You want me to commit fiscal suicide?"

"Uncommon Comics supports my efforts to reform and civilize Salonikan society," Xavier said. "They'll offset the initial loss of any business hurt by Operation Uplift." He pulled a form from his belt and showed it to Awtrey. "Here's their guarantee."

Awtrey declined to look at it. "Another loony scam-man," he said. "Follow me, scam-man." He led the way out of his office and into the salad-gassy murk of his bistro.

At a table on the edge of the main barroom, Awtrey introduced Xavier—"This annoyin' dude claims he's the real Count Geiger"—to a huge man with a burr haircut and a small, pointy nose. The big man was wearing fashionable clothes, but his body cried out for overalls. "Count, meet Big Possum Screws."

"Fester Screws," the man said. "Big Possum's a nickname."

"My best bouncer," Awtrey said. To Big Possum, he said, "I want you to arm-wrestle this guy. Prove, or *dis*prove, he's who he says he is."

Big Possum wrinkled his forehead at Awtrey, but sat down again at the table. Awtrey pulled out a chair for Xavier, who,

seated, stared across the glass-ringed tabletop at Big Possum.
"Awm wrasslin'!" an onlooker cried. "Awm wrasslin'!"

Locally, a cheer went up. People crowded around. Across
the room, a patron reached down and unplugged the giant
jukebox on a Mississippi Mudslingers hit. Xavier paid no
heed. Big Possum's biceps bulged like potato sacks. His forearms were as thick and raw-looking as prize-winning kielbasa
sausage. When Count Geiger locked hands with him, Xavier's
hand vanished inside a fist like a medieval gauntlet.

"Go!" somebody shouted.

Blaam! Big Possum slammed Xavier's hand down.

"Best two out of three," Xavier said. "He surprised me."

"You're beat," Awtrey said. "Ambushed fair and square."

"Come on," Xavier said. "I'll start the next two matches
with my arm pinned."

"Go!" somebody shouted.

This time, Xavier lifted Big Possum's arm and with an
echoing crack banged it down on the other side of the table.
Big Possum bent over so far that he was almost gnawing on
the table's edge. His fans retreated a few steps.

"You win," Big Possum managed. "Lemme go."

"It's a best two-out-of-three, Screws," Awtrey said.

Through gritted teeth, Big Possum said, "Thisere fella's
Count Geiger. Cain't you see that? I'm done beat."

Xavier released Big Possum, who sat up, rubbed the back of
his hand, and ordered a victory beer for Count Geiger.

The weekend Cutie Shoot & Crotch Potting Contest was
less than ten minutes away. Two of P.S. Annie's waitresses
stood outside the showbar with cartons of plastic Uzis, AK-
47s, and Armalite AR-18s, renting the toy weapons and directing the renters to a pressurized water keg for "ammunition."

Music boomed again throughout P.S. Annie's: New Age
primal screams, outrage raps, poke-ahs. Everyone but drunks,
pokeweed addicts, and a few mellow gays was moving into the
showbar, ready to purge the frustrations of another sour work
week.

"Call this off," Xavier told Awtrey.

"This cash machine?" Awtrey said. "Ask me to prop my
keester on a curare-tipped tent peg."

Awtrey, Big Possum, and Xavier squeezed into the rear of
the showbar. Tonight, the young women in the show num-
bered four. They were already on the catwalk in sheathlike

minis that made them look like human candy bars. Xavier recognized none of the dancers, who processed in grotesque high heels on a platform hardly wide enough for one. The showbar's mirror doubled their number, reflecting at ankle level the leering faces of the rifle-toting men.

"Ready on the left!" the showbar's tuxedoed emcee shouted from a nearby dais. The men on the left raised their weapons.

"Ready on the right!" the emcee cried. Every man on the right side of the showbar took aim.

"Ready on the firing line!"

"Stop this," Xavier said, looking at Awtrey.

"Fire!"

Twenty or thirty tight streams of water rayed upward from the crowd, turning the women's wrappers translucent or clear, rebounding from their bodies, splashing the mirror. Despite this onslaught, the women continued to pose and strut. Beneath their wet dresses, though, the piercing lineaments of nakedness were visible: breasts, rib cages, pelvises, pubic bones. It was like taking an anatomy class in a crated hurricane.

Xavier glided forward, slipping through the crowd. Up front, he wrenched a plastic Uzi from one startled rifleman and leapt with it to the catwalk. All four dancers gasped and stumbled away from him. Most of the men in the room stopped shooting. At a nod from Big Possum, someone in the main bar, out of Xavier's line of sight, pulled the plug on Awtrey's humongous jukebox again.

"I'm Count Geiger," Xavier announced. "The real one."

"Giddown. You're screwing up our Cutie Shoot."

Xavier gestured with his water Uzi. "What you're doing here is tawdry and sexist. Its only virtue—let me stress *only*—is that it isn't quite murder."

After this speech, all anyone in P.S. Annie's could hear was the rasps of salad-gas breathers in the pokeweed dens.

"They're getting paid. 'F they don't like working here, they can allus go somefuckingwhere else."

"They *like* it!" another voice cried.

Xavier called for quiet again. P.S. Annie's dancers bookended him, two on each side. He asked each woman to step forward and to introduce herself by name. The dancers complied, but as if taking their cues from either Awtrey or a salacious TelePrompTer.

"Divinity Buff." "Baby Kravitz." "Sweet Potato Pye." "Honey Melonz." Each absurd alias got a lusty jeer of approval.

"Your *real* names," Xavier said. "Let them know you as persons with honest-to-God names."

"Darned if I much care to," Sweet Potato Pye said.

But the other women cooperated: "Dorothy Broda," Divinity Buff said. "Beverly Crawford," Baby Kravitz said. "Henrietta Maloof," said Honey Melonz.

"Oh, all right," Sweet Potato Pye said: "Suzi Pybus."

"Good," Xavier said. "Answer the gentlemen this: Do you *like* being targets in these weekend Cutie Shoots?"

"No," said Dorothy Broda and Henrietta Maloof.

"It sucks," said Beverly Crawford.

"It beats hooking on Chattahoochee Avenue," Suzi Pybus said.

"Do you want to be doing this next year?" Xavier asked. "Two years from now? Five?"

"Shit, no," Suzi Pybus said.

Xavier turned back to the crowd. "They *don't* like it."

"So what?" a man up front shouted. "How many fellas here like their jobs? Why should these chicks be any different?"

"May I get down?" Hannah Maloof said. "I'm cold."

"Hey, Hannah," a man said. "You ain't given me any chanst to warm you up yet."

Catcalls. Wolf whistles. Other zoological noises.

Xavier helped Hannah Maloof, Dorothy Broda, and then Beverly Crawford down the movable wooden steps behind the catwalk. The women dashed out of sight into a warren of dressing rooms screened from the showbar by a tall black divider hung with lacy brassieres, sequined G-strings, flaglike bikini bottoms.

Hipshot beside the Count, only Suzi Pybus of all the dancers remained on the catwalk. "My mama always taught me to give a full evening's work for a full evening's wage."

War whoops. Cheers. As if given permission, two or three men squeezed off shots at Suzi Pybus. Startled, she tried to shield herself by turning away. Other men had started shooting, targeting the lizard scales of Xavier's Count Geiger outfit.

"Stop!" he cried. When no one did, he took aim with his own water rifle, sweeping every rank below him, zapping eyes,

probing nostrils, scouring the mouths of his and Suzi's attack-
ers. Many of the men began calling for a cease-fire.

" 'Men should be trained for war, 'n' women for the recreation of the warrior,' " said a young man in a wet beige jumpsuit: " 'All else is folly.' "

Xavier recognized him as Tris—no, *Trey*—one of the
yahoos who'd introduced him to this asinine sport back in the
early fall. Trey was a reader of "Thus Saith Xavier Thaxton,"
a yahoo able to quote bad Nietzsche secondhand.

"We pay our cover, rent our guns, and take our best shots
at the ladies ham-flashin' it up here," he said. "Who's it hurt?"

"And your name, Mr.—?"

"Couvillion," Trey said. "Trey Couvillion. Tell ever'body
your real name, you buttinsky stalwart."

"I can't do that," Xavier said. "I wear this Suit to conceal
my everyday identity. To increase my effectiveness as a champion of the city's victimized." One eye under Xavier's hood fell
victim to a fluttery tic.

"What highfalutin chickenshit," Trey said.

Without thinking, Xavier directed a karate kick at the
young man's nose. He stopped a half inch before the impact
of his foot would have broken it.

"Tetchy, ain't you?" Trey said. "One tetchy Suit."

Xavier knelt at the edge of the catwalk. He laid his water
Uzi down. "I'm sorry. This kind of atmosphere"—indicating
the showbar—"does that to us. All of us. And that's how it
hurts us, Mr. Couvillion."

"The world according to Superwuss." Trey pulled the water
Uzi off the ramp and pointed it mockingly at Xavier.

Xavier stood up. "You married, Mr. Couvillion?"

"Yeah."

"Children?"

"Two. A coupla rug rats."

"If you have a girl, how old is she?"

"They're both girls. Eight and five."

"In ten years, the older girl will be about Ms. Pybus's age."
That was probably being charitable to Suzi Pybus, but charity
was a virtue. "Go on then. Take a shot at the lady."

Trey glanced around as if this were a trick. "Me?"

"Need some help? Want us to call in your five-year-old?"

"Listen—"

Providentially, Suzi Pybus began to tremble. She was wet

and cold. A hambone-shaped bruise stood out on her thigh like a USDA meat stamp; otherwise her legs looked spindly and girlish. Xavier asked the man beside Trey to hand up his jacket, and when the man yielded it, Xavier wrapped it around Suzi Pybus's shoulders. Still shaking, she pulled it tight.

"Come on, Mr. Couvillion," Xavier said. "Shoot."

Trey looked around. "I would if they'd turn the damned music back on. It needs music, a Cutie Shoot." He laid the toy assault rifle back on the catwalk and pocketed his fists.

Xavier turned to Suzi Pybus and took her hand. Going to one knee before her, he recited from memory:

> "I saw her upon nearer view,
> A Spirit, yet a Woman too! . . .
>
> A Being breathing thoughtful breath,
> A Traveler between life and death;
> The reason firm, the temperate will,
> Endurance, foresight, strength, and skill;
> A perfect Woman, nobly planned,
> To warm, to comfort, and command,
> And yet a Spirit still, and bright
> With something of angelic light."

After a pause, Xavier said, "Wordsworth."

Visible even through Suzi Pybus's pancake makeup was the first faint stain of a blush. No one in the showbar moved.

"That's not me," Suzi Pybus said. "A perfect woman. A woman bright with . . . with something angelic."

"Of course it is," Xavier told her.

"No." Turning her face away, Suzi Pybus shook her head.

Xavier stood up, pulled Suzi to him, and said, "Listen, don't sell yourself short. Go backstage. Towel off. Get warm."

He helped her down the steps to the narrow aisle leading to the dressing rooms. Facing the crowd again, he readied himself for catcalls and boos. Almost singlehandedly, he had put an early end to their Cutie Shoot.

But the men staring up at him showed him either blank or puzzled faces. D. O. Awtrey, muttering audibly, pivoted and stalked back through the bar to his office, and Big Possum Screws, with a look of amiable indifference, watched him go.

"Next Thursday, Friday, and Saturday nights," Xavier told

the men, "P.S. Annie's will offer three introductory seminars, each of them free, on topics of lasting interest and importance to our male citizenry: Ennobling Images of Women in Contemporary Suthren Lit; Latter-Day Etiquette and Sensitivity Training for Male Chauvinist Pigs; and Essential Points of Feminist Concern for the Twenty-first Century. Be here. Bring your friends."

"You gotta be kidding," a man up front said.

"Just remember that I am Count Geiger," Xavier said, "and that if you aren't here, I'll personally seek you out to know why."

"Whoooaa," two or three men said together.

"I mean it," Xavier said. He jumped down from the catwalk and worked his way through shoulder-to-shoulder bodies into the main serving room.

At D. O. Awtrey's office, he poked his head in and said, "Don't fret this too much, Mr. Awtrey. We'll find ways to better our city and to keep P.S. Annie's solvent."

"Who wants to better our city?" Awtrey said.

45

Blue Fairy Dust

The smokehouse turned to charred ruins in the welding-accident fire. The Therac 4-J—every part of it but the source canister that Missy had wheelbarrowed up to the porch—was unsalvageable even for scrap.

Missy said that she was glad the smokehouse had burned. It may have held a few happy memories for Larry Glenn, of his boyhood and of his daddy, but to her it had been only a dangerous attraction to Carrie-Lisbeth.

Inside the trailer, Larry Glenn struggled with the Therac 4-J's source canister. He pulled it out of the corner into which he and his brother-in-law had wrestled it. He polished it, wedged it into a heavy box, and gift-wrapped the box, which he hid in the bedroom closet. Missy didn't miss the thing because she was busy getting ready for the birthday party, hers and Carrie-Lisbeth's, that they held on the day between their two birthdays.

On party day, twelve people filled the doublewide. The guests included five little girls from Philippi; Missy's brother and sister-in-law, Ike and Claudia Burrell; and another adult couple, Larry Glenn's best friend from high school, Ricky Stamford, and Ricky's wife, Lulah.

On the dinette table sat a three-layer carrot cake. The top of the cake was divided with a wavy line of brown M&M's, with four candles on one side for Missy (each candle stood for six years) and four on the other side for Carrie-Lisbeth. Carrie-Lisbeth got up on a chair to study this outrage.

"Mama ain't four!" she said, red-faced. *"I'm four!"*

"Whoa," Larry Glenn said. He picked Carrie-Lisbeth up by the waist and carried her like a big plastic doll to the living-room sofa. "Set right there while I get you somepin to open."

In the master bedroom, he and Ike wrestled out the gift-wrapped canister. In the living room again, they set the box in front of Carrie-Lisbeth. Claudia, Ricky, Lulah, and five little girls stood in a semicircle behind the coffee table. Missy returned from the deck, where she had just fed a stray dog a couple of burned franks.

"Is that what I think it is?" she said.

"Shhhh," Larry Glenn said.

It was working. While Carrie-Lisbeth popped the ribbon off and shredded the wrapping paper, everyone else sang, *"Happy birthday to you."* Although Larry Glenn had to help, Carrie-Lisbeth finally got the oil-stained automobile-battery box off the canister. She eyed the futuristic-looking metal object as if it had come from the Moon. Maybe she thought it needed a handle. Maybe she thought it should play "Pop! Goes the Weasel." She plunged her arm into the box, to feel around for anything else that may have been hidden in it. Finding nothing, she knocked the box to the rug and kicked it with her heel.

"Dessert time," Claudia said. "Cake and ice-cream time."

"Yaaaay!" the little girls cried.

Along with Claudia, Lulah, and Carrie-Lisbeth's friends, Missy went to the kitchen to slice the carrot cake and to lay a scoop of Neopolitan ice milk on every divvied-out slice. Luckily, the cake and ice cream grabbed the girls' attention, and eating together—scattering crumbs around, finger-printing the furniture with sludgy ice milk—kept them all busy.

With difficulty, Larry Glenn and Ike picked up the canister and led Ricky out the kitchen door to the deck. They sat down on the steps to the yard, each man at a different level, and Larry Glenn, who was wearing his tool belt, worked the top off the Therac 4-J canister with a screwdriver. He removed from the source canister a slightly smaller, but still heavy, metal capsule.

"A pregnant paint can?" Ike said. "And its 'iddy-biddy baby?" Ike was a roofer, and Ricky was an assistant to the supervisor of Philippi's waterworks.

"Right-o," Larry Glenn said, working to prise open the object that had lain like a silver fetus in the stainless-steel womb of the canister. He succeeded. Inside the capsule was a kind of chalky cake with a bluish shine. The sight of this cohesive powder or clumped-together salt brightened Larry Glenn's mood. It reminded him of the sequins on a baton twirler's costume, or the sexy blue eye shadow of the hootchy-kootchy girls who showed up at the Silvanus County Fair every October.

"And what the hell's *that?*" Ricky asked. He and Ike moved up a step so they could see into the unlidded capsule.

"Fairy dust," Larry Glenn said. "Yeah. Blue Fairy dust."

About once a week, Missy told Carrie-Lisbeth a good-night story about Little Rabbit Frou-Frou and the Blue Fairy. The story ended with the Blue Fairy totally pissed off at Little Rabbit Frou-Frou for beating up the field mice in the meadow. *"Down* came the Blue Fairy," Missy would croon in a sticky-sweet sing-song voice: "She picked up Little Rabbit Frou-Frou and she BOPPED him on the head." Carrie-Lisbeth would giggle like crazy. Listening in on the story, Larry Glenn always imagined the Blue Fairy dropping to the meadow in a halo of blue sparkles.

Carrie-Lisbeth slammed through the screen door with Missy and two of her friends from town. Sticky-fingered, frosting-smeared, she leaned over Larry Glenn's shoulder to see what he was showing Ike and Ricky.

"Oooh, Daddy. What is it?" She stuck a finger into the salt cake. Larry Glenn caught her hand and tilted his head back to give her a loud smacking kiss on the chin.

"Yuck," she said, wiping her face.

"Just keep your fingers out, okay? It's part of your birthday present, doodle-bug. It's magic."

"What is it really?" Missy asked. At the edge of the deck, she was looking down over Larry Glenn's and Carrie-Lisbeth's shoulders, the girls from town flanking her like cherubs.

"Blue Fairy dust," Larry Glenn insisted. He rubbed a pinch of the powder on Carrie-Lisbeth's face: a stripe down her nose, a spot for each cheek, a thumb smear on her forehead. Even in daylight, the stuff gleamed glittery blue. The tip of his finger was like a firefly doing skywriting stunts right before her eyes. Carrie-Lisbeth was tickled to the point of going hyper.

Crooning, *"Down* came the Blue Fairy, *down* came the Blue Fairy," Larry Glenn divided the sparkling cake into crumbly lumps for Ike and Claudia, Ricky and Lulah, and Missy and him. Later, all but two of the little girls who banged out onto the porch to see what the fuss was about begged for makeup jobs too.

All in all, the Blue Fairy dust was a big hit. Even the wives tricked themselves out in the carnival glitter, then served the chattering girls, and their giddy husbands, more carrot cake and ice milk.

That night, Carrie-Lisbeth fell asleep with a glowing piece of salt cake under her pillow. Meanwhile, in the doublewide's largest bedroom, Larry Glenn and Missy made love in an arousing dazzle that made them both feel like characters in an old Disney flick: *Snow White, Cinderella, Sleeping Beauty.* Afterward, scrunched against Missy's warm backside, Larry Glenn drifted off thinking that this had been one helluva day. . . .

46

Outings

A pleasantly mild day. At Zoo Salonika, Xavier and Mikhail stood at the rail-capped stucco wall enclosing the moat around Gorilla Island.

On the grassy island, a silverback named Mighty Clyde sat on a teenage male, Si, who had annoyed him, pinning him pedagogically to the turf. Heedless of Si's whimpers, Mighty Clyde licked from the pads of his glovelike fingers all the runamok ants gathered from a nearby ant hill. In both activities, rebuking Si and digging ants, Mighty Clyde was serene but persistent.

"You closed P.S. Annie's Cutie Shoot?" said the Mick, gripping the guard rail. "Criminy."

"What's the matter?"

"Count Geiger's supposed to fight crime, unc, not run around smashing liquor bottles and icing nightclub parties. Jeez. Are you a stalwart or some sorta holier-than-thou sin buster?"

"I'm a crime fighter, Mikhail. On the other hand, I'm also a defender—that's it, snicker—of civilized values." He wished that he could sit on the Mick the way Mighty Clyde was sitting on the chastened Si.

"Nobody's going to go to your stupid seminars. Awtrey's going to lose money."

"Bari doesn't think they're stupid. She and Howie believe

UC will fund them until they become self-supporting. Mr. Awtrey can market videos of our consciousness-raising sessions to other cities trying to clean up *their* acts."

"Gak." (Xavier regarded the Mick's ugly retort as something of a tribute.) "UC's sold out. They trashed Bowman. Now they're like fucking trying to dictate values. They've gone cryptofascist on us. You too. It's enough to make a good retropunk drop to his knees and yodel into the porcelain megaphone."

What? Xavier thought. *What?* Aloud he said, "Maybe UC wants to make amends for canning Bowman."

"Wait a minute." The Mick appeared to tumble to an upsetting truth. "You lied to Awtrey. You haven't even *talked* to anybody at UC yet. Not Finesse nor like anybody else over there's promised to stand you the green for Operation Upyours—I mean, Uplift—have they?"

"No," Xavier admitted. "Not yet."

"You not-nool raver. You filthy charl." *Charl,* Xavier knew, was one bad epithet. Where did it come from? *Charlatan?* From a retropunk? Not likely.

Suddenly, over on Gorilla Island, Si wrenched one leg out from under Mighty Clyde's bulk and made as if to escape. Mighty Clyde grabbed Si's foot, upending him. A female who had been lounging in the pale sunlight knuckle-walked over and began pounding on Si's back like a Swing Era drummer. Si responded by hugging the grass and covering his head.

The other gorillas sprawled on the steep-banked island ignored this interchange.

Still jealous of Mighty Clyde's authority, Xavier caught sight of a man and a child walking toward Gorilla Island from an awninged concession stand. What seized Xavier's eye was a silver glint, and then the blinding sheen, from the man's costume: he was dressed like Count Geiger. The little girl holding his hand was grazing on a huge pink dandelion puff of cotton candy and giving her pigeon-chested guardian a look of sheer hero worship. Xavier's anger with the Mick spilled into a sour resentment of the phony Count Geiger. He stepped into the man's path.

"You can't wear that." (Xavier was wearing grey trousers and a burgundy jacket featuring the Ephebus Academy shield.)

"Of course I can," the man said. "I'm wearing it."

"He's Count Geiger," the girl said. "He's my daddy."

"He may be your daddy," leaning down avuncularly, "but he's not the real Count Geiger." Xavier stood up again. "He's just another showboating fake."

"Is not," the girl said. "Is *not.*"

Mikhail turned around to watch this altercation. Uncle Xave was right on one level—the dude in the Suit was a fraud—but wrong on another: nothing Uncle Xave said would convince the man's daughter that her daddy was less than what he said.

Of course, Xavier knew this too. He resolved the stand-off by skinning the man out of his burn mask with a quick pincer-like grip and an abrupt backward roll of his forearm. Unmasked, Count Geiger was a balding thirty-year-old with hollow, acne-pitted cheeks and a zit on one earlobe.

Almost as if she'd never seen him before, his daughter began to cry.

"Little girl, your daddy's a fake," Xavier said. "An everyday person like me could never rip the mask off a real living stalwart, it'd be impossible."

"Like way to strike a blow for truth, justice, and really crass assholism," the Mick said.

Through the child's tears and hiccups, Xavier talked to her father: "Yesterday, Salonika's city council passed an ordinance against anyone but the real Count Geiger's dressing like the Count in public."

This was the truth. The council had determined that a glut of local impersonators would foster confusion and so diminish the real Count Geiger's effectiveness as crime fighter and role model.

"You're in violation of that ordinance," Xavier said. "You've also, pretty obviously, lied to your little girl. Go home. Change clothes. Then, if you still wish to, come back to Zoo Salonika as a law-abiding citizen. If you stay here in that Count Geiger suit, you'll be subject to arrest and fines."

"The city council's action is unconstitutional," the man said, trembling. "It'll never stand. Never."

"Do you claim to be the stalwart who broke up the mugging at Bridgeboro Sation? The stalwart seeking to reinstitute a respect for human dignity in Satan's Cellar? Do you?"

"No, but I—"

"Then you're self-confessedly in violation of a legitimate

city ordinance. For now, anyway, its constitutionality is irrelevant to that simple fact. Go home."

The man reached out and grabbed his hood back from Xavier. As his daughter sniffled, he knelt before her and stroked her hair.

"I'm still your Count Geiger," he said. "I'll be your Count Geiger at home, Sammi. There's still no law"—glancing defiantly up at Xavier—"against that. That I know of. Yet." He clasped Sammi's hand and led her back toward the tunnel of sculpted bamboo staves leading to Zoo Salonika's parking lots.

"Sheesh," the Mick said. "Like triple sheesh."

"Did I just do that?" Xavier said, entirely abashed. "I can't believe I just did that."

"Me either, unc." The Mick stuck his hands in his pockets and headed for the sunken paddock where the elephants and giraffes had their own concrete-walled, Serengeti-style environments.

Xavier, peering across the scummy moat at Gorilla Island, had an urge to hurry after the Count Geiger impersonator and apologize for embarrassing him in front of his little girl, but he couldn't work up the courage. Besides, the impersonator and his daughter were probably in the parking lot by now. . . . Stalwartly powers or no, he had behaved like a power-tripping bureaucrat. To put it more pungently, he had acted like a perfect asshole.

Mighty Clyde, bored with eating fire ants and tormenting the thoroughly abashed Si, lumbered off into a thicket of milkweed and cockleburrs to defecate.

Soon thereafter, Xavier dejectedly trailed the Mick onto the edge of Bari's fashion shoot. Bari's photographers were posing ten or twelve long-necked, long-legged models next to Splinters and Stilts, Zoo Salonika's oldest adult giraffes. Five models were actually down in the paddock, wearing sheathlike dresses patterned with jungly whorls or miragelike stripes. Deliberately or not, these outfits emphasized the women's resemblance to the giraffes. To oversee and insure everyone's safety, a zookeeper had escorted the photographers and models into the paddock.

Yet another model stood at the low wall overlooking it. She was feeding a graham cracker to Gambol, a younger giraffe whose head was on a level with the model's. A pair of photographers, one next to the model and one in the paddock, toyed engrossedly with their equipment.

"What's next?" the Mick said when Xavier joined him at a spot not too far from the model. "Scoring the tires off wheelchairs? Firebombing a kiddygarden?"

"I'm sorry," Xavier said.

"I'd accept your lame-o apology if it like really belonged to me. It don't."

" 'Doesn't.' "

"Whatever. Anyway, it ain't mine." He studied the giraffes, the models, their safari-ish clothes. "Sad to say, this is lame-o too. Bari's UC Look was dead-on nool, but these're retread threads for like, I don't know, yuppie bimbettes."

"I think the, uh, noolness isn't so much in the safari patterns as in the materials and the cuts," Xavier said.

They watched for thirty minutes. The shoot ended. Bari joined them, and they walked to an open-air café, Zooey's Place, next door to the elaborate vitrifoam reptile house. At the café, they sat at a metal table with a Day-Glo orange parasol.

"UC's glad the city passed the Just One Count Geiger law," Bari said. "They're also happy to pay you a commission every time you do something stalwartly in Count Geiger's name. They won't sue you for copyright infringement. Remember, though, F. Deane Finesse can be awfully tightfisted at times—"

"As Tim Bowman copped," the Mick said.

"—and he's *not* willing to put UC money into a project called Operation Uplift to fund consciousness-raising seminars and poetry readings. For those, Finesse thinks the Count should seek either municipal or university backing."

"What does that mean, practically speaking?" Xavier asked.

"I'm not sure. That the city'll kick in money to assist you in fighting crime, but that you'll have to find other revenue sources for your educational and rehabilitative programs."

"What about Bari's of Salonika?" the Mick said.

Bari flinched, noticeably. "Of course I'll contribute. But I can't be the major, or even *a* major, revenue source. The fashion industry's freighted with overhead. I won't deny that we've turned a healthy profit with our UC tie-ins, but reinvestment's absolutely crucial. Launching four new lines every year is tremendously like starting over each season from scratch."

"Yeah," said the Mick, biting his thumb.

"What will you do next?" Bari asked Xavier. "As Count Geiger?"

"Score a wheelchair tire. Firebomb a kiddygarden." Xavier smiled. "In-joke stuff. Sorry. A better answer is, Something spectacularly stalwartly."

The Mick jerked as if someone had dropped a wriggling eel down his shirt. "Oooee!" he said. "I've got you a backer, Uncle Xave! Somebody right here in Salonika! *Oooee!*"

"Who?" Bari and Xavier said together.

"Never you all mind," said the Mick, nailing the Suthren-ism.

A lion in the lion house growled. An alligator in the reptile house replied. Cockatoos squawked. Vervet monkeys tittered. From their sunken paddock, Splinters, Stilts, and Gambol checked in with a croon of sandpapery silence.

At their table appeared a man in a short white cutaway jacket. Bari ordered three soft drinks and three chicken-salad sandwiches, and, as quietly as he'd come, the man departed.

As the Mick told Bari about a letter from his mother describing Bangladeshi suffering in the wake of a recent monsoon, Xavier tried to get a fix on Bari's mind set and affections. Her feelings about him seemed shifting and ambivalent. Why? He was trying, with only intermittent success, to guard against becoming the sort of monster that he was now equipped to battle.

The waiter returned with their sandwiches and drinks. "Still a little cool to be eating outside," he said conversationally. Would there be anything else? Bari said no, and he clicked his heels and retreated. Xavier stared after him. The waiter's personality—or, at least, the ghostly nugget of personality that Xavier remped floating within him—radiated anger and resentment.

The Mick started to eat his sandwich. "Smell it first," Xavier said. Puzzled, the Mick removed the slice of bread on one half of his sandwich and bemusedly sniffed the chicken salad. It smelled okay to him. He was hungry. Xavier and Bari took like precautions with their sandwiches.

"What's the matter, unc? You think that charl you unmasked a while ago bribed our waiter to off us?"

"These sandwiches are fine," Bari said. She reassembled hers and began to eat. Xavier could not, even though he knew that his hunch-driven squeamishness was . . . well, foolish. "Paranoia," Bari said. "A major occupational bogey of professional supermen."

The waiter returned. "Is everything all right?"

"Yes," Bari said. "Grape halves in chicken salad have always been a favorite of mine."

"Thank you, Ms. Carlisle." Setting his notepad before her, he asked for Bari's autograph, which, neither pleased nor annoyed, she gave him. "And aren't you Xavier Thaxton? I'm an avid reader of yours. Yours too, please." Glumly, Xavier obliged the man, who was still broadcasting on a hostile frequency. "Thank you, both of you." He bowed and retreated again.

"Like what am I?" the Mick called after him. "The bastard son of Turd World do-gooders?" The waiter didn't hear him or chose to ignore him. "Like I could turn out famous too!"

Finally, the Mick shut up and finished eating. Because neither he nor Bari died of cyanide poisoning, Xavier at last began to eat and drink too.

Both Bari and the Mick left, Bari to return with her models and photographers to her studio, and the Mick to ride into Salonika to mount a direct appeal to the party whom he thought a likely backer of Count Geiger's Operation Uplift. Xavier stayed at Zooey's Place to settle up. "Waiter!" he called.

The man in the cutaway appeared. "I wasn't always a waiter, Mr. Thaxton. A short time back, I was a . . . waitperson."

"What?"

"I know who you are. I know what you are. And your secret is no longer safe with me."

"My secret?"

"Oh, come on. You're Count Geiger. The real one. You should be proud of your secret identity. So proud, in fact, that I think you should be outed."

"Outed?"

"Yes. As I was once. Well, twice, if you count my dismissal from Zapotec's as an outing."

"Ah. I didn't recognize you without your war paint."

"From Zapotec's to Zooey's Place. How different things can be at different establishments at the tail end of the alphabet. And all because I allegedly botched my handling of your bizarre public disrobing. Management blamed me for that embarrassing scene. Did you know that on a good night at Zapotec's, I earned in tips in an hour what I make here in a day? Thank you, Mr. Thaxton. Or should I say, 'Thank you, Count Geiger'?"

For a moment, Xavier could only stare at the man. Then he gave him a twenty-dollar bill. The waiter made change.

"I have nothing else to say to you, Mr. Thaxton"—slapping down the appropriate bills and coins. "Wait. I do." Almost defiantly, he raised his chin. "Up yours."

Xavier, browbeaten by guilt, left him an extravagant tip.

47

Count Geiger's Greens

Bari rode EleRail in from the zoo with the Mick, but parted from him at the Oconee Heights Station, near the parklike campus of Skye University, a private institution with exorbitant tuition fees and a world-class reputation as a fine liberal-arts school. The buildings (except for the classrooms and chapel of the Augustine-Graham School of Theology, surrealistic extrusions of spongy white concrete and pinkish glass) were grey stone, draped windows, and heavy-hanging mats of ivy. From the Oconee Heights platform, you could see the squids in their preppie wardrobes hiking the school's dappled footpaths.

"Mikhail, I'd help you with this, but I've got to get back to my studios. Howie and Marilyn are waiting."

"Yessum."

"Don't say it that way," Bari said. "You'll do better without me than with. Promise."

The Mick jogged down the platform's steps onto the campus. He had no appointment, he'd told nobody he was coming, and he'd been to Skye only once before in his life, on an Ephebus Academy field trip over a year ago when he and a busload of his classmates had fallen asleep at the musical version of Sartre's *No Exit.*

What to do? Get help, the Mick figured. He waylaid a female squiddie in woolen knee socks, a Scotch-plaid skirt, and a white cable-knit sweater.

"Can you, like, uh, where's the theology-school dorm?"

The startled Skye coed eyed the Mick as if he were a baby Mulch Creature, but grabbed him by the arm, spun him toward the concrete globe-and-turret of the chapel, and pointed past it through facing columns of oaks. She smelled, the Mick noted, of laundry soap and a popular hairdo mousse. Seminice.

"Thanx," the Mick said.

Smite Them Hip & Thigh lived in a divided suite on the third story, or ramp level, of Aquinas-Swaggart Hall, a coed dorm in the theology-school vicinage of the Skye University campus. The Mick walked into this dorm with a resident who, assuming that the Mick was a fellow seminarian, held the door open for him. Once inside, he had no trouble finding his heroes' living quarters because the building was familiar from a photo spread in the *Urbanite* devoted to the group's enrollment at Skye and their abandonment of touring for the academic life.

Light-headed and expectant, the Mick shuffled quick-time up the dorm's carpeted interior ramps and arrived outside the third-floor suite labeled 396/398. He rapped on the door. He could hear an *Electrifying Thunderstorms* CD, environmental white noise, pouring from the suite's stereo system. Either that, he told himself, or some wiring was shorting out and the room's safety sprinklers were busily sprinkling away. . . .

"Enter," a male voice said.

The Mick hit the knob key and went in. Except for the stereo system, two upturned peach crates, and a pair of tatami mats, the curved room held no furniture. The Mick recognized the group's bassist, the white-haired Kanji Urabe, at once.

Urabe was sitting cross-legged on one of the mats, wearing only a loincloth. He looked a lot like a skinny Sumo wrestler in the last days of an undistinguished career. Smite Them's three women—Matison, Suarez, and Kambo—were nowhere in evidence, probably because floor-to-ceiling curtains closed off the entrance to their half of the suite.

Krrrrr-ak! went the recorded electrical storm. Thunder quaked the walls and floor. Invisible rain pelted down.

"Hey, man," the Mick said. " 'S Gregor here?"

Urabe surveyed the room. His eyes bugged out. Their gaze at last came to rest on Mikhail. "No," he said. More lightning, more thunder, more rain. "Sit down." Urabe nodded at the room's other mat. "Sit down and wait."

The Mick sat. What now? This was a borderline weirdorama scene, but it would've been a mega mind-fogger, he copped, if he'd tripped in to find Urabe dressed like an Oconee Heights squid-kid and watching "Leave It to Beaver" on a mini-TV. Meditation, on the other hand, seemed proper Urabe, if only he weren't doing it to a multimiked frog-strangler of a thunderstorm.

Waiting, the Mick heard Urabe accompanying the storm noises with a subliminal mouth buzz: *zfffzzzfff.* This noise, like the recorded storm, went on and on. The Mick dozed. It could have been a quick nod or a steep plunge. No way to tell for sure. All the Mick knew was that when he next came to awareness, *Electrifying Thunderstorms* had given way to *Cry of the Loon:* faint water sounds and the spooky laugh of the wind-rat itself.

The door opened, and Gregor McGudgeon slouched in carrying two textbooks and a notepad. He was wearing black: black canvas shoes, black trousers, a black shirt with straplike black epaulets. He knelt at the peach crate near Urabe's and stuck his school supplies under it. Then, lightly, he perched on the edge of the crate and stared at the Mick. The Mick was like too tongue on the ground to explain his presence.

"We don't do autographs here," Gregor McGudgeon said. "Kanj'll let just about anybody in. Nothing here worth pilfering, see? But none of us, nowadays, do 'graphs anymore."

"Didn't want one," the Mick blurted. The blurt hung there.

McGudgeon, perching half on air, studied him while the loons on the CD ululated like dueling flautists.

"My uncle's Count Geiger. He needs your—like, you know, the band's—help."

"All right. We'll pray for him. Hard."

Mikhail sat hunched, his fingernails glittering like bruises or reflecting the black of McGudgeon's clothes.

"So prayer isn't what you want, then?"

"Uh-uh, not like only, anyways. It's—"

"It's nasty cash you're after?"

"Yessir. Operation Uplift. Everybody else goes like vaporlock when it's time to pay. UC's copped out, the cops've closed their tills, Salonika's nothing but dogshit PR."

"I hear you."

"Uncle Xave's a private citizen in his spares, a culture crit. You guys really pumped him at the Grotto East. This Count Geiger lock-in dropped on him later, like from nowhere."

"Maybe so, but his righteousness is—" McGudgeon appealed to Urabe: "What is it, Kanji?"

"Legendary," Kanji Urabe said. "Already."

"Yah. Legendary. Already." McGudgeon reached under his peach crate and withdrew a checkbook. Atop the crate, he wrote a check and tore it off. He handed the check to the Mick. " 'S 'at enough for a decent start-up?"

The Mick gaped at the scrawled figure on the check. He got to his feet. "Jeez. God bless you, Gregor. Really."

The loon calls and water sounds ended. McGudgeon went to the CD player and put on *Peaceful Ocean Surf:* breaking combers, gulls, foghorns. Then, stripped to a pair of khaki-colored boxer shorts, he sat down gurulike on the mat next to Urabe's. He nodded a curt don't-mention-it at the Mick and folded his hands in his lap.

"It won't bounce," he said. "The world's in a terrible state of chassis, boy-o, but Smite Them's still solvent."

The Mick left. Outside Aquinas-Swaggart Hall, the squidkids seemed less squiddy, and it came to the Mick that when Uncle Xave banked this check, it would become, like early spring collards or even Popeye's canned spinach, Count Geiger's greens. . . .

48

Ink-and-Paper Ex-po-zay

The next morning, Xavier proceeded to the Fine Arts section of the *Urbanite*'s day room to discuss with his staff members their assignments for the coming week. Pippa had already left to review an exhibit opening at Snapz, a post-yuppie photography gallery at Salonika Plaza, but Donel and Ivie were busy at their VDTs writing stories.

Why disturb them? Xavier detoured into Walt Grantham's office, which was empty, and poured himself a cup of luke-warm coffee. Alex Meisel came in. Alex was small, dark, and energetic, a Metro/State reporter who, in less than a year, had risen to be Grantham's fair-haired boy—metaphorically speaking. Alex was agitated, wired even, and although he didn't radiate either anger or pique, he did give off a kind of . . . cheerful anxiety? Anxious cheerfulness? Xavier braced himself.

"Uh, hi," Alex said.

"Hello." Noncommittal. Aloof. Or (a better read on Xavier's own state of mind) guiltily apprehensive.

"You should know, Mr. Thaxton, that I bear you no personal animosity. I take no pleasure in having my byline on a story that will alter your status here."

"I beg your pardon."

"Walt's coming, Mr. Thaxton. He told me to bring you in here for a chat. Funny you dropped by on your own."

"I wanted something hot." Xavier lifted his Salonika-Is-a-Salacious-City mug, with its caricature of the mayor hooking on Chattahoochee Avenue. "Unfortunately, this isn't." Interesting, though, that Alex should refer to Grantham as "Walt," but to him as "Mr. Thaxton." Should he be flattered or terrified?

Grantham came in. He gestured Xavier and Alex to a horsehair loveseat that had occupied the Metro/State editor's office since late in World War I. "So what does he know?" Grantham said, pacing in front of his desk and avoiding Xavier's eyes.

"Nothing, really. I was waiting for you, Walt."

"Edify me," Xavier said. He felt sure that they had discovered his impersonation of Alex at the Hazeltons'. Alex was truly sharp, a bloodhound-and-bulldog mix. No wonder Grantham liked him.

Grantham made eye contact. "On one level, it's pretty simple, Xavier: *We know*. Complications arise trying to decide what to do with you now that Alex has uncovered the truth."

"Why?" Xavier said. "I won't do it again."

Both Grantham and Alex looked at him as if he had promised to go on a permanent fast. "I wouldn't have thought that you had any significant control in the matter," Grantham said.

Xavier shifted on the scratchy loveseat. "What are we talking about, exactly?" His Suit provided a degree of insulation, but he still could have been sitting on a scroll of sandpaper.

"We know you're Count Geiger, Xavier. In one way, we're proud that you are. In another, to be truthful, confused and chagrined. Alex is writing a story," calling up Alex's most recent files and swiveling the VDT toward them, "that will inform the public of our discovery. But courtesy, simple decency, demanded that we tell you first, Xavier."

"I also wanted your reaction," Alex said. "For the record."

Xavier levered himself up so that he could read the characters glowing on Mr. Grantham's monitor: "URBANITE FINE ARTS EDITOR IS ALSO LOCAL HERO COUNT GEIGER / *Unbeknown to his fellow journalists or Salonika at large, / Xavier Thaxton has been leading at night a storybook existence / of brave and stalwartly proportions.*"

A fist to the solar plexus. Xavier said, "I'd change *storybook* to *comic-book.*"

"Then it's true," Grantham said. "You're the character running around doing good in his aluminum pajamas."

"How long have you known?"

"We had a call yesterday from your waiter at the Zapotec on the night of Blanche Lebeck's near mugging," Alex said. "He confirmed allegations brought by the restaurant's cashier and—"

"*Allegations?* Is it a crime to fight crime? Is it a crime to try to show the rainbow to yahoos and felons?"

"Easy, Mr. Thaxton. What I meant was, many people— patrons of the Zapotec, a costume merchant in Satan's Cellar, a city cop—have told me that Count Geiger is the same person who writes our regular column, 'Thus Saith Xavier Thaxton.' They didn't volunteer this information, now. They more or less admitted the possibility under direct questioning."

"Yours, I take it."

"Yessir. Except for this ex-waiter at the Zapotec. He seemed to want to get something off his chest. I drove to his place and talked to him for over an hour. You're definitely Count Geiger, Mr. Thaxton. The people with you at dinner that night were Bari Carlisle and your nephew Mikhail. The rescue at Bridgeboro Station occurred only minutes after you left the Zapotec clad in only—"

"This," Xavier said, jerking his tie loose and unbuttoning his top three shirt buttons. "My aluminum pajamas."

"Right," Alex said. "The rumor, confined and small-scale, has been circulating for several days, but your waiter—Sidney Ray Yorke—pegged it for me. What you see there," gesturing at the monitor, "I wrote last night."

Xavier turned to Grantham. "You're going to reveal the Count's secret identity? You're going to expose me?"

"It's not all that secret, Xavier, and if the *Urbanite* doesn't, the TV dinks will. Our credibility would be totally destroyed if the bozos at WSSX beat us to this ex-po-zay. Imagine it, Xavier: the vacuum tubes scooping the ink-and-paper guys when Count Geiger *is* an ink-and-paper guy. We've no choice but to run Alex's story. On the front page. Tomorrow."

"Sorry, Mr. Thaxton." Alex was a nappy-haired dynamo with eyes like a poked-up cocker spaniel's. "Nothing personal."

"And after I'm exposed?" Xavier said. "The *Urbanite* carries a living comic-book stalwart as its Fine Arts editor?"

"Again, Xavier, it's a question of credibility. That wouldn't go. We'll be elevating Pippa to the editorship. You'll . . . uh, you'll be separated—."

"*Separated!*"

"—but with three months' pay and our profoundest thanks for a job well done."

Xavier sat back down on the horsehair loveseat, almost hoping that its malaligned bristles ripped his clothes, snagged his Suit, drew blood. Could a grown man who was neither an actor nor a circus performer make a living wearing aluminum pajamas? Gregor McGudgeon of Smite Them Hip & Thigh had given the Count a generous check, but every cent of it was pledged to reform programs for those caught committing crimes, remediable incivilities, or gauche aesthetic lapses. Xavier had a savings account, an IRA, a condo share, and two small certificates of deposit, but those were just about the extent of his assets. To put the matter in perspective, Grantham had just fired him, and all he had ever aspired to do was to write arts criticism for a metropolitan audience.

"I'm fired," Xavier said. "For doing good."

"You're let go. It's not a firing, per se. And given a little time to let the resulting furor blow over, we may be able to rehire you in a, um, special capacity."

" 'Ask Count Geiger,' " Xavier said. " 'The Stalwartly Gourmet.' "

"Do you cook?" Alex said.

"I'm not just fired," Xavier said. "I'm ruined. I won't be able to continue living where I live, or shopping where I shop, or eating where I eat. I'll be overrun by soul-suckers and curiosity-seekers."

"Superhero groupies," Alex said. "Could be worse."

"Let me write a last 'Thus Saith Xavier Thaxton,' " Xavier said to Grantham. "And don't run Alex's exposé until Monday. I'll be involved in a major crime-fighting operation on Sunday afternoon. If you blow my cover now, you'll jeopardize a mass arrest unlike any in city history. I've already worked out the details with the Oconee Bureau of Investigation, the city police, the Chattahoochee County sheriff's department. Count Geiger has, I mean."

"Four days," Alex groused. "WSSX could beat us to the draw."

"They're too civic-minded to do that," Xavier said. "Or

would be, if they understood the stakes or the hazards. And if
they had the story, they'd've used it already. Which means
they *don't* have it." He appealed again to Grantham. "Bribe
your sources. Keep them in the *Urbanite*'s camp. Offer them
complimentary subs, free want ads, advance answers to our
crossword puzzles."

Susan Giono, another Metro/State reporter, popped her
head into Grantham's office. "Sir, a wrecking ball demolishing
the old Busby Building came off its chain and crashed through
the roof of Preston Motors. Keeler and Sigalos are arguing
over coverage rights."

"Thanks, Susan," Grantham said, looking back at Alex.
"We'll hold off until Monday. The least we can do." He was
gone.

Alex found a palm-sized tape recorder. "Tell me, Mr. Thaxton," thumbing it on, "how did you come to be Count Geiger?
I mean, what happened to produce—"

Xavier winced. "For God's sake, not now."

Alex turned off the recorder. "You impersonated me up at
Deke Hazelton's farm," he said. "I've known for a long time,
but I kept the secret. You owe me one, Mr. Thaxton."

He held the recorder out toward Xavier again. Xavier gave
him a look of bruised acquiescence. Alex thumbed the recorder on.

49

Dr. Woolfolk Reacts

Larry Glenn had spent half the morning hobbling back and forth between the garage and the toilet. He was in there now. Juitt banged on the door with the heel of his hand.

"Elrod," Larry Glenn said, "I'm *sick.*"

"Me too. You got my go-truck and I ain't getting my free-week-a-month's work outa you."

Larry Glenn was propped over the bowl with both hands against the wall. He wasn't goldbricking. He was honest-to-God sick. This fact finally got through to Juitt, maybe because the sound of Larry Glenn's retching was so clear.

"Awl right, damn you. Go on home. Git."

Larry Glenn, white-faced, opened the door. "Okay," he said, "I'll try."

"C'mere," Missy said. "Come see your daughter."

Carrie-Lisbeth was sick too. The fresh slip on her pillow was soaked. She was so feverish, Missy pointed out, that she looked damned-near sunburnt.

"It's food poisoning," Larry Glenn said. "We're all sick. It musta been them damn dollar-a-pack hot dogs."

"That was three days ago. This is a bug. This is the flu."

"Call ever'body who was here. See if they're sick."

Missy telephoned. Claudia and Lulah told Missy they had queasy stomachs and the sweats. Ike was all right. Ricky had complained that morning of a headache, but he'd driven in to work to man his backhoe. It sounded to Missy, though, as if most of the guests at Carrie-Lisbeth's party were flu victims.

"Food poisoning," Larry Glenn said.

"Uh-uh," Missy said, "but you'd better take us to a doctor."

Because the go-truck still had no doors, the trip into town was windy, dusty, and hot. Carrie-Lisbeth whimpered most of the way. Larry Glenn felt so bad himself that he started to believe Missy'd been right to insist on going.

The Philippi Clinic, under the direction of Dr. Zane Woolfolk, was a one-story brick building behind the post office. Larry Glenn and Missy looked into the clinic through its glass door and saw the mothers of two of Carrie-Lisbeth's friends in the waiting room with their daughters.

"I knew it," Larry Glenn said. "It was them damned hot dogs."

"It wasn't," Missy said. "It wasn't." Steeling themselves, they entered the clinic and sat down next to the patients already inside. The three women immediately started comparing their girls' symptoms. Thirty minutes passed before Doctor Zane's nurse called them out of the waiting room. A lumber jackish-looking man with a close-cropped grey beard and a monocle that he sometimes peered through comically, Doctor Zane invited Larry Glenn to come back with the girls and their mothers, but, because he was male, left him sitting on a folding chair in the hall.

When Doctor Zane returned, he said, "Larry Glenn, Missy told me you cut down a medical machine and passed out the blue powder in it to Carrie-Lisbeth and her friends. Is that so?"

"Yessir." Larry Glenn reached into his pocket and pulled out a clump of the glitter-cake. Doctor Zane's eyes got wider and wider and wider. "It was too pretty to squirrel away. Ever'body should have some, I thought. That's what a birthday party's all about."

"You poor dumb son of a bitch," Doctor Zane said.

Dr. Zane Woolfolk moved as quickly as he could to clean up the Wilkinses' mess. He had Larry Glenn drop his egg-sized chunk of cesium 137 into an empty soup can, which he carried into the X-ray room, dropped into a metal bowl, and covered with one of the vinyl-encased lead vests that his X-ray patients wore.

He hurried back down the hall, gave Larry Glenn a bar of soap, shoved him into the bathroom, and said, "Strip. Put your clothes in the trash can. Hand the trash can out. Scrub your hands, wash yourself from scalp to sole. I know it's tight in there, but do it. I'll bring you some more clothes."

As soon as Larry Glenn had wadded his clothes into the trash can, Dr. Woolfolk carried it across the hall to the little girls' mothers. He told them to undress the girls, stuff their clothes into the examination room's trash can, and hand the trash can out to him. Then the mothers should take turns scrubbing themselves, from their fingertips to their elbows, with the soap he gave them. Once finished, they should wash their daughters thoroughly and scrub themselves again. Nurse O'Brien would bring each child an inexpensive change of clothes.

Dr. Woolfolk took both trash cans to the clinic's incinerator, set a week's worth of trash on fire, and banged down the cover so that the smoke from the burning waste could escape through a single metal pipe. Back in his office, he telephoned the Silvanus County sheriff's department and suggested that a pair of deputies be sent at once to the Larry Glenn Wilkins property on Lickskillet Road, to quarantine the place.

Dr. Woolfolk's next phone call, after dialing Information for the number, was to REACTS, Radiation Emergency Center / Training Sites, a World Health Organization-affiliated outfit. REACTS' main offices were in Oak Ridge, Tennessee, less than three hundred miles away. Dr. Woolfolk explained to the radiation expert who came on the line what had happened, how he had discovered the problem, and what he had done so far.

His contact, Dr. Joseph Lusk, said, "That's good. That's real good. Now, listen . . ."

50

"Jury-Rigged Rainbows"

On Saturday afternoon, Xavier keyboarded his final twice-weekly installment of "Thus Saith Xavier Thaxton."

I am leaving the *Urbanite.* This is my last column here. It's hard to say goodbye. Writing arts criticism and promoting our species' finest imaginative products have been my only goals since embarking on my career as a journalist.

In "Thus Saith Xavier Thaxton," impelled by both ego and love, I have spoken my mind about the arts. I have applauded and scolded the makers, and the would-be makers, of art. I've railed against fraud, sloth, nincompoopery, misguidedness, and even blatant immorality. I've taken to task those of you seduced into huzzas by our most popular artists' most wretched excesses.

To my own and others' amazement, I have occasionally reversed fields and scolded myself for championing (or slighting) an artist once blindly praised (or dismissed). I have passed judgment, and I have made mistakes. For my benefit and yours, I have tried to analyze and correct my errors. I have never ceased wanting our entire species,

Xavier Thaxton included, to be better—i.e., spiritually richer—than it is.

"Just who the hell do you think you are?" is an apt paraphrase of the major thrust of a high percentage of my "fan" mail. Snob, elitist, longhair, bigot, high-hatter, blusterer, know-it-all, puff adder, and *critic*—shied at me with a sneer—are just some of the printable epithets that my judgments have provoked over the past few years. Upon occasion, I have deserved both these epithets and the unprintable ones not catalogued here.

(Parenthetically, I might add that even if my column taking to task the power-fantasy underpinnings of Uncommon Comics was a myopic one, I *didn't* deserve to be shot three times for writing it. "Once would have done," my editor and friend Walt Grantham said, "if the gunman's aim had been better.")

With my words in this spot, I have incurred your ire, your righteous indignation, your dismay, and (if you were an aggrieved artist or one of the artist's partisans) your withering contempt, if not your deathless hatred. After all, I had attacked that by which you at least partially define yourself; and only saints, angels, or the serenely secure can withstand such assaults without leaking either rage or self-esteem. Bootless to argue that I never meant to wound, simply to admonish and correct.

"Just who the hell do you think you are?" There is a Sufi saying that has calmed me when my words, discomfiting others, have spurred the wounded to act upon their fury and loathing: "Enemies are often former or potential friends who have been denied—or think they have been denied—something." Namely, praise. Namely, regard.

Further, there is a Sufi riddle, which generously supplies its own answer, that has also given me comfort: "Who is the wrong person to criticize?" Answereth this riddle, quite simply: "You." Along with an apothegm of Nietzsche's Zarathustra ("Proverbs should be peaks, and those spoken to big and tall"), these Sufi sayings restore a degree of perspective, not to mention my oft-abused and gun-shy soul.

Even as I set them down here, though, I can hear you screaming, *"Just who the hell do you think you are?"* The outrageousness of my self-image, as you falsely perceive it, must appall or amuse you (if you care at all). But I am chastened by my own failures and inadequacies even as I tweak you, tenderly, for yours. The spiritual humility behind my public arrogance is what my detractors and my enemies have never understood.

But let me answer the one question—*"Just who the hell do you think you are?"*—that echoes refrainlike from your every letter of protest, dissent, or heartfelt contumely. I am Nietzsche's would-be *Übermensch*. I am Superman in ineffectual Clark Kent drag. I am, in short, a Stalwart for Truth.

Here, I must thank the *Urbanite* for giving me this twice-weekly forum. I must also thank my staff: Donel Lassiter, Ivie Nakai, and Pippa Wiedmeyer, who succeeds me. I must also thank my colleague Lee Stamz, who taught me a few of the errors of my ways, and my nephew Mikhail Menaker for trying to teach me the others. I thank Walt Grantham for several years of gutty indulgence.

But, most of all, I thank the would-be artists who strive to show us the rainbow, and the beholders among us who seek to see as rainbows the jury-rigged arches winched into view by their hopeful makers. Sometimes the noise is bearable. Sometimes the guy-ropes are harder to see than threads. Sometimes the sky is afire with color and light and passion. Sometimes . . .

Goodbye, Salonika. Goodbye.

"The thank-yous are nice, but the counterattack on your readers is—"

"It isn't a counterattack, Walt. It's an explanation and an apologia. It's a love letter."

Grantham, staring at the printout on his desk, shook his head. "And you virtually admit you're Count Geiger. You do just what you asked me *not* to do until Monday."

"By writing 'I am a Stalwart for Truth'?"

"Of course."

"That's a metaphor, Walt, not a declaration of my synonymity with Count Geiger."

"All our readers aren't that conversant with metaphors."

"I like to pretend they are."

"In the hope they'll become what you pretend?"

"If you can't accept 'I am a Stalwart for Truth' as a metaphor, Walt, try viewing it as a hedge against being scooped."

"Come again."

"If the TV dinks—the vacuum tubes, as you call them—try to drop the bombshell tomorrow that Xavier Thaxton is Count Geiger, the *Urbanite* will've already stolen their thunder."

"But you've disguised the admission as—" Grantham stopped.

"As what? A metaphor? Exactly. Make up your mind. Do you want a straightforward admission or a metaphorical admission? You seem to be trying to cover both sides of the street."

"Damn it, Xavier! I don't want an admission at all."

"Unless Alex Meisel does the admitting for me, turning the fact into an *Urbanite* scoop instead of a confession."

"I'd like you to rewrite this last 'Thus Saith,' Xave. It's all bombast, special pleading, and innuendo."

"Walt, it's my last literary hurrah here in Salonika. Run it as it stands. You owe me that much."

On Sunday morning, "Jury-Rigged Rainbows," the last "Thus Saith Xavier Thaxton," ran in the Fine Arts pages of the *Urbanite* exactly as Xavier had written it.

51

Stung!

Before most of Salonika's churches let out, the nearer parking lots of the Hemisphere began to fill: muscle cars, Mercedes, 4 × 4 trucks, stretch limos, jalopyesque pickups. At the only gate open for foot traffic, security cops frisked everybody on line, allowing no one to enter without passing through a metal detector. Few put up a fuss. American military intervention overseas had made tight security at most major public events, as a hedge against terrorist attacks and bombings, a commonplace.

Most of those filing into the stadium were young and male, but whatever their age or sex, all had received a letter promising an afternoon of free entertainment and exciting giveaways as part of a regional promotion by a brand-new music, video, and ad consortium (Mambo-Ra Flix & Kix, in conjunction today with Blackguard Pictures and Uncommon Comics). These letters had been addressed to known bail jumpers, suspected drug dealers and burglars, verified prison escapees, possessors of delinquent parking tickets, and heretofore unapprehended con artists, car thieves, bank robbers, and felonious ne'er-do-wells. The letters had resembled sweepstake invitations, not subpoenas or crude dunning instruments, and response had been gratifying: approximately a thousand invitations had netted a crowd of over six hundred, each soul conscientiously punctual.

Inside, ushers passed out free issues of the latest Stalwart-for-Truth comic, "valuable coupon booklets," and flyers listing the activities and prizes available during the promotion. They also directed their guests to a fan-shaped section of bleacher seats behind home plate, urging everyone to sit as close to the field as possible to move things along should anyone have to walk out to accept a prize. Although the mailed invitations guaranteed that no one at the Mambo-Ra Flix & Kix promotion would leave empty-handed, they also said that, to conclude on time, the promo must start at exactly one o'clock; no one coming late could take part.

Three parachute tents, like canopies at a medieval picnic, rippled in the Cherokees' outfield: one in left, one in center, one in right. Each tent was multicolored. Under their wide, fanciful wings, the groundskeepers had set out metal folding chairs and an assortment of goods and equipment hard to identify from the seats into which the ushers had herded their guests.

Erected on the infield, between the first and third base lines, was a V-shaped stage, with a pole mike at the point of the V above home plate. At the mike, in a smart cocktail dress, stood a young woman whom even regulars at P.S. Annie's Cutie Shoots probably would not have recognized as Suzi Pybus. Steered to this booking by a tip relayed through Big Possum Screws, Suzi (a.k.a. Sweet Potato Pye) was taking somewhat less advantage of her beauty and dancing talent, and somewhat more of her parliamentary skills and her poise. She'd always wanted to be a "spokesmodel," but, until now, no one had ever given her the chance.

"Welcome," she said. "Please be s-seated. It's t-time to get st-started." Her stutter was as much the result of the under-cover-operative-for-hire aspects of her job as of performance anxiety. She'd never been under this much pressure in her life. A flourish from the PA system—drums and trumpets—quieted the crowd's hellraisers, and ushers pointed stragglers to their seats.

"Welcome," Suzi Pybus reiterated. Several pockets of guests cheered, wolf-whistled, leered. "Mambo-Ra Flix and Kix thanks you for attending our Go-Go Promo Rally. Our main purpose here today"—pausing to mentally review the script she'd already memorized—"is to make you happier Salonikans: happier and better."

"Baby, you can't get any better than the Dickybird already is!" shouted someone, probably "Dickybird" himself.

Dome-filtered sunlight ricocheted off the windshield and body metal of a sports car parked behind second base. The flyer that the ushers had passed out promised that the vehicle was a prize in a coming giveaway.

On the wings of Suzi Pybus's stage stood fifty members of a men's glee club. Wearing blue jumpsuits, with their arms behind them and their hands clasped smartly in the smalls of their backs, they looked as much like a drill team as a choral group.

"It was really smart of you to hang on to your invitations and to show up here today," Suzi told the crowd.

"Really smart!" chorused the glee club.

"Some of those who received Mambo-Ra Flix and Kicks invitations probably just threw them away," she continued. "How sad."

"How sad!" crooned the glee club.

"Many of you here today will receive free tickets to important sporting events: the Final Four of the NCAA basketball tournament, the Indianapolis Five Hundred, the World Series, the Super Bowl."

"Super Bowl!"

"Others will win free automobiles, vacation cruises, stereo and video equipment, collectible firearms, computer systems, and, maybe best of all, tax-free cash."

"Tax-free, tax-free, TAX-FREEEE cash!"

"And some of you will even have a chance to be paid extras in a brand-new Blackguard Pictures release featuring the exploits of the newest UC stalwart, Count Geiger!"

On the electronic scoreboard in center field, above a lavender and mint-green parachute tent, flashed an animated sequence showing Count Geiger subduing four would-be EleRail muggers. Piano music, as if for a silent film, issued from the sound system.

The Hemisphere's guests did the Wave, first horizontally and then vertically.

"In fact, here to tell you exactly what each of you is likely to win is Count Geiger himself! The *real* Count Geiger! Let's give him the welcome he deserves!"

Xavier, who'd been sitting out of sight beside the water cooler in the Cherokees' dugout, walked onto the field in his

Count Geiger costume. He mounted to the stage and, to the cheers of the crowd, accepted a peck on the cheek from Suzi Pybus.

"You did well, Suzi," he whispered. "Curtsy to everybody and hustle to the dugout before things turn nasty."

Waving and smiling, Suzi obeyed. A tunnel in the dugout led to the Cherokees' locker room, where OBI agents would receive Suzi and escort her safely out of the stadium.

"Good afternoon," said Xavier, leaning into the microphone.

Crooned the glee club, *"Good good GOOOOD afternoon!"*

"If you have your nontransferable invitation, verified by the Hemisphere's security people at Gate Twelve, lift it over your head so that I can see it."

Five hundred people were transformed by this command into giddy game-show contestants. Swaying in the aisles, woofing like berserk Clevelanders, they waved their invitations.

"You're all under arrest," Xavier said.

The glee club's members produced automatic rifles from behind their backs and pointed them at the crowd. The ushers on hand also drew firearms.

"GOTCHA!" cried the scoreboard, visually.

Animated fireworks exploded on the board: rockets, whirlagigs, cascades. This would have been fine after a Cherokee home run, but today it smacked of tasteless electronic gloating. From the crowd, Xavier fielded a mixed broadcast of emotions: panic, bewilderment, ignorant amusement, abject surrender, even fulminating rage. Well, the scoreboard hadn't been his idea. . . .

All the stadium's level exits and gates had been sealed. There was nowhere for the arrested felons—pokeweed junkies, pokeweed dealers, fences, bail jumpers, bagmen, car thieves, parking-ticket dodgers, parole violaters, prostitutes, extortionists, tax evaders, muggers, etc.—to run. As the scoreboard had crowed, they'd been gotten. Caught. Nabbed. *Stung.*

Under Xavier's command (the distress of the duped simplified the remping of their private guilts), a complex processing formula was activated.

Violent sorts and escaped lawbreakers trudged in sullen files into a stadium tunnel where paddywagons waited to take them to Salonika's central station house. Some of these felons hung their heads and shuffled. Others cursed or flailed angrily, inviting verbal rebukes and billy-stick proddings. Eventually, all those accused or already convicted of violent crimes were ferried away, reducing the sting victims' numbers as well as the danger of a collective uprising.

As Count Geiger, Xavier remped all the arrestees to determine specific crimes and levels of hostility toward authority figures. He then recommended that the least dangerous felons—tax evaders, call girls, parking-ticket dodgers—report to the pavilion of phony silk and white PVC tubing in center field.

"Why?" a CPA type demanded cringingly. "What're you all going to do to us out there?"

"Do you play a musical instrument?" Xavier asked.

"No."

"All right. Do the scale for me. You know, *do re mi fa so la ti do.* Sing it, though. Don't just speak it."

"Do re mi fa . . . so la ti do," sang the CPA type.

"Very nice." To Officer Sturgis, the policewoman recording tent assignments on her clipboard, he said, "Voice lessons." To the CPA type, he said, "Center field. You'll rehabilitate through voice lessons. Six weeks' worth. Or until you've mastered the second tenor's part in Verdi's *Rigoletto."*

"What? The second *what?"*

"Go on. You'll have an excellent instructor, courtesy of Skye University's School of Music, with major funding from a retropunk group on educational hiatus, Smite Them Hip and Thigh, and generous though lesser contributions from Uncommon Comics and the management of both First Stringers and P.S. Annie's."

The CPA type, along with several other minor lawbreakers, hiked under guard to center field. Beneath the canopy out there, he sat on a folding chair to take instruction from a professional voice coach and music historian. Other members of the same group set to work composing songs, playing the xylophone, or memorizing the librettos of musical comedies like *South Pacific, My Fair Lady,* and *Gypsy.* The noises from beneath this tent lasted for three hours, a spirited mongrel cacophony.

Elsewhere in the Hemisphere—namely, left and right

fields—other lawbreakers began their own surprise rehabilitations. One group (left field) strove to learn either painting, calligraphy, or cartooning. Another group (right field) tackled the rudiments of scriptwriting for stage, film, or TV, or else took acting lessons. All those assigned to a tent received their assignments from Count Geiger, who remped each felon to determine who should go where: the music, drama, or visual-arts pavilion.

Not everyone apprehended had conspicuous creative or performing talents. Thus, Xavier, already prepared for that contingency, had reserved a number of community-service jobs in the arts for anyone unable to sing, paint, draw, dance, act, compose, or play a musical instrument. After today's session, at which the "no-talent" types would simply observe and absorb, the city would find them weekend and evening jobs—salary-free—as custodians in art galleries, stagehands for little theater groups and local puppetry workshops, instrument toters for the Salonika Symphony Orchestra, and jacks (or jills) of all trades for any other valuable artistic enterprise in greater Salonika.

"Good day's work," Xavier told Officer Sturgis, the cop toting the clipboard. "It went like clockwork."

"Yeah, but we release these crims on they own recognizance at fo'. Betcha we never see 'em again neither."

"They'll be back." Surveying the tents in the outfield, Xavier said, "Mark my words, Officer Sturgis. They'll be back. I remped them. All of them."

"Well," said Officer Sturgis. "Ain't you the stud?"

52

In the Cutting Room

Either because the vacuum tubes had not a clue or were still struggling to shore up their evidence, WSSX did not break the story on any weekend news program that Xavier Thaxton and Count Geiger were the same human being. That honor belonged to Alex Meisel and the *Salonika Urbanite.*

Xavier's newspaper ran the story on the front page of Monday morning's first edition. Indeed, the entire front page was devoted to the identity and exploits of Count Geiger, for the other major headline trumpeted the sting in the Hemisphere. This operation had rounded up a total of 516 bad dudes and dudesses in a right-back-at-you con for which more than half those receiving "invitations" had fallen like chumps.

On an interior page, Count Geiger received even more press, as if he needed it, in an interview that Xavier had given Metro/State reporter Alex Meisel.

Xavier Thaxton was Count Geiger. Count Geiger was a hero. And from the premises of this strange syllogism it followed that Xavier was a hero. To many of the *Urbanite*'s readers, this conclusion did *not,* however, seem to follow—not when you factored in the critic on bilious display in "Thus Saith Xavier Thaxton." *That* guy wasn't Count Geiger. He was an opinionated Scrooge, his heart in a vise, his balls in an elastic sling.

Xavier stayed home Monday morning, for Grantham had

fired—no, had *let him go.* Maybe he should have been in hiding. On the other hand, the Mick was still in school, and he had stayed home to simulate an air of normalcy, insofar as anyone with a bad case of the Philistine Syndrome and a hero's costume for underwear could do that. The kid deserved some consideration.

Maybe, Xavier thought, I should've warned him that the top was about to blow off. . . .

The telephone rang.

Xavier let an answering machine take the call. The caller was Donel Lassiter, but Xavier was too alienated from everyone at the *Urbanite* to pick up and talk to him. Unlike the stalwart who had masterminded and supervised yesterday's massive sting, Xavier felt volitionless, empty, sere.

"Mr. Thaxton—Xavier—my God, you're Count Geiger. It's easier to believe you're a stalwart than to accept the fact you're not my boss anymore." After a pause: "Are you there? I don't blame you for letting the tape run. You're probably going to be busy leaping buildings and outrunning locomotives. It's just such a revelation, and such a loss, everything I've learned. It makes me remember and reevaluate so much. The way, once upon a time, you saved Bryan at that ball game. Your fondness for Shaw's *Man and Superman.* The way you survived the Bowman assault . . . Xavier, thanks for, you know, mentoring me. It's a shame the Powers That Be're axing you. 'Thus Saith the Count' would've looked good on the Op-Ed page. Goodbye. Stay super."

There were other calls, including a message from Bari: *"Oh, Xave, I'm so sorry. If you want to talk, I'm here."* Later, a proposition from a bodysuit fetishist, a come-on from a woman named Tiffany-Fawn, and some crank calls from teenagers. At noon, Xavier resignedly unplugged the phone.

On Tuesday, there was another article in the *Urbanite* about Xavier's startling double identity, an editorial praising him as a culture critic and a crime fighter, and a column by the *Urbanite*'s resident humorist, Red Neckerson, Jr., arguing that when Tim Bowman tried to shoot Xavier, he was committing, at least potentially, "brain childicide." Bowman had created the character Count Geiger, Xavier had taken on that role, and Bowman had allegedly tried to undo his creation with a handgun. His trial for attempted murder was only days away.

I became Count Geiger completely only *after* Bowman had shot me, Xavier thought. Neckerson's an idiot.

The telephone, if plugged in, rang and rang. So that evening, Xavier and the Mick each packed an overnight kit and a few changes of clothes and sneaked away to spend the next few nights in Bari's atelier. Xavier wore his Suit again, as underwear, to protect himself against the Philistine Syndrome and to hedge any need to reassume his Count Geiger persona.

"I'm sorry your newspaper outed you, Xave," Bari told him that evening in her central loft.

"Twice," Xavier said, at last comprehending some of the anguish of the waiter from Zapotec's and Zooey's Place.

"You can stay in the old cutting room off the main studio for as long as you like. It may be noisy some nights. Howie and I are working on our urban-camouflage ensembles for fall: brickwork, mirror-glass, smog-and-chrome, stucco-and-street-litter. It's hard cutting on the bias and preserving the integrity of our camouflage patterns."

"I'd guess so," said Xavier, baffled.

The Mick stayed one night in Bari's atelier, then moved back to Franklin Court to be closer to Ephebus Academy. As for Bari, she took pains to show Xavier what she, Howie, and Marilyn Olvera were designing but also to keep her employees out of his hair.

Xavier made that easy for her by holing up in the cutting room with his word processor, keyboarding rehabilitation plans and suggestions to the various seminar directors of Operation Uplift, which was busy reshaping the lives of hundreds of petty felons. The next step would be to carry Operation Uplift to the hard-core lawbreakers and heretofore incorrigible recidivists in Oconee's state and federal prisons. After that, it wouldn't be a bad idea to get to work on the violence-mongering captains of the military-industrial complex.

One afternoon, Bari, Marilyn, and an army of support personnel took hundreds of finished garments and garments-in-progress to a Woman's Wear International trade show in the convention center at Salonika Plaza.

While they were gone, Xavier worked long and hard producing Operation Uplift materials. He didn't hear footsteps in the main studio until the intruder laying them down stood in the doorway to the cutting room, a back-lit silhouette.

Xavier jumped a foot. So much for stalwartly sensitivity and prescience.

"Sorry to frighten you," the shadow said. It ghosted into the room, revealing itself as that retrohippie hunk, Howie Littleton. Clad in a brickwork tunic and wide ash-grey trousers, he was eating a floury chunk of bread. The bread reminded Xavier of a doorstop upholstered in a stucco-and-street-litter swatch. "I thought maybe we could parley. All right?"

"Parley?"

"That's why I'm here." Littleton thrust his bread chunk into a tunic pocket and sat down cross-legged near the step stool on which Xavier's laptop rested. "Have you heard the news?"

"Which?"

"The city council has rewritten the law permitting 'no one but the real living Count Geiger' to wear Count Geiger's trademarked UC clothes. The new statute says 'no one but the honorable Salonikan, Xavier Thaxton.' You're on the books, guy."

"You came to tell me that?"

Littleton looked down. "Not exactly. I came to tell you that it's killing me, your living here."

Feeling increasingly hexed and persecuted, Xavier listened as Littleton haltingly confessed the depth of his affection—no, *love*—for Bari. Today he'd come to the demoralizing realization that if his foremost rival for Bari were a man recently disclosed as a living stalwart, he had no chance. What could even a talented human being—Littleton stammered the phrase "a m-mere mortal"—do to compete with a bona fide stalwart?

Briefly, of course, Xavier had felt at a similar disadvantage, viewing himself as a poor specimen in comparison to the handsome, well-built, and youthful Littleton. It was hard not to guffaw—at Littleton, at himself. Littleton was jealous of *him,* terrified that Bari would never be either his wife or his lover.

"Have you declared yourself?" (Xavier wondered if he had just shifted into abnegatory Cyrano de Bergerac mode.)

"No," Littleton said. "For a long time, see, she thought I was gay. Goes with the t-territory."

"Do you think she cares about you? As her likely beloved, not just as a crackerjack fellow fashion designer?"

"Maybe. She no longer thinks I'm gay. I've got that far."

"What do you want me to do?"

Littleton seemed taken aback. "I don't know. I just thought I should tell you. It's so . . . well, tremendously unfair, your new advantage."

"How so?"

Again, Littleton seemed nonplussed. "I—I—" he attempted. "Well, because I can't h-hope to c-compete."

Xavier regarded him appraisingly. "Take a lovelorn header out a window, Mr. Littleton."

"Wh-what?"

"Your own logic leaves you no other options. Adopting the same premises, I have none either."

"That isn't—"

"Go away, Howie." Xavier returned his eyes to the screen of his laptop. "Just go. Now."

It took a while, but finally Littleton got up, turned around, and shuffled dejectedly out of the cutting room.

About an hour later, Bari, Marilyn, and a loud army of cutters, needleworkers, models, dressers, camera men, and chichi hangers-on returned from the convention center. By the giddy talk audible to him in his cloister, Xavier could tell that Littleton, not all that surprisingly, was among the celebrants.

53

On the Radiation Sickness Ward

"Come with me," Dr. Di Pasqua said. "Now."

Teri-Jo followed her boss. They rode a service elevator to the basement, then walked through the tunnel linking the Miriam Finesse Cancer Clinic to the vertical labyrinth of Salonika General. The hospital wasn't their native territory, and they navigated it like country-club bluebloods caught out on foot on the commons of a city housing project.

On the eleventh floor, Dr. Di Pasqua led her to a suite of examination rooms and treatment areas that signs and locked doors declared off-limits to visitors. He buzzed them through the first door and turned to face Teri-Jo when they were behind it.

"That room there"—he nodded toward a quarantined sick bay—"holds sixteen innocent people, adults and children, suffering from acute radiation poisoning. It appears that—"

A gaunt young man with bony wrists and hands, and a melancholy smile, came out of a tiny office down the hall. "Nurse Roving," he said, approaching them. "I'm Joe Lusk, from REACTS, the Radiation Emergency Center in Oak Ridge. Dr. Di Pasqua's told me about you."

Dear God, thought Teri-Jo. It was unimaginable that Di Pasqua had represented her favorably. He was as productive of compliments as a sycamore tree is of cherries.

"We've invited you over because working with radioactives

is a specialty of yours," Dr. Lusk said. "One of our patients said that the machine from which he took the source material responsible for this unfortunate accident was a Therac 4-J."

Teri-Jo's heart did a fluttery double-clutch. "Yessir."

"Would you like to see the patients?" Dr. Lusk asked her.

"Yessir. Definitely."

Dr. Di Pasqua told Teri-Jo to return to the clinic as soon as possible, and excused himself.

"We'll wear masks and gowns, more for the patients' protection than our own. There's a minuscule degree of danger because these people are radioactive. They're weak emitters of the radioactivity with which the cesium 137 in the Therac 4-J contaminated them. A bigger danger, by far, is that we'll infect them."

"I understand, Dr. Lusk."

In an antechamber, they put on stiff white paper coats. They masked and gloved themselves, and exchanged their street shoes for plastic slippers. The sick bay beyond the quarantine markers was divided into several separate bed spaces by movable curtains.

Whispering as they walked the corridor among these units, eight to a side, Dr. Lusk said, "The people you see here received as few as a hundred, to as many as six hundred, rads from the cesium-137 cake that Larry Glenn Wilkins shared out to their birthday guests. Mr. and Mrs. Wilkins and their daughter will almost certainly die. Four or five more, including several little girls and Mr. Wilkins's sister-in-law, Claudia Burrell, may be doomed too, but, for them, there's a degree of hope. The others, less badly exposed, will get out of Salonika General alive, but may develop cancer later on.

"This isn't Three Mile Island, of course, or even another Plant VanMeter radiation release, but it's a radiation-related disaster unlike any experienced in the United States to date. Its potential for inflicting death, and for contaminating the Oconee countryside, is as great as anything to which Consolidated Tri-State has so far subjected our region. The only applicable precedents are accidents that occurred in Latin America, one in Juárez, Mexico, in 1984, and another in central Brazil in '87. It doesn't sit well with me that we've allowed the unthinkable to happen here."

"I help with the treatment and diagnosis of cancer patients," Teri-Jo said. "Our clinic has radiologic technologists, and we use radiation in one form or another on a daily basis, but here—here I'm at a complete loss."

She could see into the make-do cloisters that the staff on this special ward had rigged for their patients. In the bed in one of them lay a three- or four-year-old girl, a little blonde connected to an IV hookup. Her face was so blistered that she looked like an overzealous sunbather.

"Please," Dr. Lusk said. "Just talk to Larry Glenn Wilkins."

"Of course. Why?"

"Dr. Di Pasqua says that last winter you contracted with a firm to haul off an antiquated Therac 4-J."

"That's right."

"Dr. Di Pasqua couldn't remember the name of the firm. Do you?

"Environomics Unlimited."

"Good. Come on." Dr. Lusk led Teri-Jo into the chamber where Larry Glenn Wilkins lay with an IV hookup like the little girl's. His face wasn't blistered as badly as hers, but his hands looked raw and greasy, like lightly barbecued pork. (Someone had applied a pain-killing salve to them.) His eyes were cloudy, pale-blue marbles. He had lost some hair, and the insides of his arms were discolored by arabesque bruises.

Dr. Lusk did the introductions. Without meeting their eyes, Mr. Wilkins said "Hey," and turned his head aside on the pillow. It had to be disturbing, Teri-Jo realized, to meet someone new who was masked like a common thief.

"Mr. Wilkins opened the source capsule," Dr. Lusk said.

"I'm dead meat," Mr. Wilkins murmured. "Dead meat."

"The cesium 137 irradiated him directly for an extended period, but, even worse, he and some of the other victims ate birthday cake sliced by hands contaminated with the powder. In other words, they *ingested* the radioactivity."

Teri-Jo's brow creased. Was it wise—was it kind?—to talk so clinically in front of Mr. Wilkins.

"Medical *glasnost,*" Dr. Lusk said. "We've agreed to discuss this matter with utter frankness. Mr. Wilkins wants us neither to soft-peddle the prognosis nor to mollycoddle him."

"I've kilt my family too," he said. "My wife. My baby girl."

Dr. Lusk turned to Teri-Jo. "We've given them all Prussian blue. Are you familiar with Prussian blue?"

"No, I'm not."

"It's an iron compound that binds cesium 137, capturing it from the bloodstream. Prussian blue facilitates cesium's excretion, but we've got to get the cesium out before it moves too deeply into the tissues or irreversibly damages the blood marrow."

"Can't you do a marrow transplant?"

"Too late," Mr. Wilkins said. "Too freaking late."

"Only if you've got a matched donor and the other organs aren't too far gone," Dr. Lusk said.

"Ha!" Mr. Wilkins said. Drained, he closed his eyes.

"I'm trying to get an emergency approval from the Food and Drug Administration so that Mr. Wilkins's doctors can use an experimental recombinant growth factor made by Behring, a German pharmaceutical company. The stuff's called GM-CSF, or granulocyte-macrophage colony-stimulating factor. It's a hormone that prompts the bone marrow to produce neutrophils and monocytes that wipe out hostile microbes."

"Dead meat," Mr. Wilkins mumbled. "Three goners."

"In the meantime, his doctors are countering with antibiotics, cell infusions, and fresh blood. Listen, Mr. Wilkins, Nurse Roving wants to tell you something." Dr. Rusk looked at her. "Describe the Therac 4-J to him. In detail."

Teri-Jo described the Therac 4-J to Mr. Wilkins.

"That was it," he said, opening his eyes. "That was it."

"How did you get it?" Dr. Lusk asked Mr. Wilkins.

"Elrod bought it off this pair of spades from Satan's Cellar. Hard-assed dudes. I thought they was gonna kill me." He looked at Teri-Jo. "Guess they did, huh?"

"Do you remember their names?" Dr. Lusk asked.

" 'Say Yes to Droogs.' They called themselves Droogs. Brother Droogs. I don't remember the guys' names—only that."

"That's a help," Dr. Lusk said. "Thanks."

Teri-Jo felt like a gate-crasher. "Can I do anything for you?" she asked. "Check your medication? Read to you?"

Mr. Wilkins regarded her as if she had just had an epileptic seizure. But he said, "Have 'em put me, Missy, and Carrie-Lisbeth in the same goddamn room."

"That can probably be arranged," Dr. Lusk told Teri-Jo.

They left Mr. Wilkins and the treatment bay. Outside, Dr. Lusk told Teri-Jo that she had given him circumstantial proof that the Therac 4-J implicated in the Philippi accident was from her cancer clinic. Also, he now had three names to investigate: Environomics Unlimited, Elrod Juitt, and, strangest of all, Brother Droogs.

"What else can you tell me about Environomics Unlimited?"

Teri-Jo recounted the radium-waste pickup and the more recent episode of the Therac 4-J's removal. "I have a working telephone number, and all the paperwork for both the state and the NRC is in our files somewhere, along with the clinic's canceled checks."

"Give me the number. There's a criminal irregularity— maybe even criminal intent—in the firm's disposal methods. We need to reach them before the media alert them to the exact degree of the hot water they're in."

Teri-Jo returned to her office in the cancer clinic. Dr. Di Pasqua was sitting at her desk with his hands folded on her blotter like a pair of tarantulas frozen in flagrante delicto in an obscene act. Her squeamishness, she realized, probably had less to do with his hands than with his smug invasion of her space.

"Mrs. Gainsboro helped me remember the name of that disposal company," he said. "I found their number in your Rolodex."

"Good. I came to get it for Dr. Lusk."

"I telephoned them," Dr. Di Pasqua said. "I assured the young snot who answered that we'd never do business with them again, that we didn't appreciate the disrepute into which their slipshod, even criminal, disposal methods were likely to plunge the premier cancer clinic in the Southeast. I gave him a piece of my mind."

"Not really," Teri-Jo said.

A questioning shadow swept over Dr. Di Pasqua's self-satisfied face. "I could have left it to you to do, Nurse Roving, but I did it myself."

"Well," Teri-Jo said, "that was mighty thoughtful."

Aware of something vaguely mocking in her tone, Dr. Di Pasqua countermanded the smile that he had intended to give Nurse Roving. Women, he decided, were unfathomable creatures, fickle sphinxes in debilitating thrall to the moon and the tides. . . .

54

A Lethal Diversion

Alex Meisel exploded a bombshell that made Salonika—indeed, everyone in Oconee—forget the news that Xavier Thaxton was Count Geiger, and that his crusades against both crime and kitsch would continue despite the newspaper's disclosure of his real identity. The story relegating the Thaxton/Count Geiger affair to virtual irrelevance was word that a radiation accident unassociated with Plant Van Meter had occurred in early May in Silvanus County. It was a long investigative story, which Xavier read with disbelief and a troubling, if still faint, taste of guilt:

At least 20 residents of Philippi, a farming community 60 miles west of Salonika, were stricken with radiation poisoning last week when a junkyard worker, Larry Glenn Wilkins, 29, dismantled the core of an obsolete radiation-therapy device improperly disposed of by a firm calling itself Environomics Unlimited.

Wilkins, his wife Missy, 24, and their 4-year-old daughter Carrie-Lisbeth, along with 13 other people, are undergoing treatment for acute radiation poisoning in an isolation ward in Salonika General Hospital.

Ironically, the treatment machine responsible for their contamination was once in operation at the Miriam Finesse Cancer Clinic, an affiliate of Salonika General. The machine's source, or energy supply, contained about 1400 curies of cesium 137, a radioactive substance with a half-life of 30 years.

Meisel's story defined *curie, half-life,* and *therapy device.* It chronicled the steps by which, according to a reconstruction of events by representatives of the Oak Ridge-based agency known as REACTS, a used Therac 4-J had reached the out-skirts of Philippi from the cancer clinic. Meisel detailed the events leading to tragedy at a birthday party near Philippi, and he profiled a dozen different actors in the story.

Dr. Edward Di Pasqua, 52, director of the cancer clinic, delegated the task of disposing of the clinic's radi-ation waste—"radwaste," in industry jargon—to Head Administrative Nurse Teri-Jo Roving, 39, a veteran em-ployee. Six years ago, Mrs. Roving used Environomics Unlimited to dispose of some used radium implants left in high-priority protective storage by Dr. Di Pasqua's predecessor, the late Dr. Wyman Huguley.

"I was desperate when I found this firm to carry out the disposal," Mrs. Roving said. "No licensed site any-where would agree to accept our radwaste. Then EU ap-peared, as if by magic, and handled all the necessary arrangements. At that time, Environomics Unlimited seemed a godsend. Literally."

From the beginning, Mrs. Roving believed that EU was licensed by the Nuclear Regulatory Commission and the Oconee Department of Natural Resources to trans-port and dispose of nuclear-waste materials.

"No company would handle radwaste unless they were licensed," Mrs. Roving said. "And we tracked our ship-ment of lead-encased radium needles from Salonika to Memphis to Wichita to Denver—all the way to the Han-ford Atomic Energy Reservation in Washington State. Except for the fact that the company used an unmarked truck, everything appeared to be in order."

However, a recent check with officials at the Hanford site revealed that they have never heard of Environomics

Unlimited, nor do they have any record of a delivery
from the Miriam Finesse Cancer Clinic on the date specified by Mrs. Roving and confirmed by signed documents
on file at the clinic.

"If that's true," Mrs. Roving said yesterday, "we have
no idea where the men purporting to be licensed haulers
took our radwaste or where they finally chose to dump
it. Frankly, that horrifies me."

Mrs. Roving hired Environomics Unlimited again, in
late October of last year, to dispose of the obsolete Therac 4-J that a clinic janitor had found stored in a basement utility closet. This device, like the radium needles
encased in lead cylinders, was a holdover from the direc-
torship of Dr. Huguley. Dr. Huguley performed more
than competently as a physician, former colleagues note,
but took a catch-as-catch-can approach to record-
keeping.

"It was a natural thing to turn to Environomics Unlimited again," Mrs. Roving said. "They'd been lifesavers
before, and I felt reasonably confident that they would
dispose of the Therac 4-J swiftly and safely too. I never
imagined that our machine would show up on the property of an unsuspecting family in Silvanus County.
Never. I don't understand it."

At this point, Mrs. Roving was emotionally unable to
answer further questions. Dr. Di Pasqua says that he in-
tends to pursue an in-house investigation of his own, "to
discover the facts and to fix responsibility for the machine's improper disposal."

When a chief executive rants about discovering the facts and
fixing responsibility, in most cases that person is looking for
a head to chop. Here, Xavier had no trouble deducing the
identity of the likely guillotine victim. Meisel's story then
shifted from its tight focus on Environomics Unlimited to the
impact of the accident on Silvanus County:

"The lot on which the Wilkinses had their home," said
Dr. Lusk yesterday, "is severely contaminated. The core
of the therapy machine was kept in a bedroom closet.

The machine itself was more or less destroyed in a fire initiated by Mr. Wilkins's efforts to cut it down for scrap with a welding torch."

According to Dr. Lusk, agency teams in helicopters equipped with radiation detectors have been overflying every part of Silvanus County where they can logically expect to find hot spots.

"These flights began the day after Dr. Woolfolk alerted us to the danger," said Dr. Lusk. "So far, our teams have found three contaminated dogs, a radioactive pig, and a wide array of 'dirty' furniture, cars, and money. Plastic-suited men on bulldozers are scooping radioactive soil into concrete-lined drums for shipment to nuclear-waste disposal sites."

The cleanup, according to REACTS, should be nearly complete within another two weeks. The well and the septic tank on the Wilkins's property have been tested and do not appear to be dangerously contaminated. The trailer itself may have to be destroyed, though, along with a 1990 Toyota go-truck. Additional radioactivity exists in the homes of some party guests, but Dr. Lusk observes, "We are dealing with it expeditiously."

Late yesterday, a raid on the suspected offices of Environomics Unlimited by Salonika's police and a team of FBI agents came up empty-handed. Agent Henry Avila believes that the company consists solely of an office with a telephone and a small fleet of unmarked vehicles parked elsewhere. The building housing the office is in an apartment complex owned by HighSites Realty Corp. of Miami, Florida.

"I think someone had been there shortly before we arrived," Agent Avila said. "It was almost as if the occupants had been tipped that we were coming. It appears to us that Environomics Unlimited may have been just one of a number of cheapjack outfits to work their scams from this office."

The accident in Philippi is unprecedented in the United States. Most Americans expect any radiation-related disaster to have its origins either in the nuclear-power industry or in the military arsenals of our nation.

According to Dr. Lusk, medical-related radiation mishaps are not that uncommon in other parts of the world.

"Algeria, the Republic of China, and Mexico have all had accidents of this kind," Dr. Lusk says. "They have involved dangerous quantities of such substances as cobalt 60 and cesium 137. For something like that to happen here, though, detailed regulations for the shipment and disposal of nuclear-waste products have to be wilfully flouted or ignored."

Dr. Lusk said that officials at Salonika General and the Miriam Finesse Cancer Clinic have not behaved unethically. "I *do* fault them for failing to check out Environomics Unlimited more carefully." The government investigation of the company continues. . . .

Xavier digested Meisel's story while sitting cross-legged on his pallet in Bari's cutting room. He was relieved to find that he had ceased to be Topic Number One on the *Urbanite*'s roster of hot local stories, and appalled by the cruel irony of the catastrophe that had befallen the Wilkinses and their friends.

A type of accident that had altered Xavier's life (giving him, via the Suit from SatyrFernalia, stalwartly powers) had meant only terrible sickness and death for others.

Where was the justice in that? Why was he a living superhero when the Wilkinses were dying, in one of the most excruciating ways that he could imagine, as radiation victims? Their ignorance and innocence, along with an outrageous chain of events totally beyond their anticipation or control, had betrayed them. The greatest injustice was that these events and qualities had betrayed them to the grave. . . .

Bari entered. It wasn't yet nine. She was up early. She wore a pair of blue silk sleeping shorts and a matching short-sleeved top, with a pale blue monogram, that exposed her svelte belly. She looked tasty as an éclair. Arms akimbo, she gazed down at Xavier with a moue at once endearing and hostile.

"Did you tell Howie to take a header out the window?"

"Come on, Bari. With all that's—"

"Did you?"

"Actually, I told him to take a *lovelorn* header out a window. He's hopelessly enamored. Of you."

"And you, secure in your self-surmised position of preference, suggested that he kill himself?"

Xavier stared at Bari's enameled toenails. Patiently, he said, "I told him to take a lovelorn header out a window. A metaphorical brush-off, like 'go fly a kite.' Not, Bari, a real invitation to splatter his brains all over the pavement."

"A metaphor? A brush-off? A macho dare, cynically thrown down from the lofty heights of your stalwartliness."

"Is that what Howie told you?"

Bari shifted her weight. "Xavier, think of me no longer as your lover and certainly not as your affianced."

"*Affianced.* A lovely word."

"I regard our relationship—our special relationship—as over, Xavier. We've stagnated as an 'item,' in both gossip-column and personal-growth terms, and I'm sick of your inability to find yourself under the ugly mask of this Count Geiger . . . *creature.*"

Xavier felt as he had the instant after being shot: stunned, empty, frightened. "You'll want me to go, I suppose."

"Of course not. What does that have to do with anything I've said? Stay until it's safe for you to go. You're not underfoot. So you can stay as long as you need to."

Xavier thought that maybe now she would soften a little, enough to give him a peck on the nose, a semiconciliatory smile. Instead, brow creased, she strode purposefully back into the atelier's central loft.

"Thanks," Xavier whispered after her.

55

"Only Connect"

The phone's stopped ringing off the hook every time I plug it in. Folks're starting to get the message, Uncle Xave."

"Meaning?"

"You could like come home. If you wanted."

"I could, couldn't I?" Xavier said. It surprised him to hear the Mick make this suggestion both uncoerced and unprompted. He had feared that Mikhail, left to himself, would convert his condo apartment into a high-rise replica of Salome's or P.S. Annie's; that the Mick would take every step conceivable to prevent him from recrossing its threshold. Instead, Thomas Wolfe notwithstanding, the Mick was inviting him to come home again. Xavier hesitated before replying. He missed Mikhail. That was indisputable. Phil and Lydia's son was his nephew. Family. It was important that they share the same household, and *not* a household belonging to an unrelated third party.

Xavier spoke into the receiver: "I'll tell Bari."

Bari was out again, discussing with the chief buyer at the biggest department store in Salonika Plaza the delivery of winter merchandise. There were a dozen workers in the studio's main loft, all under the supervision of Marilyn Olvera and Howie Littleton. Xavier had a special telephone line in the old cutting room, an instance of Bari's thoughtfulness that he would repay by vacating the premises and giving the space back.

Living with Bari—in her business headquarters cum bu-doir—hadn't been as romantic as, shortly before Christmas, he would have supposed. It'd been *anti*romantic, like pitching camp in an EleRail station at rush hour. Now, in fact, they were kaput as a couple, loverly has-beens. How had that happened?

When Bari came home that evening, Xavier was packed and ready to go. He had been in her windowless room so long—five days, but it *felt* longer—that he imagined himself as pale as a sheet of computer paper, the physical antithesis of a stalwart. At least they could powwow in private, in the studio proper, for Bari had dismissed her staff at five, an hour or two earlier than usual, and Howie had retreated to his own flat to brood upon the events that had brought his foremost rival under his beloved's roof.

"Xavier, I've given it some additional thought, and I think it would be good if you *did* move out."

The only appropriate response was laughter, but the only civil one was curiosity. "I guess it would. Why now? Am I interfering with daily operations?"

"Far from it. In fact, everyone works harder because you're here. They're afraid you're my spy. I told them that if any of them leaked your whereabouts to the media, or to anybody else for that matter, I'd let them go. Fire them. All of them, if it came to that. Every last one."

"So what turned you around?"

"Howie's bothered that you're here. He can't focus. And so his creativity's fallen off."

"He loves you, Bari."

"That's not very convenient for either of us. I should either can him or marry him, but I don't like my choices."

"So you've reconsidered and decided I should leave?"

"Yes, I have. The radiation accident at Philippi—"

"Ah. You've heard of it."

"In passing, yes. Anyway, media preoccupation with that story has reduced the glare on your own predicament. I don't think your leaving now will work a major hardship on you."

"So also saith Mikhail Menaker."

"Despite his retropunk antiintellectualism, he's a bright kid."

"Well, I think we should begin seeing other people, anyway."

Bari smiled. "Speaking for myself, Howie's out, as I've tried to let him know, him not being a stalwart. That leaves me a pretty narrow field. The Decimator? Mantisman? Where do these fellas hang out when they're not putting the hurt on evil-doers?"

"At First Stringers, I think, having the grilled chicken-breast sandwich and a sedate gander at 'Masterpiece Theatre.' Never fear, Bari, I'll leave. It's undoubtedly for the best."

It startled her to see Xavier emerge from the old cutting room with his gear already packed and his laptop in hand. She frowned at him bemusedly.

"Goodbye," she said.

He wanted to kiss her, a valedictory gesture, but her perplexed look wouldn't allow it, and he too said goodbye.

Dressed as Count Geiger—minus, now that publicity had made it superfluous, the uncomfortable hood—Xavier paid a visit to Teri-Jo Roving at the Miriam Finesse Cancer Clinic. He popped in unannounced, primarily to thwart her or Dr. Di Pasqua's opposition to his coming, trusting implicitly that his identity as the Count would melt any opposition once he was on-site.

Amazingly, or maybe not so amazingly, it did, and Mrs. Roving's secretary buzzed him into her office as if he were the President of the United States. Mrs. Roving sat at her desktop computer. His glittery materialization seemed neither to nonplus nor to delight her. Before looking up at him, she deliberately finished whatever task her computer was helping her perform.

"Good morning, Mr. Thaxton."

"I'm here in my inescapable capacity, or persona, as Count Geiger," he said gently.

"Is that supposed to be a joke? A sly reference to the people dying next door of radiation poisoning from our misdirected Therac 4-J?" Mrs. Roving squinted at Xavier. "A judgmental dig?"

"No'm. I just wanted to talk to you."

"Join the crowd."

"I know what you mean."

Mrs. Roving's squint softened a little. "Maybe you do. We're each having our hour under the microscope, aren't we?"

"Yessum. In fact, the accident at Philippi rescued me from

a few extra minutes on an ever-hotter glass slide." He thought that Mrs. Roving might ask him to sit. She didn't. He had convinced her that he wasn't a finger-pointing zealot, but until he revealed himself fully, she intended to keep him on probation, to give him a bit more time to substantiate his reputation as . . . well, as a Stalwart for Truth. He said, "I may be able to help you. If, of course, I could ask you a few questions—"

"You'd be joining the nonexclusive ranks of Dr. Di Pasqua, the FBI, the city police, the NRC, and the state and national media. I'm going to yell at Mrs. Gainsboro for letting you in. Loud and long."

"It's the uniform."

"Ask your questions. Hurry up and ask."

"Alex Meisel's story in the *Urbanite* said that the clinic twice employed Environomics Unlimited to dispose of radwaste. True?"

"Dead on." Mrs. Roving grimaced. "Cruel pun unintended."

"We know what happened to the Therac 4-J, but the paper stated that the whereabouts of the radwaste from EU's first job—if the Hanford site didn't receive it—are still unknown. That suggests that another major radiation hazard for the public could exist, an accident in waiting, perhaps right here in Oconee again."

"I understand that all too well. It's especially likely since Environomics Unlimited apparently didn't see fit to haul the Therac 4-J any farther from the cancer clinic than a warehouse in Satan's Cellar. For all I know, they could have dumped the junk from that first job right off a city bridge into the Chattahoochee."

"How was the radium waste shielded? In what form did EU haul it away?"

"The used radium implants were plugged into lead cylinders and stoppered with more lead. There were heaps of cylinders. Frankly, Dr. Huguley let them back up on us."

"Are there any more here at the clinic?"

"Radium-waste cylinders? No. For the last ten years, we've been using cesium implants. Cesium's the stuff that's killing the Wilkinses and those other poor people from Silvanus County. If you break a cesium needle, it doesn't release a radioactive gas the way a broken radium implant releases radon."

"Do you dispose of cesium the same way? In lead cylinders?"

"Yes. Except that we keep better records than we did under Dr. Huguley, and the pharmaceutical company that supplies the implants is responsible for taking back the used needles and disposing of them itself. It's licensed to do that. A good system. It spares you the agony of finding an authorized disposal site and a company willing to haul your radwaste there."

Xavier was sweating. The amorphous suspicion that had plagued him ever since his visit to the Hazeltons' place—the vague hunch that he'd seen illegally dumped radwaste on the land next to Plant VanMeter—eroded into a hard nugget of certainty. Perhaps if he hadn't impersonated Alex Meisel to get into Deke Hazelton's house, he would have revealed this suspicion to the authorities months ago. Figuring mentally, he realized that that still would not have been soon enough to stop Environomics Unlimited from picking up the Therac 4-J and depositing it in an ill-secured warehouse in Satan's Cellar, but it might have been soon enough to spread the news that a potentially dangerous piece of medical equipment was unaccounted for and that anyone stumbling upon it should (1) avoid monkeying around with it and (2) report its location to the NRC or the Oconee Department of Natural Resources. Had he done that, the folks dying of acute radiation poisoning in Salonika General might have escaped victimization. Xavier suddenly felt as, in the days before buying the Suit, he often had when listening to Mahler or contemplating a Vermeer: feverish, weak-kneed, queasy. Mrs. Roving's office did a stately but disorienting wheeling maneuver around him.

"May I sit down?"

Mrs. Roving, whom he had not even seen leave her desk, had a hand on his forehead. "You feel like you're about to *fall* down. My Lord, you're on fire. Here." She helped him to a chair.

"I know where your misdirected radium waste is," Xavier said. "Apparently, it's been there for six years."

"Where?"

He told her.

"How do you know that?"

"About two years ago, radon seeping from the canisters dumped into that stream made me sick with the intermittent, and decidedly peculiar, ravages of the Philistine Syndrome."

"Come again."

Xavier gave a feeble, dismissive wave. "More recently, the radiation percolating through the water altered my cell structure and my body chemistry—on a second exposure to it—so that I became the augmented being known to this city as Count Geiger. I became a living stalwart."

"Sounds like wild-eyed balderdash to me, Mr. Thaxton—I mean, Count Geiger. A second exposure to radiation would have probably just made you sick again. Depending on its intensity, it could've even killed you."

"I wish it had." Xavier observed that his self-pity provoked nothing more sympathetic than an eyeball roll. *"Sometimes* I wish it had," he corrected himself. "No mere physical augmentation can make up for a person's moral poverty, Mrs. Roving."

"I'll write that on the flyleaf of my Bartlett's.—How long have you known about the radwaste up there? How do you know you're not jumping to a wild-eyed conclusion?"

"Cockroach," he said.

"What?"

"Cockroach, the six-legged racehorse now running for Hallelujah Stables in Tennessee. Also, a three-eyed catfish."

"Would you like a glass of water? A cold compress?"

"I've never seen Cockroach, except on television, but I did see the catfish, Mrs. Roving. It looked like the get of a feverish surrealist's supercharged imagination. It was bioluminescent, it glowed, it watched me. Swear to God."

"Calm down, Mr. Thaxton. Relax a few minutes."

Xavier leaned his head against the wall and took a series of slow, deep breaths. His nausea abated. His flushed skin clocked down to a cool off-white.

Without leaning forward again, Xavier asked, "Who actually did the pickups for Environomics Unlimited? Could you describe these people? Do you remember their names?"

"I've answered—I've *tried* to answer—these questions at least twelve times each."

"Then let's make it a lucky thirteen. This is extraordinarily important."

"Two men came the first time. Two men came the second time. Only one man came both times. He was the one in charge. He was the driver of the unmarked truck."

"Who was he?"

"I don't know. He called himself . . . *Will.* That's about all I know about him. His first name was Will. I signed the transfer forms. He didn't. He and his partner—a kid the first time; a Latin-American fellow, nicknamed Gooz, the second—took our stuff and skedaddled."

"What did he look like, this Will?"

Mrs. Roving broke into a glib sing-song recitation that Xavier interpreted as annoyance with the number of times she had had to repeat it: " 'A white guy ten or twelve years older than me. A thin but paunchy, brown-eyed, rusty-haired white guy in company overalls. The second time he was here he didn't seem to feel too well. He knew enough to boss his partner around, but he wasn't a college graduate. Or so I'd wager. He *may* not've graduated high school. Will: a middle-aged, thin but paunchy, brown-eyed, rusty-haired white guy.' End of portrait."

"Why don't you think he was a high-school graduate?" Xavier was now leaning forward in his chair, like an outer-directed *The Thinker,* alert and attuned.

Mrs. Roving hesitated, as if none of her many interrogators had thought to ask this particular question. "He had this countrified Oconee way of talking. An accent that was recognizably rural but at the same time all his own. Distinctive, now that I think about it. A signature way of talking."

"Give me an example."

That presented a challenge. Mrs. Roving stared at the picture molding above Xavier's head. "He said *awl* for *all.* He said *arf* for *off.* He said . . . my God, he said *thonks* for *thanks.* It was as if he sometimes got his *a*'s and *o*'s mixed up, sort of. Sart of, I should say." She chuckled reminiscently. "I remember that even better than the way he looked."

"I know who he is," Xavier said, startled by the insight that Mrs. Roving's testimony had triggered. "Son of a bitch."

Mrs. Roving said nothing. She waited.

"Sorry," Xavier said. "Wilbon T. Stickney. Will is Wilbon T. Stickney. The only other man in the world—so far as I know—victimized by a form of the Philistine Syndrome."

As if Xavier had just spelled the final word in a competition that over several hours had eliminated every contestant but him, Mrs. Roving shut her eyes. Xavier felt relief, gratitude, a fresh sense of mission. Stickney was even more responsible for the fate of the Silvanus County's radiation victims than he. Knowing this didn't entirely alleviate his guilt, but it eased it. It also gave him a solid reason to put Operation Uplift on hold. His attention belonged to matters of higher moment, greater urgency.

"Tell whoever needs to be told about the radwaste cylinders in the Hazeltons' stream," Xavier said. "The Hazeltons, the NRC, the state, whoever. I've got to find Stickney."

"Maybe you'd like to meet the Wilkinses," Mrs. Roving said. "I could probably arrange it."

"Yessum. It's just that—"

"Wait too long and . . ." The consequences of waiting too long twisted before him like a trio of hanged innocents.

As Count Geiger, Xavier paid his visit to the radiation ward on the eleventh floor of Salonika General. Mrs. Roving acted as his tour guide. Gowned and masked, they stopped at the bedside of each medicated and IV-dependent patient. Most were too drug-befogged or ill to talk. Dr. Avery, the specialist treating these people, had determined that all but four had suffered damage to their internal organs and hematopoietic systems that was too severe to allow bone-marrow transplants. Despite the poor prognosis in every case, the FDA had refused to grant an emergency approval for the experimental hormone, GM-CSF. Xavier, along with Mrs. Roving and Dr. Avery, cursed the obstinancy and shortsightedness of the FDA. Given that several of these patients were otherwise doomed, why did the agency manifest such a hard-hearted scrupulosity?

The Wilkinses—Larry Glenn, Missy, and Carrie-Lisbeth— lay in beds in an enlarged cloister at the end of the set-apart sick bay. Mrs. Roving said that Carrie-Lisbeth was critical; she could die in the next day or so, possibly within hours. If Dr. Avery determined that the time was shorter rather than longer, he would privately advise his staff to put Carrie-Lisbeth behind her own set of curtains again. The trauma of watching their only child die, even if medication eased her going, was hardly one that he relished inflicting on the parents. Of course, they would suspect the worst when she was moved. Consequently, he had frequently second-guessed the wisdom of uniting the family at all. Mrs. Roving shared these doubts.

As the initiator of this gone-awry kindness, she had often second-guessed herself.

Larry Glenn, as he had understood on his first day in the ward, was also a short-term patient; in his own words, a "goner," "dead meat." Purple lesions tattooed his face, chest, and arms. Patches of his hair had fallen out. Cell infusions that he had received to counter hemorrhaging had puffed him up like some weird antierotic sex doll. Despite measured administrations of the iron compound Prussian blue, Larry Glenn remained radioactive. Internally, he was bombarding himself toward a state of irreversible nonbeing that he would probably find a merciful release. Missy Wilkins shared his condition and his prognosis.

The only patients who might eventually walk out of Salonika General were Claudia Burrell, Ricky and Lulah Stamford, and two of the four little girls who, at Carrie-Lisbeth's party, had blithely adorned themselves with cesium glitter. In store for them later, though, was a question-mark state heavy with disease possibilities (cataracts, leukemia, colitis) and a diminished life span.

No one—*no one,* Xavier reminded himself—walked away from violent radiation exposure unscathed. The idea that such exposure could boost one's abilities, as it so often did in the contemporary popular arts, was totally bogus, a brutal lie. Xavier, of course, was the unhappy exception that proved the rule.

At Larry Glenn Wilkins's bedside, Xavier touched his surgical mask and said, "I know you probably can't tell this, but I'm Xavier Thaxton, also known as Count Geiger. I'm sorry—terribly sorry—about what's happened to you."

"Me too." Mr. Wilkins's irises appeared to be floating on the edema of their vitreous matter. "You gonna be in a movie, Count?"

"I doubt it. I mean, *I* won't. My character might. Uncommon Comics owns the character. But I'm not an actor. I mean, I'm just a person. Like you. Like any other."

"If there's a movie—" Mr. Wilkins—no, Larry Glenn—ran down. His bug-eyed gaze drifted off to another part of the room. Even lying prostrate, his body seemed to be buoyed on the uncharted ocean of his radiation sickness.

"Yes?" Xavier prompted. "If there's a movie . . . ?"

"If there's a movie," said Larry Glenn, focusing sidelong on his wife and daughter, "go see it for us, hear? That's a flick I'd probably really get off on." He smiled at Xavier. "Yeah."

56

Antinoolity Cubed

H ow're you gonna find this Stickney turkey?" the Mick asked. "He coulda moved. He could be dead."

"He hasn't moved," Xavier said, rummaging through a kitchen drawer for the Greater Salonika Telephone Directory. "He was here to haul off the cancer clinic's radwaste six years ago. He was here last summer to pick up that Therac 4-J treatment machine, and he was inhaling salad gas in P.S. Annie's right after you pulled your stupid cut-and-run stunt."

"Hey." For the Mick, a pretty low-key bristle.

Xavier ran his finger down the last tight column of names on a page of *S*'s. There were eleven Stickneys in Greater Salonika, but no "Wilbon T." among them. (The closest was a "Willie Ray.") He tossed the open directory onto the counter and dug deeper into the utility drawer for an older book. The Mick sidled over to study the listings in the book on the counter.

"You could like call some of these Stickneys here and ask for Will or Wilbon T. Whoever answered, if they said 'No,' you could scope their voice to see if they was lying."

"Mikhail, my powers don't function all that reliably over Ma Bell's phone lines. What would probably happen is that I'd alert Stickney something was up and he'd bolt. No thank you." Xavier found a three-year-old directory (preserved for the addresses and numbers scribbled on its cover) and plopped it open atop the book already on the counter.

Mikhail edged between Xavier and the counter and scanned the Stickneys with his index finger. The ebony nail at the tip of this finger halted and tapped on the paper. "Here he is. 'Stickney, Wilbon T. 1117 Jarboe Lane.' Big deal. The number ain't good no more. The gasser probably moved away years ago."

Jarboe Lane was across the Chattahoochee in Satan's Cellar. (Of course.) It could be a valuable lead, though. An old neighbor of Stickney's might remember him. Somebody over there might even know where he'd moved. If he'd moved. If Xavier's questions didn't panic his chosen informant and trip a cascade of alarms up and down the ghetto grapevine. To Xavier, a visit to Stickney's old address seemed worth the risk and aggravation. He had to find the man. No doubt about it.

"Why don't you just give the police his name?" the Mick said. "If he's like this hopelessly blown weed-eater and repeat offender, they may already know where he is. That'd save you a wade through the Cellar too."

"What? Mikhail Menaker—the outlaw bohemian, the regent of retropunkdom—wants me to query the morally bankrupt enforcement agency of our fascist establishment? Do my ears—"

"Yeah, yeah: 'deceive me?' " The Mick refused to be baited. "Never mind. But if you're going, I'm going with."

Xavier started to protest, but caught himself and relented. As new as he was to Salonika, the Mick was instinctively savvy about the Cellar. As a conscientious guardian, Xavier ought to forbid him to come. Dangers abounded over there, motiveless slayings were commonplace—but whereas an expedition of one might end in injury or failure, the two of them together might accomplish their mission and return to savor the triumph.

Xavier had a small brainsquall. "Bring your Geiger counter, and I'll be happy for you to come."

"My Geiger counter? My Geiger-Müller counter?"

"Yes. Bring it."

"Why?"

"Never mind. Do you want to come or not?"

"Affirmative," the Mick said. "Absodamnlutely."

Even with a map of Satan's Cellar (from the Salonika Tourist and Convention Center, with tiny fire decals to denote

danger areas and crime hot spots), Jarboe Lane was no cinch
to find. It was squeezed between two alley thoroughfares not
far from the trolley terminus, among a jumble of flophouses,
flea-bag hotels, and fly-by-night pawnshops. At least three
times before identifying it, Xavier and the Mick strolled past
the cavelike entrance to Jarboe Lane: a cobblestone tunnel
barely wide enough for a hot-dog cart. It was gloomily awninged over with mildewed canvas scraps.

Farther in, the narrow, tread-worn stairs of 1117 Jarboe
Lane took Xavier and the Mick up one flight of steps to a
turn-around office occupied by three Oriental males playing a
board game with plastic wedges and pielike plastic counters.
The door to this office was open. Xavier and the Mick entered.
The gameplayers ignored them: Xavier was dressed in the
same outfit in which he'd emulated a Smitten at the Grotto
East, and the Mick's weird getup was *de rigueur* in the Cellar.

" 'Which comic-book stalwart is known to his mundane
colleagues at Zoo Salonika as Leonard White?' " the thinnest
young man of Asian ancestry said, reading the question from
a card that he immediately returned to its box.

"The Snow Leopard!" a second Asian man shouted. *"Hai
yah!"*

"Does Wilbon T. Stickney live here?" Xavier asked the
group.

"Never heard of," the card reader said.

"Maybe," said the man facing the open doorway.

"Down hall on left," said the man who had just called out
the answer to the thin Asian's question.

The Mick seemed puzzled by the multiple responses that
Xavier's question had elicited. "Mr. Stickney doesn't have a
phone listing at this address anymore," he said. "He hasn't for
like maybe three years."

"Probably not here then," the thin Asian said.

"Out on business call," the man facing them said.

"Sleeping with TV on," the third man said. "Always sleeping with TV on. Apartment five."

Neither of the other two men rebuked their companion for
giving out this information.

"Thanks," Xavier said. He and the Mick did an about-face
and walked down the boxy hall to the specified apartment.
Outside its door, they could hear strangled crowd noises, undoubtedly from the television. Above that sound was the bro-

ken nasal trilling of an announcer, his every word unintelligible. The Mick stepped up and knocked. Once. Twice. A third time, even louder than before. At last, he tried the knob. It rotated in his hand. The door drifted inward, flooding the hallway with frantic audio and a grainy wash of televised light.

Stickney, if it *was* Stickney, wallowed in a beat-up recliner, an Edsel-era La-Z-Boy probably scavenged from Goodwill Industries. He lounged facing the blue-grey TV screen, nodding before it as if disastrously poked out. The room stank of salad-gas fumes and of sweat-soured clothing.

"Phieuw," the Mick said. "Gaawghh."

Xavier soft-shoed over the threshold behind the Mick and closed the door. Had he been a thief or a hit man, he could have walked off with all Stickney's worldly goods or his bargain-basement life, if not both together. Who would have cared? Maybe Stickney was already dead. Disregarding the meager contents of the flat, Xavier crossed to the recliner to see.

It was Stickney, all right, the pokehead who—while sitting, no less—had accosted Xavier on his first visit to P.S. Annie's. He had an army recruit's haircut, a drowned man's bloated jowls, a sunburn victim's lobster-broil tan. The fingers that had seized Xavier's wrist in P.S. Annie's were flabbier now; they gripped the chair arm with an almost pitiable looseness. Under the flap of his brittle Oriental robe, Stickney's other hand basketed his groin. Xavier was about to jostle his shoulder when a sudden click and an insistent mechanical whirr halted him.

"Only the VCR," the Mick said. "The tape's run out. It's on like automatic rewind or something."

Xavier and Mikhail waited. They were doing homage to the rewind, Xavier realized, like Episcopalians hearing out a communion homily. When the process had completed itself, a softer click and a fresh whirr brought the tape's FBI warning against unauthorized copying wobbling into view.

The Mick said, "It's on like automatic replay too. Stickney's set it up on a kind of never-ending flashback loop."

The tape's opening titles appeared. It was a *Sports Monthly* compilation of clips from the career of the world's most inept heavyweight boxer, Rashid "Eggshell" Harrell. The clips were very brief: Harrell had never lasted more than three rounds in any official bout. He had had hundreds of fights, of which

more than twenty had ended with his ejection, over or through
the ropes, from the ring. A montage of these graceless exits
appeared. Mikhail, round-eyed and cavern-mouthed,
watched. Like a misfired Scud, Harrell repeatedly achieved
parabolic flight before crashing down into a different set of
ringside seats.

Xavier turned again to Stickney. "Mr. Stickney." He
squeezed Stickney's shoulder. "Mr. Stickney, wake up."

Stickney showed his eyes the way a KO'd boxer, under the
chin-lifting knuckles of a referee, slowly and involuntarily
shows his, his irises the sickly beige of used bath water.

"What?" he said. "Wha thuh?"

"Turn that off," Xavier told Mikhail. "He's not watching,
and who knows how long it's been on."

"Turn it off? But—"

Xavier gave him a look. Mikhail went to the set—it and the
VCR seemed to be the only fully functional pieces of equipment or furniture around—to kill the boxing tape. Immediately, the set's screen was a riot of flying phosphor dots. The
Mick clicked it off too.

Now, the only light came from a plastic night-light plugged
into the socket beside the La-Z-Boy. Molded to caricature a
naked adult female, the night-light glowed a warm vulvar
pink. A truly tacky item, Xavier thought. It embarrassed him,
and all the more for wholly monopolizing the Mick's attention.

"Turn on another light," Xavier said. "Right now."

The Mick shuffled to the kitchen and turned on the fluorescent above a sink stacked high with unwashed pie plates and
empty cans of spaghetti. Roaches had colonized some of these
cans.

"Stickney!" Xavier was saying. "Stickney, wake up!"

Stickney roused a little. His pupils, initially as large as
dimes, shrank to the size of typewriter o's. Then, belatedly
aware that his apartment had been invaded, he lurched forward, banging his chair's footrest down. In a groggy panic, he
stared around his lodgings.

"Who th' hell're you guys? Whad're you all doing here?"

Xavier put a hand on Stickney's arm to calm him and
introduced himself and Mikhail. "The door was unlocked," he
said. "The Mick and I would like to ask you a few questions."

" 'At 'uz stupid, leaving th' door unlaacked. Go on, then, and kill me."

"I don't want to kill you," Xavier said. "I want to know about Environomics Unlimited. Tell me about it."

"It's defunk," Stickney said, self-consciously rearranging his Oriental robe. "Or, leastwise, my jaab with 'em is." He began to sweat, profusely. "Aow! My toe! It hurts somepin orful!" Xavier glanced at Stickney's big toe. Twitching noticeably, it shone red, as if an angry wasp had injected it with venom. "It's th' gout! 'Nother damned attack!" Stickney peered past Xavier at the TV. "Where's my boxing video? Lissen, I'll 'clapse like a stove-in chimbley if thatere nephew of yours don't turn it back on. And I mean double damned quick too!"

Mikhail relished the opportunity. He tripped back into the living room to restart the video of Eggshell Harrell lowlights. Xavier made him turn down the sound, but the mere sight of Harrell stumbling about disoriented, bleeding from the ears, or landing on the ringside press table seemed to satisfy the Mick's curiosity and to alleviate Stickney's physical distress. His big toe had already stopped throbbing so vividly.

"I can't watch this garbage," Xavier said.

"Yeah. And I can't *not* wortch it."

"Radiation exposure caused you to develop your version of the Philistine Syndrome, didn't it, Mr. Stickney?"

"Philistine Syndrurm? What th' hell's that?"

"The chronic ailment that's got you tooting poke and indulging dozens of other twelfth-rate amusements to balance off the symptoms brought on by first-rate ones. Am I right?"

"I don't know," Stickney equivocated.

"Of course I am. Look around this place. The evidence of your attempts to counter the syndrome are everywhere." Xavier nodded at the framed drawings on the chipped wall behind the La-Z-Boy. Seven of the pieces consisted of penciled stick figures engaged in hard-to-identify consensual (or maybe not consensual) erotic (or maybe not erotic) acts. Clearly, though, Stickney had hoped that this inept homemade pornography (if that's what it was, and, yes, it seemed to be) would forestall at least a few of the unpredictable metabolic attacks triggered by his love of "classy" cutie-book photography. Meanwhile, the boxing tape, Xavier decided, was his serendipitous antidote to the physical depredations caused by "Hee Haw" and "Green Acre" reruns.

A search of Stickney's old-fashioned vinyl-record albums turned up a collection of barnyard sounds—hogs in rut—to counteract the toothaches, acne attacks, or diarrhea occasioned by listening to pre-Syndrome favorites, *Lefty Frizell's Greatest Hits,* say, or *Minnie Pearl Live!* Other illness-offsetting albums were by artists whom Stickney, before going to work for Environomics Unlimited, had probably despised: Engelbert Humperdinck, Luciano Pavarotti, Joni Mitchell, and Don Henley.

Other evidence that Stickney was taking his own approach to the treatment of his Syndrome was a plastic soda bottle full of flowers on a nearby table. The flowers included desiccated milkweed pods, dandelions, and cockleburr stalks. Stickney had arranged them with no pattern or skill, but they still looked pretty good.

Xavier knelt before Stickney, to block his view of Eggshell Harrell. "Working for EU, you often dealt with radioactive waste, right?"

Stickney struggled to see around him. "Not awl that orfun. Ee Yue was a partime jaab for jes' about ever'body who worked for 'em. If somepin else come up, we took it."

"The Miriam Finesse Cancer Clinic called upon you twice in six years to get rid of radwaste. The first time, you dumped the stuff into a stream in the Phosphor Fogs. You fudged your documentation to make it look like you'd followed NRC guidelines."

"Yeah," Stickney said. "Move over."

"He loses by a knockout. You've already seen it, God knows how many times. —Now, why did you hide that obsolete Therac 4-J in a warehouse on the far outskirts of the Cellar?"

"Are them'ere Silvanus County folks gonna die? Are they?" He had stopped trying to see the TV screen.

"Some will," Xavier said. "The young Wilkinses for sure, all three of them."

"Damn," Stickney said. "Lissen. We didn't know. What th' hell's a Therac 4-J anyhow? Gooz and me couldn't tell cesium 137 from cesspool overflow. It 'uz a accident, plain and simple, what happened to them poor crackers."

Xavier shook his head. "How many other times did you dispose of radioactive waste fraudulently?"

"Not awl that many, damn yur. Most o' th' time, we 'uz getting rid of pritty harmless shit, filling the woods up with broke-down equipment, used syringes, old drugs. 'Cept for six or eight other places, that chunky nurse's cancer clinic was th' only place that gave us hot crap to hawl. Swear to Gawd."

"Who's behind Environomics Unlimited? Who paid you?"

"I don't know."

"I think you do, Stickney."

"Mebbe I do. Trouble is, 'fie talk about it, I'll likely get kilt for spilling it out." He chuckled mirthlessly.

"Just like Larry Glenn Wilkins," Xavier said. "His reward for spilling out that deadly cesium cake. *Who paid you?*"

Stickney vented a sour sigh. "I don't care, nohow. It don't matter no more, 'fie'm dead or not. Dead'd be a blessing."

"Who?" Xavier insisted.

"F. Deane Finesse. He 'uz th' big cheese behind Ee Yue, Ink. He 'uz th' guy who wanted th' radwaste from six years back dumped upcountry next to thatere Plant VanMeter."

"Finesse?" the Mick said. "The big shot on the cancer clinic's board of directors? The prez of Uncommon Comics?"

"Swear to Gawd. Wunst, he paid me hisself. Paid me out cash on a sidewalk outside th' Hemisphere. Finesse it was, you'd better b'lieve it. He had a grudge on—mebbe still does—'gainst ol' Con-Tri."

"Holy schmoly," sidekickishly from the Mick. (Eggshell's taped swan dives had suddenly lost their charm.)

"I'm sick," Stickney lamented. "I'm as sick, in my own way, as them'ere Silvanus County folks. But who cares? Who cares 'fie die in this orful damn rathole?"

"Put your radiation detector on him," Xavier told the Mick, and the Mick obeyed. The counter began clicking like a caffeine-crazed secretary in a typing pool. "My God."

Xavier told the Mick to stick with Stickney while he went down the hall to telephone the city police, to report that he had found Environomics Unlimited's chief disposal agent. The Asians in the office were still playing their game. The thinnest Asian, who had won four more pie wedges, appeared to be gloating.

" 'What was the code name of the U.S. military's assault on

the forces of Panamanian dictator Manuel Noriega?' " the
man facing the door read from a game card.

"Operation Just Cause!" cried the gloating Asian. *"Hai
yah!"*

"Buffalo dung," said the third player.

As unobtrusively as possible, Xavier made his call and returned to Stickney's apartment. Stickney was asleep again. His
boxing tape was rewinding for the umpteenth time. The Mick
stared long and hard at the stick-figure pornography on the
wall. His eyes had begun to water. He pinched his nostrils to
ease the burn from the pokeweed stench and the stale acridity
of Stickney's B.O. He kept shifting his Geiger counter from
one hand to the other.

Xavier agreed that, yes, they could probably safely leave the
apartment even before the cops arrived: Stickney definitely
wasn't going anywhere.

In Jarboe Lane, Xavier and the Mick walked along medita-
tively: two shadows in a claustrophobic, starless tunnel.

"Finesse," the Mick said. "Betcha ol' Tim Bowman's gonna
love *that* piece of scandal."

Xavier, thumbs hooked inside the pockets of his jeans,
remped the neighborhood for hostility or danger. He registered none. The denizens hereabouts were unaccountably mellow.

"Boy, that place was the cheesiest," the Mick said. "I mean,
you'd have to be like a skidder with complete and utter antinoolity to camp there."

"Flamingos," Xavier mused. "A few plastic flamingos
would've perked it right up. . . ."

57

The Rap on Mr. Finesse

To few people but UC's employees and teenage fans like the Mick was F. Deane Finesse, over and above everything else, the owner and publisher of Uncommon Comics. To Finesse himself, the comic-book business was little more than a gratifyingly profitable sideline. Some, in fact, regarded him as the South's chief entrepreneur and his surname as synonymous with Salonika (although, today, if the prompt in a word-association test were *Salonika,* more would say *Bari* than *Finesse*).

According to the current received historical mythos, the city had begun as a trading post and river port established in 1788 by Phillipe Jean Yves Paul Finesse, one of several French volunteers with General Lafayette at Jamestown Ford, and elsewhere, during the American War of Independence. Today, then, Finesse's name was on everything in the city from street signs to pocket parks to cancer clinics.

The morning after visiting Stickney in Jarboe Lane, Xavier called the *Urbanite* and asked for Donel Lassiter. From Donel, he requested as much information—the "straight skinny"—about F. Deane Finesse as Donel could extract from the newspaper's files, computer or otherwise. He invited Donel to his Franklin Court condo that evening to discuss his findings. Donel arrived right on time. Moved, he hugged Xavier, and then the Mick, as if they had been freed after long prison terms.

Said Donel, "You really think Finesse is behind the accident in Silvanus County?"

"Yes. That and the deliberate misdirectioning of used radium implants to the Hazelton farm," Xavier said.

With a homemade milkshake in a plastic cup, the Mick wandered away from this talk to his room. Finals were coming up, and he was actually making an effort to prepare.

Donel told Xavier that the scuttlebutt at the *Urbanite* was that a clean-up operation on the Hazelton place would begin tomorrow. Preliminary tests on the section of Placer Creek identified by Xavier as contaminated showed that measurable traces of radiation were indeed present. An associate of Dr. Lusk's from the Oak Ridge Associated Universities had found gamma-radiation levels from one to ten roentgens per hour at and around the canister-filled rock pool in the creek itself. Water flow diluted these measurements, but drinking from or swimming in the creek, at least on Hazelton's farm, was potentially risky.

"Why would Finesse involve himself in a penny-ante scam like a misdirected radwaste shipment?" Donel asked.

"Lots of penny-ante scams, taken together, can one day amount to a sizable wad," Xavier said. "Come on, Donel—tell me what you have on Salonika's wealthiest citizen."

"Second wealthiest."

"Really? Who's richer?"

"Letitia Bligh Brumblelo, widow of Prather Brumblelo, founder and CEO of KudzuCo Enterprises."

"Oh," Xavier said. KudzuCo, an organization begun in the late 1950s, specialized in the processing and recycling of kudzu, the run-amok Japanese vine introduced as a soil-erosion measure and as fodder and forage for cattle. KudzuCo converted the leaves of this ubiquitous plant into everything from loose tea to attic insulation to shawls to wallpaper paste to complexion astringent to infield tarps to pet food to jeep fuel. KudzuCo had conversion facilities and subsidiary divisions from Louisiana to North Carolina.

So, to give Mr. Finesse his due, Xavier decided, it was hardly a knock to call him less wealthy than Prather Brumblelo's widow. KudzuCo was the thirteenth largest business in the United States, a financial colossus.

"Of course, Finesse is no bush leaguer himself," Donel said.

"In addition to Uncommon Comics, he owns,"—reading from a printout—"the Salonika Cherokees, Finesse Chemical, Goober Pride Foods, Cherokee Software, and Oconee-Oregon Transport Systems. He's also on the board of directors of dozens of foundations, libraries, public utilities, historical societies, and medical institutions, including the Miriam Finesse Cancer Clinic, which he dedicated to his mother's memory in 1959, six years after her death of ovarian cancer.

"Even more: He has partnerships in, or links to, the publishing and communications industry, the construction industry, corporate Hollywood, the pharmaceuticals industry, and, as you already know, the fashion industry. Uncommon Comics recently licensed Bari's of Salonika to make design use of the copyrighted costumes of some of its stalwarts for a line of ready-to-wear clothing, exempting, of course, the costumes of the Decimator and Count Geiger, the former because of its importance to the UC empire and the latter because the Salonika city council has passed an ordinance forbidding anyone to impersonate you.

"Finesse has been married four times," Donel rattled on, still consulting his printouts. "He is currently a bachelor. He has two sons and four daughters, all of whom are grown and living somewhere other than Oconee. In the winter, Finesse dresses exclusively in black. On the opening day of baseball season, however, no matter the temperature, he begins wearing either white-linen plantation suits or lightweight seersucker ensembles, often with a Panama hat and a silver-tipped walking stick. He often escorts—*dates* would overstate his level of commitment—women two, three, or even four decades younger than he. Over the past several years, he's spent as much time traveling abroad or networking on the West Coast as he has overseeing his financial empire here in Salonika.

"The world at large knows F. Deane Finesse just as you and I do, Xavier, as a curmudgeonly sports enthusiast and a high-profile humanitarian businessman. Ex-wives and disgruntled ex-employees, though, depict him as tight-fisted and petty, a control freak with a two-ton ego and featherweight verbal skills. He has succeeded, his detractors allege, by projecting a charismatic aura of menace and willpower. In conversation, his speeches are either purposely gnomic or totally nonsensical, depending on your view of the man. It occasionally seems that he needs a translator." Donel stopped, looking up from the stack of printouts to see what effect his words were having on Xavier. "What else did you want to know?"

"Oconee-Oregon Transport Systems. What's that?"

"OOTS? It's a trucking line. A cross-country trucking line. From Oconee to Oregon, and back again."

"Does Finesse have anything to do with Environomics Unlimited, the bogus hazardous-waste-disposal firm?"

"Nobody but Wilbon T. Stickney, the guy you sicced the police on, seems to know anything at all about Environomics Unlimited—if it even exists. And Stickney, you'd be interested to know, is in a secure area of Salonika General, being treated for a kind of radiation poisoning and an undetermined piggyback ailment that kept the police from jailing him."

Xavier mulled this. A fresh indictment of the sensitivity marking his behavior of late, as if that quality undergirded his entire personality. He should have stayed with Stickney until the police arrived. He should have realized from Stickney's nodding head and slurred speech—from his grogginess and stink—that he needed medical attention. Instead, he had gotten himself, and the Mick, out of Satan's Cellar as fast as possible.

"Donel"—Xavier beating back these self-recriminations—"does Finesse have any reason to wish Consolidated Tri-State ill?"

Donel flipped through the stapled printouts on his lap. "Until construction began on Plant VanMeter, he was a member of Con-Tri's board of directors. The president of Con-Tri had him removed from the board shortly after company stockholders thwarted an attempt by Finesse Chemical to acquire a majority interest in Con-Tri. The year you came to the *Urbanite* from Atlanta, Finesse left Con-Tri's board of directors. He left it kicking and screaming, but he left, and Con-Tri, not long after his departure, broke ground for Plant VanMeter."

"Ah."

The Mick rejoined them, carrying his milkshake cup in one hand and a dog-eared copy of *The Selected Prose and Poetry of Jonathan Swift* in the other. " 'Nor do I think it wholly groundless,' " he read, " 'that the Abolishing of Christianity may perhaps bring the Church in Danger.' I don't get it." He slurped at his cup. "I mean, is this guy for real or like a total poked-out charl?"

"Charl," Xavier said, feeling uncomfortably charlish himself. "Charl this, charl that." He appealed to Donel. "Where do these retropunk upstarts get the term, anyway?"

"The Ten Commandments," Donel said. *"Ben Hur. Major Dundee.* Or, a little closer to home, *Chiefs."*

"What?" the Mick said.

What? Xavier himself was thinking. Then the answer opened out like a night-blooming flower, and he had a vision of Tim Bowman, inexplicably armed, shooting three bullets into him at point-blank range. Sweat popped out on Xavier's upper lip, a line of tiny liquid domes.

Charlatan Heston.

"I'd like to meet Finesse," he said. "What are my chances?"

"Finesse is in town," Donel said, "but he doesn't exactly run an open-door operation anywhere. What can you offer him?"

"Nothing. An accusation, I guess."

"Then your chances are zilch. He won't want to see you."

"Grab a hang strap," the Mick said. "Have Bari get you to him, Uncle Xave. Would she be an instant in, or what?"

Xavier looked at the Mick as if he were the prototypical kid genius who's just blown a fuse: "No, she wouldn't, Mikhail. We're kaput. You know that. Bari may not want anything to do with me."

"Get real, unc. She's a good guy. She'd be tickled to help you bring a charl like old F. Deane down."

"Even if it killed Bari's of Salonika's fashion-franchising of Uncommon Comics characters?"

"Sure. Doin' good's a bigger kick for her than making money. Don't you know that?"

Xavier could only shake his head.

The Mick continued to astonish: "And, hey, you keep forgetting that Uncle Xave is also Count Geiger. Even if Bari can't or won't do the intros, Finesse'd *love* to meet him. I mean, the sorry old fart like gets his ego revved rubbing hips with fellow hotshots and media stars. Besides which, Count Geiger's really just a big-name field hand on the old UC plantation. You could even talk business, if you stalled out on other stuff."

"Thank you, Mikhail," Xavier said sincerely. "Apply that same level of brain power to your finals and you'll ace them all."

"Uh-uh. Get me past that second book in *Gulliver's Travels* and Swift and me don't exactly mesh."

58

Skybox

Less than two months into the season, the Salonika Cherokees had an unheard-of, for them, .632 winning percentage. They'd also just begun an important homestead against the Dodgers. Xavier and Bari sat high above the tawny diamond of the infield and high above the soothing fan-shaped green of the outfield—where, not long ago, Count Geiger and the Salonika city police had carried out a successful sting.

Tonight, Xavier had a fresh perspective on the ballpark, on his unasked-for role as an urban stalwart. He and Bari were guests in F. Deane Finesse's skybox, a ritzy bulletproof bunker tiers and tiers above home plate. Along with Finesse, they occupied the middle three wingbacks in a row of seven posh chairs in front of the skybox's window. Behind them, as Xavier had noted earlier, the rear wall was lined with photographs of past and present Cherokee players, each black-and-white photo alternating with a full-color action portrait of a UC stalwart. Legendary center fielder Moses Hammacker, for example, stood between an $E = MC^2$ poster and another of the DeeJay throwing a 45-rpm record like a discus. Little Vin Caputo, meanwhile, seemed to be fielding a fungo batted by a club-wielding Warwoman. (Bizarre.)

Finesse, tricked out in starched seersucker and old-fashioned suspenders with brocaded roses on the elastic webbing, was playing the magnanimous host. He spoke charmingly to

Bari, confidentially man-to-man to Xavier, making pronouncements like "It's no good winning if a loss would've
up-spirited everybody more" and "A stitch in nine's better
than a hitch in the trenches." Over and over, he sent his polite
black waiter, Linzy, back to his silent, even darker barman,
Geoff, for fresh cocktails, clean napkins, and new servings of
finger food, from tissue-thin cold cuts and cheeses to spicy-hot
toothpick sausages.

The atmosphere was one of casual formality. Casual in that
Finesse was relaxed and jovial. Formal in that the other men
in the skybox, not only Linzy and Geoff but also a pair of
prissily dressed young white guys, to whom Finesse did not
even bother to introduce Xavier and Bari, were so clearly at
his total disposal. The white guys, across from each other near
the back, were eyeing the crowd for any possible menace.
Bodyguards, of course, even if they looked like a pair of
uptight CPAs.

"Glory!" Finesse yelled. "Another leg hit for Newton!"

It was just the third inning, but the score was already 4–1,
Cherokees. Vilified for years in the *Urbanite*'s sports pages as
the architect of his team's unending ineptitude, Finesse was
hugely enjoying its possession of first place in its division. That
an ex-employee of the paper—Xavier Thaxton, alias Count
Geiger—was on hand to witness the latest chapter in the ongoing miracle only heightened his pleasure.

The Cherokees were winning consistently. That proved that
all those nitpicky sportswriters were ignorant shits. It had
taken a decade, but at long last the verdict was in.

Xavier was happy for the team's fans, but utterly indifferent
to Finesse's stumblebum bliss. Bari, herself no baseball fan,
was equally unmoved by the upturn in the team's fortunes.

"The pennant clincher," Finesse said. "When do you all
think it'll be? Care to lay down a bet on the day, Count?"
From the beginning, Finesse had insisted on calling Xavier
Count, perhaps because the title elevated Xavier to the lordly
peerage but also subtly reminded him of his debt to Uncommon Comics. "Come on, you all, lay me a wager."

"I have absolutely no idea," Xavier said aloud. "You
wouldn't make me bet an uneducated guess, would you?"

"Sportswriters do. All the time. *All* the time." He appealed
to Bari. "Come on then. Pick a day, Bari honey."

"I hate baseball," Bari said. "Even when it's exciting, it's boring. That isn't nonsense, it's true. The only reason I'm here, Mr. Finesse, is so that you and Xavier—"

"The Count," Finesse corrected her.

"So that you and the *Count*"—Bari smiling half-apologetically at Xavier—"could meet."

"And we have," Finesse said. "And it's historical, our run-in here. And if you're bored, Bari child, you can leave with no fear of bruising my feelings. Feel free."

"Oh no," Bari said. "I'm staying. What happens between you two fellas ought to make up for all the aimless crotch-tugging and tobacco-spitting down there."

Crossing her miniskirted legs, Bari sipped at the murky amber orangeness of her Manhattan. She could go, but her departure would violate some crucial tenet of her Suthren sense of decorum (in a way that devouring Xavier erotically on the back seat of a taxicab, once upon time, had not). So she stayed, frowning down on the between-innings antics of the team mascot, a costume-party Cherokee who led cheers from atop the dugout and made ritualistic fun of the umpires. Glancing sidelong across Finesse's chair, Xavier saw that Bari was having a hard time maintaining even her charade of aloof interest in the game. The tension of their reunion, he felt, also played a role in her distraction.

The Dodgers were at bat. Their first two hitters had grounded out. Now the third batter was up, with the count on him stalled at 3–2 after a tedious run of foul tips.

Bari, Xavier saw, had set her drink on the floor. Now she was hugging herself in the vast wingback, her knees drawn up and her head lolling against its rear cushion. She looked like a sleepy waif at an overlong adult party.

Seeing Bari that way, Finesse cupped her knee with one hand and winked at Xavier. Xavier tried to remp him. Was there lust in his apparently avuncular, but oddly ambiguous, behavior toward Bari? Or malice in his heart toward Xavier? Xavier got nothing back from Finesse but combers of bonhomie, as if his enjoyment of the game were drowning his deeper feelings in waves of psychic energy and a deafening tidal white noise.

Every inning, the Cherokees' lead grew by a run or two. Soon, Finesse was talking earnestly to Xavier, leaning over to share impersonal confidences, humidifying Xavier's space with a mist of exhaled scotch and the medicinal reek of throat lozenges. He congratulated Xavier for his recent heroics, including the sting in the Hemisphere ("Another honest-to-God gut-check win"), and he noted that on its six o'clock news WSSX had attributed the arrest of the Environomics Unlimited "con artist" ultimately responsible for the disaster in Philippi to Xavier's clever detective work.

"Plus you made a brave phone call from Stickney's hell-hole apartment building. The paper said."

"Nothing brave about it," Xavier said. "The men in the front office posed about as much danger as a coven of piano teachers."

"But you and yore little brother—uh, nephew—whatever he is—you fellas went into the Cellar. Right?"

"Yessir, but—"

"Yessirbutt, yessirbutt, yessirbutt." Finesse's singsong was supposed to be friendly mockery. "You did it, didn't you? Went in there after dark and all? So yessirbutt *what?* Come on now. Don't false-modesty all over yorese'f, Count. You got the guy who caused that radiation accident, right?"

It surprised Xavier how angry this boorish badgering, under the guise of admiring solicitude, made him. "Actually," he said, "the guy 'ultimately responsible' for the screw-up in Philippi may have been you, Mr. Finesse."

Finesse's lower jaw dropped like the hinge on a hot-dog bun. He closed his mouth and cocked his head as if appraising a counterfeit painting.

"Mr. Stickney told me you were his boss," Xavier accused. "He said you once personally handed him his pay."

"That bastid," Finesse said. "That two-bit stoolie bastid. A dadblamed liar. A dope fiend. A pokehead." With each epithet, he thumped Xavier on the chest. "A blame-shifting small-time crook. B'lieve a thing he says 'n' you're as sick as he is, Count."

"I believe he's your dupe. Your designated fall guy."

So big grew Finesse's eyes that their grey-flecked green irises seemed primed to drop into the bags dissolutely pouching them. He looked over at Bari, who was still asleep. He noted the positions of his bodyguards. Side by side at the leather wet bar, Linzy and Geoff were watching the game on closed-circuit television. Xavier saw that Finesse had made a rapid 360-degree assessment of the situation. He shifted into remp mode

again and reflexively lifted his arm to ward off Finesse's surg-
ing anger.

Finesse seized Xavier's forearm, levered him out of his
chair, and shoved him into the skybox's long tinted window.
Xavier struck the shatter-resistant polymer, rebounding from
it so that he was facing not only Finesse but also the bodyguards and barmen.

Geoff and Linzy tried to ignore what was going on, but the
bodyguards drew down on Xavier with guns that had been
holstered under their coats—two CPAs with lethal Desert
Eagle automatic .357 Magnums equipped with baffled sup-
pressors.

"Hold it, Mark. Hold it, Bud."

Retreating from his near-ballistic rage, Finesse put a finger
to his lips and nodded at Bari, as if killing Xavier were forbidden because the noise would wake her up. He certainly wasn't
afraid of Xavier, the so-called living stalwart. And Bari . . .
Bari was an overworked couturière in need of her "inspiration
rest."

"You had Stickney misdirect at least two radwaste ship-
ments," Xavier said, feeling a curl of sweat slither down his
spine inside the near skintight lamination of his Suit. "The
Therac 4-J ended up in Silvanus County where—"

"Shhhhhh," Finesse hissed, waving a hand and looking
down at the playing field. "Damn you, son, *shhhh!*"

"—twenty unsuspecting people where contaminated. Several years ago, you had Stickney and some other fool dump
radium-implant charges on Deke Hazelton's property, not far
from the reactors at Plant VanMeter."

"Sweet Jesus!" Finesse said. An opposition homer had triggered this outburst, not Xavier's synopsis of Finesse's alleged
criminal activities. Two antlike figures in Dodger blue jogged
from base to base ahead of the home-run hitter. On the electronic scoreboard in center, an animated caricature of the
Cherokee pitcher shed sweat and tears. "Damn, damn,
damn!" Finesse muttered.

"You're the ranking member on the cancer clinic's board of
directors," Xavier said. "When you finally learned from Dr.
Di Pasqua about Mrs. Roving's trouble getting rid of Dr.
Huguley's radwaste, you had someone telephone her posing as
an officer in Environomics Unlimited. Arrangements were
made, and Stickney dumped the stuff in Placer County, as

near to Plant VanMeter as he could get without giving himself away to Con-Tri's security force. The point of your—"

"Dog it! Can you b'lieve sech se'f-destruction? Morrison's th'owing the bastids rabbit balls. DAMN!" Beside Xavier at the window, he gazed down on the sight of the second Dodger in a row to park a slow change-up and to circle the bases.

Despite these back-to-back homers in the top of the eighth, the Cherokees continued to lead, 10–5. Maddeningly, Finesse found the prospect of a Dodger comeback a bigger personal affront than he did Xavier's reconstruction of his role in illegal waste dumping.

"Look," Xavier said. "At the expense of a cancer clinic named for your own mother, you made a small, almost meaningless profit. You put the general public in jeopardy—the Hazeltons and their neighbors, an ignorant drudge named Wilbon T. Stickney. In that first case, if it *was* the first, you must have wanted to make Plant VanMeter look like the guilty party if anyone ever found hazardous levels of radiation in the area. Stickney's effort was amateurish, scientifically sloppy, but you wanted to get back at Consolidated Tri-State, not only for rebuffing Finesse Chemical's takeover bid, but for unseating you from their board of directors."

Distracted by the game, Finesse said, "Gratefully shut your mouth." *(Gratefully?)* "Garavaglia's leaving Morrison in! Where do I get these cut-and-paste lineup shufflers, anyway?"

Xavier tried to remp the skybox. He felt the two bodyguards—Mark and Bud—tense, their baffled weapons trained on him. One man radiated a vague discontent with others' opinion of him; the second wanted to exult in the violent physical feedback of Xavier's exploding skull. Jesus.

As for Linzy and Geoff, they were only mildly alarmed. To see Xavier blown away would have briefly horrified them, but the simple prospect of his murder wasn't enough to make them cry "Stop!" or run for help.

And Bari? Xavier remped her too. Her dreams rippled past in vivid swatches, which wouldn't piece together. She was recharging her psychic batteries, heedless of any danger.

Xavier tugged Finesse's sleeve. "Sir, forget the game. A lot of folks from Silvanus County are dying from radiation poisoning. You triggered the chain of miscalculations that made them sick. You, nobody else, no matter how far away from the disposal process or its results you try to place yourself."

"Damn you!" Shaking free of Xavier's grasp, Finesse appealed to his bodyguards: "Stifle the fool."

Bari stirred. Xavier registered the flickering of her eyelids as one interesting event in a swirl of developments. One bodyguard—Bud? Mark?—took a squat shooter's stance. Across from him at the rear of the skybox, his counterpart—Mark? Bud?—hurried to offer cover, positioning himself to take a shot at Xavier, who was still between the wingbacks.

Finesse's lips were frozen in a jutting sneer. Xavier realized that some stalwartly aspect of himself was slowing time, as if he had given everyone a drug inducing a grand lethargy. Every person in the skybox was an ice statue thawing toward life. Xavier could have walked among them the way a curator strolls from statue to statue in a closed museum.

A slug from one of the bodyguards' pistols was inching toward him, haloed by a red flash and a nimbus of almost motionless muzzle smoke. Beautiful. Scary.

Once, years ago, Xavier had seen a daredevil on a TV program called "Can You Believe It?" catch a slug between his teeth. The bullet had been fired from a stationary handgun held about forty or fifty feet away, across a studio soundstage. The daredevil had stationed himself in front of the handgun, with a plastic appliance in his mouth to absorb the bullet's impact when it hurtled between his lips to lodge in the unlikely vise of his teeth.

This stunt had amazed Xavier. If it was real, there was no margin for error. If it was an elaborate put-on, to boost ratings, it betrayed its audience. Another problem was that the audience's fascination—hell, even his own—had struck him as tawdry and voyeuresque, its credibility as entertainment tainted by the fact that the daredevil might die. If the slug shattered the appliance in his mouth, it would either burst out the rear of his skull or rattle around inside his cranium like a pea in a gourd.

Anyway, a suspenseful drum roll had sounded. The gun fired. The daredevil's braced head snapped back as if someone had slugged him in the jaw. The camera zoomed in. There, between his teeth, more like a bitten-off pencil eraser than a deadly piece of handgun ordnance, was the bullet whose flight he'd halted. The daredevil had braved death, defying the humdrum, the quotidian, the stodgy, and Xavier, although skepti-

cal of what he had just seen, could not help admiring the man.
. . .

The bullet coming toward Xavier now looked like an under-powered housefly, bumbling forward on a low rising curve. A second bullet emerged from the .357's muzzle, the third right behind it, so that the other bodyguard, driven to it by his partner's action, squeezed off two slow-motion shots of his own.

Xavier sidestepped the first slug, which hit the bullet-proof window and ricocheted across the bunker to dimple War-woman's arm (on a poster), as the barmen dove like dreamily delayed albatrosses behind the bar. The second slug, which seemed to pick up speed as it flew, Xavier grabbed out of the air and hurled into the carpet. The other slugs, each buzzing a little faster than the one before, Xavier dodged or slapped aside.

"Noooooo!" Bari was crying. The sound of this cry restored the natural flow of time. Bari was on her feet. "Stop! Stop!"

Having hoped to see Xavier dead, the bodyguards stopped firing, then began shooting at him again.

Although unable to track visually the unfolding parabolas of these shots, Xavier dodged or parried them with an ease that made him realize how quickly he could get used to this. Who wouldn't enjoy the total invulnerability imparted by stal-wartliness? Who wouldn't be corrupted?

Bud had fired all nine rounds in his .357's magazine, Mark a total of six, and Xavier was still upright. He warned Bud not to reload. He warned Mark that if he fired again, he would take his weapon and break his trigger finger.

"If for nothing else, sir," he then told Finesse, "you're under arrest for attempted murder."

"Attempted murder? I didn't lay a hand on you. You threatened me. My fellas here were, uh, just doing their—"

"What rot." Hugging herself, Bari walked into Xavier's arms. "These men"—nodding at Bud and Mark—"could've taken out a whole platoon, firing like that. At your cruel bidding."

"Hey there," Finesse said. "You were asleep until the shoot-ing started." He turned to his bodyguards again: "That man"—thrusting a finger at Xavier—"moved on me in a very unfriendly, a pugilistic fashion. Am I telling it straight, fellas?"

"Yessir," Bud and Mark said together. "Yessir."

"That ain't the way it happened," Linzy said from the rear of the skybox. "You said 'Stifle the fool,' them'ere goons of yorn gave it a try. Missed, though, Gawd knows how."

"Nigger, you're dead," Finesse told Linzy.

"Mebbe. But you're dead too. I'll tell what I has to say to anybody. Say it in court, even. Geoff too. Won't you, Geoff?"

"I guess so," Geoff said. "Probably."

Finesse's goons put up their guns and fled by opposite doors.

"Lemme call down to security," Linzy said. "They'll get 'em."

Finesse paid no heed. The Dodgers had scored two more runs. Garavaglia, his manager, had yanked Morrison. the score was 10–7. With two outs and a runner on, a new pitcher was warming up. The scoreboard animated a Cherokee pitcher soaking in the showers.

"Talent but no artistry," Finesse mumbled. "My boys're 'bout as reliable as"—waving disappointedly—"paid he'p."

"Let's go," Xavier said. "To the central stationhouse."

"Uh-uh, Count. I stay to the end. A good owner does that."

"Mr. Finesse, forgive me," Xavier said, "but at this point I'd sooner sit down with an L. Ron Hubbard novel." He dragged Finesse out of the skybox. Bari followed along gratefully.

In the perimeter concourse, Xavier glanced back with a twinge of self-questioning dread. "Was that all right?"

"What?" Bari hurried to catch up. "Was what all right?"

"The way I . . . the way the Count handled that."

Bari came abreast of Xavier and hooked her arm through his free arm. That was her answer.

In the stands, the fans vented a collective groan, which rolled through the concourse like the lowing of slaughter-bound cattle.

"They've blown it," Finesse said. "That's it for Garavaglia. The inept bastid's history. . . ."

59

A Singleminded
Uniqueness of Focus

The stadium's security police apprehended Finesse's bodyguards in a locker-room tunnel one floor below entrance
level. A shootout, deafening there, had left Bud winged in the
arm and a security cop scalded along the jaw by a ricochet. No
one else was hurt, and the shootout had concluded in minutes.

As Xavier learned from the next day's *Urbanite,* Finesse did
not spend the remainder of that night in jail. He used his
allotted telephone call to reach his attorneys. Moreover, his
presence in the station house provoked a lionizing stir. He was
an outspoken proponent of law-enforcement agencies and a
generous contributor to police causes. He had disagreed publicly with Chief Millard Rapp's demand for stricter local gun
controls, casting himself as both a skeet shooter and a hunter,
but his stance on this issue had never tarnished his image with
the cops in the street. Thus, when his attorneys made his
$100,000 bail less than ten minutes after his official indictment,
Finesse had left the station like a medieval crusader spurring
off to war to the cheers of his castle's admiring householders.

Published only an hour and a half behind the *Urbanite*'s
regular morning edition, a special edition of the paper put the
skybox fuss between Finesse and Xavier into its biggest headline. (The regular edition had given special prominence to the
death of Carrie-Lisbeth Wilkins at Salonika General. Its
sports pages had gone to bed with the Cherokees leading 10–7,

when the homeboys had eventually eked out a 12–11 win in thirteen innings.) The story—by Alex Meisel, with whom Xavier had done a telephone interview—reported Count Geiger's charge that Finesse was the heretofore secret power behind Environomics Unlimited, and also Finesse's irate denial.

Meisel noted that although Linzy Keene and Geoff Satterhedge, long-term employees of the Salonika Cherokees and F. Deane Finesse, were ready to corroborate in court the attempted-murder charge against their boss, the only witness with the purported credentials to link Finesse to the crooked waste-disposal company was Wilbon T. Stickney. Stickney was a jobless teamster and pokehead lying ill and delirious in the same hospital, Salonika General, treating the victims of the recent Therac 4-J radiation accident. Most pundits believed it unlikely that, even if he recovered fully, Stickney would be able to pin this rap on a man as rich and influential as F. Deane Finesse.

"You caught bullets barehanded, like?" said the Mick, sitting at the dining-room table with the *Urbanite*'s special edition. "You 'deflected' bullets with 'lightninglike karate chops'? Hey, that's totally nool, unc. Totally."

"Thank you."

"You even caught a bullet between your teeth? Wow. Have I got a stud for a guardian or what?"

"*I* didn't do that," Xavier said. "When Finesse's goons opened fire, I remembered this guy who'd caught a bullet between his teeth on an old TV show. That memory steeled my nerve. Mikhail, you've got to quit skimming and pay more attention to context."

"Still. Snagging bullets barehanded ain't too shabby. I mean, you could microminiaturize yourself and chase down escaping valence electrons like a flea-sized center fielder."

"Strictly speaking, I *am* out of work," Xavier said. "I'll keep that in mind as a career option."

"An improvement on your main job nowadays."

"You think so? And what's that."

"Would-be murder victim. First, Bowman tries to blow you away, and now the hirelings of the cryptofascist who fired Bowman give it a shot too. Are you unpopular, or what?"

"Fifteen shots," Xavier said. "I remember them all."

"Nool. Did you remember that Bowman's trial—like, you know, his big-time stand on 'Salonika Law'—starts next week?"

If he had ever known, Xavier had forgotten. "Finish your Wheat Crisps and get out of here. You're late for school."

Around noon, Bari met Xavier at First Stringers for a low-cal lunch. They weren't exactly an item again, but they weren't just business associates either. Clearly, events of recent days had rekindled Bari's always qualified regard for him, while he, in turn, had never lost his romantic feelings for her.

Xavier wore sunglasses and, over his Suit, unprepossessing street clothes—to minimize the hubbub that often ensued when he went out in public nowadays. Bari sabotaged his good intentions, however, by showing up in an outlaw outfit of her own design, sort of Azzedine Alaïa meets a demure Saint Torque, and so crooking the neck of every enchanted male and curious woman within a three-block radius. The miracle was that Bari managed this feat, Xavier felt, without looking either showboaty or cheap.

Even so, he was exasperated. "You might as well've walked in here naked on a pair of Manolo Blahnik heels."

"Pardon me."

"You know what I mean." In the Bill Moyers room, they were watching the PBS series *Joseph Campbell and the Power of Myth,* the "Sacrifice and Bliss" episode, and signing autographs for patrons with sufficient chutzpah to intrude on them as they tried to eat.

Scrawling away, Xavier concluded that Bari didn't know— not exactly, anyway—what he meant. She understood perfectly well what impact her fashions, worn by another woman, might have on others, whether friends or detractors, but the notion that anyone besides a lover might view the same dress on her as provocative occurred to her only as an abstraction. It wasn't innocence, for Bari knew as much about life and the world as he did. Instead, it was a singleminded uniqueness of focus.

Signing the backs of used envelopes or soggy napkins, Xavier at last got a feel for her self-submerging mind set. Bari worked for herself, but the products of that work belonged wholly to those who bought and wore them. She was a creator, not a customer, even when she wore an outfit of her own design.

"Sign it Count Geiger," a hefty young woman with a Gold-finger's shopping bag said. *"Not* Xavier Thaxton."

Xavier obeyed. He and Bari had met not just to eat lunch, but to pay a sympathy call on the Wilkinses at Salonika General. An earlier telephone talk with Dr. Avery had confirmed that the couple would see him, and Xavier had asked Bari along as moral support.

What did you say to parents who had lost a child?

Outside First Stringers, strolling toward the hospital along Dogwood Boulevard, Xavier said, "You look great, but what made you choose this particular dress?"

Passersby were rubbernecking.

"I wanted to look cheerful for the Wilkinses. Not that they're likely to care. I just wanted to give them something upbeat—sunny. Even if they only pick up on it, you know, peripherally."

"Bari, they won't be able to pick up on it at all."

"Why?" She was startled. "What's wrong?"

"Every visitor to the Wilkinses' ward has to wear a mask and a disposable gown. Throw-away slippers. No exceptions. To maintain a germ-free environment, it's vital."

"Oh." They turned onto Lower Juniper Street, a block or two from the hospital. Bari squeezed Xavier's arm with the crook of her elbow. "Actually, I also wore it for you."

Dr. Avery, looking overworked and haunted, met Xavier and Bari in the corridor outside the radiation-poisoning ward. He directed them quietly aside to an eleventh-floor waiting room no bigger than a walk-in closet.

"Look, I've been trying to reach you for an hour. I can't let you see the Wilkinses. They've taken a bad turn, both of them, almost simultaneously. They're . . . failing. Neither is fully conscious. They're each on intravenous painkiller-relaxants. You could go in to look, I guess, but why?"

"No," Bari said. "No, we wouldn't do that."

"Bless you for trying to visit them. From Philippi, only Dr. Woolfolk has dropped in. Everyone else from Silvanus County seems scared to death they'll be zapped by gamma rays. Some hazard does exist, but, properly addressed, a small one. In fact, the only regular visitor any of these people has

had is Mrs. Roving from the cancer clinic. She's been here
almost daily."

"What about Carrie-Lisbeth?" Bari said.

"We still have her, Ms. Carlisle. In a lead-lined casket that
Dr. Lusk, the liaison from REACTS, sent down from Oak
Ridge. We made her going as easy as we could, given the
circumstances. Her parents want to be buried in the Full Gos-
pel Holiness churchyard on Lickskillet Road, where Larry
Glenn's father was buried. So that's where they want Carrie-
Lisbeth buried too, of course."

"When?" Xavier said.

"Soon. I don't expect the Wilkinses to last another twelve
hours. To keep from contaminating soil and ground water,
they'll require lead-lined caskets too—larger ones. They're
expensive. Frankly, REACTS is having trouble procuring
them."

"Wish Environomics Unlimited were still around," Xavier
said.

Dr. Avery took Bari's hands in his. "Thank you for coming,
Ms. Carlisle." He glanced at Xavier. "And you, Mr. Thaxton.
I guess the Wilkinses won't know, but it *does* mean, your
coming—it means to me."

He left them.

On the elevator down, Xavier and Bari were silent. So were
two other passengers, a ward nurse and a patient in pajamas,
robe, and slippers. On the seventh floor, two interns came
aboard, talking about an obscure jazz-fusion group. (Was
there any other kind?) On the third floor, Mrs. Roving, in a
teal pantsuit reminiscent of one of her clinic uniforms, entered.

"Mrs. Roving," Xavier said. "How are you?"

"Fine."

"Your day off?"

Mrs. Roving looked sidelong at Xavier and Bari. "We'll
talk in the lobby." She turned her gaze to the antique pointer
ticking off the floors above the elevator's door.

"Pat Metheny," one intern said. "Earl Klugh. Like that."

"Cripes," the other said. "You call that taste?"

60

The Suit (Revisited)

Di Pasqua suspended me yesterday," Teri-Jo said, embarrassed that someone as plain and square as she was sharing a lobby sofa with Bari, of Bari's of Salonika, and the stalwart known as Count Geiger. "If my instincts aren't on the fritz, it's a prelude to my outright release. Why? For negligence in hiring a waste-disposal firm. As if anyone else in the clinic searched as long and hard, or was under as much pressure, to find one."

"You're being scapegoated," Bari said. "It's classic."

"Not that I didn't buy the Environomics Unlimited scam. I did, all the way. The way a thirsty man drinks off the first cold glass of liquid set before him. Yeah, classic."

"You had help finding that 'firm,'" Xavier said. "The chairman of the cancer clinic's board of directors—it appears—played a major role in sending EU to you."

"Well, it sure wasn't Di Pasqua." Funny how quickly she had dropped the man's title, once the demands of duty and the workaday foolishness of insubordination no longer applied. "He was in the dark too, flailing about. When I found, or thought I'd found, EU, well, he was as happy as I was. The notion of running a background check never crossed his mind. Or mine either. How could anyone make money picking up toxic wastes and used radioactives if they didn't actually dump the stuff? Pretending to be a waste-disposal firm was like pretending to be a junk dealer. If just pretending, why not pretend to be something, you know, glamorous?"

"Isn't there money in hazardous-waste disposal?" Bari asked.

"Only if you've got beaucoups of clients. Only if the jobs are tough. Or only if, using EU's apparent strategy, you hire losers to do the dirty work, pay them a pittance, use borrowed or stolen equipment, and dump as close to your pickup point as you think you can get away with."

"If EU did only your radium-waste disposal and your Therac 4-J disposal," Xavier said, "there's no way they could have stayed in business, even if they cut corners. And if they'd done other jobs for other area hospitals or businesses, wouldn't somebody've come forward by now to say so? No one—no hospital, no company—has done that."

"Environomics Unlimited was the monicker they used to deal with the Miriam Finesse Cancer Clinic," Teri-Jo said. "They used other names—Eco-Specialists Incorporated, Keep It Green Waste Services, Back-to-the-Earth Disposal Industries—to carry off the wastes of commercial firms. The point was to prevent easy cross-referencing and background checks. What these 'companies' all had in common, though, was the lie of safe disposal and the questionable expertise of Wilbon T. Stickney. Poor fella." She rubbed a finger along the bottom of the sofa sectional. What if Finesse had had the lobby of Salonika General bugged?

Bari and Xavier looked at her as if she had smeared lipstick on her teeth. "How do you know all that?" Xavier asked her. "Can you document it?"

"From Mr. Stickney," Terri-Jo said. "And, no, I can't. He just told me. And telling me exhausted him."

"Then we'll need to get a statement from Mr. Stickney on tape," Xavier said, "before that's no longer possible."

Teri-Jo explained again that Stickney was incapable of talking to them. He might improve. He might not. In any case, he had a police guard on his tenth-floor room, which she had visited before stopping off at the third floor to talk to a friend. Although, as Count Geiger, Xavier might wangle his way in, there were clearly no guarantees, and Teri-Jo felt that, just now, more visitors would reduce Stickney's chances of recovery. She'd been able to see him because of her association with the cancer clinic—staff in the hospital proper were still unaware of her suspension—and because she could claim a prior friendship.

"After all, he duped me twice. Politely." Teri-Jo stood up. "I've got to go. My son's been in day care all morning. I'm going to take him to the zoo. That's one beneficial thing to come out of this fiasco—the time to be a mother."

"What's his name?" Bari likewise standing.

"Chad. Chaddie. He's a pistol."

"It's great at the zoo right now," Bari said. "Take him to see the giraffes, Splinters and Stilts. He'll love them."

Teri-Jo promised that she would and told them goodbye. In the parking lot, where, amazingly, no one had yet tried to commandeer her assigned spot, she leaned her forehead against the warm metal above the door of her brand-new Honda, a gift from Fletcher, and tried to imagine herself as a full-time mother. That would be good, wouldn't it? *Wouldn't it?*

Bari was ready to get back to her atelier, but Xavier took her wrist and made her sit back down beside him on the sofa section in Salonika General's lobby.

"Stickney needs a Suit," he said.

Bari could think of no intelligent response to this.

"After the onset of my Philistine Syndrome, the Suit stabilized me, Bari. Its effectiveness began to wear off before Christmas, yes, but until then it provided me some welcome relief. The Suit's failing powers were reactivated by a reexposure to radiation on the Hazelton place. I've been fairly healthy—a stalwart, in fact—ever since." Xavier took Bari's hands in his. "We've got to put Stickney into a Suit, a Suit like mine. So he can come out of his death spiral and testify against Finesse. If not in court, then at least on tape."

"There aren't any more Suits like yours," Bari said. "Howie told me that when the city council passed that resolution outlawing Count Geiger impersonators, there was a quick citywide crackdown on costume sellers—from legitimate operators like Oconee Theatrical Supply to kink-and-slink merchants like SatyrFernalia. And Howie's forbidden by that statute—*everyone*'s forbidden by it—to make any more Count Geiger costumes, except at your request. Howie says you can't find a Suit to rent or buy anywhere in Salonika, except, possibly, at exorbitant black-market prices. In fact, he's refused a couple of attractive commissions to reproduce it."

"I'll ask—specifically request—him to create a duplicate for me. And I'll give it to Stickney."

"What makes you think Howie would oblige you?"

"Why wouldn't he?"

"Think. He doesn't like you. He may believe—with reason—that depriving you of a change of stalwartly underwear would also deprive you of your . . . your stalwartliness."

"Then *you* could make me a spare."

"I could. I would. But the material's a chemically treated metallic fabric produced in very limited quantities at the Du Pont Experimental Station in Delaware. It's expensive, Xavier, and it would take at least a week to have an order approved and shipped to me. I'd need another two or three days to turn the fabric into a serviceable garment."

"Stickney may not last that long."

"Exactly. You might be able to find a black-market costume in Satan's Cellar. On the other hand, you might not."

Xavier had heard enough. He pulled Bari up and led her through the lobby to the hospital's elevators. They waited until they were the only two people to board an ascending car. On the ride between the first and fifth floors, Xavier hurriedly stripped to his Suit. He handed his street clothes to Bari to stash in the oversized bag that she had carried with her. On the sixth floor, two people were waiting. Seeing Count Geiger, minus burn mask and slippers, they nodded a bemused hello and allowed the elevator's doors to close on them without boarding. Xavier and Bari continued their ride to the tenth floor.

Once there, it wasn't hard to find Stickney's room. A police officer stood at the far end of the corridor (directly under the radiation-sickness ward) guarding the room in which Stickney lay. A heavy irony here was that the guard had been stationed to keep Stickney from escaping when it was more to the point to protect Stickney from the Machiavellian devices of F. Deane Finesse. But maybe this tall, baby-faced officer could do both.

"We're here to see Mr. Stickney," Xavier said. "If, of course, he's up to another visit so soon."

"Sure," the guard boggling mildly at the sight of Count

Geiger in his stocking feet. "Go on in. Just don't expect a lot
of chitchat from him."

The laxity of the officer's vigilance was disturbing, but Bari
and Xavier took advantage of it to enter the room. Between
the raised safety rails of his bed, Stickney lay hooked to both
an IV drip and an oscilloscopic blood-pressure monitor. He
was breathing shallowly, his complexion's natural ruddiness
thinned to the color of diluted milk. He looked even worse
than he had in the La-Z-Boy in his foul-smelling Jarboe Street
flat.

"Mr. Stickney," Xavier said.

"Will," Bari said. "Will? Can you hear us?"

No response. None. Xavier initiated a process quite familiar
to Bari: he began to skin out of his Suit.

"Xave, what're you doing?"

"Shhhh." Over the past few months, he had become more
and more adept at rapid ecdysis. "You're going to help me put
this on him," he whispered, the Suit now draped over his
forearm like the molt of a hammered-metal iguana. "Now."

"But he's hooked to all that"—Bari looking flummoxed—
"stuff."

"Then we'll have to be careful, won't we?"

They were careful. Bari painstakingly removed the ab-
breviated hospital gown in which Stickney was dressed, while
Xavier, baldly reminiscent of one of the sinewy males in an old
roadhouse film, held aside the blood-pressure-monitor line
and inserted Stickney's feet into the scaly leotard's legs. He
niggled the garment up to Stickney's hips with some alternating tugs; then, Bari helped him get the Suit's elastic torso on
Stickney's arms and flaccid upper body. They achieved their
goal without completely disconnecting Stickney from his life-
lines or setting off a monitor alarm. He wasn't as nattily
attired—as wrinkle-free—as they would have liked, but he
didn't look too uncomfortable, either.

"You folks all right?" It was Stickney's police guard. He
had stuck his head in the door to check on them. At the sight
of Count Geiger nude—except for his socks—the guard
blushed. Stepping all the way into the room, he moved to grip
his gun butt. "What's going on here anyway?"

"Don't," Bari said. "We're unarmed."

"Speak for yourself." But Xavier snatched Stickney's hospital gown away from Bari and wrapped it around himself.

"We're testing an experimental medical procedure, that's all," he told the police officer.

"You're not doctors."

"Ms. Carlisle's expertise obviates the need for a diploma, and I hold two doctorates, one in comparative literature, one in mass media. It would be wise to evaluate the procedure on its results, not on the unorthodox credentials of its implementers."

"You're naked, Mr. Thaxton."

"Under that uniform, so are you, Officer—"

"Leveritt."

"Officer Leveritt. As is Mr. Stickney under my Suit. Clothes make the man, right? A naked emperor is a fool."

"What?"

"Ms. Carlisle—Bari—give me your bag." Xavier accepted the bag from Bari across Stickney's outstretched form and quickly pulled on the clothes that he had shed in the elevator. Without the Suit on under them, his slacks felt like pantaloons, his shirt like a voluminous poncho.

Officer Leveritt was perplexedly gawking.

"A human being is an animal that wears clothes," Xavier trying some banter. "An animal in clothes is either a circus performer or a Park Avenue matron's trot-along doodad."

In his glittery duds, Stickney lay before them like a body in state. Xavier patted him on the shoulder. "Well, we'll go now, Officer Leveritt. Make sure no one but Mr. Stickney's doctors and qualified staff members come in to see him. He's a witness. His testimony will be absolutely crucial in implicating the person or persons responsible for the mess in Philippi."

Xavier grabbed Bari's hand and pulled her around Leveritt and into the hall before the officer could move or protest. The whole episode had stunned Officer Leveritt. What now? Was Stickney in violation of the ordinance prohibiting anyone but the "real" Count Geiger from dressing like him?

61

A Feeble Cheer for Altruism

Not many people, Xavier knew, can focus for long on the plight of others. Even those moved by the starving millions in Africa, *los olvidados* in Latin America, and the flood and cholera victims in Bangladeath (as Mikhail insisted on calling it) seldom dwell on these issues longer than it takes to voice their heartsickness at a cocktail party or to write a conscience-salving check.

Xavier's sister Lydia admitted that making the humanitarian frame of mind last longer than five minutes is difficult, even for relief workers at the scenes of misery and devastation. Yielding to pragmatism, they shift into a crisp, get-the-job-done state of consciousness that removes the need to hand-wring. Mother Theresa, for example, didn't brood tenderheartedly on the disease and hunger of her untouchables; she gave them medicine and food.

"In many ways," Lydia told Xavier during a long-distance call, "it's easier to be here doing something, even if it's semifutile, than watching it on TV. Being here reduces the guilt. It brings home the situation's unmanageability, too, but I'd rather be work-ridden than paralyzed by guilt."

"Most people turn off the TV," Xavier said. "They flip to the funny pages."

"Sure," Lydia said. "But Mom and Dad raised us to drive around wagons heaped to the scuppers with nobility and guilt."

Xavier had to admit—to himself, not to Lydia—that she was right. Altruism is rare, and self-interest, which doesn't have to be selfish, nevertheless almost always overwhelms other-directed generosity. Which was why, even though suffering for his altruism and sometimes thinking himself a fool, Xavier was glad that he had given his Suit to the comatose Stickney.

Another reason was that Bari had come fully around again. By witnessing his sacrifice in Stickney's hospital room, she had found her natural bias in his favor validated. Oddly, in giving up the clothes of a stalwart, he had become for her the very hero that she had despaired of ever finding in him.

Stickney began to improve at once. This encouraged Dr. Avery, Stickney's doctor, for Larry Glenn and Missy Wilkins died within an hour of each other in the early morning hours of the day after Bari and Xavier's visit to the hospital. Dr. Avery's other patients on the radiation-poisoning ward— Claudia Burrell, the Stamfords, three of Carrie-Lisbeth's birthday-party guests, the mothers of two of the little girls, a neighbor of the Burrells, four neighbors of the Stamfords— were still in danger, although the prognosis for the group was cautiously positive. For Dr. Avery then, Stickney's turn-around was a ray of sunlight lasering through a thunderhead.

It also made Teri-Jo Roving happy. As soon as he could sit up, Stickney taped his story ("Confessions of a Waste-Dis-posal Flimflam Man"?) on a police cassette that the department copied and locked away in a half-dozen different files.

Stickney himself, now that Chief Rapp understood the nature and severity of the threat against him, went into protective custody on the south Oconee coast.

"Mr. Finesse and his legal trust will pull strings and search out loopholes," predicted District Attorney Hamilcar Clede in an interview with the *Urbanite*. "He'll bully, cajole, rant, plead, and try to finesse us. But unless God cracks open the municipal-courthouse dome and announces that Mr. Finesse is as innocent as His only begotten Son, we've *got* the old fraud!"

It looked, in fact, as if Mr. Clede might be right. The police had Finesse under round-the-clock surveillance to prevent him from absconding to parts unknown. Moreover, agents of the Oconee Bureau of Investigation had recently arrested the "voice" of Environomics Unlimited, the hack who had also functioned as the telephone front for Eco-Specialists Incorporated and Back-to-the-Earth Industries, among other phony waste-disposal firms. His arrest appeared to strengthen, immeasurably, the DA's case. So did the impounding of paperwork connecting Oconee-Oregon Transit System vehicles and warehouses with the fraudulent disposal jobs overseen by Stickney. Investigators from REACTS and the NRC had added their reports to the accumulating evidence. His wealth and local influence aside, Finesse looked to be facing some heavy-duty prison time.

Xavier wrote the following in his journal shortly after his and Bari's visit to the hospital:

> As for me, I am no longer a stalwart. The fact that the Philistine Syndrome has returned (afflicting me, as before, in some painful, dignity-stealing way every time I try to indulge my aesthetic tastes) has short-circuited any tendency in me to altruism. A man enduring the pangs of cancer, or drugged to insensibility to alleviate those pangs, seldom pays courtesy calls on the local old-fogies home or AIDS hospice. I am such a man.
>
> What's worse is that Mikhail is a major culprit in my undoing. By teaching me that even such low-order fare as rock 'n' roll, comics, junk cuisine, Hollywood movies, and science fiction may sometimes resonate artfully, he has multiplied by a staggering sum the number and types of experiences that can now kick off my syndrome. Not just *Rigoletto,* but *Revolver.* Not just Bosch's *Garden of Earthly Delights,* but Moore and Gibbons's *Watchmen.* Not just *pâté de foie gras,* but *salsa picante.* Not just *The Discreet Charm of the Bourgeoisie,* but *They Drive by Night.* Not just *Ulysses,* but *Ubik.*
>
> Thanks, Mikhail. In expanding my septum [*sic*] of appreciation, you have also expanded the scope of my susceptibility [*sic sic sic*]. With a nephew like you, who needs pathogens?
>
> (The Mick is beside me. " 'Low-order'?" he says, reading over my shoulder. " 'Low-order'? You still don't

glom it, do you? You have to make distinctions between
Number Two yellow pencils, don't you? Coca-Cola bottle
caps, even. Sheesh."

"Not *between,* Mikhail, *among.* But it could be done.
That is, one could discriminate among pencils or bottle
caps, if one looked closely enough."

"Pardon me," the Mick says disgustedly. "I'm going to
fetch in a copy of *The Sound and the Fury* and read to
you from it until you like herniate or something, okay?"
He departs. To carry out his threat?)

In any case, nowadays I am so far from a stalwart that
I am almost an invalid. To stay ambulatory, I have to eschew everything of any aesthetic consequence. As a result, I eat stale breakfast food and freezer-burned TV
dinners. I listen to the Mick's Up Periscope albums. I
read, from cover to cover, every number of the *National
Instigator.* I diligently peruse the "Let's Get Personal"
blurbs in every issue of the *Urbanite.* Every afternoon, I
watch "For Love Designed"—with Bari if possible, a
shared activity that has the compensatory virtue not only
of holding my syndrome at bay, but also of cementing
the bond between us. And, at night, I lie down to sleep
with a cracked plaster-of-Paris flamingo in my arms. . . .

62

An Episode in the Terry

One night, unable to sleep either with or without the help of an artificial bird, Xavier left his building and strolled into town. He was wearing casual clothes: faded jeans, a rumpled George Bernard Shaw T-shirt, and a pair of frayed huaraches. The walk, he had decided, was not simply to clear his head but to test himself on the streets minus the cozy somatic undergirding and the familiar moral support of his Suit; in short, a self-dare.

Xavier, he asked himself, what are you doing?

Looking for trouble, he immediately replied.

It was crazy—an impulse to suicide, a quest for sudden self-validation—but Xavier was powerless to resist it. In a way, the feeling reminded him of what he had experienced dashing through the gerbil tube from the Zapotec to the Ele-Rail station. Opportunistic vigilantism, call it. Looking for trouble. Pining for it.

Salonika did not cooperate. It was a balmy evening. Traffic was light. At the Parataj, where in early December he had fled a wonderful performance of *The Nutcracker,* there lingered in the ginkgo-studded patio court only a remnant of the crowd that had earlier attended a week-night performance of an Aaron Copland ballet. Men in white linen suits or pastel tuxedos, ladies in Donna Karan trouser outfits or short-skirted Ungaro gowns. If not for his release by Grantham, Xavier would have covered the opening of this production himself. Instead, Pippa had done so—with a column, in his opinion, too effusive in its praise and too niggling in its censures. Xavier stared into the court at the stragglers, some of the men with their jackets off and one elvin-faced woman dangling her sapphirine shoes from her fingers.

"Here," said a white-haired man striding past him toward the limousine at curbside. A regal woman who refused even to look at Xavier clung to the man's arm. Xavier glanced down. The man had given him a dollar: a wadded, velvety bill. A discard. Xavier laughed. The alms giver had taken him for a street person. Fine. In many ways, that was better than being recognized.

"Thanks, guv!" he cried, but the limousine was already rolling unhailably down the avenue. Xavier followed along on the sidewalk, keenly aware that, tonight, Salonika's police were swarming in the theater district. Only a well-armed, and foolish, mugger would try to stalk his victims here.

Xavier kept walking. Forty minutes later, he entered a black section of Salonika called the Terry (short for the Territory), a semihilly neighborhood of rundown mill houses and shabby businesses—barber shops, pawnshops, grocery stores, poolrooms, clothing or appliance outlets—where an occasional cooing couple sashayed by, winos lay in the bushes or sprawled under broken streetlamps, and crack smokers limped the porches of shadowy, weed-grown bungalows only a few feet from the sidewalk.

Squad-car patrols were so rare here that a flash of headlights on any of the Terry's narrow streets alarmed rather than reassured Xavier. Here, he was more likely to be buttonholed for a handout than given one. His floating whiteness—the ghostly pale of his face and hands—marked him out as an alien. Suspicious residents would have to decide if he was one bad mother or an unlucky tourist with a lousy sense of direction.

"You buying?" a shadow on a porch yelled at him.

"Just walking," Xavier said, demonstrating.

"Selling, then? You selling?"

Xavier's demonstration went on. So did the row of mill houses, until, down the stumble of a litter-strewn hill, another stretch of streetfront shops jockeyed into view. Xavier jolted down the slope toward it. A squat vehicle standing in the too-tight intersection beyond the shops—along with a faint broadcast of psychic energy from two figures in front of the glowing door of a video parlor—told Xavier that he'd found his trouble. The shadows at the door, if he could judge the intent of their activity, seemed to be trying to remove a panel of glass large enough to step through. They were using glass cutters, manipulating a pair of suction cups on wooden handles, trying not only to get in, but to thwart the shop's alarm system. Burglary, with that open-topped jeep for the getaway.

Xavier drew near the figures on the sidewalk—gangbangers, lean young hoods in fatigue pants and twenty-pound tennis shoes. They ignored Xavier, but the remp that he dropped on them—a feeble thing, a net of rotten threads—told him they knew he was there. Across the back of one guy's ripped T-shirt was a peculiar slogan: SAY YES TO DROOGS. It rang a distant bell.

"Keep footing it, Caspar," the gangbanger said.

"Aren't you fellas an awfully long way from your usual stomping grounds?"

The hood in the T-shirt looked at Xavier. The other, still ignoring him, removed the excised panel of glass from the door and propped it against the building. Without a backward glance, he stepped through the hole into the store. Xavier hoped for sirens, flashing lights, the activation of a sprinkler system, but what he got was . . . absolutely nothing.

"We stomps jes' about anywhere we wants," Mr. SAY YES TO DROOGS told Xavier. "You better—"

Xavier stepped past him, through the rectangular cutout, and into the video parlor. Looking back through the store's window, he saw the gangbanger outside emphatically signaling his two cohorts in the getaway jeep. Xavier thanked God the Droog hadn't chosen to follow him into the shop. At the EleRail station, he had handled four muggers at one time, singlehandedly, but even a stalwart liked less formidable odds.

The Droog inside had just opened and rummaged through a cash computer. Apparently, he'd found nothing. Now, hurrying between a pair of display shelves, he may have been looking for a safe.

Most of the video cartons in here, Xavier distractedly noticed, featured black performers—Paul Robeson and Lena Horne, Diahann Carroll and Flip Wilson, Spike Lee and Robin Givens.

"Stop!" he yelled. "Give it up!"

Beyond yet another long shelf, the Droog turned and glowered at Xavier. His face, lit by the video parlor's safety lights
and the headlamps of the jeep outside, was so malevolently
crimped that he looked like a purple demon. Xavier had no
time to think about the threat implicit in his angry fleer, for a
VHS cartridge—followed by another and another—came
winging at his head. Each cartridge was a hard-edged bomblet.
The first grazed his temple and clipped his ear. Xavier tried to
slow time, as he done in the skybox in the Hemisphere, but, no
matter how hard he tried, he was able only to marginally
impede the videos' tumbling.

"Qwarq!" somebody yelled. "Hunker, bro! *Hunker!*"

An earthshaking crash immediately behind Xavier. He realized that the gangbangers in the jeep had driven it, like a
four-wheel battering ram, up onto the sidewalk and straight
into the red-brick shopfront. The video parlor's picture window had collapsed from its frame. Lights revolved. An alarm
cycled noisily. The jeep backed up and rammed the building
again.

Inside, the gangbanger called Qwarq tried to dart past
Xavier to the door. Xavier sprang from his self-protective
crouch and seized the Droog. Gripping Qwarq under the
arms, he lifted him as high as he could, brushing his extravagant hairdo, with its razor stripes and its topiary bat wings,
against the ceiling. If only the parlor had had a chandelier—
well, a sizable light fixture—from which to hang the
punk. . . .

Qwarq gouged Xavier in the eye and twisted free, dropping
into a jumble of video cartons—Sidney Poitier, Cicely Tyson,
James Earl Jones, Whoopi Goldberg, Godfrey Cambridge,
Pam Grier—but immediately scrambled up and broke for the
door. Aching, Xavier scrambled after him. When Qwarq leapt
through the door's precision cutout, Xavier, trying to emulate
him, blundered and knocked out the glass neatly framing the
hole. On the sidewalk, still upright, he found himself facing all
four gangbangers who had attempted this penny-ante burglary.

"Who the fuck you think you are?" one of them said.

"Man, you dead now," Qwarq said.

Another Droog stepped toward Xavier and sliced his forearm with a lightninglike swipe of a foot-long shiv.

Xavier yelped. Then he lifted his arms high, spread them wide, and cried: "I'm Count Geiger!" His face, he knew, was a grandiose mask of outrage and disdain. "I'm not wearing my costume, but I'm still Count Geiger and you're all doomed!"

"It *is* him," Qwarq said.

The gangbangers turned and ran, scattering into the night and abandoning both their mangled jeep and all hope of salvaging from the video parlor any spoils beyond bad memories. A moment later, a pair of squad cars squealed into the intersection, but a concerted effort to apprehend the gangbangers came to nothing. Meanwhile, a heavyset patrolman questioned Xavier, and the video parlor's owner, who lived in a remodeled mill house less than a block away, arrived to survey the damage.

"Good job, Count," the patrolman said.

"They escaped. All of them."

"Yessir, but you foiled the robbery attempt. You even helped recover"—nodding toward it—"that stolen jeep."

"Good for me," Xavier muttered. He sat down on the curb, amid a sidewalkwide rime of shattered glass. His temple throbbed, the nick on his ear stung, and the long but shallow cut on his forearm had suddenly begun to bleed alarmingly. The patrolman wrapped it with a handkerchief and told him to hold the bandage in place by gripping his right shoulder with his right hand. This wasn't as hard as putting an elbow in his ear, but—tonight, anyway—it was close. Damn close. It dismayed him that the knife cut hadn't instantly healed itself.

"What else can I do for you?" the patrolman asked. (Inside the blasted video shop, another patrolman was taking a statement from the shell-shocked owner.)

"Keep me out of the papers."

"But why? Folks'll eat this up. Folks'll—"

"For God's sake, keep me out of the papers."

"I'll try," the cop said. He stepped through the debris to examine the smashed grille of the high-centered jeep.

Xavier brooded. He had foiled the robbery, but he had hardly made a clean job of it. Moreover, he was hurt—not badly, but demoralizingly. Stalwarts weren't supposed to get hurt. They were supposed to stymie bad guys without breaking a sweat or calling for the Mercurochrome. Even worse, it was reputation rather than performance that had actually thwarted the gangbangers. Reputation and a highly desperate bluff.

Xavier got up. He started to walk.

"Hey," the cop at the jeep said. "Where you going?"

"Out of the Terry. Home."

"Just hold your horses, Count. You're in no shape to walk. We'll give you a ride."

In the end, persuaded by the fatigue that had settled on him, Xavier accepted the ride.

63

O Suitless Me

Mikhail and Bari decided independently that Xavier needed a new Suit to offset his recidivous illness. The Mick went to Satan's Cellar for a black-market facsimile of the Howie Littleton creation that they had bought from Griff Sienko at SatyrFernalia. Sienko had nothing to sell the Mick. The statute prohibiting Count Geiger impersonations had stifled demand, he said, and thus all production of the item.

"I may be a pizza-faced host for parasitic zits," the Mick told Sienko, "but I didn't hatch like three days ago. Come on, Griffer, I know you got like *some*thin'."

Sienko did. He brought it out, a leotardlike costume sculpted from the kind of polyester film used to make the helium "balloons" sold on birthdays and anniversaries by florists. Mylar? the Mick asked. Yep, Mylar, Sienko replied.

When Mikhail balked—"That stuff conducts electricity. In a storm, a guy could get like fried"—Sienko swore that this Count Geiger costume was the only one he had. He insisted so loudly that his gerbil, Spudsy, hid in a toilet-paper tube on the countertop and refused to come out. Anyway, the price was fifty bucks, take it or leave it. Mikhail took it and carried the filmy, mirrorlike suit home to Xavier.

It fit. (Boy, did it.) It fit so well, clinging to Xavier's every anatomical nuance, that unless he tried to pass himself off as Rudolf Nureyev, sans codpiece, he would have been arrested

for indecent exposure a New York minute after hitting the
street. On the other hand, had the Mylar suit worked, the city
council could have exempted Count Geiger from the decency
statute. The real problem was that the facsimile *didn't* work.
Xavier gave it eight hours, but his syndrome-freighted metabolism declined to recover. Mozart's *The Magic Flute* made
Xavier as sick the next morning as it had made him the night
before.

With Lee Stamz's help, the Mick placed an ad in the person-
als section of the *Urbanite*. The ad offered to negotiate the
purchase of a high-grade Count Geiger outfit from any former
or secret Count Geiger imposter who phoned the real Count
Geiger's personal rep at the number given. Discretion assured,
the ad cajoled.

Three people telephoned. One wanted a million dollars for
his costume, sight unseen. The second was an unemployed
seamstress who proposed making a facsimile costume from
aluminum foil, Swingline staples, and ordinary kitchen grip-
per pads. She would do this for $39.95, labor included. The
third caller identified himself as the man whom Xavier Thaxton, a.k.a. Count Geiger, had boorishly humiliated in front of
his impressionable daughter at Zoo Salonika.

"I wouldn't sell that jerkbrain my suit if he crawled through
a kennel of rabid pit bulls to kiss my foot for it. Besides, both
my wife and my daughter *like* me in it."

Bari had no more success acquiring a substitute costume
than had the Mick. She asked Howie Littleton to fashion a
suit like the One that had first relieved Xavier's Syndrome, and
that had later enhanced his stalwartly powers. Howie couldn't
believe that Bari was making this request of him. He didn't
like Xavier. Xavier had invited him to take "a lovelorn header
out a window."

"No costume," Howie said. "Not a freaking chance."

Bari made an exasperated strangling noise.

"Hey, even if I wanted to help, there's not a scrap of the
right material anywhere and Du Pont's stopped making even
limited quantities. You want the impossible."

Bari telephoned fabric centers, piece-goods emporia, Du
Pont's Experimental Station. Howie hadn't exaggerated the
scarcity of the fabric or lied about Du Pont's decision to stop
producing Chemesh No. 9. It was no longer a cost-effective

synthetic fabric, even if sold for exorbitant sums to the U.S. defense industry.

Xavier was Suitless and would remain so. It might be, in fact, that Stickney was now the only man in the world who had a bona fide working Count Geiger costume.

"How many suits did you make from that experimental chemesh?" Bari asked Howie.

"Just one. I did it on a secret commission from SatyrFernalia just before you hired me. Later, there were other suits like mine in their inventory, but all made of cheap materials by fly-by-night operators ripping off my tucks and stitching."

Shortly after this conversation with Bari, Littleton packed up his belongings and moved to New York City. Xavier had decidedly mixed feelings about his leavetaking.

In the absence of his Suit or any working facsimile, Xavier made a secret midnight trip to the stream on the Hazeltons' farm. The most recent report in the *Urbanite* had noted that the water below the millrace, despite the removal of the rad-waste cylinders that had contaminated it, remained an uncertain health hazard. The Army Corps of Engineers was considering diverting the creek and filling in the rock pool that Stickney had once bombarded with radioactive depth charges, but Mr. Hazelton had argued that it would "unbalance the fragile ecosystem" on that portion of his property, and the NRC had asked the engineers to cool their 'dozers until the results of another environmental-impact study were available.

Thus, Xavier thought—hoped—that the radioactive residue in Placer Creek would counteract his Philistine Syndrome symptoms and the general chronic weariness that had afflicted him ever since yielding his Suit to Stickney. It was something of a surprise to him, but Xavier *wanted* to be a stalwart again.

As he had months ago, he took a rented car up into the Phosphor Fogs. He parked the car in a stand of fragrant hardwoods and crept through the trouser-snagging foliage to the overlook on which he had once pitched a tent and eaten a light picnic dinner, with wine and a backdrop of mysterious splashings. Tonight, he could observe the evidence of the NRC's and the state's clean-up efforts: a fence around the area originally affected, chain-link glittering on both sides of the stream, and an unmanned cranelike vehicle silhouetted on the far bank like some kind of mechanical tyrannosaur. They had used that, Xavier deduced, to dredge up and to dispose of the muck-smeared canisters responsible for the pool's contamination. There were warning signs on the fence, but no security cops anywhere. It was easy, then, to shed his clothes, scale the fence, and slip into the pool.

It was a hot night. The water effervesced soothingly around Xavier. He kicked lazily through the scarflike currents wrapping and unwrapping his feet. Where were the lavender eels? The outsized frogs? The three-eyed catfish? All the mutant wildlife was gone. Xavier felt like an intruder. It seemed unlikely that this would-be cure-all would restore to him the Nietzschean great healthiness that he had known as a newcomer to Salonika.

He crawled out of the water and sat on the bank reflecting that his midnight swim, with all the risks of getting here, of flouting the many NO TRESPASSING and HAZARDOUS AREA signs, had been a fool's errand.

Nothing more, nothing less.

64

"A Revenge-Crazed and Fleeting Avatar"

Tim Bowman came to trial between the deaths of the Wilkinses and their highly controversial funerals in the Full Gospel Holiness Church on Lickskillet Road east of Philippi. The DA, Hamilcar Clede, a forty-year-old man with the hatchet jaw of a farmer and the luxuriant prematurely grey hair of a soap-opera actor, called Xavier to the stand on the first day of the trial, at ten o'clock in the morning.

Xavier took the oath in an oversized summer suit a pale khaki color darker than his own complexion. He felt lightheaded and detached, like a Mylar balloon hovering around the door lintel as it leaks toward complete deflation.

Even though F. Deane Finesse had fired Bowman from his position as supervising editor at Uncommon Comics—*before* Bowman's armed assault on Xavier—the defendant was being represented by a small brain trust of Finesse's attorneys. Xavier reckoned that Finesse had assigned them to Bowman as a kind of humanitarian homage to his most talented protégé. After all, Bowman had conceived just about every character in the UC stable and elevated the upstart Finesse-backed company into full competitiveness with the big-time players in New York City. He deserved the best legal counsel that Finesse could give him. Bowman's creative and managerial efforts at UC had enlarged Finesse's empire by stalwartly bounds.

Now, however, it appeared to some—Xavier among them—
that Finesse might be trying to make amends with Bowman by
supplying him with legal counsel, to enlist him as a friendly
witness in his own forthcoming trials. Further, if Bowman
beat *his* attempted murder charge, Finesse's lawyers would
have a head start defending their boss on that same indictment, particularly since the alleged victim in both cases was
exactly the same man. If the judge would allow Finesse's
attorneys to raise the issue of Xavier's alleged history as a
failed murder victim (as if he habitually incited potentially
lethal attacks on himself), the jury might come to regard him
as a goad and a provocateur, like a decent woman portrayed
as a strumpet by the cynical barristers of a rapist.

You can't impute that much ulteriority to Finesse's motives,
Xavier told himself. He wasn't even arrested until weeks after
making arrangements to help Bowman.

Yesbutt, still . . .

"Can you identify the person who shot you as you sat at
your work station in the Ralph McGill Building?" asked
Hamilcar Clede. He was trying the case himself, perhaps as a
highly visible warm-up for the Finesse trial. If he won the
latter, it could catapult him to the governorship or a U.S.
Senate seat.

"Yessir, I can," Xavier said.

"Do so, please."

"That man there," Xavier pointing at Tim Bowman, a redheaded clotheshorse in a suit more expensive than his, who,
this morning, was sitting calmly at the defense table, a prepos-
sessing specimen of Suthren manliness and rectitude.

"Hey there, ol' Xave the Knave," Bowman lifting a hand in
wary acknowledgment. "How 'bout it, buddy?"

Clede put Xavier through his paces describing the shooting
and its aftermath. At one point, Xavier unequivocally confirmed that although he had panned the debuts of three new
UC stalwarts—the DeeJay, Gator Maid, and Count Geiger—
he had never given Bowman cause to hate him. He had certainly never done anything to provoke violent retribution.

"Wasn't panning those new comics enough?" Bowman interjected from the defense table. "I bet you didn't even read
them."

Judge Devereaux gaveled the defendant silent for speaking out of turn, and the proceedings continued.

"What was the last thing Mr. Bowman said to you as you both lay on the floor of the day room?" Clede asked Xavier.

"His exact words? Expletive and all?"

"Please. That would be very helpful."

"He said, 'Shit, you didn't die.' " There was a minor stir in the courtroom, including a faint but heartfelt groan from Bowman himself, not so much to express the conviction that this disclosure would hurt him, Xavier felt, as to signal remorse for ever having uttered such a callous sentiment.

"No further questions, Your Honor," Clede said.

Bowman had pleaded innocent by reason of temporary insanity. Even given the mitigating circumstances of that mental state, he claimed that he had never intended to inflict debilitating injury. This was an unusual plea, even in Salonika, and Finesse's legal team, alternating testimony elicitors with a frequency akin to Papa Bach's visits to the conjugal bed, pursued it with a purse-lipped zeal.

The first attorney up, a curly-haired young man with an action-adventure film star's ponytail overlapping his coat collar, ambled up to Xavier for the cross-examination.

"Did Mr. Bowman succeed in killing you, Mr. Thaxton?" he asked.

"Not so that I've noticed."

"But you believe he tried to?"

"That 'Shit, you didn't die' indicates as much, yes."

The ponytailed lawyer widened his eyes at Xavier in an effort to repeat his question without saying it aloud.

"Yes," Xavier reiterated. *"Yes!"*

"Then why did he shoot you between the lower abdomen and the rib cage, where a bullet, even three bullets, might not occasion the allegedly desired effect?"

"Objection!" Hamilcar Clede rose from the prosecutor's table. "Counsel is soliciting aimless speculation. Let him defend his client without trying to have the victim do it for him."

"Sustained," said Judge Devereaux.

The ponytailed counselor nodded at a colleague at the defense table, whereupon an intent young Eurasian woman in a saronglike dress of orange and yellow arose to assume the cross-examination. This attorney's name was Sheila Ling, and Xavier admired her dress mightily.

"Along with your nephew, a fan of Mr. Bowman's, you visited Mr. Bowman in Salonika's main police station shortly after his alleged attempt on your life. Is that correct?"

"It is."

"Why did you visit him?"

"Mikhail wanted to go. And I was curious about Mr. Bowman's motives and state of mind."

"How would you characterize this meeting?" Ms. Ling seemed to home in, raptorlike, on Xavier's bewilderment and irresolution. "What adjective would you use to describe the common mood in that visiting room?"

"Strange," Xavier said. "Am I supposed to factor in the mood of the police officer providing security?"

"Of course not. What I'm asking is, How did you and Mr. Bowman react to each other after the joint trauma of your last encounter? With suspicion? With hostility? With mutual tolerance? With reconciliation? With—"

"Objection!" Hamilcar Clede on his feet again. "Counsel is leading the witness. Let her defend her client without encouraging the victim to do it for her."

"Sustained."

"Don't let me put words in your mouth, Mr. Thaxton," Ms. Ling said, "but do try to answer the question. What was the prevailing sentiment, or mood, between you and Mr. Bowman toward the end of your session?"

Xavier expected Clede to intervene again, but he did not. "I don't know. Something akin to . . . understanding? Whatever evil had been boiling in him the morning of my shooting seemed to be gone. I saw him much as my nephew Mikhail did, as a confused but idealistic young man with a unique creative drive and a misdirected sense of betrayal."

"Gak," said Hamilcar Clede audibly from the prosecutor's table, then muttered something unintelligible, though the disgust in this mutter was plain enough.

"Mr. Thaxton," Ms. Ling said, "do you believe that Mr. Bowman should be convicted, convicted and sent to prison, for attempting to murder you?"

"*Objection!*" Hamilcar Clede roared. "The victim's opinion as to the final disposition of the defendant is entirely irrelevant to the issue of Mr. Bowman's guilt or innocence!"

"Sustained."

Ms. Ling turned toward Judge Devereaux. "Your Honor, I

concede the point. But Mr. Thaxton's opinion about the final disposition of the defendant may shed a subtle light on the degree to which he assumes that Mr. Bowman was trying to kill him. And the nuances of that opinion, I think, are altogether relevant."

Thoughtfully, Judge Devereaux inclined her head. "Counselor, please repeat that for me. Slowly."

Ms. Ling obliged the judge, quoting herself verbatim.

"Objection!" Hamilcar Clede roared again.

"Overruled," Judge Devereaux said. She looked down on Xavier on the witness stand. "You may answer the question."

Xavier had forgotten it. The clerk read it back: Did Xavier believe that Mr. Bowman should be convicted and sent to prison for attempting to murder him?

The Mick was sitting next to Bari in the front row of the courtroom, about three feet behind his idol, the genius-afflicted creator of the Decimator, Yellowhammer, Saint Torque, the DeeJay, Snow Leopard, and countless others. Xavier saw the Mick studying him with both expectation and hope.

"I can't see what purpose that would serve," Xavier said. "So, no, I guess I don't."

"Objection!" cried Hamilcar Clede.

"Overruled. I'm sorry, Mr. Clede, but you may not object to the honestly expressed opinion of a witness replying to a question legitimately approved by the court."

("What crap," Clede muttered, not quite loud enough for Judge Devereaux to cite him for contempt.)

"Xave the Brave," Bowman said. "How 'bout it, Crusader Kid? Your unc's ol' Xave the Brave."

Judge Devereaux gaveled him quiet again. Other witnesses took the stand, including Lee Stamz, Walter Grantham, Ivie Nakai, and Donel Lassiter, each of whom testified to the uproar and confusion in the *Urbanite*'s day room after the shooting, but also to their certainty that it was Tim Bowman in the baggy Big Mister Sinister costume. Ms. Ling and her associates chose not to cross-examine any of these people, waiting until the afternoon session to call their own witnesses.

At that time, they had co-workers at Uncommon Comics and a pair of psychiatrists testify to the severity of Tim Bowman's depression after his removal from the comic-book company that he had founded. Bowman had "snapped." Under treatment during his incarceration, he had improved to the point that neither witness—a Freudian depth-psychologist and a nonaligned behavioralist—believed that he now posed a danger to society. His shooting of the newspaper critic Xavier Thaxton had been an aberrant response to a hugely traumatic event, a response not likely to be repeated.

Toward the end of the afternoon, the defense team called the defendant Tim Bowman to the stand. This time, the lawyer directing the testimony was a dapper black man, Michael Rutledge. Rutledge wore a pair of silver-rimmed granny glasses and a ruby pinky ring. Standing next to the witness stand, he faced Hamilcar Clede and the courtroom's spectators rather than Bowman or the jury box. Xavier noticed that his handsome brown eyes bulged in their sockets every time he got to the end of a question.

"Mr. Bowman, did you wish Mr. Thaxton dead on the day that you allegedly shot him?" Rutledge asked.

"Of course. And it wasn't 'allegedly.' I shot him. Or, to put it more accurately, a revenge-crazed and fleeting avatar of myself shot Mr. Thaxton."

" 'A revenge-crazed and fleeting avatar' of Mr. Bowman did the shooting," Rutledge told the court. " 'A revenge-crazed and fleeting avatar.' " Without turning to face his client, he said, "Would you explain yourself less cryptically, please?"

"It was me who shot Mr. Thaxton, but it wasn't me. I am no longer the person who went after Mr. Thaxton disguised as my own comic-book arch-villain Big Mister Sinister."

"Was it significant that you disguised yourself as a comic-book bad guy to perpetrate the would-be murder?"

"Of course. Absodamnlutely. You see, I knew that what I was going to do was wrong—the *real me* knew that—or I would never have dressed as a villain to do it. That's important, I think."

"Tell the court why."

"Because it also shows that at some fundamental level, even in my pain and despair, I was still discriminating between right and wrong. A bad set of circumstances submerged that knowledge at the conscious level, but it was still subconsciously at work."

"Meaning?"

"That I—Tim Bowman—am not a bad person. I did wrong. A *part* of me did wrong. But the essential Tim Bowman, the

real me, is an advocate of . . . of the Good, the True, the
Beautiful. When Mr. Thaxton and his nephew the Mick came
to visit me, I told him that I was sorry. I meant it."

"If the court convicts you of attempted murder, what would
you say, here and now, to secure a just sentence?"

Bowman turned toward Judge Devereaux. "In my time at
Uncommon Comics, I came up with far more stalwarts, or
good guys, than I did villains. Big Mister Sinister, along with
two or three lesser bad guys, recurs from comic to comic, but,
in the gallery of my belief, stalwarts abound. It's not that I
don't recognize the multiplicity of evil, Your Honor, it's just
that I'd rather stress the strength and marvelousness of the
Good—as you can see for yourself every month in UC's *Stalwarts for Truth* comic."

"Objection," Hamilcar Clede perfunctorily half-rising.
"The witness is turning his testimony into an advertisement
for the pulp adventures of a comic-book company. It benefits
no one but his ex-boss and the stockholders in Mr. Finesse's
financial empire."

Judge Devereaux nodded at Clede and folded her hands in
front of her. "Mr. Rutledge," she said, "are you about finished
with your client? It does seem that this line of testimony bor-
ders on special pleading."

"Yes, Your Honor." For the first time, Rutledge deliberately looked at Bowman. "Anything else?"

"I would like to remind everyone that I created the comic-
book stalwart Count Geiger. In trying to kill Mr. Thaxton, I
created—inadvertently—the real-life stalwart called by my
copyrighted character's name. And everyone here today
knows what Mr. Thaxton, as Count Geiger, has done to fight
crime in Salonika and to restore our faith in the transforming
power of decency. Out of evil, in other words, there has issued
good. I can't claim any credit for purposely releasing the
potential of the second, or living, Count Geiger, but, as I
suggested in an interview with the *Urbanite* after Mr. Thaxton
was fired as Fine Arts editor, it's unlikely he would have
recognized his capabilities so quickly without my . . . well, my
intervention." A wedge of sunlight dropped onto Bowman's
hands through the high glass dome of the courthouse, tipping
with bronze fire the reddish hairs on his knuckles and wrists.

"Your witness," Rutledge said.

Hamilcar Clede maneuvered around the prosecutor's table,

walked to the witness stand, and stopped directly in front of Bowman. " 'A revenge-crazed and fleeting avatar,' " he said. "What the hell's an avatar, Mr. Bowman?"

"An avatar?"

"Please. If you would."

"Well, it's like . . . it's like one of the manifestations or forms of a Hindu deity."

"A deity, Mr. Bowman?"

"Yes. A god."

"A god?"

"Yessir. An avatar's a manifestation of a Hindu god."

"Ah, a god. You see yourself—or, to be fair, in attacking Mr. Thaxton several weeks ago—you saw yourself—as a revenge-crazed god?"

"No, I—"

"No more questions." Clede returned to his table while Bowman and, Xavier felt, three quarters of those in the building wondered what Clede thought he had just achieved with his ambiguous parting shot. Did he think that Bowman had wounded himself by grandiosely identifying himself with a deity—even, or especially even, a foreign one?

Closing arguments began at nine o'clock the following morning. Neither Clede nor the defense team took more than fifteen minutes. The arguments themselves were summary recapitulations of points made the day before.

Clede asked for a guilty verdict on the attempted murder charge and stated forcefully that nothing he had seen in Timothy Bowman's courtroom behavior suggested that he was to be trusted again (not, at least, for the foreseeable future) in the society of law-abiding citizens.

Ms. Sheila Ling, summarizing for the defense, argued that a guilty verdict would of course be just, but that imprisoning their client for any length of time—any length of time at all—would be to punish a man no longer in need of formal correction and to deprive the world of both an original artistic talent and a dreamer with an innate commitment to the public weal. Xavier wondered if Ms. Ling had forgotten that F. Deane Finesse had fired Bowman and that at present he had no ready outlet for either his skills or his opinions. Perhaps this trial, a media circus throughout the state, would provide an outlet, but you never knew.

In less than an hour, the verdict came back: guilty.

With this verdict, however, the jury sent a recommendation for leniency; perhaps probation was the appropriate sentence. Judge Devereaux took the recommendation under advisement and returned one day later to establish a year's supervised probation as the court's official sentence.

The Mick was elated.

Xavier, however, felt anxious as well as gratified, like a man paying for his dinner in a café that the health inspector has just entered with a warrant. Even had he been wearing his Suit, Xavier knew that he would have felt no better. No matter how talented or remorseful, Tim Bowman—Xavier could never forget—had shot him three times.

65

Dinner at Lesegne's

After Bowman's trial, in the crowded courthouse lobby, Bari pulled Xavier aside and asked him if he felt well enough to meet her that evening for an early dinner at Lesegne's. The name of the restaurant gave him pause. Lesegne's, of course, was the site of their first date, and they had not eaten there together in . . . well, in a long, long time.

"What's the occasion?" Xavier asked.

"I'd like to buy you dinner."

"For what? Declining to say that I wanted Bowman clapped in irons until his last mortal breath?"

"Among other things, yes."

"Sorry, but I wonder if that wouldn't be a wiser sentence than a measly year's probation."

"Forget that. Meet me in the Delacroix Room at Lesegne's."

"Should I bring Mikhail along?" The Mick, Xavier saw, was standing on the edge of a group of reporters, two of them from the *Urbanite,* who were badgering a subdued Tim Bowman about his present feelings and his future plans.

"Mikhail can operate a microwave, can't he?" Bari said.

"My Nintendo ace? You betcha. In any event, I think he was planning on catching the performance-art festival at Abraxas. One of its featured artistes pantomimes the decomposition of a Bolivian mudslide victim, apparently to the accompaniment of a slowed-down Cold Grease on Cary CD."

"Lovely. Be there at five-thirty. Sharp." Bari gave him an affectionate nibble on the chin and disappeared into the milling reporters and hangers-on blocking the wide glass doors out to East Magnolia Avenue.

Xavier arrived at Lesegne's at 5:28 P.M. The maître d', who clearly expected him, escorted Xavier to a candle-lit, two-person table in the antique radiance of the Delacroix Room.

Bari was already there. So was their meal, piping hot on bone-china plates that gleamed like either scrimshawed baleen or delicately crazed ivory. By both its looks and its aroma, the fare was instantly recognizable: blackened pompano. In the wine stems at each place setting, Meursault white burgundy. Bari had arranged everything to recall the experience of their first shared visit to the restaurant.

She stood to greet him. In fact, she pulled his chair out before the maître d' could perform that service. "We'll be fine now," she said. "Give us thirty minutes of uninterrupted privacy."

Xavier sat down. A faint apprehensive nausea coiled in his stomach. Without his Suit, he was once again susceptible to the scattershot depredations of the Philistine Syndrome. Wearing one of her own creations, Bari looked like the insured contents of Fort Knox. The entire situation—the setting, Bari's appearance, the cuisine—seemed designed to trip in him a hectic cascade of gonzo infirmities.

"I know," Bari said. "Thus, no appetizer, no salad, no premeal small talk. Come on. Let's eat."

Xavier took Bari's hand across the table and said a silent grace. He was suddenly hungry. The pompano, the green beans, the spiced carrots—everything was good. The wine gave every taste an edge, something ineffably extra.

"Do Mikhail's parents ever intend to reclaim him?"

"Of course. I think so." A carrot halfway to his lips, Xavier considered. "I don't know." Lydia seldom wrote, and when she did, Mikhail was a footnote rather than a headline in her texts. And he rarely got letters from her, just personalized postscripts at the end of her letters to Xavier.

"How do you feel about the Menakers' cavalier treatment of your nephew? Does it trouble you at all?"

"Lately, I haven't thought about it much." He heard himself add, "Maybe I've gotten used to having Mikhail around."

"Not to mention that you had other things to worry about."

"Sure." But that was too easy an out. With a strange, and audible, conviction, Xavier said, "I *like* having Mikhail with me."

"It shows." They ate in silence for a few moments, and Bari said, "He's lucky to have you, but he deserves a family."

"The Menakers—"

"Are blood kin, but they're hardly family anymore. They're busy. Busy doing good. And the 'good' they do translates into a benign neglect of Mikhail."

"Benign neglect," Xavier repeated dully.

"Benign in intention, malignant in its potential effects. The Mick deserves—he *needs*—a family."

Xavier opened his mouth, not to eat but to speak. He found himself wordless.

Laying a hand on his wrist, Bari said, "Xavier, I want you to spend the rest of your life with me. With me and with Mikhail. I want you to be my husband. This is a proposal."

"Xavier Carlisle," he said. "Has a nice ring, doesn't it?"

Bari removed a small velvet box from her handbag and pushed it across the table. "Open it." Xavier opened it. The box contained a simple gold wedding band. "With that ring, I would make you my life-mate. Say yes."

"If you make me your 'life-mate,' Bari, you may have to find another one pretty soon. Or else you'll enjoy a spectacularly long widowhood." He closed the box. "This is silly. I feel that I'm being patronized—sweetly, but patronized nevertheless."

"This is for me, not your problematic condition. And for the Mick, who's one nool retropunk, right?"

"My condition"—Xavier hesitating, weighing his words—"isn't all that problematic. This may sound petty, but I doubt that I'd pass the blood test." He put his tongue to his palate and made a rapid series of Geiger counter clicks.

"Do I care?"

"Perhaps you should."

"You don't want my name. I don't want yours. What we want is family. We can have that without blood tests, paperwork, hassle." Bari tapped her wine glass with a spoon. "Just say yes."

"Yes."

Looking smug, the maître d' arrived, a black-clad, blank-faced waiter in tow. "This guy'll marry us," Bari said. "With all the power vested in him as a majordomo. The other fella's a witness. Stand up, Xave. Let's do it."

Feeling both light-headed and mildly queasy, Xavier stood, and the maître d', in a French accent tinged with a perceptible Oconee drawl, joined Xavier and Bari in, as he put it, "a legitimate facsimile of holy matrimony." The ceremony took three minutes, and Xavier had the impression, not at all unpleasant, that the maître d' had rehearsed his part several times before the "official" run-through.

"I now pronounce yoo huzbun 'n' wife," he said. "Lady, you may kizz 'e groom."

Bari kissed Xavier, and the maître d' and his unsmiling cohort repaired to other dining nooks.

"Your place or mine?" Xavier said.

"Yours. Why live where I work?"

Bari left Lesegne's on Xavier's arm. He was happy—glowing, in fact. His wedding band spun on his finger like a well-greased washer, but so what? He had earned Bari's respect, and that part of himself that had earned it had just received from her the grace of a lifelong commitment, however long that might be.

66

Eulogies

Without yet raining, it threatened rain. The air was freighted with vapor. Every person standing in the weedy graveyard, among the honeysuckle and the illegible stone markers set flush with the wet clay, and every person facing the cemetery in the gravel drive of the Wilkinses' clapboard church, and every person held clear of their last rites by an amateur security force of beefy men in cheap polyester suits and scuffed work shoes, felt as a gravedigger feels in the fatiguing summer instant before his sweat pops.

The pines behind the graveyard were hung with a heaviness like mist, loops of see-through pewter gauze. Xavier thought he would fall down if the air took on one more drop of wetness, fall to the burr-matted grass like . . . like a hard rain.

" 'T ain't the heat," said a sharp-chinned country woman next to Xavier, Bari, the Mick, and Teri-Jo Roving. "What it is, is the humidity." She was a Burrell, a relative of Missy's by marriage, and, like everyone in Xavier's party, she had a chit—a curious metal coin with an intaglio W in its center—authorizing her to stand inside the fenced cemetery of the Full Gospel Holiness Church during the formal prayers and eulogies. Her flesh gleamed like a porpoise's.

Three coffins—two adult-sized, one very small—rested on chrome bars over the pits that had been dug for the Wilkinses. A large, open-sided mortuary tent sheltered the immediate family—the members who had actually come—from both the floating May sun and the onlookers pressing near from the roadway and drive. (The tent was useless, though, against the deep mugginess.) Each casket was closed, and had been closed. Each was a sportily fishtailed box of fake mahogany. Just by looking, it was impossible to tell that the caskets were lead-lined, even heavier than the steamy air: blunt little boats meant to sink and self-seal.

"Cremate them!" cried a voice from the pickup-barricaded road below the church. "Burn 'em, damn you all!"

"Shoot them into orbit!"

"Don't let these corpses poison our land and water!"

"Don't let them pollute holy ground!"

The cries of the protesters—two dozen people from in and around Philippi, including congregants of the Full Gospel Holiness Church and some blood kin of the Wilkinses— drifted into the cemetery from the dirt road going by the church. Their cries came like bad odors on slow gusts of air. The protesters were acting as if the Oconee state government, as it had already done elsewhere, had named Silvanus County the site of a hazardous-waste dump. To his surprise, they included not only ill-informed or superstitious country folks but also white-collarites from Philippi: quasi-rural yuppies in brogans, shorts, and slogan-screaming T-shirts.

Bari leaned toward Xavier. "Are you all right?"

"I don't know."

The Mick was wearing his Ephebus Academy blazer, a pair of clean blue jeans, and some brand-new lizard-skin ankle-toppers. He steadied Xavier with one arm and a supportive shoulder. Xavier marveled at how strong the kid was getting. He could feel the rod of Mikhail's forearm and the vulcanized hardness of his biceps. Without this help, Xavier would have fallen. His soul would have evaporated like a shallow saucer of booze.

God! such mugginess. Who'd summoned today's weather, anyway? Jacques Cousteau?

Teri-Jo Roving said, "Why not go into the church, Mr. Thaxton? You could stretch out on a pew. Get your strength back."

"No, I want to see this funeral through."

"Maybe you do," Bari said, "but you don't want it ending up being yours too. Listen to Teri-Jo."

"I'm all right," Xavier said. "More or less. Possibly less. It's as if all the people here had chunks of kryptonite in their pockets. It's probably the humidity."

"Nobody's got any kryptonite chunks," said the sharp-chinned Burrell woman next to Bari. "They've picked 'em all up and throwed 'em away. Dr. Woolfolk hopped on the first uns like a frog on a June bug. Then them REVACS people came."

What was she talking about? Xavier didn't know, exactly, but her certainty was comforting. He let his gaze swim back to the mortuary tent. There he saw the preacher, a short, compact man with a greying military haircut, and a queue of eulogists waiting to praise the Wilkinses.

One of them was speaking, slowly and ungrammatically, about Carrie-Lisbeth's "sweetness." Xavier knew that sincerity had to count for something, but he wished that the speakers' individual testimonies had more fire, more wit, more concision, possibly even more outrage. When Carrie-Lisbeth's eulogist finally hushed, Elrod Juitt, the owner of the Cherokee Junque & Auto Parts Reservation, stepped up to speak.

"This was a really crappy thing that happened to Larry Glenn and his family—I mean, *really* crappy. This was a boy who loved engine-tinkerin', and chassis grease, and free-style customizing assignments. He was good at what he did too. It pis—*hacks* me off that the slackbutts in Salonika's police department could let a junked radiation machine get improperly warehoused, that way, and then ripped off by a greedy tribe of shines that rode over here to Silvanus County to take advantage of a ordinary working stiff like me. And, yeah, like Larry Glenn. No wonder our society's getting sent to Zoobalooba on a Afro-engineered fax machine.

"Well, Larry Glenn wasn't greedy, though. He wasn't a saint, Gawd knows, but he had his standards. He did his work. He loved his family. He thought his missus was the Madonna of Lickskillet Road. He thought Carrie-Lisbeth was the universe, the Philippi Inn's brightest Budweiser sign. I felt the same—even if Missy didn't like me much, even if Carrie-Lisbeth could sometimes tighten your jaw with her puley damn whine. Who'd've wanted this horrible radiation crap to happen to 'em, though? None of us. Least of all me. They was the salt o' the earth."

As soon as Juitt walked out from under the mortuary tent

into the crowd, two men in dark suits flanked him and took his arms. They struggled, mostly successfully, to direct him through the churchyard gate and then down a treacherous roadside cut to an unmarked late-model car.

"What the hell!" Juitt shouted. "What the hell!"

Beside the Wilkinses' caskets, another eulogist was already talking, a cousin of Missy's, a woman remembering how much, as a girl, Missy had liked to play mumblety-peg. . . .

The men bookending Juitt forced him into the car, a long black sedan with polarized windows. No one else among the mourners gave this arrest much thought, but Xavier, fascinated, watched the car slink down the road through a picket line of roped-off protesters brandishing homemade signs that said, among other things, KEEPING OUR GROUND WATER PURE IS GROUNDS FOR ACTION, DON'T LET THE WILKINS [*sic*] GET PLANTED WITH OUR CROPS, and WHEN IS A CORPSE NOT REALLY A CORPSE? WHEN IT'S AGLOW.

Juitt's abductors, Xavier decided, were OBI agents. They had spirited him away without incident in spite of the number of people present. First, of course, they had let him incriminate himself in his off-the-cuff eulogy (which they'd probably taped as evidence), and then they had kidnapped him.

Your tax dollars at work. For once, effectively.

"Look!" the Mick shouted, pointing toward the coffins. "Jesus, is this unreal or what?"

Striding to the center of the tent, through a row of mourners on folding chairs, was Gregor McGudgeon, fresh from the Augustine-Graham School of Theology at Skye University in Salonika. He was wearing khaki work pants, a short-sleeved white dress shirt open at the collar, and a pair of maroon sandals. He stopped at the foot of Larry Glenn's casket, facing the family members under the tent and the crowd beyond the graveyard's cast-iron fence.

With no accompaniment but the protesters' background buzz and the creakings of the pines, McGudgeon sang "Amazing Grace." His voice, sometimes high-pitched, sometimes throaty, shaped each word as if on a lathe. He concluded with this stanza:

When we've been there ten-thousand years,
Bright shining as the sun,

We've no less days to sing God's praise
Than when we first begun.

By the end of McGudgeon's singing, only the ragged pines were crooning with him. The protesters had fallen silent. Xavier was drained by the humidity, the parade of eulogists, the resurgence of his syndrome. He sank down to the grass, his heart thumping away like a forty-year-old gas-powered generator. Several people nearby witnessed his collapse, but only Bari, the Mick, and Teri-Jo Roving cared. He hardly cared himself.

We've no less days, he thought. No less days . . . God forgive him, he doubted that sentiment.

67

Fast-Forward Decline

Without his Suit, Xavier grew progressively sicker and more feeble. He did not bloat or vomit. He did not develop cataracts, or dermatitis, or any verifiable signs of leukemia—but he aged at the untoward rate of five physiological years a week, or thirty years in the next six weeks. His hair turned grey and receded, his facial muscles slumped, his eyes lost their electric quickness, his heart grew fibrotic, his lungs swelled and ached, and his genitals shriveled—it seemed to Xavier—like scuppernong clusters under a parching southern sun.

Bari hurried to intervene. She petitioned the Oconee Bureau of Investigation to ask Wilbon T. Stickney to return Xavier's Suit, on the theory that Xavier's dressing out in it again would reverse his unaccountably accelerated aging. Even understanding that he might suffer a relapse, Stickney yielded the Suit, and the OBI had it airlifted from his safe house on the Gulf of Mexico and rushed to Salonika General in an Emergency Medical Service vehicle as if it were the heart or kidney of a traffic fatality meant for immediate transplantation.

Meanwhile, using scraps of Chemesh No. 9 salvaged from various unsold designer fashions at boutiques and department stores around the city, Bari's employees set to work making two additional Count Geiger costumes. They worked from patterns that Howie Littleton, at Bari's urgent requisitioning, had faxed them from New York. One suit was for Wilbon T. Stickney; the other was a backup for Xavier, should the original halt or counteract the onslaught of his early senectitude.

Unhappily, the original Suit didn't slow the process. A facsimile costume, rushed to Stickney, prevented any return of his version of the Philistine Syndrome, but when Bari, using Dr. Avery as her contact, had the second facsimile costume sent by bicycle messenger to Xavier at Salonika General (on the off chance that the original had again lost its potency), it proved equally ineffective and morale-blighting.

Xavier had Stickney's old room on the tenth floor. He hated it. He hated hospitals. He hated their impersonality, their inescapable antiseptic background stench, the way they teetered on the emotional interface between timid hope and ineffable gloom, the separation from Bari. The nurses and orderlies always had one of two approaches: a forced joviality or a diffuse sort of petulance. Nobody ever acted . . . normal. That was because (if you blithely assumed that "great healthiness" was the quotidian standard), hospitals simply weren't normal human environments. They were way stations to either Frankenstein monsterdom or death. Xavier hated them. *Hated them.*

"All I can say"—Dr. Avery assuming the professionally feigned and thus bogus normality of the MD—"is that you're not hooked up to a life-support system, you can walk about if you take the urge, and your friends and family have stuck by you."

"Shuffle," Xavier said. *"Shuffle about."* He perched on the edge of his bed in a fanny-concealing hospital gown that preserved only a tender modicum of his fading dignity.

Xavier's ankles were thin and bony and white-haired (like his daddy's, right before the fatal heart attack). He crossed them to keep Bari and the Mick, who were visiting during this consultation with Dr. Avery, from staring at them. In the five weeks since the funerals in Silvanus County, the stalwart in Xavier, he ruefully acknowledged, had become a novice dotard.

"But you're not completely incapacitated," Dr. Avery pointed out irritatingly. "You're aging much too fast, granted. That's a result, I think, of the damage done to your system not only by radiation exposure, but also by the repression of symptoms and the boosting of abilities mediated by your original costume."

"Burn the damn thing."

"Mr. Stickney's wearing it again, but once he's finished with it, we'll ship it to an official nuclear waste-disposal site to be incinerated or stored." Dr. Avery laid a gaunt hand on Xavier's frail shoulder. "We'll do what we can, but, as blunt and heartless as this may sound, it looks like it's simply come time to pay the piper, Mr. Thaxton."

The Mick had the room's TV turned to the one-millioneth rerun of an old "Star Trek" episode. "These dudes did a story like yours once, unc. Everybody on the *Enterprise,* down on some alien planet, turned into these really antinool geezers."

"This isn't another planet! This isn't 'Star Trek'!"

"Mikhail, your uncle Xave is reminded of *The Picture of Dorian Gray,"* Bari said. "A loftier allusion."

"Semiloftier," Xavier said. "What I'm really reminded of, you yahoos, is that I'm dying. Dying!"

Bari said, "My theory, Dr. Avery, is that his body's belatedly catching up to his natural curmudgeonliness. He's starting to look the way he always sounded in 'Thus Saith Xavier Thaxton.' "

"Thank you so much," Xavier said.

The Mick turned off the TV set with a hand-held remote. "Hey, I'm sorry, Uncle Xave. Am I like a jerkbrain or what?" He set the remote down and wandered remorsefully into the hall.

"I think we should send you home," Dr. Avery said. "Unless you think you'd be happier here, there's no forceful reason for you not to go home."

"To die."

Dr. Avery seemed to want to reply to this negativism. Aloud, he said only, "It's your call."

"Then I'll go home. Only a masochist would stay."

"Good for you," Bari said.

When they got back to the condo apartment on Franklin Court, the first thing Xavier had the Mick do was toss out all the tacky flamingos, bean-bag chairs, and framed dogs-playing-poker prints. It was something he should have done during the brief phase of his stalwartliness, while the Suit was holding his syndrome at bay, but he had never quite had the nerve.

Now, it hardly mattered. He could indulge his most basic, as well as his most discriminating, tastes without any real fear of the consequences. He was going to die. He was dying. Nothing he ate, read, beheld, or listened to was going to change that fact. Death was a fearsome predator, but his incontrovertible awareness of its approach gave him freedom, confidence, maybe even God. If not God, then the genius of Mozart and the melancholy virtuosity of Mahler. Maybe that *was* God.

The day after his return from the hospital, Walt Grantham came to visit with some of Xavier's former colleagues: Lee Stamz, Donel Lassiter, Ivie Nakai, and Pippa Wiedmeyer, who were dumbfounded by his looks, but adept and tactful enough to disguise their shock. A few weeks ago, this man had been collaring muggers, defending the honor of damosels, and healthfully rearranging the city's eating habits. Today, he looked like a refugee from the Nearer My God to Thee Nursing Home.

Bari fixed them all gin and tonics, Xave's favorite hotweather drink. Ivie and Pippa carried the conversational ball, oohing over the interior decoration—the door to Mikhail's room was closed—and gossiping about colleagues.

"Your color's *wonderful,*" Pippa said. "You look *good.*" Bari silenced her by handing her a drink whose ice cubes were colliding like falling hailstones.

Walt Grantham jumped in: "I want to rehire you, Xavier."

"Why?"

"You're not a stalwart anymore. So there'd be no conflict of interest."

"Rehire me as what? Fine Arts editor?"

Pippa smiled sunnily but her jaw tightened, and Grantham said, "No, that position's filled."

"As Entertainment editor?"

Lee Stamz laughed. "We've already been that route, Xave. You don't wanna switch back again, do you?"

Grantham cut short all speculation: "As a columnist, Xavier. I want you to resurrect 'Thus Saith.' A column a week. Two, if you feel up to it. It can be about anything you like: anything."

"Walt, do you remember 'Jury-rigged Rainbows'?" (One advantage of looking old was that you could address everyone familiarly.)

"Sure. All too well."

"That column was my swan song. Thanks but no thanks."

Out of politeness, the crew stayed a while longer. Chitchat with them was pleasant but wearying, and Xavier was wholeheartedly relieved when Bari rose to show them out.

"Hang in there, Xave," Lee Stamz said.

Ivie and Pippa pecked Xavier affectionately on the cheek as they were passing his chair. That wasn't surprising. What was—momentarily, at least—was that Donel, who had been reticent and watchful throughout the visit, also kissed him on his ravaged cheek.

A tender, warm, memorial kiss, the feel of which stayed with him like a gentle brand.

68

A Conviction, a Dream, a Conviction

Toward the end of Xavier's fast-forward decline, F. Deane Finesse came to trial on the attempted-murder charge. Xavier's testimony was an ordeal that eventually lasted the better part of two days. At the trial's outset, a small furor arose over the legitimacy of his intended witness.

Sheila Ling, Finesse's most active team attorney, questioned Xavier's identity. She remembered what he had looked like at Tim Bowman's trial, and Mr. Thaxton, in her view, now more nearly resembled an older relation, perhaps his own father, than he did his putative self.

Hamilcar Clede, once again the prosecutor, countered with fingerprints, voice prints, and DNA patterns. These exhibits persuaded the court of Xavier's uninterrupted selfhood, from his previous vigorous stint on the witness stand to this startling manifestation as a stooped Methuselah. Obliged to question Xavier, Ms. Ling attacked him as if his sudden physical decrepitude were evidence of some deep-seated moral failure, an unreliable memory, and a bent to deception.

These tactics, whether pursued by Ms. Ling, Mr. Rutledge, or any of the other three well-dressed barristers at the defense table, backfired. The jury regarded Xavier with sympathy. They recalled his brief but glorious reign as Count Geiger. They were moved to see him beset by an untreatable illness that was bearing him, unappealably, toward death. They believed what he said on the stand, including his story of the slowing of time during Finesse's bodyguards' attempt on his life, when bullets came inching toward him through the sky-box like tranquilized bees. Cleverly, Hamilcar Clede suggested that this slowing of time had somehow precipitated Xavier's subsequent accelerated aging. What was bought on layaway then, so to speak, was being paid for at a furiously com-pounded temporal interest now. Although Rutledge's angry objections were sustained, most observers felt that the jury had registered Clede's speculation and would remember it in spite of the judge's stern warnings to disregard it.

Bari, Linzy Keene, Geoff Satterhedge, and the bodyguard named Mark, who had turned state's evidence in a pretrial plea bargain, all marched to the stand to further incriminate—"badmouth," as Geoff put it—F. Deane Finesse, but Xavier's testimony might well have carried the day even without their corroboration. He had withstood subtle personal attacks and a withering, fact-centered cross-examination. Everyone agreed that he made a better witness as an old man than he would have as his former fit, but quasi-fussy, middle-aged self. Feisty old men, especially sick ones, were bang-up prosecution witnesses.

By the final day of the trial, Finesse seemed reconciled to its likely outcome. On the stand in his own behalf, he concluded one rambling denial of evil intent—toward anyone but oppos-ing ballplayers—with this comment: "And maybe Grady Garavaglia. He kissed away a nine-point lead in the last two innings of the Dodger game. He hauled us into extras. Amaz-ing."

The verdict came back as expected: guilty. Owing to some last-minute maneuverings in the judge's chambers, as Hamil-car Clede and Finesse's legal team jockeyed with each other, the sentence handed down was a surprisingly lenient ten years without parole, all to be served in the Phosphor Fog Correc-tional Institution, a spanking-new penal facility with comfort-able two-man cells and a cinder-block gymnasium for the use of the prisoners.

In an unsigned editorial, the *Urbanite* blasted this sen-tence—in some ways a small miracle, given Finesse's reputa-tion, wealth, and power—as "sheer capitulation to a nose-thumbing plutocrat." But another trial, undoubtedly a bigger one, was yet to come, when Finesse faced a jury of his less affluent peers on charges of environmental abuse and reckless endangerment of the Oconee public weal. At these proceedings, Xavier would not have to testify in person. He was sick, very sick, and he was, in Clede's phrase, "a peripheral witness, an incidental victim."

After showing up in court to hear Finesse's sentence, Xavier said, "I'd take ten years if the judge could guarantee them," then returned to Franklin Court. Bari put on Hindemith's *Mathis der Maler,* and he fell asleep in his chair. On some troubling level, he was listening to this music even as he dreamed.

At Zoo Salonika there was a tiger that the zookeeper hated. The tiger had clawed him during one of his early attempts to feed it, but someone decided—this wasn't clear in Xavier's dream—that the mishap had resulted not from the tiger's viciousness but from the keeper's own carelessness.

The keeper had failed to close a grate that would have kept the tiger securely penned during the feeding. As a result, the tiger had raked the keeper's forearm while dragging a bloody chunk of horse meat close enough to it to eat. The injury to the keeper had not been severe. He quickly came back to work, but with a bandaged arm and a bitter enmity.

Under the cloud of this hatred, the tiger began to age. Years passed, or seemed to, for the tiger. Its clear green eyes, which always spooked the keeper, prodding him to various petty cruelties, went opaque and flat. Its beautiful striped coat took on the look and feel of frosted straw. The tiger began to lose its teeth, and its claws were ground to nubs by its habitual pacing on the ledges outside its cage.

The keeper did not age at all. He looked exactly like the Count Geiger impersonator whom Xavier had accosted at Zoo Salonika and embarrassed in front of his daughter. In any case, it seemed that the keeper would have found his revenge on the tiger in its relentless aging, but no, he somehow came to despise the tiger even more furiously.

Now that the tiger had no teeth, the keeper had to mash its horse meat to a paste and shovel this vile mixture through the bars, almost as if slopping pigs. The keeper hated these duties, and his resentment of the tiger took on an intensity that no other zoo employee noticed or could have fathomed even had the keeper's hatred been more conspicuous.

An odd sort of revenge occurred to the keeper. From the office of the zoo's veternarian, he stole a radioactive medical substance, iodine 131, and injected it into the tiger's mashed horse meat. He did this every day for eight days, replenishing his supply of radioactives from the vet's office as needed. He took the stuff early in the morning and put it into the tiger's food in the cold grey dusk just before sunrise. Near the end of this period, the tiger began to vomit up its feedings.

Late one evening, several children noticed that the droppings on the tiger's exercise ledges, fecal matter and vomit alike, were glowing. A child reported this to the authorities. Count Geiger was summoned to investigate. He showed up at Zoo Salonika in his silver uniform, carrying a Geiger counter. Even though Xavier's dreaming self had been observing the keeper appalled, Count Geiger was ignorant of all that had been happening. He had no idea that the keeper was poisoning the already decrepit tiger.

Soon, working among the concrete ledges where the tiger spent most of its days, Count Geiger discovered that its droppings were radioactive. His detector went crazy, chattering away, and he finally understood that the person assigned by the zoo to care for and protect the tiger was trying to kill it. No one else had such ready access to the big cats.

One day, Count Geiger heard the tiger alternately snarling and bleating—sounds from the echo chamber of its cage. Count Geiger ducked into the tunnel leading from the outdoor ledges to the cage, and the tiger's cries, along with a recurrent thumping, grew louder the deeper into the tunnel he crept. Emerging, he saw the keeper beating the tiger with a cat-o'-nine-tails. The stripes inflicted by the whip overlay the stripes of the tiger's wintry pelt like broken scarlet bars, and, except for its feeble snarls, the tiger was powerless before the keeper.

Suddenly, in the dream, Xavier's costume was gone. His Geiger counter was gone. He was a naked man stooped in the mouth of a cage tunnel watching an evil man beating a once beautiful but now damaged tiger.

With great effort, Xavier pushed the keeper aside. He felt the braided tails of the keeper's whip bite into his back. As the whip continued to score him, he sank to his knees beside the tiger and embraced it. He put his face into its bloody neck fur and wept. At last, the whip ceased to fall, as if the keeper were taken aback by this unexpected act. Meanwhile, the sounds of Xavier's sobbing went on and on. . . .

Xavier awoke in a full-body sweat, unable to tell if it were tears, sweat, saliva, or all three that had soaked his pillow. A part of his consciousness, he understood, was trapped forever in the dream, and an ache like a tormented sea rose through his chest, almost unbearably.

The primary witnesses against F. Deane Finesse in his second court case were Teri-Jo Roving; Wilbon T. Stickney; the captured functionary who operated the phones for Finesse's ersatz hazardous-materials firms (another sullen plea bargainer); a Latino named Agostino Guzman; two former members of a street gang called the S.C. Droogs (also plea bargainers, but more eager ones); a small group of hospital and manufacturing-firm administrators, including a very ill-at-ease Edward Di Pasqua; Dr. Zane Woolfolk; Dr. Joseph Lusk; and, a surprise to Xavier, Deke Hazelton and his daughter Ailene, of the Placer County farm where "Environomics Unlimited" had dumped its radium-waste shipment from the Miriam Finesse Cancer Clinic.

Before the trial began, Xavier sent in a signed deposition, summarizing his own testimony. He also answered, on tape, a sheaf of written questions constituting the defense's cross-examination. This tape was edited under the supervision of the trial judge—Judge Devereaux again—with the semicooperative input of both the prosecutor and Finesse's attorneys, and then played in court for the benefit of the jury.

These complex arrangements were necessary because Xavier was now too weak to appear in court.

Under a special dispensation approved by opposing counsel and granted by the Oconee state legislature (Finesse seemed stricken with a patrician remorse, for a man younger than he now looked old enough to be his biological father), closed-circuit TV cameras were set up in the courtroom, and Xavier, Bari, and the Mick were able to watch the proceedings at home.

The trail was noteworthy for the bizarre quality of several of those offering testimony or presenting evidence. Stickney, for example, took the witness stand in the Count Geiger costume that had originally belonged to Xavier. Under the Suit, his tumorous paunch had the appearance of a large metal mixing bowl strapped to his abdomen. He said that he had worked as the chief disposal agent for EU, Back-to-the-Earth Disposal Industries, Keep It Green Waste Services, Eco-Specialists Incorporated, and Pollution Nixers Amalgamated, performing over a hundred jobs a year throughout the Southeast, for wages that barely kept him clothed, fed, and fumed, every weekend, to total zonkedness.

"Why did you do it?" Hamilcar Clede asked.

"I liked th' hours," Stickney said. "I liked th' driving and th' 'venture. Ittuz awmost a nanstap hoot." *(Nanstap,* Xavier belatedly flashed, was Stickneyese for *nonstop.)*

Stickney volunteered that on one occasion Finesse himself, delighted that Stickney had dumped used industrial solvents on a skeet range in southern Tennessee for the use of Consolidated Tri-State muckymucks, had paid him in person: three hundred dollars in cash and tickets to a Cherokee homestand against the Pittsburgh Pirates.

"And thattuz when them'ere boys really stunk too—worse 'n a beagle breeze."

Even weirder than Stickney's testimony was the show put on by Deke Hazelton and his daughter Ailene. They brought with them a videotape of their former thoroughbred, Cockroach, scuttling to a second-place finish in the Pulaski High Stakes in April, its first professional outing for Hallelujah Stables. They argued that if not handicapped by two extra legs, flimsy antennalike appendages curving out from its rib cage, Cockroach would have won that race, hands down. The offending mutation, of course, was the result of used radium illegally dumped in the drinking water of Cockroach's mother. Hazleton would not have cared all that much, of course, except that the colt's new owners were upset by its failure to come in first and peeved with him and Ailene for reputedly overselling the critter's speed.

"Caveat emptor," Hazleton said. "On the other hand, second place ain't so bad. On the other hand"—as if he too had an extra appendage—"it's no picnic having my honor besmirched on account of a radiation disaster that wasn't my fault."

Next, as dramatic living exhibits, two giant bullfrogs and a three-eyed catfish were brought into the courtroom in an aquarium on casters. Ailene pushed the aquarium past the jury box as if she were moving a sofa. The oversized amphibians and the glowing fish immediately drew everyone's attention.

A defense attorney argued that the bullfrogs were examples of a commonplace African species and that the catfish's central eye was false, a clever stick-on. A pisciculturist and an ophthalmologist testified that the third eye was real, and that the bullfrogs and the catfish deserved to be admitted as evidence. Judge Devereaux agreed, and the critters, in their algae-grown glass domicile, were formally admitted as exhibits.

Toward the end of the trial, in his own defense, Finesse said, "A frog is a frog is a frog. Stewball was a racehorse. So is Cockroach. Stickney . . . Stickney stinks. So does pollution. I hate cancer. I hate Freon sludge, battery acid, contaminated dirt, plastic-goods byproducts, hot waste, and old Anthony Perkins movies without *psycho* in the title. (Or *fear.*) I hate Consolidated Tri-State. You should see my electric bills. You should see the Hemisphere's. I'd go buggy if you were me. So would I. So would your average three-eyed bullhead."

Despite the eloquence of this apologia, the jury returned a guilty verdict. Finesse had struck out on only two swings. He was sentenced by Judge Devereaux to twenty-five years in the Phosphor Fog Correctional Institution, the first ten to run concurrently with his previous sentence.

At the completion of that term, he would be eligible for a parole review. Before any part of this sentence could take effect, however, Judge Devereaux ruled that Finesse must undergo a thorough psychiatric evaluation.

Sitting in the Franklin Court condominium apartment watching the sentencing on WSSX, Bari and the Mick broke into spontaneous applause.

"Hear hear," Xavier said, his birdlike head turned toward the set on a plumped-up pillow. "Hear hear."

Ends and Beginnings

On sentencing day (unbeknown to Xavier, Bari, or the Mick), the Miriam Finesse Cancer Clinic—whose honor had been besmirched by the son of its late namesake—did the right thing. It reinstated Teri-Jo Roving as chief administrative nurse, with full back pay and a salary increase to compensate her for conscientious past work and the cruel indignity of her suspension.

The clinic's board of directors determined that Teri-Jo's duties should not rightfully include the principal responsibility for hazardous-waste disposal and rebuked Dr. Di Pasqua for an improper delegation of this important authority. It would be agreeable to report that the board also fired his ass, but Dr. Di Pasqua, as a weekend golfing partner of two long-term board members, sidestepped this fate. As a result, Teri-Jo had to tolerate his condescension, morose humor, male chauvinism, and occasional outright fatuousness until his retirement, six years later.

As Xavier lay dying, Bari sat on his bed stroking his papery, blue-veined hand.

In the front room, Lydia Menaker, just arrived from the Asian subcontinent, paced with a glass of pineapple juice at whose rim she occasionally moistened her lips. She was upset.

It was hard to believe that Xavier was going to predecease her, even harder to credit that the ravaged stranger in the bedroom was her younger brother, the same man with whom she had boarded her son. Despite a host of distractions and a squeak-by on his English exam, the Mick had passed all his finals at Ephebus Academy, and he was trying to calm Lydia down and reassure her about the future. His maturity, in Lydia's state of mind, was almost an irritant.

"Why don't you like scoot in there with Miss Bari?" the Mick said. "Uncle Xave's still hitting on a cyl or two. He'll know who you are. He'll be glad you're here."

"I don't know who *he* is."

"Your brother. An all-right dude. Who else?"

Bari understood a little of what Lydia was going through. Xavier had become his own fossil, his face a death mask and his hands the carapaces of two long-dead crabs.

"Any arrangeable last requests?" she asked him.

"So long as it isn't . . . *smarmy?*"

"Yes."

"Closed casket. As at the Wilkinses' funerals."

"All right. Anything else?"

"Make me something flamboyant, flamboyant and border-line tacky, to be casketed in. Something indisputably . . . not-me."

"Another Count Geiger costume?"

"Ha ha."

"Feathers? Sequins? S-curve zippers?"

"Whatever you think . . . *in*appropriate. But"—swallowing painfully—"everything else—everything outwardly visible—has to be dignified. Dignified and—"

"Tasteful?"

"Yes. Tasteful. Aesthetically fine."

"But your casket vestments—gaudy, vulgar even? Wildly out of Thaxtonian character?" She was planning already. Nothing about Xavier's ordeal, not even the televised grotes-queries of Finesse's second trial, had been fun. With this goofy last request, though, he seemed to want to reverse that state of affairs.

It took Xavier a while to reply: "Suits me." Then he closed his eyes. He never opened them again.

*　*　*

In the front room, Mikhail told his mother, "Everything's gonna be fine, Lyd. Everythin'."

The funeral took place two days later, in Christ's Episcopal Church on Jackson Square. Its monumental fresco of Christ, with his arms outspread, and the teeming choir lofts on either side of the sanctuary dominated the well-attended ceremony. A string quartet played Bach. A mellow-voiced priest recited Paul's words on the incorruptibility of the resurrection body, over and against the undeniable corruption in which one's mortal body is sown. As he recited, a headliner from the city ballet performed an evocative pantomime dramatizing the passage. Scarves leapt around her like pentecostal flames.

No one in the sanctuary, of course, had a chance to look upon the outfit that Bari—not the head mortician at the Mitford-Joyce Funeral Home—had dressed Xavier in for commemoration and burial; the service, as he had requested, was closed casket, and there was no viewing of the body.

On the morning that F. Deane Finesse was to be transferred from his jail cell to the mental hospital in Corinth, Oconee, for his psychiatric evaluation, Big Mister Sinister walked into an upscale gun store that had opened that spring in Salonika Plaza, not far from Goldfinger's.

On the wall behind the gun store's main counter was a banner declaring AN ARMED SOCIETY IS A POLITE SOCIETY, a motto indirectly accounting for the flood of etiquette books from Beirut, Peshawar, Belfast, and East Los Angeles.

"I'd like to buy a gun," Big Mister Sinister said.

"What for?" The proprietor meant to be helpful. He could have added, "Target shooting? Hunting? Display?" but it never occurred to him that the customer might misunderstand him.

"To shoot somebody," Big Mister Sinister said.

"That's a good one." The proprietor smiled. "I suppose you'd like a handgun then."

"Please. I'm in a hurry."

"I could refuse to sell you one," the proprietor joked, "but a criminal like you would just barter for one on the street or steal one from a law-abiding citizen's home and I'd be out a sale."

"That's right," Big Mister Sinister said.

He bought a Ruger Redhawk .44 Magnum revolver with a 7.5-inch barrel and a box of ammunition, charging them to a Visa card issued only a few days ago by a bank in Aberdeen, South Dakota. The name on the charge card was Timothy Bowman, but the discrepancy between this name and the bearer's zoot-suited impersonation of Big Mister Sinister was of no consequence to the gun-shop owner. He seldom read comic books, and the bearer had not even bothered to introduce himself.

Big Mister Sinister touched his hat brim and walked out of the store with his purchases.

A half hour later, in front of Salonika's central station house, Big Mister Sinister shot F. Deane Finesse three times in the chest with the Ruger Redhawk. To his assassin, it seemed an intolerable cruelty that the man who had given Big Mister Sinister, via Timothy Bowman, his start in life should have to spend his own declining years in prison. Shooting Finesse, therefore, was meant to be both a gift and a mercy.

As soon as he had fired the third shot, several plainclothes officers wrestled Big Mister Sinister to the pavement. Finesse staggered a few steps, despite support from a uniformed cop, and collapsed in agony.

With his cheek pressed to blazing concrete, Big Mister Sinister looked with one eye at his victim. It was a heavy disappointment to him that the expression on Finesse's contorted face betrayed not a shadow of gratitude.

Suzi Pybus had an afternoon talk show on WSSX. It was called "The Suzi Pybus Show." It came on at four o'clock, an hour or two before most day laborers and office workers got home, and it blew away all the competition in its time slot, ratingswise. In less than a month, Suzi Pybus had become the biggest instant celebrity in town since the late Count Geiger.

On the program that aired the afternoon of F. Deane Finesse's murder, Suzi whirled down some steps and paused in front of her cheering audience in a Bari's of Salonika outfit that flattered her figure while hinting at both independence and style.

"Today," she said, "we'll be talking with seven impersonators—five men, two women—of popular comic-book stalwarts. Why do they do it? Do they hide their fetishes or parade them in public? Is their behavior evidence of an aberrant personality or just good kinky fun? In a moment, we'll ask the impersonators themselves." The camera panned the costumed guests on Suzi's stage. "Stay with us for an exciting hour of issues, arguments, and laughs."

The prereleased theme music from the Count Geiger film debuting in Salonika on the Fourth of July filled the studio with stirring electric trumpet flourishes and fortissimo synthesizer chords. Suzi did a cute twisting-in-place jig to this music and exaggeratedly mouthed, *We'll be right back.*

Up in Placer County, the reactors at Plant VanMeter generated electricity for millions of homes and businesses in three states. The public devoured this energy, and the keepers of the reactors, blameless in the accident that had brought heartbreak to Silvanus County, took a quiet pride in undemonstratively feeding it.

In Oconee's next gubernatorial election, Hamilcar Clede ran an aggressive campaign. He reminded the voters how he had prosecuted the big shot responsible for the disaster in Silvanus County. He also reminded them that, properly handled, a facility like Plant VanMeter was the cheapest and most efficient power source for the region's growing needs. Come November, he won a smashing victory over the doubting-Thomas incumbent.

Bari and the Mick inherited Xavier's apartment. The day after his funeral, Bari heard Smite Them Hip & Thigh's "Count Geiger's Blues" booming from Mikhail's room. She knocked on the door. No answer. Bari pushed the door open and saw Mikhail sitting over a carton of comic books, the latest issue of UC's *Stalwarts for Truth* series in his hands. Grimacing, he ripped out a handful of its flimsy pages and dropped them to the floor. Bari entered the room and stood directly in front of him.

"Mikhail—"

"I'm like destroying this crap," he shouted over the bass notes of "Count Geiger's Blues."

"Don't. Your collection's worth money."

"It isn't worth shit."

"Neither is destruction, Mikhail."

"It's good to destroy antinoolity and lies," he said, tearing out another sheaf of ink-stained pages.

"It's better to make something."

Mikhail stood up and flung the rest of the torn comic away. He was crying. Smite Them Hip & Thigh was wailing. The room seemed to be jitterbugging. Bari stepped over the debris, took Mikhail in her arms, and held him until the angry music was over.